WHAT COMES AROUND

WHAT COMES AROUND

A Zoe Chambers Mystery

Annette Dashofy

LEVEL
BEST BOOKS

First edition

ISBN: 978-1-68512-641-4

Cover art by Level Best Designs

This book was professionally typeset on Reedsy.
Find out more at reedsy.com

In memory of Dawn Dowdle, my agent and my friend

Chapter One

Lyle Abercrombie followed the aroma of fresh coffee down the staircase of his home, through the living room, and into the kitchen. Sunshine spilled onto the table where his wife of forty-five years sat with her morning tea and newspaper. Grace wasn't a coffee drinker but, God love her, she always made sure the pot was ready for him.

He paused to press a kiss to the top of her head before pouring his first cup.

"What time are you meeting with that woman?" Grace asked.

The glowing blue numbers on the coffee maker indicated it was currently a little past seven. "Two o'clock."

Grace propped one elbow on the table and nested her chin in her palm. "What exactly does she want you to look into?"

Lyle rarely went into the details of his work with his wife, and she rarely asked. "She wants me to look into her husband's death from a few years back. That's all."

His dismissive last sentence was a lie. Family members didn't pay the fee of hiring their own forensic pathologist without good reason, and the widow in question had an abundance. Her husband's death had been ruled a suicide, quashing any police investigation. He would never have killed himself, she'd told Lyle. He wasn't depressed and *was* a devout Catholic. Adding to the widow's distress, the victim's life insurance had denied her claim to his death benefits. She was on the verge of losing the home she'd shared with her husband. Friends and family had raised the funds to hire Lyle and pay the expenses of a new autopsy.

1

He'd done this kind of work before, but this case had one major difference. He currently worked with the pathologist who'd tagged the case a suicide.

"The brouhaha between Charles Davis and Zoe is really getting nasty."

Lyle faced away from the coffee maker to discover Grace's attention was again on the newspaper. He feigned ignorance. "Oh?"

"I told you the nonsense Davis was spouting on Friday about Zoe neglecting her duties at the coroner's office because she'd stayed at the side of her poor friend during the flooding."

Lyle took a sip and said, "Um-hum," around the brew. Grace had read the entire article to him, but he'd also heard two firsthand versions of it.

"Well, Zoe fired back. She gave an interview to a reporter." Bent over the page, Grace pinned a finger to the paper and read. "According to Coroner Chambers-Adams, Dr. Charles Davis has done his best to undermine her authority within her office from day one. 'I hired him as my chief deputy because I felt his years of medical expertise would be beneficial. Instead, all Dr. Davis has done is act unprofessionally and drag down my reputation and that of the office.' In response to his recent comments regarding Chambers-Adams being ineffective and his willingness to take over her position, she pointed out, 'I am an elected official and answer directly to the voting public, not to my own employee, and I have had no complaints from anyone else on how I do my job.'" Grace lifted her face. "What do you think?"

Lyle maintained his well-practiced passive expression. "I'm trying to stay neutral."

She removed her reading glasses and tossed them, clattering onto the table. "Bullshit. I know you, Lyle Abercrombie. You like to play the Swiss Pathologist, never taking sides. But you work with these people. You know what really goes on."

He took another slow sip, savored the dark roast on his tongue, and swallowed, taking the time to form a reply. "Dr. Charles Davis is an ass."

Grace held Lyle's unblinking gaze for several long moments, before choking a laugh. "I've never met the man, but I had a feeling that was the case. I *have* met Zoe, and she is always professional."

He didn't add to his wife's assessment, although he'd known Zoe for years.

He recalled the times early in her career as a deputy coroner when she'd bolted from the autopsy suite, unable to keep her lunch down when struck by the various odors of an opened human body. But in recent years, she'd overcome those issues. While only officially heading the office for a few months and still being green, she was tough and compassionate.

And more than able to carry out her duties without Davis's "help."

Still, Lyle worried about her statement to the press. The flooding last week, combined with the loss of life thanks to a stone-cold killer—several of the lives lost hitting too close to home for Zoe—had left her vulnerable to Davis's barbs. Part of Lyle wished she'd refrained from doing the interview. The other part wanted to pat her on the back for finally going on the offensive.

Charles Davis was going to be livid. Used to browbeating those he saw as opponents, he was unaccustomed to having the tables turned. Lyle was caught in the middle. As a medical subcontractor hired by the county to perform autopsies for a coroner who was not a forensic pathologist, Lyle could simply walk away. But that was exactly what Davis wanted. If he had his way, Davis would be the county's sole pathologist.

Lyle stuck around because of his affection for Zoe as well as his fondness for Franklin Marshall, her mentor. Franklin would want Lyle to stay and help her out.

Besides, between the battle brewing and the case Lyle was being hired to investigate on his own, he suspected Davis's days at the Monongahela County Coroner's Office were numbered.

"What on earth is eating you?"

Lyle caught Grace watching him again. He gestured at her newspaper. "Isn't that enough?"

She studied him so hard, he turned away and opened a cabinet door, rummaging for a cereal box sitting right in front of him.

"It would be," she said to his back. "Except there's something else."

To deny it would be a lie.

Before he could think up a reasonable half-truth, she added, "It's your meeting with that woman later, isn't it?"

He grasped the line she'd tossed. "Yes." Not a lie. But not the whole truth either. There was something else keeping him on edge. Some might call it paranoia. Unless he wasn't merely imagining the car following him since well before the flood. He wasn't sure how long. A week? Likely longer, but he'd only recently noticed it.

His phone pinged with a notification. Grateful for the distraction, he pulled the device from his pocket. "Speak of the devil." He opened the message. "It's Zoe."

Potential drug OD needs to be autopsied. Are you willing/able to come in? Or wait until tomorrow morning?

Lyle read between the lines. Zoe either didn't want to call in Davis, or he was being pissy and refused to answer her call. Lyle checked the clock. Five after seven. He tapped out a reply. **Be there in 30 minutes**.

"A case?" Grace asked. "On a Sunday?"

"Afraid so. Death never takes a day off." He finished his coffee and deposited the cup in the dishwasher.

His wife gave him an impish grin. "And everyone is dying to meet you."

It was an old, overused joke, but he chuckled anyway. "I'm popular but only with a select few."

Five minutes later, he'd changed from his ratty t-shirt and jeans to a polo and khakis and climbed behind the wheel of his blue Cadillac CT4. He backed from the garage and braked at the end of the driveway to check for traffic.

There it was again. The same black Toyota SUV he'd seen repeatedly in his rearview, in the parking lot downtown, and now parked at the curb in front of the Myers's residence. Neither of the Myers owned such a vehicle.

The Toyota was facing the same direction Lyle needed to go, as if waiting to follow him.

Enough already. Instead of turning left, he turned right and coasted toward the SUV. He stopped next to it, drivers' doors mere feet apart. Behind the SUV's wheel, a young man wearing a ball cap sat, head tipped forward, obviously focused on his phone. Despite Lyle's car idling motionless next to him, the kid didn't look up. Lyle became vaguely aware of a loud bass-beat radiating from the other vehicle. Its driver appeared oblivious to the world.

Oblivious to Lyle.

Maybe he really was paranoid.

After contemplating and rejecting the idea of stepping out and pounding on the SUV's window, he sighed and drove on. Three lefts and a right placed him back on his street, en route to the county seat and to the morgue in the basement of Brunswick Hospital.

He didn't look into his mirror until he reached the lightly traveled Dunlap Valley Road.

And realized it was too late.

Chapter Two

Zoe Chambers-Adams pocketed her phone and met the watchful gaze of her secretary. "Doc said he'll be at the morgue in a half hour. You should go home. The paperwork can wait until tomorrow."

Paulette made no move to collect her purse. Instead, she clasped her hands as if in prayer and drifted from her desk to a pile of boxes. Despite the move to this historic building last winter, they had never fully unpacked. Now, a recently completed, totally modern county building had a new suite waiting for them. The move-in date was little more than a week away, so the number of boxes cluttering Zoe's office was multiplying and creating an obstacle course.

Zoe eyed Paulette. Always efficient and punctual, but rarely on edge, Paulette's nervousness made Zoe uneasy too. "Are you okay? You seem... tense."

Paulette spun to face her and inhaled, inflating like a balloon. "There's been something I've wanted to talk to you about for a while."

Zoe leaned her hips against her desk. "What is it?"

Paulette began a slow pace around the room. "When you first took over as coroner after Franklin died, I offered to stick around and help until you could get your feet under you. It was never my intention to stay on permanently."

Zoe knew this. She'd anticipated—and dreaded—the day Paulette tendered her resignation. Zoe kept quiet, hoping Paulette was going to say she loved working with Zoe so much, she now wanted to stay.

"Well, you've got your feet under you. The new office is ready for you to move into." Paulette stopped pacing and gave Zoe a weak grin. "To be honest, the only reason I've stuck around this long is because I absolutely hate Dr. Davis and have been awaiting the day you can his sorry ass. Or force him to quit. Either way, I figure after those newspaper articles, the day has arrived."

Zoe returned her weak grin. "You mean if I don't fire Chuckie, you'll stay?"

They both knew how much he hated being called Chuckie.

Paulette snickered. "No. But I do want to see the explosion in person rather than reading about it."

Zoe looked around the office crammed with three desks—one for her, one for Paulette, and a spare for the deputy coroners, including Davis, to use. The third mostly remained empty. Davis wouldn't lower his standards to working at a dented, scratched gray metal dinosaur that echoed a low boom any time someone bumped it with a knee. Her other two deputies came and went, perching briefly at the desk to write their reports before escaping from the musty room.

"Could you do me a favor?" she asked.

Paulette made no promise, silently waiting to hear Zoe's request.

"Can you stay on long enough to help me train your replacement?" Zoe knew there was no such animal as a replacement for Paulette.

"Absolutely. In fact, that's part of the reason I came in on a Sunday." She shrugged. "Besides hoping to watch you toss Dr. Davis out on his butt. I plan on posting the job opening first thing tomorrow morning and wanted to give you the heads-up."

Zoe cringed. This was happening way too fast. Not to mention, tomorrow morning already cast a pall on her thoughts. She'd been summoned to the office of one of the county commissioners after Davis very publicly accused her of incompetence and dereliction of duty.

"I promise to go through every application and only pass along the ones I believe will do a good job for you," Paulette went on. "And I'll make sure they know the ropes before I leave."

"Good. You've run this office for at least a decade. Heck, you probably

know more about how to do my job than I know about how to do yours."
Zoe's phone vibrated in her pocket, and she reached for it. The screen
revealed the incoming call was from her husband of seven months, Vance
Township Police Chief Pete Adams. "Hey, handsome."

He responded with his stern cop voice, all professional. "We have a
homicide victim at the Vance Motel."

Zoe snapped into coroner-mode and checked her watch. "I'm on my way."
She looked at Paulette. "Can you call Gene and have him meet me at the
Vance Motel? He knows the address."

"Will do. What about Doc?"

Zoe was already punching in the number. "On it." She pinned her phone
between her ear and shoulder as she snagged her purse from the bottom
drawer of her desk. After several rounds of ring-back tones, Doc's recorded
voice asked her to leave a message.

She obliged but thought it was odd. He always answered his phone.

* * *

The Vance Motel was a throwback to a time when families traveled two-
lane roads, seeing the country in their station wagons, stopping at motor
inns along the way. The few remaining single-story, exterior-entryway
structures had largely fallen into disrepair or had become the haven of drug
users, dealers, and prostitution. Such was not the case with this one. Clean
and well-kept, Vance Motel was one Pete Adams would willingly check into.

A stiff breeze kept the sunny September morning's temperature in check.
Pete waited outside the room with Officers Keegan Ireland, one of the
township's new weekend patrolmen, and Nate Williamson, who usually
worked nights during the week. A pair of Pennsylvania State Troopers also
stood guard, awaiting the arrival of the coroner.

Gray-haired Sandy Giden, the motel's owner, approached from the office,
carrying a sheet of paper. Her usually tanned and freckled face was void of
any trace of color, save for a hint of green. Pete broke away from the other
officers to meet her.

"Her name is—was—Virginia Lowe." Sandy handed him a printout of the registration form before looking toward the open door, her fingers resting lightly on her lips.

He scanned the information. The victim's home address was listed as Somerset, a hundred miles or so to the east. Vance Township was in the largely rural Monongahela County. No big attractions to lure tourists for an extended stay. Less than two hours from home, Virginia Lowe had chosen an unlikely place to rest her head for the night.

"I can't believe it. I never used to have to call the police." Sandy's soft voice was muffled by her fingers. "Then last year, there was the business with that horrible man...what was his name?"

Pete remembered the incident. "Trent Crosby." But it wasn't the name he'd given her when he registered. Maybe Virginia Lowe wasn't this woman's real name either.

"Right." Sandy shook her head. "Now this. I tell you, Pete, I'm giving a lot of thought to retiring. There's a developer who has expressed interest in buying the place. Tearing it down and putting in God-knows what. I turned him down. I mean these old motels are practically historic landmarks. But if I can't keep it family friendly, maybe it's time I take him up on the offer."

Pete understood. Finding a brutally murdered woman in one of the rooms would send anyone running from the property, but he hoped Sandy wouldn't act rashly.

He continued skimming the victim's registration. "Says here she was driving an older model silver Honda Civic." Besides his own department-issue Explorer, two others belonging to his officers, and another bearing the state police emblem, the lot was vacant. "Where is it?"

Sandy looked around. "Her son must've taken it."

"You didn't mention a son."

She lowered her hand and exhaled. "I forgot. I'm sorry. I guess I'm a little rattled."

"A little?" Pete gave her an understanding grin. "What can you tell me about him?"

"He didn't come into the office with his mom, so I didn't get a good look at him. I'd estimate he was in his late teens. Tall and skinny." She pointed at Pete's VTPD ball cap. "He was wearing one of those. Not a police department one. I think it was a Steelers hat. Black and gold. I'm afraid that's all I know."

"How do you know the boy was her son?"

"She asked about adjoining rooms because she had her son with her, but when I quoted the price, she said they'd have to make do with two double beds. I felt bad for her. I don't think my rates are high."

"They aren't." Pete rolled the situation around in his mind. A woman and her teen son checking into a bargain-priced motel a hundred miles from home. Maybe she'd been running away from a bad situation. Maybe that situation caught up to her.

Or maybe the bad situation had come with her.

Sandy apparently had the same thought. "You don't think a son could do…" She pointed at the open door. "…*that* to his own mom, do you?"

"I don't think anything other than we need to find him." Pete held up the registration form. "We have the make, model, and plate number. We'll track him down." He gestured toward the other rooms. "Are any of those occupied?"

"No. I only had two other guests last night. A husband and wife who checked out at first light. I put them at the far end." She pointed toward the motel's other wing, beyond the office in the middle. "For a few days there, the place was filled up with locals who had to evacuate their homes because of the storm. Now? Just the couple and this poor woman and her boy."

No one to interview.

No one to overhear a fight.

"I'd still like to see the couple's registration information before we're done. They might have seen something without even knowing it."

"I'll print it out for you."

Pete thanked Sandy for her help and suggested she go back to the office, get a cup of coffee—or something stronger—and try to get some rest.

She didn't argue.

Once she'd walked away, Pete approached one of the state cops, Trooper

Jamison, according to his nameplate, and handed him the sheet of paper. "We need to put out a BOLO on this car. The young man driving it allegedly is the victim's son who arrived with her last night."

"Got a name on him?" Jamison asked without looking up from the page.

"You expect me to do all the hard work?"

The trooper chuckled. "Anyone ever tell you you're a smart ass, Chief?"

"Once or twice."

A familiar soft rumble drew Pete's attention to the lane leading into the parking lot. The white Forester belonging to his bride rolled to a stop beyond the yellow tape, and Zoe stepped out. She grabbed her black duffel from the cargo compartment, ducked under the fluttering crime scene tape, and crossed toward him. Despite the horrendous scene inside the motel room, Pete smiled. Zoe had been damned sexy in her paramedic uniform before she'd given up the EMS for her current gig. And she was damned sexy now.

She must've read his mind and narrowed her eyes at him. "Pete." Her tone was clear. *Keep it professional, bub.* Then, all business, she asked, "What's going on?"

"We're waiting on you, madam coroner." He extended his arm toward the door. "Brace yourself."

She shot a look at him, a silent *oh crap*, before leading the way to the room. Once she'd slipped Tyvek booties over her shoes, Keegan and Nate stepped aside to allow her entry.

Pete had already seen the victim. Female. She wore a pale blue blouse blotched with crimson, as were her beige cargo shorts. Her face was unidentifiable between the blood and her clearly fractured skull. No x-rays needed. Not that Pete could see much of her face. Sprawled prone on the carpet, the victim had taken a tremendous beating. Pete knew that much without moving her, which he wouldn't do. In a homicide, the body belonged to the coroner. The rest of the crime scene, covered in blood spatter, belonged to the police.

Zoe withdrew her digital camera from the duffel and fired a series of shots. Overall views followed by closer, detailed images. She eased her way around the body, careful to avoid blood or other evidence on the floor. Once she packed the camera away, she squatted next to the body. "Do you have an ID on her?"

"We have the registration she filled out last night. As far as I can see, there's no handbag, no wallet."

Zoe pulled on gloves and patted the woman's pockets. "Got a phone." She waved the device at Pete.

He extended a palm at Nate. The officer handed him a paper evidence bag. Pete opened the bag, and Zoe deposited the cell into it.

She kept patting the pockets, pausing at one of the pouch-like ones on the side of the victim's thigh. "Found something." She unbuttoned the flap and pulled out a laminated card. A Pennsylvania driver's license. Zoe held it by the edges and read. "Victoria Lowe, Somerset."

"Matches the information she gave Sandy."

Zoe glanced around, taking in the trashed room, same as Pete had done earlier. Both beds had been slept in. The sheets of the nearest one were speckled with blood. No voids. The bed had been empty when the attacker struck. A mid-sized roller bag was overturned on the floor with the metal folding luggage rack collapsed next to it. The mix of women's and young men's attire spilling from the bag didn't appear to have been scattered or gone through. Pete surmised the victim and her assailant had tussled, knocking over the luggage.

A lone nightstand, holding a phone and a digital alarm clock, was positioned between the beds. Something about the scene bothered Pete— beyond the obvious.

"Where's Wayne?" Zoe's question interrupted Pete's thoughts. "Or one of the other county detectives?"

"Dispatch said they'd send someone out." Pete dug out his phone. "You're right. They should've been here already."

Before he had a chance to key in the number, he spotted a dark, unmarked sedan pull in and park next to Zoe's Subaru.

"There he is." Pete started toward the county detective's car, but instead of Wayne Baronick, another detective stepped out. "Knight. Good to see you."

Detective Max Knight always reminded Pete of a slightly heavier version of Columbo. Dark-haired and unassuming, criminals often underestimated him. Knight accepted Pete's offered hand with a firm grasp. "Chief. What've we got?"

Pete gave him the short version. The female victim's identity. The missing son. The lack of motel guests to interview. Only the facts, as the old TV show used to state. Pete kept his opinions on what he'd seen to himself. Knight didn't miss much and could reach his own conclusions.

* * *

Over the next hour, Gene, Zoe's deputy in charge of transportation, arrived along with the county crime scene truck. Pete listened as Zoe reported on the victim's condition. No surprises, at least so far. Virginia Lowe's skull was fractured, presumptively the cause of death. Time of death was trickier. "I would guess less than twelve hours," Zoe told Pete and Knight.

Anything else would have to wait until after the autopsy.

Pete watched the coroner's van pull out with Zoe right behind. Knight and the crime scene techs in their white Tyvek body suits entered the room the moment the body was removed.

Pete remained outside, observing the action through the open door. Behind him, the sound of a loud muffler drew his attention. He turned in time to see a battered silver Honda Civic make the turn into the lot.

"Keegan. Nate." Pete didn't gesture but remained focused on the newcomer. "That's the victim's car."

They and the two state troopers turned toward it.

The driver braked. For a second, Pete thought he was going to reverse and take off. Instead, the driver hit the gas, sped toward them, and lurched to a stop with the car's front end leaning into the crime scene tape. A tall, lanky young man tumbled out as if having trouble maneuvering his long, coltish legs from the small car. He grabbed at the door, regaining his balance, ducked under the fluttering yellow ribbon, and loped in their direction.

Pete realized the kid wasn't looking at them but at the open motel door.

Pete cut him off and raised one hand. "Stop right there."

The young man, eyes wide, mouth gaped open, showed no sign of slowing.

Pete grabbed for his shoulders, but he juked out of Pete's grasp. All four of the other officers dived at him, wrapping him up in their arms. For a scrawny kid, he managed to drag all of them a few more feet before they could stop him.

"Let me go," he wailed. "What happened? Where's my mom?"

Pete released him, trusting the others to maintain control now that the young man's momentum had stalled. "Who's your mother, son?"

He squirmed one arm free to point at the open door. "Virginia Lowe. That's our room. What's happening?"

"You are?"

"Alex," he said, the fight draining out of him. "Alexander Lowe."

Pete nodded to the others, who loosened their grips. Standing between Alex and the motel room, Pete gave him the news no one wants to hear about a loved one. "I'm sorry, Alex. I'm afraid your mother's dead."

Tears flooded the young man's eyes. "What?" he squeaked. "How?"

Pete had been lied to hundreds, thousands of times in his twenty-plus years in law enforcement. This kid's reaction appeared genuine. "Let's go talk in my car," Pete said.

Alex jerked free of the hands still holding him. "I need to see her."

Before they could react, he bolted for the door. Pete charged after him, prepared to tackle the kid before he had a chance to enter the room and contaminate the crime scene. But Pete needn't have worried.

Alex froze at the threshold and blanched at the sight before him. He gripped the jamb with one hand.

Pete caught him as his knees started to buckle.

"Oh, my God," Alex said, gasping through tears. "All that blood. Is it...hers? Where is she?"

"She's being transported to the hospital." Pete didn't mention the morgue was in the hospital's basement. He again said, "Let's go talk in my car."

This time, Alex agreed and allowed Pete to guide him away from the scene where his mother had been murdered.

14

Chapter Three

Pete settled Alex Lowe in the front passenger seat of his Explorer. Nate brought the distraught young man a bottle of water. Alex thanked him in a hushed voice and held the bottle without opening it.

Pete turned a page in his notebook and started with the easy questions. Alex was seventeen years old. He started his senior year at Somerset Area High School a few weeks ago. He lived with his mother at the address on the registration. Just the two of them. He had no siblings, and his father ran out on them when Alex was three.

"I'm sorry," Pete told him.

Alex's expression grew dark. "What happened to her?"

"That's what we're trying to figure out."

"Someone killed her. Right?"

"Looks that way."

Alex lowered his eyes as if reading the label on the water bottle. "It was my stepdad." He inhaled a ragged breath, letting his head drop back against the headrest. "Not that he even came close to being a father to me."

"You said you and your mom lived alone."

"We do. They're divorced." Alex's voice turned venomous. "He's scum. A liar. He was the worst thing that ever happened to my mom."

When Alex didn't continue, Pete prompted. "Why do you say that?" He wanted to ask if this stepdad had been abusive but wasn't about to taint the topic by leading the witness.

"He liked to intimidate Mom. Made her feel like she was stupid. Always bossed her around, even when they were out in public. I used to hear her crying in the middle of the night."

"How long have they been divorced?"

"Three, maybe four years."

Pete studied the young man. "Have they seen each other recently?"

"No." Alex's short, firm response carried no doubt.

"Yet you think this guy might be guilty of killing your mother after all this time. Why?"

"Because he's why we're here." The boy choked out a sob and looked away. Pete gave him time. Then Alex's tearful gaze came back to him. "It's my fault. I saw all the stuff about him online in the news and showed it to her. I just wanted her to know. I didn't think she'd do anything about it. But it set her off. She insisted we come here and make sure that coroner lady knew who she was dealing with."

The heat of the sun coming through the windshield wasn't enough to counter the chill enveloping Pete's brain. Coroner lady. He only knew of one woman coroner in the area. "What's this guy's name?"

"Charles." Alex's voice dripped with disgust. "Charles Davis."

"*Doctor* Charles Davis?" Pete knew it was a stupid question.

"Yeah. He makes sure no one forgets he's a doctor. But Mom and I always joked about him only being qualified to work on the dead, because if he ever worked on a living person, he'd end up killing them anyway."

Despite the gravity of the situation, Pete struggled to keep a straight face. Zoe would like this kid. And Virginia, had she survived. He swallowed down the urge to snicker and focused on the facts of the case. "I know the man you're talking about. And the woman coroner? Zoe Chambers-Adams? She's my wife."

"Oh."

"I still don't understand why you think Dr. Davis killed your mother. If she hasn't spoken to him—"

"You asked if she'd seen him. She hasn't. But she did speak to him. She called him after hearing he was trying to get this woman—your wife—to step down because of her incompetency. Mom said that sounded just like

16

him. It's how he used to talk about her. She fumed about it a while and then called him and gave him hell."

"You were there during the call?"

"Yeah. It wasn't on speaker or anything, but I could sure hear him yelling over the phone."

"Did he threaten her?"

"I couldn't make out exactly what he said. But Mom told him to back off his claims or she would come to Monongahela County and make sure everyone knew the incompetent one was him. She called him a…" He paused, obviously searching for the word. "A charlatan. Then he really started screaming over the phone. Mom finally hung up. He called back, but she wouldn't answer. That's when Mom decided to come here and speak directly with this lady coroner. Your wife."

"Besides Dr. Davis, who else knew you and your mom were coming to Monongahela County?"

"No one." Alex hesitated, thinking, then shook his head and repeated, "No one."

Pete closed his notebook and pocketed his pen. "I appreciate your time, and I'm deeply sorry for your loss. Is there someone I can call for you?"

Having told his story, Alex appeared to deflate. He sat motionless, staring toward the motel room. "I have two aunts. My mom's sisters."

"Where are they?"

"Aunt Fiona lives in Confluence. Aunt Darlene lives in Uniontown."

"Do you want me to call them?"

Alex bent forward to place the water bottle on the floor at his feet before digging out his phone. "I can do it. I should be the one to break the news to them."

"I could make the call for you."

He shook his head. "No, thanks."

Pete stepped out of his car and waved to Nate. After asking him to sit with the young man, Pete wandered toward the crime scene tape while pondering what the victim's son had told him about why his mother had come to Vance Township and Zoe's possible involvement. Zoe, who was currently on her way to the morgue, twenty miles away in Brunswick.

Where Dr. Charles Davis also worked.

Pete's phone vibrated in his pocket. County Detective Wayne Baronick's name lit the screen. Pete thumbed the green icon.

"I'm at a one-vehicle collision along Dunlap Valley Road," Baronick told Pete, not bothering with hello.

Dunlap Valley Road was well outside of Pete's jurisdiction. "Why are you calling me about it?"

"Is Zoe there?"

The chill returned. His only comfort was the tone of the detective's voice. He didn't sound like he was about to deliver a death notification. "No. She's on her way to the morgue with a DB. Do you need her there?" But even as Pete asked the question, he didn't understand why Baronick hadn't simply called Zoe.

"Not exactly."

Rather than ask yet again, Pete waited, listening to the unintelligible voices in the background.

"The driver's alive," Baronick finally said. "But he's in bad shape. Fire and Rescue are trying to extricate him now." Baronick paused. "Pete, it's Doc Abercrombie."

His thoughts flashed to the easy-going pathologist who worked with Zoe, helping to ease her way into her new career. Both she and Pete considered him a good friend. "Is he going to make it?"

"I don't know. He's not responsive. From the looks of him, he's got some serious head injuries."

"What happened?"

"The accident reconstruction team is en route. I can tell you he ran off the road, over an embankment. He only stopped when he hit a tree."

Pete closed his eyes, trying to block out the image Baronick's words created. "I guess you don't have time to work on a homicide."

"The one at the Vance Motel? I heard about it. Isn't Max Knight there?"

"Yeah, but I wanted—" He stopped, about to tell the egotistical detective that Pete wanted *the best* working this case. Baronick would never let him live it down. "I want another set of eyes and ears on this one."

"Why?"

"Because according to the victim's son, the reason Virginia Lowe is in town is to speak with Zoe."

Baronick didn't reply immediately. From the muffled background noises, Pete had a feeling Baronick had covered his phone's mic and was speaking to someone else. The line cleared. "Pete? The accident reconstruction team just arrived. They can handle things here without me. I'm on my way."

* * *

Zoe stood in the autopsy suite with two morgue assistants. Waiting.

Doc was late. Doc was never late.

She'd called him three more times. All three calls went to voice mail.

Why wasn't he calling her back?

She'd ordered the OD victim to be returned to the cooler. And she'd overseen the murder victim's intake, weighing her, photographing her, and removing the clothing, which she bagged as evidence, and, after even more photos, washing her.

There were now two bodies awaiting Doc.

Zoe checked her watch. Almost eleven. Something must've happened to delay him. But, surely he'd have phoned and let her know.

Good lord, she didn't want to have to call in Davis.

Ever. Again.

Except to fire him, which would have to wait until after her meeting with County Commissioner Juliann Holland tomorrow morning. Decades ago, Zoe'd been ordered to the high school principal's office more times than she could count. She dreaded this summons more than any of those.

Zoe had known two of the three commissioners for years and always got along well with them. Juliann, a top-notch defense attorney by trade, was new to the office and, from what Zoe had read of her in the news, was doing her best to make a name for herself, mostly by objecting adamantly to any proposal made by the others.

Across the suite, she heard the door to the morgue's office open. For a brief moment, she thought Doc had finally arrived, but he would use the rear entrance. Instead, Pete and Wayne appeared at the doorway from the office to the autopsy room. The sight of her husband always cheered her, but the looks on both men's faces told her they weren't bearing good news. She ran through a mental inventory. She'd left Pete at the Vance Motel crime scene two and a half hours ago. Now he was standing before her, no blood, no bullet holes. He was safe. Same with Wayne. If someone had died, she'd have been called to the scene. But from the looks on their faces, this was bad.

"What is it?" she asked without bothering to say hello.

Wayne shot a glance at Pete, who gave him a go-ahead nod. "There's been a vehicular collision. Car versus tree." He drew a breath.

All those calls that hadn't been returned. Zoe knew before Wayne had a chance to continue. "Doc," she said.

"Yeah."

She looked at Pete. "How bad?"

He tipped his head at Wayne. "He's the one who was at the scene."

Her focus returned to the detective.

"He's alive but unresponsive." Wayne pointed at the ceiling, indicating the hospital above them. "He was transported here. With your EMS connections, you can probably get more information than I can right now."

Zoe fought the urge to head to the elevator, but she had two bodies in the cooler that needed a forensic pathologist, and her preferred one was out of commission. She swore. "I have to call in Davis."

"There has to be somebody else," Pete said.

"I wish there was."

"No." He stepped closer and gripped her shoulders. "I mean, there *has* to be somebody else. Davis can't work the Virginia Lowe case."

Zoe studied her husband's ice-blue eyes, trying to read him. And failing. "Why?" she asked, dragging out the word.

"Because he used to be married to her."

Wayne cleared his throat. "To be completely above board, *she* probably shouldn't work the case either," he said to Pete.

Zoe tried to put the pieces together. The murder victim from the Vance Motel was Charles Davis's ex? Although Zoe struggled to imagine anyone being married to the overbearing ass, she understood why Davis couldn't perform the autopsy. But...

"What have I got to do with Virginia that precludes me from doing my job?"

Pete exhaled a breath and told her about his conversation with the victim's son.

As Zoe listened, the swirling questions in her brain stilled and settled into place, clicking together with the answers like so many puzzle pieces. Virginia had read about the battle between Zoe and Davis. She'd argued with him about it and arranged to come here to speak with Zoe. Except Virginia hadn't lived to tell her what she knew.

"You think Davis killed his ex-wife?" Zoe glanced from Pete to Wayne and back.

"He's a person of interest," Pete said.

"But why me?" She suspected she knew the answer but needed to hear it. "Why can't I work on her autopsy?"

"You're in the middle of a very public dispute with the person who may be a prime suspect," Pete said, his voice soft. "We don't want the defense attorney to have any reason to call the autopsy results into question."

Turning away from them, she paced across the room trying to think. Her predecessor had never faced this kind of issue. Or, if he had, she wasn't privy to how he'd handled it.

First, she needed to find a forensic pathologist who would agree to fill in for Doc until he recovered. Second, she needed to find a replacement for herself.

No. Not two problems. One.

She faced Pete and Wayne. "Legally, Davis can still do the postmortem on the OD victim, correct?"

"He's not under arrest," Pete said. "So, yes."

She noticed a glimmer in his eyes but ignored it. "I'll call around to neighboring counties and see if one of their coroners' offices will take Virginia Lowe. Then Davis and I can continue with business as usual. Such as it is."

Pete looked at Wayne. "You thinking what I'm thinking?"

Wayne smirked. "Yeah. Since it's really Knight's case, I'll invite him to join us."

"What are you talking about?" Zoe asked. Again, the answer came to her without either of them responding. "You're going to question Davis when he comes in."

"No," Wayne said. "We're going to watch Max Knight question him."

Zoe pulled up her chief deputy's number and tapped the green call icon. She wouldn't have been surprised if he let it go to voice mail.

But he answered, his tone superior as always. "What?"

She put the call on speaker. "We have an OD victim in autopsy. How soon can you get here?"

"I'm busy," he snapped. "It's Sunday. Call Abercrombie."

Zoe almost rose to the bait but closed her eyes and took a slow breath. "He's not available."

"Neither am I."

Zoe's nails bit into the palm of her free hand. She intentionally stretched her fingers. "When will you be available?"

An extended silence greeted her, as if he was checking his calendar. Or making her squirm. "I'll be in tomorrow morning. Nine o'clock."

Did he know Zoe had a meeting with Juliann Holland at nine? "Make it ten."

"I'll be there at nine. If you're too busy to maintain reasonable business hours, I'm happy to take over your job."

Wayne waved, catching her attention. He mouthed and mimed, "Nine is good. I'll be here."

With Detective Knight. The idea appealed to her. Two detectives, greeting Davis with questions about his ex-wife. "Okay," Zoe said. "You get started. I'll be back as soon as I can."

"You don't even need to bother. I ran this place last week, and it—"

She ended his bluster with a tap of the red icon.

Pete stepped over to her and pressed a kiss to her forehead. "Don't let him get to you."

"Easier said than done. I was hoping to send him packing tomorrow morning. Paulette's going to be heartbroken when she hears I have to keep him around."

"I'll arrange to be here with Knight first thing tomorrow," Wayne said. "Good luck with the county commissioner." He flashed one of his dazzling smiles at her. "You've got this," he said and headed for the door.

"Right behind you," Pete told him. He brushed Zoe's cheek, and she leaned into his touch. "Are you heading home?"

"I have to make some phone calls and check in on Doc first. See you when I see you."

Chapter Four

Zoe arrived at the new county building—the one into which the coroner's office would be moving in one week—five minutes early. County Commissioner Juliann Holland's secretary directed her to have a seat in the anteroom, stating Ms. Holland would be with her shortly. Zoe wondered how long "shortly" was. So far, it was twenty after the hour, and the door to the commissioner's office remained closed.

Yesterday, after Pete left, Zoe had sent her staff home and made a phone call to a colleague at Allegheny County's Medical Examiner's Office. He arranged to have Virginia's body picked up and transported to Pittsburgh. While Zoe waited, she'd gone upstairs and tracked down Doc's wife, Grace, in the Emergency Department's waiting room. The poor woman was distraught. Doc was headed to surgery, having suffered several broken ribs and a closed head injury.

"Thank God for airbags," Grace had said. "It could be so much worse." At which point, she'd dissolved into tears.

Zoe had called her this morning for an update and learned Doc had made it through surgery but wasn't out of the woods yet. He was in ICU, still unconscious. The last part had Zoe on edge.

Doc's condition wasn't the only thing causing Zoe to squirm in her chair. She thought of Davis at this very moment, handling the autopsy alone. She wasn't concerned about his abilities. He was capable. But he had to know she intended to terminate him, and she feared he might retaliate somehow.

The phone on the secretary's desk buzzed. She picked it up, listened, and replaced the receiver in its cradle. "Mrs. Adams? Ms. Holland will see you now."

Zoe rose and smoothed her black dress trousers, picking a short ginger hair, courtesy of one of her orange tabbies, from the fabric. She always joked cat owners should buy their clothes to match their pets. Too bad she hadn't taken her own advice.

She stepped into a remarkably claustrophobic office. Bookshelves lined the bulk of all four walls. One section was void of legal tomes and, instead, displayed framed diplomas and certificates boasting of her attorney status. Stacks of paperwork and a large flower arrangement on the modest desk framed the petite brunette behind it. She stood and extended a perfectly manicured hand toward Zoe. "Mrs. Adams. Thank you for agreeing to meet with me."

Zoe forced a smile and accepted Holland's firm grasp. "You're welcome. What did you want to talk about?" As if she didn't know.

Holland gestured to a chair and waited for Zoe to sit before reclaiming her own. "Let's not waste each other's time. I asked you here because of the public comments Dr. Davis made last week following the series of homicides. According to him, you weren't on hand to attend those autopsies. Is that true?"

Heat crawled up Zoe's neck. "As you said, let's not waste each other's time. I was unable to get to Brunswick because of road closures due to the flooding, so I asked Dr. Davis to handle things here in the city until the roads were safe to travel. Once that happened, I returned to the morgue and attended four of the five victims' autopsies." Then she threw in, "With Dr. Abercrombie's assistance."

Holland lowered her gaze. "Terrible news about Dr. Abercrombie. Have you heard how he's doing?"

"Not well. But he survived surgery. He's a fighter"

"Yes. Getting back to Dr. Davis's comments. According to him, you made a conscious decision to stay at an accident scene in Vance Township rather than return to Brunswick well before conditions deteriorated."

Zoe tensed. She'd read Davis's public comments. He'd thrown around a lot of falsehoods. *Repeated instances of dereliction of duty,* and *She has been ineffective in this office from the moment she was elected,* to name two. But there had been no mention of the "accident" scene nor her decision to stay with her friend during those long dreadful hours pinned beneath a tractor while his daughter went missing. "I gather you've spoken directly with Dr. Davis." It was the only way she'd have that knowledge.

Holland sat back in her chair and steepled her fingers. "Charles and I are well acquainted. Yes, we've spoken. Are his accusations about your choice to act as a paramedic rather than fulfill your sworn duties as a county official accurate?"

"I was not acting as a paramedic. I was working with the police to gather information from the victim regarding the identity and location of the suspect."

"You weren't acting as a paramedic. You were acting as a cop. Also, not your job."

Now Holland sounded like Pete. Except he'd backed Zoe this time. "The victim asked me to stay with him. The police also asked me to stay with him and get information while they were out searching for a killer and a missing child. They were extraordinary circumstances. And, I might add, by staying in Vance Township, I was able to respond to one of the homicides and do a preliminary exam, which helped with the investigation. I wouldn't have been able to do that had I been here in the city." Zoe felt her blood pressure rising, her voice growing louder with each word. She stopped and took a breath, aware of Holland's hard eyes watching her. When Zoe continued, she'd reined in her emotions. "Regardless, the coroner's office was in good hands during those hours." She'd give Davis that much. "But his allegations of dereliction of duty are unfounded. What I find reprehensible is the way he took his so-called grievances to the press. Grievances, which, by the way, are largely lies to make himself look good."

Holland didn't speak for what felt like minutes. Zoe was about to ask if she was free to get back to the job she'd been accused of neglecting when the commissioner shifted in her seat, rested one elbow on the desk, and leaned forward, her eyes narrowed. "Dr. Davis is a political opponent of yours, correct?"

The question took Zoe back to the election in which he'd been running against her late mentor. Back to the deal she'd made with the devil that had put her in this position. "He has been in the past. Coming to work under me as my chief deputy was his idea."

Holland's reaction told Zoe she hadn't known that part. She visually gave the revelation some thought before going on as if Zoe hadn't spoken. "Dr. Davis is a proponent of converting the current coroner's system to a medical examiner's office, similar to the one in Allegheny, Delaware, and Philadelphia Counties as well as many other more advanced parts of the country."

Zoe caught the emphasis on advanced and swallowed down what she took as an insult to her current profession. "I'm aware of that," she said, forcing her voice to stay low and steady.

"What you may not be aware of is the fact I support this move. It will save time and money and give our county the prestige it currently lacks."

Zoe saw where this was going. "And you'll be able to hire whomever you want. They won't be responsible to the voters. Only to the commissioners."

"That's right. And if they prove to be ineffective or step beyond the bounds of their duties, we'll be able to fire them."

Zoe leaned forward. "Which you have no power to do right now."

"Sadly, you're correct."

"I, however, have every right to hire or fire those in my employ."

Holland hiked one eyebrow. "With just cause, yes."

"Dr. Davis's unprofessional behavior and insubordination fall under just cause."

A predatory smile crossed the commissioner's lips. "You may want to rethink that."

Zoe sensed Juliann Holland had baited a trap, and Zoe had stepped into it.

"Your current circumstances leave you a little shorthanded, don't they?"

Zoe didn't reply.

"Your dear friend Dr. Lyle Abercrombie is unable to perform his duties for the foreseeable future. Dr. Abercrombie has been gracious in subcontracting with Monongahela County for quite some time. He was friends with your predecessor. As such, he offered us a contract at a much lower rate than most and never asked that we raise it. I've placed calls to other qualified pathologists within a hundred-mile radius. Not one of them is willing to work with us for the same rate. In fact, their fees would substantially affect your office's budget."

Zoe's hands ached from clenching. She wanted to point out the commissioner had overstepped, except Zoe wasn't familiar enough with the legalities to know for sure. What she did know was had she been given the opportunity to make those calls, she may have been able to negotiate a better deal. Somehow, she didn't believe Holland had made the effort.

"In other words," the commissioner went on, "until Dr. Abercrombie is fully recovered, you *need* Dr. Davis."

Zoe needed to pay Doc a visit and beg him to heal faster.

"Frankly," Holland added with a smirk, "I believe our citizens need Dr. Davis with or without Dr. Abercrombie on staff. Have I made myself clear?"

Zoe thought about Virginia Lowe, who'd wanted to talk to her about Davis, but who was now mysteriously dead. Zoe wanted to throw the information in Holland's face. Except the police were keeping much of the case out of the news. Pete wouldn't appreciate it if Zoe divulged what she knew.

She inhaled. *Stay calm.* She slowly climbed to her feet and looked down at the still-seated commissioner. "You have made yourself clear. Now, let me make *myself* clear. I'm an elected official. Until I'm voted out, I'll run my office in the way I feel best suits its needs, and I'll hire and fire personnel accordingly. If you'll excuse me, I have work to do." She turned and strode to the door, keeping her trembling hands out of Holland's sight.

"That's your prerogative." The commissioner's words trailed after Zoe, growing louder all the way to the anteroom. "Just as it's mine to vote to cut your funding."

* * *

Abby Baronick, Wayne Baronick's younger sister and Vance Township's weekday daylight officer, appeared at Pete's office door, a legal pad and pen

28

in one hand, a travel mug in the other. "I've come up with some background on Virginia Lowe," she said.

Pete waved her in, grateful for a break from his Monday morning administrative duties. "Any word from the crime lab?"

Abby lowered into the chair across the desk from him. "I called them about five minutes ago. Nothing yet. Apparently, they're backlogged."

"Imagine that." Pete rose and circled the desk to refill his mug from the Mr. Coffee in the corner. He gestured to Abby, silently asking if she wanted any.

"I'm good. Thanks."

Pete returned to his seat. "What've you got?"

"Virginia Lowe was born Virginia Roth. Her first marriage to Keith Lowe produced her only child, Alexander. They divorced when the boy was three. She worked as a secretary for the Magisterial District Court in Somerset for eight years until she married Dr. Charles Davis." Abby spoke the name as if it tasted sour on her tongue.

Davis had that effect on people.

"They were married for two years and divorced four years ago, at which point she took back the last name of Lowe. She also returned to her secretarial job and has maintained the position since then."

"I wonder why she didn't take back her maiden name," Pete mused.

Abby eyed him as if wanting to say *duh*. "Because Lowe is her son's last name."

Pete considered the rationale and couldn't argue. "Any contact between her and Davis following their divorce?"

"No protection from abuse orders or anything like that."

Pete thought about what Alex had told him yesterday. "Virginia came here to talk to Zoe about Davis. The son said his mom used the word charlatan."

Abby sat motionless, thinking. "Huh."

"Yeah."

The intercom on Pete's desk beeped before his secretary's voice came through the device. "Chief, there's someone here to see you."

He pressed the button. "I'll be right there." To Abby, he said, "Why don't

29

you—"

"Do a little digging into Dr. Davis," she replied without waiting for him to finish.

"Exactly. Then I think you and I should take a ride out to the Vance Motel. I want to have another talk with Virginia's son. Sandy Giden told me she gave him another room at the far end of the place so he wouldn't have to drive in his condition yesterday."

"Roger that."

As soon as Abby headed back to her cubicle in the bullpen, Pete stood, took a long sip from his coffee, and strode toward the front of the station.

A statuesque brunette waited in the vestibule. Wearing her chestnut hair in a long, sleek ponytail and attired in dark jeans and a curve-hugging black t-shirt, the woman could've easily been featured on the cover of one of the fashion magazines Abby tried to keep hidden in her desk.

"I'm Chief Pete Adams." He extended a hand, which the brunette took with a firm grasp.

"I'm Isabella Elson. Thank you for seeing me."

Pete surmised she was in her early thirties. "How can I help you?"

She studied him with an intensity he found unnerving. After several seconds, she blinked as if his question had finally sunk in. "I'm new to the area, and I fear I may have a stalker."

Pete ushered her from the front entry down the hall to the conference room, where she took a seat at the long table and turned down his offer of something to drink. He sat kitty-corner from her and opened his notebook to a new page. "Tell me about this stalker."

She folded her hands on the table. "I'm renting a little bungalow in Elm Grove. I keep seeing the same car parked across the street with a man sitting in it. He doesn't get out, and as far as I can tell, he doesn't live near me. Then I started noticing the same car following me."

"What kind of car?"

Her right eye twitched. "White."

Which narrowed it down to at least three-quarters of the vehicles in the county. "Sedan? SUV?"

"SUV."

"Can you tell me the make or model?"

"Subaru, I think."

Pete made a note and caught himself imagining Zoe staking out this woman in her Forester.

"It's not funny, Chief."

He realized the thought of his wife as a stalker had brought a grin to his face. "You're absolutely right. I was just thinking of how many people I know with white Subarus. Have you been able to get a plate number?"

"No."

"Can you describe the driver?"

"The windows are tinted."

Pete took that as a no. "Do you have any idea who might be stalking you? An old boyfriend, perhaps?"

"No. But I'm afraid of what he might do."

"Tell you what. Give me your address, and I'll have my officers beef up their patrols on your street and keep an eye out for a vehicle matching this description."

She gave him the street and house number, watching him as he wrote it down. "Do you ever do patrols out there?"

Pete met her intense gaze, not sure what she meant. "Elm Grove is in Vance Township. We routinely patrol it several times a day."

"I don't mean your police force. I mean you. I would feel safer if I knew the police chief was looking into this guy."

Her laser focus again made him uneasy. He gave her a relaxed smile he didn't feel. "We're a small department. Even the chief has to get out and work the streets. So yes, I'll be one of the officers patrolling your neighborhood."

Her lips parted into a wide smile. "Good. Thank you."

After determining she didn't want anything else from him, Pete escorted her out the front door and watched as she climbed into a deep red Toyota Corolla backed into the space. He made a mental note of the plate number.

"What was that all about?" His secretary, Nancy, asked.

"I'm not sure." But Pete felt certain of one thing. Isabella Elson was not the victim of a stalker.

Chapter Five

Zoe hoped to find Wayne and Knight interrogating Davis when she returned from her appointment, but they were nowhere to be seen. She geared up and entered the autopsy suite to discover Davis hadn't waited for her. The victim's chest cavity was open, as was the top of the skull. A glance at the nearby countertop revealed an assortment of specimens ready to go to the lab.

But from the expressions on her two young interns' faces, there was more going on than a simple postmortem.

Davis glared at one of them. "What's your name, miss?" he demanded.

Her response was barely audible. "Nikki."

"Have you never seen a dead body before?" Davis leaned toward the young woman. "How long have you been working here? If what you're doing could be called work."

"Two months. And, yes, sir. I have seen dead bodies before."

"Then what seems to be the problem?"

Always curt, he was behaving even more boorish than normal.

Zoe strode across the room. "I suspect *you're* the problem, Doctor."

He wheeled toward her. "Mrs. Adams. I'm so glad you finally decided to put in an appearance."

She glowered at him. The way he stressed the *missus* part of her name made it sound menial. She realized Juliann Holland had used the same version—Mrs. Adams rather than Ms. Chambers-Adams or Ms. Chambers—and had used the same demeaning tone. How often did Davis and Holland get together and discuss her?

He waved a hand at Nikki, who appeared grateful to be out of his bullseye, even if temporarily. "You need to dismiss this useless excuse for an assistant. She apparently can't handle the job."

"That's not true." Nikki's response was aimed at Zoe, not Davis. "It's just that poor girl—" She gestured at the decedent on the stainless-steel table. "My older sister died of a drug overdose, and she looks so much like her. I got a little choked up. I'm fine now."

She wasn't at all fine, but Zoe knew the victim's resemblance to her sister was no longer the problem. "Don't worry about it, Nikki. We need to have compassion and empathy for the dead."

Davis sneered. "They couldn't care less about our compassion." He wheeled on Nikki again. "You are too weak for this job." He came back to Zoe. "As are you."

With all of Davis's ranting, Zoe failed to notice the sound of the door opening and closing until she caught Nikki and the other assistant looking in that direction.

"Are we interrupting something?" Wayne asked.

Zoe turned to find Wayne and Detective Knight standing a few yards behind her. "Yes," she replied, "and I owe you both lunch for it."

Davis shot a dark look her way before facing the county detectives. "If you're here for the evidence, it's bagged and on the table over there."

"Thank you," Knight said. "But we're here to question you."

Davis cast a snide grin at Zoe. When he realized both men were looking at him instead of her, the grin faded. "Me?"

"Yes. You, Dr. Davis."

"About what?"

"About the death of your ex-wife, Virginia Lowe."

His expression turned stony. "What on God's green earth are you talking about?"

Wayne stepped in. "We're sorry to have to tell you Virginia was found dead yesterday."

Davis looked from Knight to Wayne. "Fine. You've told me. You can take your evidence and go now."

"I'm afraid we still need to ask you a few questions," Knight said.

"What could you possibly need from me? She lives in Somerset. I haven't seen her in years."

Knight glanced at the two interns, who appeared very interested in this turn of events. His gaze settled on Zoe. "Do you mind if we use your office?"

She extended an open palm toward the glass-enclosed room. "Be my guest."

The three men strode toward the office. Zoe longed to follow them and listen in but knew that wasn't going to happen. Instead, she turned her attention to the young woman lying on the stainless-steel table and the two assistants at her side.

"Looks like Dr. Davis was about done," Zoe said.

"Yes, ma'am," Nikki replied. "Except for closing her up."

Zoe faced the young assistant. "If I remember your resume, you're beginning your residency in forensic pathology in a few months. Am I correct?"

"Yes, ma'am. I truly am sorry for letting this case get to me, but a black mark on my records would—"

Zoe silenced her with a raised palm. "You won't be receiving any black marks from this office."

Nikki's hunched shoulders relaxed. "Thank you."

"The reason I asked…" Zoe looked at the body. "I know this is a tough one for you, but I feel certain you're quite capable of finishing up here." A task that involved bagging the organs Davis had removed, replacing them in the body cavity, and stitching the incisions.

Nikki's chin came up. "Yes, ma'am."

Zoe also recalled the resume stating Nikki had served in the military and smiled. "Good." To the second assistant, a college med student getting extra credit, Zoe said, "You help with whatever she needs."

Leaving the pair to complete the job, she headed toward her office, stripping out of her autopsy garb. She deposited it into the biohazard bin, even though she hadn't been present for the postmortem.

Wayne had left the blinds open, giving her a clear view of the interrogation.

No. Pete would call it an interview at this stage of the investigation.

None of the men in her office were looking at her so she risked taking in the scene. Wayne and Knight were calm and cool. Davis was not. However, he wasn't his usual blustery self either. He looked agitated. On edge. And, if she was any judge, on the defensive.

His eyes shifted her way and locked with hers. Anxiety flared into anger. Wayne followed his gaze. He gave Zoe an annoyed look, approached the window, and flipped the blinds closed.

So much for being a fly on the wall. Even a deaf one.

She stalked to one of the stools where law enforcement officers liked to perch while observing an autopsy and took a seat. A loud but muffled voice filtered from the office. Davis's voice. Across the room, Nikki and her helper quietly went about their work. Minutes ticked by.

The stillness exploded as the office door crashed open. Zoe expected to hear the tinkle of shattered glass.

"If you want to speak to me again, do it through my attorney." Davis stormed out, not bothering to change from his scrubs. He didn't glance in Zoe's direction but stomped toward the exit at the rear of the suite.

Wayne strolled out of the office. Knight followed, holding a small card pinched between his forefinger and thumb.

"I've had a lot of suspects tell me to speak with their attorneys," Knight said, "but this is the first time one has been prepared to hand me his lawyer's business card."

Zoe rose from the stool. "What did he say?"

The detectives exchanged a look. Zoe understood its meaning. They were debating how much, if anything, to share.

"He did *not* confess to bludgeoning his ex-wife to death," Knight said.

Zoe gave him a look of her own. "I didn't expect he would. Do you believe him?"

Wayne traced his upper lip with one finger. "Everyone lies."

"In other words, no."

"I didn't say that."

Knight wasn't as cryptic. "I must admit he didn't exactly appear grief-stricken."

"Or surprised."

Zoe considered Wayne's comment. "I don't mean to sound like I'm defending him, but I don't think I've ever seen him truly surprised. It might not be in his emotional repertoire."

Knight snickered. "Now that you mention it, you may be right."

An unsettling thought came to Zoe's mind. "How much did you tell him about Virginia's death?"

Wayne scowled. "That she was found beaten to death yesterday. Why?"

"Did you mention where she was killed? Or that her son was with her?"

"No," Knight said firmly. "I wanted to see if he let the location slip. And we didn't want to put the kid in danger in case Davis is involved in the homicide."

"Did he ask where the body was? Knowing him, he probably thinks he's the only pathologist capable of performing the autopsy."

Knight shook his head. "He didn't ask, and we didn't tell."

"Come to think of it," Wayne added, "he didn't ask a lot of questions. It's almost like he already knew."

* * *

Sandy Giden met Pete and Abby as they stepped out of his Ford Explorer. The Vance Motel's parking lot was vacant except for Alex's silver Civic at the far end of the row. As far away from the crime scene as Sandy could place him.

It was the same room as the only other occupants from the previous night. Pete had reached them by phone. The couple was shocked to learn of the crime and claimed they hadn't seen or heard anything. They remembered the Honda but couldn't say for certain if it had been there when they left before dawn.

"I turned on the no vacancy sign after your guys finished up yesterday," Sandy told Pete. "So, Alex had the place to himself. I called him about a half hour ago. He said he was going to take a shower and would be waiting whenever you need to talk to him."

"Thanks." Pete looked toward the room where Virginia had spent her final hours. "Can you do me a favor?"

"Anything."

Pete wasn't so sure she'd feel that way when she learned of his request. "Come with us and take a look at the room."

Her eyes widened. "*That* room?"

"Something bothered me about it yesterday and I thought you might be able to help me figure out what."

"Something bothered you? There was a dead woman on the floor and blood everywhere."

He lowered his face to hide an embarrassed grin. "I should've said besides the obvious."

Sandy squirmed but agreed.

They approached the room, and she dug a keycard from her pocket.

"No sign of forced entry," Abby said.

"Small comfort." Sandy inserted the card and unlocked the door. "I don't have to replace anything out here. Only everything inside." She pushed the door open but didn't cross the threshold.

The stench of death wafted out, and Sandy took a step back. Pete reached inside and hit the switch. Even the overhead light fixture failed to penetrate the gloom. "You don't have to go in. Just take a good look and let me know if you notice anything out of place." This time, he added, "Besides the obvious."

Sandy hugged herself as she scanned the room, frowning. Pete waited and watched as she chewed her lip. After several moments, she unfolded her arms. "The bedside lamp is missing. Every room has one. An alarm clock, a phone, and a lamp on each stand." She pointed. "It's gone. Unless your CSI guys took it."

"No, you're right. I knew something was off when I was looking over the scene yesterday, but I couldn't put my finger on it. That's it." Pete looked at Abby. "We need to check with the Allegheny County ME's office about Virginia's autopsy results. We might've identified the murder weapon."

"I have the same lamps in every room," Sandy said.

38

"Mind if we take one with us?" Pete asked. "I'll see you get it back."

She wrinkled her nose. "You can keep it. My gift to the cause." She continued to study the room. "There's something else missing. One of the pillowcases. See? The pillow on the second bed has one but not the bed closest to the door."

Pete had missed that one. "Good catch."

She looked at him. "Do you want one of those as well?"

"No, thanks. If we need to match it, I'll come back."

She nodded. "I'll go get the lamp."

As Sandy walked away, Abby surveyed the room from the doorway. "If the lamp really is the murder weapon, the killer must've taken it with him. Maybe wrapped in the missing pillowcase." She turned and scanned the lot, settling on a gray bin. "Or tossed it in the dumpster."

Pete doubted the killer would make it that easy for them.

"I'll go check it out," Abby said and hurried toward the bin.

He wasn't going to stop her. He suspected the crime scene unit had already searched the trash, but the last thing he wanted was to miss a vital clue.

Pete brought his attention back to another clue Abby had mentioned.

There was no sign of forced entry.

Virginia's killer had easy access to the room. Either the victim had opened the door to him, or he had a room key.

Footsteps on the pavement drew Pete back to the present. He turned to find Sandy returning with a lamp. Simple, basic dark bronze base with a white shade and a cord bundled in her hand, the fixture would've made an effective club.

Sandy held it out to him. "If you find out that poor woman was killed with one of these, I'm going to buy all new ones."

Pete accepted the lamp and hefted it. Definitely a contender for the murder weapon. "Yesterday, you were talking about selling the whole motel."

"I still may. Do you need me for anything else?"

"Thanks, no. I'm going to put this in my car, gather my dumpster diving officer, and go speak with the victim's son."

Once Abby completed her search, coming up empty, Pete watched as she stripped out of her nitrile gloves and tossed them into the dumpster. She met him at the SUV, where she retrieved a container of hand sanitizer wipes and used several to clean up despite the gloves. The glaring look she gave him clearly told him to keep his snide comments to himself.

They found Alex Lowe waiting in his new room. Instead of the t-shirt and jeans he'd worn yesterday, he had on a plaid button-front shirt and a pair of workpants, both too big for the kid.

"How are you holding up?" Pete asked once they were settled, he and Abby in a pair of side chairs, Alex on the edge of the bed. Pete noticed the bronze lamp on the table, right where it should be.

Alex exhaled a loud sigh. "I'm okay. I guess." He looked around the room. "It's kinda creepy. This room looks exactly like the one where Mom—"

"I'm pretty sure every room here looks the same," Pete said softly.

"I'm not complaining." Alex lowered his face. "It was nice of Ms. Giden to give me a place to stay."

Pete opened his notebook. "Are you up to answering a few more questions?"

"Yeah. I guess."

"I want to nail down the timeline. When did you and your mom check in on Saturday?"

"It was a little after seven. We aren't familiar with the area and wanted to get here before dark."

Pete noted the information. "Did either of you go anywhere last night after you arrived?"

"Nope. Mom was tired and stressed. We pretty much crashed and watched TV."

"Do you or your mom know anyone around here?"

"Nope. No one."

Pete studied the kid long and hard.

Alex fidgeted under the scrutiny. Then his eyes widened. "Oh. Well, yeah, there's my stepdad. But I don't even know where he lives."

"Did your mom know?"

Alex started to shake his head but stopped. "I don't know. She never said."

"You told me your mom argued with Dr. Davis over the phone."

"Yeah. I guess she had his phone number, but it doesn't mean she knew where he lives."

True, but that wasn't really what Pete needed to know. "When was the phone call?"

Alex brought one hand up, running it through his hair. "Today's Monday, right?"

"All day," Pete replied, giving him a comforting smile.

"Saturday afternoon. I was online, reading articles about the flooding, when I came across the stories about him trash-talking your wife and her throwing shade right back at him. I told Mom about it. She called him, and they yelled at each other."

"And she decided to come here that same day?"

Alex lowered his face. "I wish I'd talked her out of it. I wish she'd held off and thought about it a few days." His face came up, his eyes shifting toward the door. "None of this would've happened."

Pete watched the sorrow weigh on the young man. Keeping his voice soft, Pete asked, "When your mom was talking to Dr. Davis, what exactly did she say about coming here?"

Alex appeared puzzled. "She warned him to back off the coroner lady. Your wife, right? Or she'd come here and talk to her."

Pete wondered what buried secrets Davis wanted his ex to keep to herself. "It sounds like she intended to give him time to make things right first."

Alex shook his head emphatically. "No. I mean, yeah. But then he started yelling at her. I don't know exactly what he said, and she didn't tell me. But I got the impression he told her to go to hell."

"So, she decided to drop everything and come to see my wife."

"Yeah. Mom's impulsive." His lips twitched as if attempting to grin. And failing. "She always tells me I'm just like her that way."

Pete flipped to a new page. "Let's talk about yesterday morning."

Alex winced.

"Tell me what happened."

The scowl deepened.

41

"I mean up to the point where you returned and found us at the motel. Where did you go?"

"To get some breakfast."

"Talk me through it."

He seemed confused by the request. "We woke up and were hungry. And we both needed coffee." He gestured at the small brewer next to the TV. "No offense to Ms. Giden, but that stuff is crap. Anyway, there's no restaurant here, so I got on my phone and found a fast-food place in a town called Phillipsburg."

Burger Boy. Pete knew it and its coffee well. "What time did you leave?"

Alex's brow creased in thought. "About six? Neither of us slept very good, so we were up early."

"And your mom was fine?"

"She was anxious about tracking down your wife, which is what she was doing when I left. She was on her phone looking at the county's website."

"You left around six a.m." Without looking at his notes, Pete knew Sandy had called in the homicide almost an hour later.

Phillipsburg was only seven miles away.

"Six or a little after. I wasn't paying attention."

"Tell me where you went."

"I already did. I went to the fast-food place."

"Did you use the drive-through?"

"No. The line was ten miles long." He huffed. "The lines inside weren't much better."

"How long did it take?"

Pete saw the realization flicker in Alex's eyes. "You're checking my alibi." The young man's voice rose an octave. "You think I could've done that to my mom?"

Pete didn't want him to shut down. "I need to get a timeline to figure out when your mom was killed. And I want to clear you, so we don't waste valuable time."

Alex's expression transformed from anger to grief and back to sorrow.

"I was here when you returned," Pete said softly. "It was eight-thirty. You

42

can see why I need to pin down where you were during those two-and-a-half hours."

Alex swiped his eyes with his shirt sleeve and sniffled. "I wasn't thinking. I never meant to be gone so long."

Chapter Six

When Zoe returned to her temporary office, she found Paulette staring out the window.

"You okay?" Zoe asked when her secretary didn't move.

Paulette flinched and turned to face her. "I didn't hear you come in."

Zoe noted her secretary's puffy eyes. "Is something wrong?"

"I've been worrying myself sick about Doc." Paulette dug a tissue from her cardigan's pocket and quietly blew her nose. "Have you heard anything?"

Zoe dropped into her chair. "I spoke with his nurse. He's stable and showing signs of regaining consciousness."

Paulette brightened. "Good." She tossed the tissue into her garbage can and moved to stand in front of Zoe's desk. "How did your meeting with Commissioner Holland go?"

Zoe braced her elbows on the desktop and buried her face in her hands, trying to block out the memory. "Not well."

"She didn't fire you, did she?"

Zoe lifted her head. "No. She doesn't have the authority."

"I know that. I just wasn't sure *she* knows it."

"She wants to though. She's backing Chuckie's push to convert us to a Medical Examiner system." Zoe dreaded speaking her next words. "And she's backing Chuckie. She basically told me I can't fire him."

"Why the hell not?"

"First, there's Doc's situation."

"Hire another pathologist."

Zoe told her about Holland's so-called attempts to do just that. "I have a

44

feeling she intentionally alienated everyone she contacted."

Paulette leaned down, pressing both palms to Zoe's desk. "You call them again. You're more diplomatic than she is."

"I plan to. But it would've been so much easier if she hadn't muddied the waters." Zoe remembered her other news. "Speaking of Chuckie, did you know he was married?"

Paulette straightened. "Was. Yes. The woman, whoever she is, wised up."

Before Zoe could tell her about Virginia Lowe's death, someone rapped on the office door. Paulette crossed the room to open it. A woman with dark blond hair pulled into a bun on the back of her head stood there clinging to the shoulder strap of her handbag.

"You must be Elizabeth," Paulette said brightly. "Come in."

The woman hesitated before taking one step across the threshold. "I'm sorry. You have me confused with someone else. My name is Rachel Ferrari. I'm supposed to meet Grace Abercrombie here."

Zoe rose and strode to her. "Doc Abercrombie's wife?"

"Yes. She told me she'd introduce me to Coroner Zoe Chambers-Adams."

Zoe held out a hand. "That's me. Consider us introduced."

Rapid footsteps in the hallway stopped Paulette from closing the door. Puffing, Grace appeared, grasping the jamb as if to keep from collapsing. "Rachel, I'm so sorry I'm late."

"No problem." Zoe waved her in. "I hear Doc's showing signs of improvement."

Grace's smile was fleeting. "He is, but I won't feel any peace until he opens his eyes and speaks my name."

With Doc's wife and Rachel seated in folding chairs, Zoe returned to her side of the desk. "How can I help you?"

The women exchanged glances. Rachel appeared uncomfortable. Grace gave her a nod and looked at Zoe. "Rachel had an appointment with Lyle yesterday afternoon. One he obviously didn't keep. When she found out why, she came to the hospital and tracked him—and me—down. Lyle had already told me a little about the reason for the meeting. Rachel filled in the rest. We talked and…"

Rachel picked up the story. "Grace told me about you. Last night, I did some research. I read about how you solved a cold case this summer and cleared a young man's name."

Zoe squirmed internally at the memory but maintained her outer calm. She stayed silent, knowing Rachel was far from finished.

"Five years ago, my husband died."

"I'm sorry."

"Thank you. I came here to Monongahela County to hire Dr. Abercrombie to reopen the case. As if my husband's case was ever really open."

Grace placed a hand on the woman's arm. "Start at the beginning, dear."

"Yes, of course." Rachel paused, gathering her thoughts. "Five years ago in April, my husband's body was recovered from the Youghiogheny River between Ohiopyle and Confluence. Do you know the area?"

Zoe drew a legal pad closer and picked up a pen. "I've been to Ohiopyle State Park a few times."

"Then you know the river. My husband was an outdoorsman. Hunting. Fishing. Especially flyfishing on the Yough."

Zoe imagined a man in his waders, standing in the middle of the often treacherous river, being swept off his feet, carried downstream into the whitewater and rocks. But all she said was "Yes, I know it."

Rachel appeared satisfied she didn't have to elaborate on the location. "A witness called 911 to report seeing a man—my husband—jump from the bridge on Route 281 in Confluence. It crosses the river just below the dam. There had been a lot of rain, so the water was a little higher than usual. The witness said he went under, and she never saw him resurface. They called out river rescue. It took a couple of days before they recovered Tanner's body downstream." Rachel's voice grew ragged.

Paulette grabbed a box of tissues from her desk and set it in front of the widow, who smiled in appreciation.

After dabbing her eyes, Rachel continued. "The autopsy determined cause of death was brain trauma sustained during the jump and called it a suicide. The case was closed." Jaw clenched, she locked eyes with Zoe. "My husband did not commit suicide."

Zoe had heard variations of these same words innumerable times since she'd worked at the morgue.

"Tanner loved life. He loved his job. He loved being out in nature. On top of that, he was a devout Catholic. Suicide? Even if he had been depressed, he would never assert dominion over God's creation by taking his own life." Rachel fell silent, watching Zoe intently.

Zoe studied her notes and touched the tip of her pen to one word. "You said there was a witness."

Rachel's expression darkened. "Someone, a woman from what I've been told, called it in. But that's one of the things troubling me. According to the 911 operator, the caller didn't leave a name. When the police wanted to question her, she'd disappeared. The call was placed from a burner phone, so they couldn't track her down."

Zoe tapped her chin with the pen. "Why would someone use a burner phone to call 911?" she mused.

"Exactly." Rachel sat back in the chair as if she'd used all her energy and had none left to support her spine. "Since the Somerset County Coroner proclaimed Tanner's death a suicide, the police didn't look into it any further."

Grace touched her arm. "Rachel, dear. Tell Zoe who the Somerset County Coroner's pathologist was back then."

From Grace's tone, Zoe knew the answer before Rachel spoke the name. "Dr. Charles Davis."

Zoe groaned. A knock interrupted the woman's story and Zoe's whirling mind.

Paulette scurried to open the door. Another woman stood in the hallway, this one tall and striking with short gray hair and carrying a large handbag.

"Can I help you?" Paulette asked.

"I hope so. I'm Elizabeth Preston. I—"

"Oh." Paulette gave herself a light tap on the forehead. "Elizabeth. Of course. I've been expecting you. Please come in."

As she did, Paulette faced Zoe and froze. "I'm sorry. Where's my head?" She gave the newcomer an embarrassed smile. "Perhaps we should go downstairs to the coffee shop until the coroner finishes her meeting."

Rachel stood. "It's fine. I don't have anything else to add." She eyed Zoe, her expression imploring. "Please tell me you'll look into this."

Zoe glanced at Grace. "There's one big problem here. The death happened in Somerset County. I have no jurisdiction. Doc's really the person for the job."

Grace rose slowly to her feet. "He wanted to do this investigation. I'm sure once he's better, he still will. Zoe, what Rachel is asking you—what *I* am asking you—is for a favor."

Zoe squirmed. "I wish I could, but you're putting me in a professional bind." She didn't mention the predicament she was already in with Commissioner Holland.

Grace didn't back off. "If you could, just do some preliminary work off the record. Find out what you can. It would save Lyle a lot of time and effort. Once he's able, turn over your findings to him, and he'll do the rest. You could keep him from wasting his energy on false leads." She took Zoe's hand in both of hers. "Please."

Zoe closed her eyes, imagined being called once more in front of Juliann, pictured Davis gloating at the commissioner's side. What Grace and Rachel were asking could be professional suicide. Zoe exhaled and opened her eyes to find Grace's beseeching gaze still locked onto her. "I don't know what good I can do, but I'll make some phone calls. See what I can find out."

Grace pumped her hand. "Thank you."

"Yes, thank you." Rachel handed Zoe a real estate agency's business card. "You can reach me here. I'm sure you'll have questions."

Zoe was sure, too.

Once the two women left, Paulette closed the door and ushered the new arrival to Zoe's desk. "County Coroner Zoe Chambers-Adams, this is Elizabeth Preston. She's applying for my job."

"Oh." Zoe shook the hand Elizabeth held out. First, an uncomfortable meeting with Juliann Holland. Then, a request to investigate a case she had no business being involved in—one of her despised deputy coroner's old cases, no less. Now, she needed to be composed enough to interview a potential replacement for the irreplaceable Paulette.

"I'm sorry. I can see this is a bad time," Elizabeth said.

Before Zoe could agree, Paulette fluttered a hand and said, "Nonsense. One thing about the coroner's office. There's never a good time."

A laugh escaped Zoe's throat. "You have a point." She gestured at the chair Grace had vacated. "Please have a seat."

Elizabeth complied and dug into her handbag, coming up with a neatly folded bundle of papers, which she held out to Zoe. "This is my resume. I emailed it to you but in case you didn't have a chance to read it, I brought along a copy."

"Actually, you emailed it to me," Paulette said. "I did read it and was quite impressed. That's why I set up this meeting."

Zoe scanned the immaculately formatted four-page document. Elizabeth Preston was forty-eight years old, had a master's degree in business administration from the University of Pittsburgh, and had worked for several major companies in Baltimore and Atlanta. Most recently, she'd spent five years with a finance company in Pittsburgh. Her current address was listed as Lafayette Township, the most upscale community in Monongahela County. Elizabeth Preston was undeniably overqualified for the job of secretary.

Zoe looked at Paulette, who sat at her desk, beaming. Clearly, she thought the same thing. If Paulette wanted out of this job, Elizabeth was her best bet. Zoe brought her focus back to the applicant. "I have to ask. Why do you want to work here?"

Elizabeth offered a reserved smile. "I probably shouldn't admit this, but I'm burned out. I've been in the middle of high-pressure, high-stakes business all my adult life." Her short laugh was low and throaty. "I do realize a coroner's office is also high-pressure and high stakes, but this is Monongahela County, Pennsylvania. It's not the same as the big-city madness I'm used to. You do important work. Work that matters. I want a job dealing with real people instead of trying to make rich people richer." She paused. "Does that make sense?"

"It does." Before Zoe had a chance to say more, the office phone rang.

Paulette answered and grabbed a pen and paper to jot notes. After repeating "Uh-huh" several times, she told the caller, "The coroner's on her way," and hung up. To Zoe, she said, "Traffic fatality on Millcraft Road, two miles south of Marsdale."

On her way out, Zoe snatched the sheet of paper Paulette had torn from her pad. "I leave it to you to finish the job interview," Zoe told her. Lowering her voice, she added, "I'm also leaving the final decision to you. You know your job better than I do."

Paulette grinned and whispered, "If she'll accept getting paid a pittance, I'm hiring her."

Chapter Seven

Pete listened as, face lowered, Alex Lowe poured out a story about meeting a girl—a super cute girl, according to him—at the fast-food place and completely losing track of time. They'd sat and talked for well over an hour before Alex realized how much time had passed.

"Did you at least get her number?" Pete asked the question, giving the kid a man-to-man wink. Keep him thinking Pete was on his side.

Alex grinned through his tears. "I did." He dug a slip of paper from his pocket and showed it to Pete.

He held out his hand. "Do you mind?"

Alex's phone chimed. He gave the note to Pete before picking up the device and thumbing the screen.

Pete unfolded the scrap. A girl's name was printed at the top. Heather. Below it, her number. A local landline if the prefix was any indication, not a cell. Odd for a teen.

Alex tapped something into his phone and set it down. "That was my aunt." From his tone, he was far from overjoyed at hearing from her.

Pete held up the paper bearing Heather's contact information. "Did you happen to get Heather's last name?"

"Uh. No."

"Do you mind if I keep this?"

Alex's eyes widened. "Uh," he sputtered, "I thought I might still give her a call. You know. Not right away, but..." A sigh lifted and dropped his shoulders. "I mean, she's super cute."

Poor kid. Pete remembered being his age and enamored with a "super cute" girl. "How about you let us take a photo of it? Then you can keep the original."

"Okay." Alex relaxed. "Thanks."

"No problem." Pete handed the paper to Abby, who captured the image on her phone and returned the note to Alex. Pete didn't mention Heather might turn out to be Alex's alibi for the time his mom was murdered.

Abby rose and left the room.

Once Alex folded and pocketed the paper, Pete closed his notebook. "I think that's all for now."

"Can I go home?"

"Absolutely. I have your number if I have any other questions." Pete left the teen in the motel room and met Abby in the parking lot. "Well?"

Her expression soured. "The number is out of service."

Pete grunted.

"Poor kid," Abby said. "It's one of the oldest tricks in the book. A guy is overly interested. The girl? Not so much, so she gives him a fake phone number."

Pete wouldn't admit it to Abby—or Zoe—but he'd experienced the same thing a time or two. "That's one possibility."

"What do you mean?"

"Alex might've figured he needed an alibi for yesterday morning. Or at least a good story. We need to track down a sample of his handwriting."

Abby's expression turned glum. "Aw, man. I really hope he's not our guy. He seems like a nice kid."

Pete didn't mention how many stone-cold killers came across as "nice kids." "Provided the handwriting doesn't match, we'll need to ask around at Burger Boy. Try to locate Heather."

Squealing tires drew Pete's attention as a small, older-model Nissan careened into the parking lot. The car braked to a stop for a moment, then veered in their direction. He grabbed Abby's arm, about to jerk her out of the way, when the Nissan swung around them and skidded to a stop between Alex's Civic and Pete's Explorer.

Pete swore. This driver was either drunk or reckless or both. Pete charged toward the car as its door swung open. The young, willowy woman who stepped out shot a glance at him before fixing her gaze on Alex's room. She started toward it.

"Hold up there," Pete called in his most commanding voice.

The woman spun to face him, her jaw set, her eyes defiant. "What?" she demanded.

Confronting anger with anger was a bad idea. Pete tamped his down. "Where's the fire?"

She looked confused. "Huh?"

He rephrased. "What's your hurry?"

Alex appeared in his doorway. "Aunt Fiona. What are you doing here?"

The young woman turned away from Pete and strode to the boy, gathering him in her arms. Alex, Pete noticed, didn't immediately return the hug, although after a few seconds, he gingerly embraced his aunt.

"Where else would I be?" she said. "Poor Virginia. I can't believe she's gone. I got here as soon as I could."

"I told you, there's nothing you can do." Alex grasped her shoulders and pried her away. "I was about to head home."

"Then I'll drive you."

"I have Mom's car."

Pete surveyed the two vehicles. Both had been on the road for many years. Taking a closer look at the aunt, he decided what they shared in preferences for small deathtraps on wheels, they lacked in appearances. He'd only seen Virginia in death, but she bore little resemblance to the lead foot in front of him. Fiona's dark, almost black, hair was cut in a short pixie. Her sleeveless tank top revealed well-muscled arms without an ounce of fat. Ironically, the only visible tattoo was a dainty pink rose on her shoulder.

Fiona gestured at the Honda. "We can leave it and pick it up another time."

"No." Alex stomped a foot, acting more like an obstinate pre-teen than an almost-grown man. "I'm driving it home. You can follow if you have to."

She planted her fists on her narrow hips. "And where do you think home is? You can't live by yourself."

It was a low blow, a reminder of what he'd lost, and his petulant attitude dissolved in a fresh gleam of tears. "I don't know. Maybe not. Maybe I can stay with Aunt Darlene."

"You'll stay with me." She drew him into another resisted hug.

Pete caught the glance Alex shot his way and the flash of embarrassment that crossed the young man's face.

Alex squirmed free and stepped back, creating physical and emotional distance from his aunt. "We don't have to settle this right now. I just want to go home. We need to plan a funeral for Mom." He wheeled and disappeared into his room.

Fiona started after him.

"Hold up there," Pete ordered.

She spun to face him. "What do you want?"

"I need to see some ID."

Her expression made Pete wonder if he'd sprouted a third head. "My nephew told you who I am."

"It doesn't change the fact your driving was, shall we say, reckless when you pulled in." He held out a hand. "Driver's license, registration, and proof of insurance, please."

She glared at his hand as if ready to spit in it. Instead, she growled like a bear and retreated to her car.

While Fiona rummaged through the car's interior, Abby, who'd been standing next to the Explorer, returned to Pete's side and gave a low whistle. "What a piece of work. Poor kid."

Fiona exited the Nissan and stomped toward them, the requested documents clenched in her fist. She thrust the IDs at Pete. "Happy now?"

He didn't reply but handed the cards to Abby, who carried them off to their SUV.

Fiona hiked a thumb at the motel room. "When you're done with those, I'll be helping my nephew pack."

"Not yet." Pete crossed his arms and fixed the dark-haired stick of dynamite with a hard glare.

"Now what?"

Mostly, he wanted to give Alex a few minutes of peace. Mostly, but not entirely. "What can you tell me about your sister's trip here?"

Fiona mimicked Pete's crossed-arm stance, adding a cocked hip. "Not a thing. First I heard of it was when Alex called to say she was dead."

"Any idea who might've wanted to kill her?"

"Nope." Fiona wasn't making this easy.

Pete relaxed his arms to his side, hoping she'd again mirror his pose, possibly relaxing her attitude as well. "Tell me about her ex-husband, Dr. Charles Davis."

Fiona took the time to consider her response, but it didn't help. "He's a jackass."

Nothing new. "What else?"

"That's it. He's a jackass. I don't know the man well enough to tell you anything else."

"He was your brother-in-law."

She shrugged. "I never spent any time with him. I only know he's a jackass from what Alex told me."

"What about Virginia? What did she tell you?"

"Nothing much. She wasn't the talkative type."

Unlike her sister, Fiona, Pete thought.

Alex appeared at his room's door.

"You ready to go?" Fiona asked.

"Almost." He looked at Pete, pinching the oversized shirt he wore. "Ms. Giden loaned me some clothes that belonged to her husband. I need to thank her and find out if she wants me to return them." He avoided looking at his aunt. "The detectives said our clothes—Mom's and mine—were evidence. Do you know when I can get them back?"

"I'll walk with you," Pete said. When Fiona started to follow, he turned to her with a firm "Stay here."

She gave the bear growl again but obeyed.

Once they were out of hearing range, Pete asked, "As for your clothes, I'll check into it. But they may insist on holding onto them for a while."

Alex breathed a resigned sigh.

"Are you okay? With your aunt, I mean?"

"I'm not going to stay with her. She's...pushy."

Pete snickered. "I gathered as much. You mentioned your other aunt."

"Aunt Darlene. She's not so bad. I guess I can stay with her for a couple of months. I'll be eighteen soon, and then I can live alone."

"What about college?"

Alex gazed into the distance. "Good question." One he didn't answer.

"Before I forget, while you're on your way—" Pete almost said home. "On your way to your aunt's house, stop at the Monongahela County Police Station and let them fingerprint you." When the boy looked confused, Pete added, "So they can eliminate your prints from the motel room."

"Oh. Okay."

At the door to the motel office, Pete stopped. He dug out his notebook and pen, which he handed to Alex. "Write down your Aunt Darlene's full name and address so I can be sure to reach you as soon as the county police release your clothes."

Alex took the pad, scribbled down the information, and returned it to Pete before offering his hand. "Chief, thank you." He shot a glance toward his car and, Pete presumed, his "pushy" Aunt Fiona. "For everything."

Pete appreciated the firm grip. "You're welcome. You have my number if you need anything. Or if you think of anything that might help with the case."

"Yes, sir."

Alex continued into the office. Pete returned to the vehicles. Fiona sat motionless inside her Nissan, although Pete felt certain she watched his every move through her rearview.

Abby waited in the Explorer's passenger seat.

"Well?" he asked once he'd climbed behind the wheel.

"I returned her IDs." Abby looked at her notes. "Fiona Roth lives on Ramcat Road in Confluence. No wants or warrants."

"When we get back to the station—"

Abby finished his sentence. "I'll dig deeper."

Pete handed her his notebook, still open to the page Alex had written on. "What's this?"

"The other aunt's address."

"Jefferson Street, Uniontown."

"Yep." Pete wagged a finger at the page. "And it's in Alex's handwriting."

Abby's eyes widened in realization. "Oh." She picked up her phone and scrolled. Pausing, she squinted at the screen, enlarged it, and shifted her gaze from the phone to Pete's notebook. "I'm no expert, but the handwriting doesn't look anything alike to me."

"Good." But Pete still wanted to have someone who was an expert confirm it.

Finding Heather would be helpful as well.

* * *

By the time Zoe returned to the office, Paulette had gone home for the day. She'd left a note on Zoe's desk.

Hired Elizabeth on a six-week probationary basis. She starts tomorrow AM. I'm officially giving you my two-week's notice.

This was happening way too fast. Zoe wasn't at all ready for more upheaval in her life, no matter how efficient Elizabeth Preston might be.

Zoe flopped into her desk chair and stared at her phone. The accident fatality awaited autopsy in the morgue's cooler. All Zoe needed was a pathologist to perform it. Gritting her teeth, she called Davis.

"What?" he answered.

"We have a traffic fatality at the morgue. When do you want to schedule the postmortem?"

"Call your friend, Doc Abercrombie."

With her free hand, she dug her fingers into the rock-hard muscles running up the back of her neck. "Can we be serious, please?"

"Fine. Seriously. I'm busy for the next few days. Get someone else." He hung up.

She wanted to burst into tears. A good cry might help her stress, but it wouldn't do a thing for the young man in the morgue.

Zoe moved to the other desk and Paulette's Rolodex. For the next hour,

Zoe placed one call after another to every forensic pathologist in the card file. One by one, they turned her down, citing other jobs, other appointments, or simply flat-out saying no. Each used the same cold tone, which she'd never heard from any of them before.

Thank you, Juliann Holland.

Finally, a woman answered Zoe's call and sounded as frustrated as Zoe felt.

"Commissioner Holland gives professional women a bad name," Dr. Maneet Patel said. "Of course, I will help you. I can be there for nine tomorrow morning."

Zoe thanked her profusely. After ending the call, she leaned back in Paulette's chair and closed her eyes.

Her phone rang, jerking her upright. She feared Dr. Patel had reconsidered, but caller ID showed Grace Abercrombie's number. An even deeper sense of dread fell over her.

But the lilt in Grace's voice calmed Zoe's nerves. "Zoe, dear, are you still in town?"

"Yep. Wrapping things up for the day."

"Can you swing by the hospital before you go home? Lyle's awake, and he wants to see you."

"I'm on my way."

Chapter Eight

Zoe found Grace at Doc's bedside, beaming and holding his hand.

"Zoe's here," Grace said, her tone perky.

Doc, on the other hand, looked anything but.

Zoe crossed to stand next to Grace but held Doc's gaze. "It is really good to see you," she told him.

He managed a weary smile. "Better here than where we usually spend our time." His words came out slurred.

"Definitely. But I have to tell you, I can't wait until you can get back there. Vertical. Not horizontal."

His chuckle was soft and ended with him wrapping his free arm across his torso. "Damn broken ribs. Don't make me laugh."

"Sorry."

Grace released his hand to gently smooth his blanket. Satisfied, she leaned back in her chair and looked at Zoe. "I told Lyle about your meeting with Rachel."

So this was what he wanted to talk about. "She has an intriguing story," Zoe said.

"Right now, you and my wife know as much as I do." He slid the nasal cannula from his nostrils to under his chin. "Maybe more. But I agree. It's intriguing."

"But it's out of my wheelhouse, not to mention my jurisdiction, to investigate a cold case from another county." Zoe left out the part about Davis's involvement.

Grace reached over and replaced the oxygen tubing. "I told Zoe I think she should do it. You're on the mend and can take over once you're able. Don't you agree having Zoe do the legwork would make it a lot easier on you?"

Doc coughed. And grimaced. Grace snatched the plastic cup of water from his tray and handed it to him. He cleared his throat and took a sip from the straw. Wrinkling his nose, he said, "I need a soft drink."

Grace jumped to her feet. "I'll ask at the nurse's station for some ginger ale."

Doc waved a hand. "Not ginger ale. Do me a favor? Go down to the cafeteria and get me a Coke."

Grace cocked her head in disapproval.

"It'll be fine. They offered to bring me coffee, so I don't believe a soda would be an issue." His expression reminded Zoe of an imploring toddler. "Please."

She sighed. "Fine. I can't refuse you anything when you're like this."

Zoe noticed he watched Grace leave, and the moment she was gone, he yanked the cannula from his nose. "I need to talk to you," he said.

The urgency in his voice unnerved Zoe. "About Rachel Ferrari?"

"No. About my accident."

Stunned, Zoe dropped into Grace's empty chair. "Oh?"

After another glance at the doorway, Doc raised the head of his bed a few inches. "That's better. Okay, look, I don't remember the actual wreck. Have you heard anything from Pete?"

"No. But it's not his case. The county police are handling it."

Doc nodded. "I may not remember the crash, but I remember something else." He lowered his voice to a whisper. "I sent Grace to the cafeteria because I don't want to worry her. I'm pretty sure someone's been following me. I don't remember much about Sunday morning. But before that."

Zoe leaned forward. "How long before?

"Maybe a week? I'm not sure. Hell, I might be paranoid. But I swear I've seen the same black SUV either tailing me or parked near my car at different places around town."

"What kind of SUV?"

"A Toyota 4Runner."

She pondered Doc's words. "Pete and I joke half the population of Monongahela County owns a white Forester like mine. I think the other half own black Toyota 4Runners."

He huffed. "Not half. Maybe a quarter. Which is what I've been telling myself. But then I wake up in here after I apparently ran off a road I drive on a daily basis? It makes me wonder."

A rap at the door drew Zoe's attention. Wayne Baronick stood there. "It's good to see you're awake, Doc. Mind if I come in?"

Doc gave him a weak wave.

Wayne crossed to stand next to Zoe. "Any word on the Virginia Lowe case?" he asked her.

"I was going to ask you the same thing."

"Who's Virginia Lowe?" Doc asked.

"A homicide victim," Wayne said without elaboration.

"I'll call the Allegheny County ME in the morning," Zoe told the detective.

Doc wasn't about to be dismissed so easily. "Why is the Allegheny County ME involved?"

Zoe called up her best poker-night-bluff smile. "Because my best pathologist is on vacation."

Doc's scowl told her he wasn't amused.

"I need to ask you a few questions about yesterday morning, if you're up to it." Wayne's request distracted Doc from the topic of Virginia Lowe, for which Zoe was grateful.

"I don't know how much help I can be, but go ahead and ask."

"What do you remember?"

"Not a damn thing. According to my doctor, I may or may not recover those memories."

"That happens a lot with concussions," Zoe said.

"Any kind of traumatic injury." Doc glared at her. "I do know my medicine." He turned back to Wayne. "Since you probably know more than I do, why don't you tell me? What the hell happened?"

Wayne glanced at Zoe before coming back to Doc. "According to the accident reconstruction team's report, it was no accident."

Zoe gripped the lowered side rail to still her spinning brain.

Doc's voice sounded like gravel. "What are you saying?"

"There was a dent in your rear bumper that can't be explained by the collision with the tree you struck." Wayne paused, watching Doc. "And there was paint transfer on your Caddie's driver-side quarter panel. As close as we can tell, someone rammed you from the rear, then came alongside and tapped you, sending you out of control and over the embankment."

Zoe looked at Doc. She knew what he was thinking. "What color was the paint transfer?" she asked Wayne while keeping her eyes on Doc.

"Black."

"Oh, God," Doc breathed.

Wayne looked at him askance. "What?"

Doc closed his eyes and shook his head, clearly not wanting to answer the question.

So, Zoe did, telling the detective about the black Toyota 4Runner.

"You think someone's been following you?" Wayne asked.

Grace's panicked cry from the doorway spun Zoe sideways in the chair. "Lyle Abercrombie. Someone's following you, and you never told me?"

Doc swore under his breath. "How long have you been standing there?"

"Long enough." She stormed into the room and slammed the cup of soda onto the tray, sloshing some of it out in spite of the plastic lid. She faced Wayne, hands on hips. "You mean to tell me this wasn't an accident?"

Chagrined, he lowered his face. "No, ma'am. It doesn't appear so."

Grace turned her fury toward her husband. "How long have you known you were being followed?"

"I don't know for sure."

She crossed her arms. "Give me an educated guess."

Zoe considered escaping before Grace's wrath was aimed at her.

"Two weeks, maybe."

Grace mulled over all this new information. She inhaled and gained at least an inch in height before locking eyes with Zoe. "Two weeks," she repeated. "Rachel Ferrari contacted him two weeks ago."

* * *

Pete had the takeout containers from Walden's and silverware already on the table when Zoe came downstairs from her shower. He knew neither of them felt like cooking after this very long Monday.

Zoe scooped up the orange tabby who'd settled into her chair. She had two, and he still couldn't tell them apart.

With the cat deposited on the floor, Zoe popped open the lid and inhaled. "Meatloaf. My favorite."

"I'm pretty sure anything you didn't have to prepare would be your favorite tonight."

"You know me so well."

They sat in comfortable silence for several minutes, taking the edge off their hunger, before Pete asked, "How was your day?"

She groaned.

"That good, huh? You told me Doc was conscious and doing well. That's one for the positive column."

"The only one. Speaking of Doc, did you hear what the accident reconstruction team learned?"

"Baronick called and told me."

Zoe filled him in on the black 4Runner.

"Interesting," Pete said. One word holding so many possibilities.

"Did Wayne tell you he's posted security outside Doc's hospital room?"

"No, but it makes sense. Someone tried to kill him once. They might try to finish the job."

Zoe visibly shivered, then proceeded to tell him about her meeting with Juliann Holland, a woman Pete had encountered a handful of times, both in her new capacity as commissioner and in court when she'd been defending someone he'd arrested. She always seemed angry and tried too hard to prove herself.

Zoe went on, talking about Pauline's resignation, a shocking revelation tempered at least by the promising new hire. When Zoe fell silent, gazing at her food as if it had offended her, Pete knew there was more.

Before he could press, she blinked and looked at him. "What about you? I asked Wayne about the Virginia Lowe case. He didn't tell me anything, but we couldn't really talk because Doc started asking why I sent the body to Allegheny County."

"Have you heard anything from them?"

"Not yet. I'll call first thing in the morning."

"You might want to ask if they think a brass lamp like the one I sent them might be the murder weapon."

Zoe lowered her fork. "Oh?"

He told her about the missing light fixture and about his talk with the victim's son.

"A teenage boy and a cute girl? I have to say, I buy it."

"I would too, but the number she gave him is out of service."

"I've done that. It works best when you know you're never gonna see the guy again."

"Doesn't help when you need an alibi though."

"True." Zoe moved some mashed potatoes around her plate with her fork.

"Then the kid's aunt showed up."

"Oh?"

"I'm not sure what to make of her. She didn't seem too torn up about her sister's death, but she sure was protective of her nephew."

Zoe thought about it before echoing Pete's word back at him. "Interesting."

He circled back to what was bothering her. "What else happened today? I can tell there's more than what you've already said."

She smiled sheepishly. "I'm convinced you can read my mind."

"If I could, I wouldn't have to ask."

Zoe gingerly placed the fork on her plate and leaned back in her chair. "I had a visitor today." She told him about Rachel Ferrari, a widow who wanted to hire Doc to dig into her husband's supposed suicide.

Pete considered the ramifications. "I can see her hiring Doc. He could exhume the body and do another autopsy. But why you?"

"Because Grace thinks I can do some investigating like I did this summer."

"That was different. It was a Monongahela County case."

"I know. I told them this was outside of my jurisdiction."

Pete raised both hands. "There you go." But he watched her expressions run the gamut and knew it wasn't so cut and dry. "You still want to do it. Why? And when? It's not like you have a lot of spare time."

She lowered her face. "I know, I know, I know," she chanted under her breath.

"But?"

Her baby blues came up to meet his. "But it would save Doc time if I could at least get some of the preliminary questions answered while he's healing."

Pete knew there was more.

She exhaled. "The forensic pathologist who labeled Ferrari's death a suicide just happened to be Dr. Charles Davis."

And there it was.

"Davis seems to be in the center of a lot of shit right now," Pete said.

"He certainly does." Zoe looked at her food and pushed the takeout plate away. "I hate to think it, but..." She shook her head.

"But what?"

"You said Virginia's son believes Davis had something to do with her death."

"He's a grieving kid."

"But Virginia was coming here to see me. To talk to me about Davis."

Pete saw where Zoe was headed and remained quiet.

"Before she could tell me anything, she turns up dead."

He gave her a slow nod of confirmation.

"Davis has to know I planned to fire him. Before I get my chance, Doc ends up in the hospital. Meaning I have no choice. I have to keep Davis on staff. Juliann Holland saw to it by alienating almost every other pathologist within a hundred-mile radius."

"'Almost?'"

Zoe told him about finally tracking down a doctor willing to help.

"I wonder if we should offer this Dr. Patel a protection detail," Pete said sarcastically.

"Don't even joke about it." Zoe came forward in her chair, resting both elbows on the table. "But it does make you wonder." Her eyes narrowed. "You don't think Davis could be responsible for running Doc off the road. Do you?"

"What kind of car does he drive?"

"A silver Lexus."

"Does he have a second vehicle?"

"You mean like a black 4Runner?" She shook her head. "Not that I'm aware of."

Pete made a mental note to make sure, but as much as he disliked the man, he couldn't see Davis behind the wheel, running a colleague off the road.

Zoe must've been thinking the same thing. She shook her head again and drew her takeout container closer. "I know you hate coincidences, but this might prove they do happen."

Pete watched her devour what was left of her dinner. He, however, had completely lost his appetite. Coincidences.

Yes, he really did hate them.

Chapter Nine

Zoe arrived at the morgue by eight o'clock Tuesday morning so she could have the body prepped and ready for Dr. Patel. But the pathologist was already there, sitting in the morgue office, reading the report on the victim. She rose when Zoe entered.

"You must be Dr. Patel." Zoe extended a hand.

She grasped it. "Please," she said with only a hint of an accent, "call me Maneet."

"Maneet. I'm Zoe." She gestured at the report on the desk. "You're early. I wanted to have everything set up for you."

"Forgive me. I like to accustom myself to a new facility before getting down to work." She offered a sheepish grin. "The head of security here at the hospital is my brother-in-law. He let me in. I hope you don't mind."

"Not at all." Zoe wanted to kiss the dark-haired woman's hand. Maybe she'd be able to fire Davis after all.

For the next half hour, Zoe showed Maneet around, encouraging her to rearrange instruments and tools as she pleased. When the two assistants arrived, Zoe introduced them. If their jaunty attitudes were any indication, both were thrilled to have someone other than Davis to work with.

By nine, the decedent was positioned, and Zoe and Maneet were suited up for the autopsy.

Until the morgue's rear door slammed open, and a red-faced Charles Davis stormed in. "What's going on here?" He glared at Maneet. "I know you. Dr. Patel, isn't it? What do you think you're doing in my morgue?"

Her eyes widened in the wake of Davis's fury.

Zoe felt her own face flush hot with embarrassment. "What are *you* doing here?" she asked him. "You told me you couldn't make it."

He gave a dismissive grunt. "What are you talking about? I merely said we'd start a little later than usual. It's more evidence of your incompetence. You've mixed up the schedule again." He pointed an accusatory finger at Dr. Patel. "Or are you part of her plan to sully my good name?"

"Absolutely not. Clearly, there has been a terrible misunderstanding," Dr. Patel said, her accent suddenly more pronounced. "I would never intentionally step on a colleague's toes." She faced Zoe. "I had heard the two of you were dealing with a work disagreement. I do not appreciate you putting me in the middle of it."

"I *didn't.*" Zoe heard the pleading note in her voice.

But Maneet had already turned her back. She retreated to the office, stripping out of her protective gear as she went.

Zoe wheeled on Davis and his smug, victorious sneer. She sputtered, aching to slap the smirk from his pompous face. "You told me you were busy and to get someone else to do this autopsy," she said through a tight jaw.

"I never said any such thing." He turned to the ashen-faced assistants. "Did either of you hear me say I wasn't coming in?"

Both shook their heads, quick, jerky movements that looked more like tremors. Of course, they hadn't heard. The conversation had taken place over the phone in her office.

Davis zeroed in on Nikki, holding up one finger as if poised to jab her nose. "You." He turned to glare at Zoe. "I told you to fire her." He pivoted back to Nikki. "You're fired."

Zoe fought to maintain control of her temper and her mouth. "You don't have the authority—"

"I most certainly do. I'm Chief Deputy Coroner."

"And I'm County Coroner. Your *boss.*"

Davis lifted his chin, so his pinched gaze appeared even more superior. "For the moment." He stalked toward her, stopping when his face was mere inches from hers. His overpowering aftershave burned her nostrils. In a low, growling voice, he said, "Bringing in another pathologist was a classless move. You can't get rid of me. Neither I nor the powers that be will allow it."

As hot rage roared up Zoe's neck to throb in her temples, Davis backed off. He returned his attention to Nikki. "I told you, you're fired. Get out of here."

Zoe inhaled. *"No."*

Nikki stepped away from the body, looking at Zoe. "Don't bother. I quit."

The best assistant she'd ever had spun and strode out the rear exit.

As Zoe watched her leave, Davis closed the distance between them again, enveloping her in the pungent scent of imitation leather. She couldn't look at him for fear she'd slug him.

"I'm not going anywhere," he whispered into her ear. "The only way you'll get rid of me is if you resign." Then he turned and moved toward the body on the table. "Let's get to work."

The searing anger cooled to a calm chill and settled at the base of Zoe's brain. The thought surging into her consciousness almost brought a smile. But she maintained her temper and her poker face.

It's not the only way, you son of a bitch.

* * *

Pete looked up from his paperwork when Abby knocked on the frame of his open office door. He waved her in. "Find anything?"

She stepped up to his desk but didn't bother to sit. "Not really. First off, Dr. Charles Davis doesn't own a black Toyota 4Runner. He leases a two-year-old Lexus sedan."

Naturally. Nothing was ever that easy. "What else?"

"I didn't find any reports of a stolen 4Runner either."

"Doc's stalker could be using his own vehicle."

"There are a lot of 4Runners on the road." Abby wrinkled her nose. "Without a plate number, we don't have much to go on."

Pete's intercom buzzed, and Nancy's voice filtered through. "Chief, can you come up front?"

He pressed the button. "Be right there." Rising from his chair, he thanked Abby.

"Do you want me to keep digging?" she asked.

"Right now, I want you to get out on patrol." He thought of yesterday's visitor. "Make a few extra passes through Elm Grove and the address I gave you. Keep an eye out for a white Subaru SUV."

Abby gave him an amused look. "Zoe's?"

"No. The one Isabella Elson described had tinted windows. Zoe's doesn't. Then contact all the body shops in the area and the Toyota dealer in Brunswick and over in Allegheny County. Ask about any black 4Runners coming in recently with front end damage."

"Roger that." Abby veered right out of Pete's office, heading back to her desk in the bullpen. He turned left to the front of the station and immediately recognized the woman waiting for him.

"Ms. Elson," he said. "What brings you in today?"

She studied him intently, once again making him uneasy. Then she blinked. "That car is still following me."

"The white Honda?" he asked, knowing she'd originally claimed it was a Subaru.

"Yes. You promised you'd keep an eye on my place, but you haven't been by even once."

Pete caught Nancy eyeing them over her glasses without lifting her head from her work. "You haven't been paying attention then. My officers have been making passes through your neighborhood every couple of hours."

The woman's eye twitched, which Pete interpreted as annoyance. "But have *you* come by?"

He gave her a practiced smile. "I have not. But I assure you, my officers are the best. If they spotted your stalker, they would handle the situation."

Her scowl deepened. She shot a glance at Nancy, whose eyes snapped back to her paperwork. Coming back to Pete, she asked, "Can we speak in private?"

Pete's gut told him to send this woman packing. He couldn't get a read on her, which was as unsettling as the way she studied him. But he needed to find out what the hell was going on. Stepping aside, he gestured to the hallway and the conference room.

The front door swung open, and Baronick breezed in. "Good. I'm glad you're here," he said but stopped when he spotted Pete's visitor. "Excuse me." He flashed his overly bright smile at Isabella. "I'm Detective Wayne Baronick."

Pete fought an eye roll. Baronick all but bowed to the dark-haired beauty.

Isabella, however, merely tipped her head in acknowledgment before focusing once more on Pete. "Chief?"

He gestured at the open door to the conference room. "You go on ahead of me. I'll be there in a minute." Once his visitor had left them alone, Pete faced Baronick. "What's up?"

"I thought you'd like to know. We located the black Toyota 4Runner this morning."

"You sure it's the right one?"

"Positive. It was parked behind a vacant bar in Rogers Mine."

A small, mostly abandoned mining town in the southeast corner of the county. Pete had seen it on the map but had never been through it.

Baronick read from his notes. "The vehicle had damage to the grill and passenger-side fender. They also found blue paint transfer. We ran the plates and contacted the owner in Spragg's Run."

Another small town on the eastern edge of Monongahela County, this one about twenty miles north of Rogers Mine. Pete pictured the lay of the land. Both towns were a good twenty-five miles from Brunswick. Even farther from the Abercrombie residence.

Baronick flipped a page. "Correction. Make that the owner's wife. The man whose name's on the title has been in a rehab facility for the last month, recovering from a stroke. The wife didn't realize the 4Runner was missing until we contacted her. Her husband keeps it in a detached garage on their property, and she never goes out there."

"Any fingerprints left behind?"

"We didn't think so at first. It appeared to be wiped clean, except he missed one spot."

Pete didn't have to struggle to guess the spot in question. "The rearview mirror." Inexperienced car thieves tended to wipe down the seats, steering wheel, and doors, but missed the mirror.

"Exactly. There are a lot of smudges, but there are also a few usable partials and fulls. We'll have to get the owner's prints to eliminate his, but..."

Pete didn't need him to elaborate.

"One thing I find odd," the detective said with a scowl, "is the keys are missing. If the assailant was abandoning the car, why take the keys?"

"Did you search the area where the vehicle was found? Maybe he tossed them."

"Of course, we searched." Baronick acted as if Pete had offended him. "I had a team go over the entire perimeter with a fine-tooth metal detector. I admit, he could've taken them with him and dumped them anywhere along the road."

"Any witnesses?"

"None."

Pete ran the scenario through his head and came up with one huge hole. "Don't suppose you found any abandoned cars nearby."

"Nope." Baronick's gaze shifted toward the hallway.

"I assume you had your men search the area around Rogers Mine."

"You assume correctly." Baronick's eyes came back to Pete. "No sign of anyone taking up residence in any of those vacant buildings. There was one thing, though."

"What kind of 'thing?'"

"There was evidence of a small fire in the parking lot, about twenty feet from the 4Runner. Not a very big fire. Maybe whoever stole the truck was camping out there, cooking hot dogs and toasting marshmallows. We collected samples, but I don't hold out much hope for finding anything useful."

Pete mulled over Baronick's report. "You steal an SUV. Use it to tail someone for days, maybe weeks. You run the person off the road and then abandon the SUV basically in the middle of nowhere..."

The detective nodded knowingly. "Doc Abercrombie's stalker either hitched a ride—"

"Unlikely. There can't be a lot of traffic out there."

"Or," Baronick continued, "he had an accomplice."

Exactly the hole in the scenario Pete had come up with.

Baronick's eyes shifted again. "Who's the woman you were talking to when I came in?"

"A newer resident of Vance Township, and she has a stalker of her own." Although Pete knew full well there was something else going on with Isabella. "The last thing she needs is you hitting on her."

He expected Baronick to backpedal and play the innocent card. Instead, he continued to look over Pete's shoulder, his expression darkening. "She just tiptoed across the hall into your office."

"What the hell?" Pete wheeled. The hallway was clear. With Baronick on his heels, he strode toward the conference room, taking advantage of the stealth aspect of his rubber-soled shoes. A glance into the conference room confirmed Isabella wasn't there. He took another step to his office doorway.

She stood behind his desk, her back to it and to him, studying the various maps and photos tacked to the wall.

"Excuse me," he said in what Zoe called his cop voice.

Isabella pivoted so fast she stumbled and grabbed for his chair. For the first time, she appeared rattled as the cool façade crumbled.

"Do you mind telling me what you're doing?" he asked.

She remained frozen in place, glancing about the room, obviously searching for an answer. But only for a moment. She quickly gathered her wits. "I got tired of waiting for you, so I wandered in here. I assure you, I didn't touch anything. I was only studying the map of the township since I don't really know my way around yet."

Pete held her gaze, aware she was lying—at least partly. He'd played this game of who-blinks-first enough times to know it wouldn't be him.

Isabella lowered her face, shot a glance off to one side, and brought her chin back up, her expression less confident. "I'm sorry. It won't happen again." She circled from behind his desk, her eyes averted and approached the door. And Pete.

"What are you really doing here, Ms. Elson?" he asked.

This time, when she looked at him, he caught a gleam of tears. She blinked and tipped her head, her long hair shielding her face from him like a curtain. "I'm looking for help," she said, her voice choked. "Clearly you can't provide it. Sorry I bothered you."

She brushed past him and Baronick, almost breaking into a jog.

Pete didn't move, stunned by the emotion coating her words.

"I hate to tell you," Baronick said, watching the woman slam through the front door, "but I don't think she has a stalker. I think *you* do. And I think it's her."

Chapter Ten

Zoe charged into her office to find Paulette and Elizabeth using the third desk as a dining table. They looked up from their Chinese takeout, startled but smiling.

"Did you have anything to eat?" Paulette waved a hand over the assorted containers. "We have plenty."

If Elizabeth hadn't been there, Zoe would've ranted to Paulette about the scene in autopsy. But Davis had accused Zoe of being unprofessional. She didn't want to prove him right in front of the woman destined to become her new secretary.

Let Elizabeth find out about him for herself.

Zoe tamped down her foul mood. "Thanks, but I'm not hungry."

Paulette gave her a questioning look, well aware Zoe rarely skipped a meal.

Elizabeth looked sympathetic. "I can well imagine doing what you do would leave you without much of an appetite."

Paulette chirped a laugh. "Zoe used to work as a paramedic. Blood and guts don't bother her."

Elizabeth pushed her takeout container away. "Even the mention of it upsets my stomach."

Maybe this woman wasn't destined to be Zoe's secretary after all.

"You'll get used to it," Paulette said. "It's not like Zoe brings anything more than the paperwork back here. You'll never need to go to the morgue."

Zoe studied the two women. Paulette had never been squeamish. Then again, Zoe hadn't known her when she first started working for Franklin at

75

his funeral home. Paulette had become accustomed to being around dead bodies decades ago. How long had it taken her to get comfortable in that setting?

How long—if ever—would it take Elizabeth?

As if sensing Zoe's trepidation, Paulette smiled and pointed at the new hire. "She's amazing. I only had to show her the filing system once, and she had it down. She's catching onto the computer programs faster than I did, for sure."

"I'm glad to hear it," Zoe said. If Elizabeth was indeed a fast learner, Zoe's plan became more feasible. She moved to her desk and slapped the morning's autopsy notes on it harder than she normally would, even with Davis playing on her last nerve. "You know, come to think of it, I am hungry. But not for Chinese. I really need to get started on my paperwork. Elizabeth, could you run out and pick up a stromboli for me at the pizza place on the corner?"

Paulette's mouth opened. Zoe shot a look her way, hoping to stop her from offering to run the errand instead. It worked. Paulette closed her mouth but gave Zoe a darker version of the questioning look from a few minutes earlier.

Elizabeth stood. "I'd be happy to."

Zoe dug a twenty from her wallet and handed it over. "Thanks."

Once the sound of Elizabeth's footsteps faded in the hallway, Paulette faced Zoe, arms crossed. "Okay, spill it. What has Davis done now?"

Zoe told her about the confrontation with Maneet Patel. And Nikki. "You can't convince me he isn't in cahoots with Juliann Holland. Between the two of them, there's no way I can fire him, and he knows it."

"I know Dr. Patel." Paulette pursed her lips. "I bet I could convince her to come back."

"Not as long as Chuckie's still here."

Paulette sighed. "Probably not. Darn it. I was hoping to outlast him."

"There's one way." Zoe had a feeling her smile was a little on the evil side.

"You can't kill him," Paulette said with a smirk. "Not without a silver bullet or a wooden stake."

Zoe snickered. "Pete wouldn't approve of either of those options."

"What've you got in mind?"

"If you and Elizabeth can manage things here, I'm going to take a day trip."

"Oh?"

"To Ohiopyle State Park." Not entirely true. "And the surrounding area." That part was true.

Paulette's eyes widened. "The Ferrari case."

Zoe tipped her head in one slow nod. "You have to swear to not tell Chuckie where or why I'm going."

Paulette's grin was bigger than any Zoe had seen. "My lips are sealed."

* * *

Baronick's words, improbable though they were, stuck in Pete's mind the rest of the morning. The idea Isabella Elson was stalking him was ludicrous.

Wasn't it?

But once Baronick left, Pete abandoned the reports and his office. "I'll be on patrol," he said to Nancy on his way out.

She responded with a grunt.

Elm Grove barely ranked as a village. Its lone market had shuttered a couple of years ago. The Elm Grove Presbyterian church merged with another small congregation a few years before that, leaving only an abandoned structure with peeling paint, boarded windows, and a steeple. Only three dozen houses, grouped within roughly four square blocks, remained of the community.

The address Isabella had given him was on the outskirts of town. The tidy single-story brick house sat on a large lot about a quarter mile from the village. Surrounded by cornfields on two sides, a wooded lot on another, and a pasture with a few beef cattle across the road, it didn't look like the kind of place a city dweller—especially a single woman—would choose.

Was Isabella Elson single? Pete had assumed so since she'd brought her stalker concerns to him instead of a husband.

Unless the stalker *was* the husband, which might also explain a woman

77

from the city moving to the middle of nowhere.

Dammit. He should've done more digging into Isabella's background before dismissing her concerns.

As he cruised past the address, he took a long look. No garage. No red Toyota parked beneath the open carport. Curtains hung in the house's picture window and a red, white, and blue wreath decorated the front door. Pete backed into a driveway a few hundred yards away, put the Explorer in park, and opened the newly installed computer. Modern technology had arrived in Vance Township. He typed in the plate number he'd noted from Isabella's first visit to the station.

The car was indeed registered to Isabella Elson, but the address listed was Pittsburgh. She probably hadn't changed it yet. He found no wants or warrants against her. No reason to dig deeper. Maybe he was wrong about her.

And surely Baronick was wrong as well.

Pete's phone rang, distracting him from Vance Township's newest resident. Zoe's smiling face lit the screen. He answered the call. "Hey."

"Hey, yourself."

"How'd it go with your new pathologist?"

The growl that filtered through his phone answered his question.

"She *had* to be better than Davis," he said.

"She was." Zoe spilled out the story of Chuckie showing up and running off half her team. "The worst part is I can't fire him, and he knows it."

Pete checked his watch. "I was thinking of driving to Brunswick. Have you had lunch yet?"

"I just sent Elizabeth out to get me something."

He was almost afraid to ask. "How's she doing?"

"Good." Zoe lowered her voice. "I think Paulette has a girl crush on her."

He chuckled. "I could swing by and visit before I head back to Vance Township."

"Tempting, but no. I have a ton of paperwork to do."

"So do I."

"Yes, but you aren't taking tomorrow off."

"Why are you taking tomorrow off?"

"I'm going to look into the Ferrari case." A pause. "If his widow is correct and Davis shut down the investigation by declaring the death a suicide, being able to show he cut corners and in doing so, botched the investigation, might be the leverage I need to get rid of him without Juliann Holland raising hell."

Pete mulled over Zoe's plan. "This all happened in Ohiopyle, right?"

"Close. According to the report, Ferrari jumped from a bridge in Confluence."

"That's about nine or ten miles upstream from Ohiopyle. The Somerset County Coroner oversaw the case, right?"

"Yeah?" Her voice carried a question.

Virginia Lowe was from Somerset. "Tomorrow's supposed to be a nice day. It's been a while since I've been to Ohiopyle. We could stop at the park on our way back."

"We?"

"How would you like some company on your day off?"

* * *

Zoe smiled at the suggestion. "You're willing to play hooky to spend the day with your wife?"

"Not exactly hooky," Pete replied. "I have a homicide case of my own to investigate, and the victim happened to live and work in Somerset."

Footsteps drew Zoe's attention to the door as Elizabeth returned with a white bag from the pizza place. Zoe's stromboli. She realized Pete's plan had stirred her appetite. But with Elizabeth back, she didn't want to risk pointing out the common denominator between Pete's case and hers was Davis. "I would love to have you tag along." Plus, she could use a more experienced set of eyes and ears for this investigation.

"Then I better head back to the station and finish my own paperwork."

"See you at home later."

"Count on it. Love you."

Aware of her audience, Zoe lowered her voice. "Love you too. Bye."

When she looked up from the call, she spotted Paulette grinning. "Aw, newlyweds," the secretary said, patting her bosom as if her heart were fluttering. Turning to Elizabeth, she said, "Zoe and her husband got married on Valentine's Day. Isn't that the most sickly-sweet romantic thing you've ever heard?"

Elizabeth appeared uncomfortable discussing her new boss's personal life. "I suppose so."

Zoe shot a glance at Paulette before focusing on Elizabeth. "Paulette already knows this, but I'm taking tomorrow off."

"Oh?"

"I need a mental health day. Pete's agreed to take a vacation day, too, so we're going to Ohiopyle State Park."

Elizabeth gave her a tight smile. "Sounds lovely."

"I'm trusting the two of you can handle the office in my absence."

"The office, yes," Paulette said. "What about..." She looked toward the window and the general direction of the county morgue.

"I know." Zoe stared at her phone's blank screen. Calling Davis was never something she took pleasure in. After his recent accusations, the last thing she wanted was to hand him another example of her neglecting her duties. But if the trip to Somerset resulted in evidence of his own negligence, it would be worth it. "I'm turning the morgue duties over to my chief deputy."

Chapter Eleven

After arranging for a meeting with the Somerset County coroner, Zoe spent the evening mulling over maps and routes on the computer, with Pete standing at her shoulder, grumbling about how he missed the days of paper maps spread over a kitchen table. By the time they'd agreed to drive the Pennsylvania Turnpike and take care of business in Somerset first, at least he'd admitted Google Maps was quicker, if not necessarily more efficient. In addition, they agreed once they completed their work there, they could meander their way home via the more scenic route, which would take them through the town of Confluence.

The morning sun quickly warmed the interior of Zoe's Subaru on the drive east. As requested, she called Somerset's coroner once they exited the Turnpike. He directed them to his office in the courthouse.

Kenneth Nicholson, a tall, square-jawed man who looked to be in his fifties, greeted them with a smile and a firm handshake. He guided them into a room with a conference table covered in neat stacks of papers. "You said you were looking into a death from five years ago? Tanner Ferrari?"

"That's right." Zoe gave Nicholson a brief synopsis of the situation with Doc Abercrombie and Ferrari's widow.

Nicholson gestured to the table once she finished. As they sat, he picked up a folder and handed it to Zoe.

She placed her legal pad and pen on the table and opened the folder. Pete took a seat next to her and pulled his reading glasses from his shirt pocket. She angled the folder so he could see the contents.

"I remember the case," Nicholson said. "We get several deaths on the river each year. Usually, they're rafters who are thrown out in the whitewater. You've probably heard of the notorious Dimple Rock."

She had. "Is that where Ferrari's body was found?"

"Oh, no. Dimple Rock is in the Lower Youghiogheny. Ferrari jumped from a bridge in Confluence. His body was found upriver from the town of Ohiopyle, not downriver." Nicholson reached over and fingered the pages Zoe hadn't gotten to yet, sliding out a topographical map with a red arrow. "This is where the body was recovered."

"I understand a witness reported seeing Ferrari jump."

"Correct."

"Can you tell me anything about him? The reporting party, I mean?"

"I understand the caller was female. You'd have to check with the police for anything more."

"That's our next stop," Pete told him.

"I also understand the RP didn't leave a name," Zoe said.

Nicholson gave them a sullen smile. "Again, you'd have to ask the police. You know as well as I do our investigation focuses on the body, especially in the case of suicide."

Zoe shot a glance at Pete and knew what he was thinking. She had yet to master the skill of focusing only on the body rather than the whole picture.

Returning her attention to Nicholson, she asked, "Dr. Charles Davis was the forensic pathologist in the case, correct?"

The coroner's face puckered as if he'd bitten into a sour lemon. "He was."

"So your determination of suicide was made from his findings." She said it as a statement rather than a question.

"Correct."

She breathed a sigh. If Nicholson's facial expressions were any indication, he wasn't one of Davis's fans either, but she resisted asking outright. After scanning several more pages in silence, she looked up and said, "I'm not sure if you're aware, but Dr. Davis is currently my chief deputy coroner."

Nicholson leaned back in his chair. "I am aware of that."

"I can understand your hesitance to speak about a colleague," Zoe said, choosing her words carefully, "but how convinced are you his findings and recommendations were correct?"

Nicholson lowered his gaze, mulling over the question. When the coroner lifted his face, looking her in the eyes, he asked, "Off the record?"

"Absolutely."

"Dr. Davis was an adequate forensic pathologist, but impossible to work with. He insisted the Ferrari case was cut-and-dried. The victim was seen jumping. You can see in the report COD was a fractured skull consistent with either striking his head in the fall or against the rocks soon after. One thing was certain. He did not drown. We found no water in his lungs."

Pete leaned forward, resting an elbow on the table. "A fractured skull can result from other causes."

"I agree. I questioned Dr. Davis about it, especially after the widow came to see me, but he was adamant." The coroner shrugged. "As he frequently pointed out, he's the one with the medical degree, not me."

"He hasn't changed in the last five years," Zoe muttered and immediately regretted saying it out loud.

"I'm sorry to hear that," Nicholson said. "Truly. But my comments about him don't leave this office. Understood?"

"Understood." Zoe skimmed through the last pages of the report before closing the folder. "Can you tell us anything about the victim? I don't mean medically or regarding his death, but about his life."

"Only what was reported at the time. Tanner Ferrari owned and operated a restaurant near Seven Springs Ski Resort. Apparently, he was quite the chef. I'm not a foodie myself, but it seems people came from all over the country to eat there, whether they were skiers or not. He was even featured on one of those Food Network shows."

This was news to Zoe. She scribbled a note on the legal pad.

"I realize this isn't in your investigative wheelhouse," Pete said, "but did you ever hear of anyone who spoke ill of the victim?"

A grin flitted across Nicholson's face. "As you point out, not in my wheelhouse. All I know is what caused his death and what I read about his career. Anything more, you'll need to ask the police."

"Understood." Pete shifted in his chair and retrieved his notebook from his pocket. "If you don't mind, I have an active case I'm working on. The victim's home address is here in Somerset, and she worked for the magisterial district judge. Do you happen to know Victoria Lowe?"

"The name doesn't sound familiar."

Pete didn't say anything for a few moments. Zoe wondered if he was going to let it drop. Then he said, "She used to be married to Dr. Davis."

Nicholson's expression clouded. "Victoria Davis? She's dead?"

"Murdered late Saturday night, early Sunday morning in a motel in Vance Township."

The coroner looked away, absorbing the news. "That's a shame."

"So you knew her?"

"Not well. I met her a couple of times at county functions. She seemed… unhappy. No, I take that back. Not so much unhappy as…resigned. I heard they'd gotten a divorce. Didn't surprise me one bit."

"Did you ever meet her son?"

Nicholson looked at Pete, surprised. "No. I didn't realize they had a child."

"They didn't." Pete clicked his pen and removed his glasses, tucking both in his pocket. "Alex was from a previous marriage."

"Sorry I'm not any help."

Zoe pushed the folder toward him. "Thank you for your time and for letting me see this."

"That's quite all right." He slid the folder back to her. "This is a copy of my report. You can keep it. I hope it helps in your search for the truth…whatever the truth is in this case." He rose from his chair and extended his hand to Zoe. "Good luck. And I wish Dr. Abercrombie well. I've only worked with him a few times, but he's a true professional. Unlike someone else we know."

Zoe thanked him, tucked the folder and her legal pad under one arm, and stood. One last question screamed to be asked. "Can you tell me one more thing? Off the record again."

Nicholson stood as well and crossed his arms.

What she really wanted to know was how the hell he'd gotten rid of dear ol' Chuckie. Instead, she asked, "Why did Dr. Davis leave your office?"

Nicholson's expression turned to granite. "I wish I could tell you, but I can't. Even off the record." He glanced at Pete before returning his focus to her. "There's a non-disclosure agreement in place."

This surprised her, but she tried to not let it show. "I understand. Can you tell me *when* he left?"

Nicholson considered the question and must've decided this one wasn't bound by the legal system. "A little less than a year after the Ferrari case."

* * *

Once outside, standing at the top of the courthouse steps, Zoe turned to Pete. "What do you think?"

"This is your investigation. I should ask you the same question."

A breeze played with her hair as she looked down at the street where her Subaru was parked. Nicholson hadn't provided any real answers in the Ferrari case, but he had confirmed her feelings for Charles Davis weren't unfounded. "I think it's a relief to know Chuckie's a jerk with everyone, not just me."

"I'm pretty sure we already knew that."

She swept her wind-tossed bangs from her eyes. "Do you find it interesting he left his job here so soon after the Ferrari case?"

"I do. I also find it interesting there's a nondisclosure agreement involved."

Zoe wondered how she could find out what that was all about and decided to file it away for another day—one in the not-too-distant future. "I didn't know Ferrari was a chef. Did you?"

"No. I wonder what happened to his restaurant." Pete started down the steps. "I'm hungry."

She trailed after him. "Seven Springs wasn't on our itinerary."

"No, but it could be."

"Didn't you arrange for us to meet the state trooper you know?"

"Yeah. But first, I have a couple of stops to make."

* * *

While planning their route last night, Pete noticed the magisterial district court where Virginia worked was only a couple of blocks from the county courthouse. He waited for Zoe to lock the files Nicholson had given her in the Forester, then they walked along East Union Street to the historic two-story red-brick structure housing Magisterial District Judge Jonathan Caine's office.

A woman with short brown hair and large dark blue eyeglasses looked up from her computer when they entered. Pete introduced himself and Zoe, being sure to mention she was Monongahela County's coroner rather than merely his wife. "We're investigating the homicide of Virginia Lowe. I understand she worked here."

The receptionist's expression turned somber. "Yes." The woman placed a palm on the desk in front of her. "This was hers. I'm only a temp until Judge Caine can find a new secretary."

"Did you know Virginia at all?"

She shook her head. "No. I'm sorry."

"Is there any chance I could speak with the judge?"

She climbed to her feet. "He's on a short recess right now. Let me see if he has time." She crossed to a door leading deeper into the suite and rapped lightly.

Pete heard a faint "Come in" before the temp stepped inside.

Less than a minute passed before she reappeared. "He says he can give you ten minutes, then he has to get back to the courthouse."

"It'll do."

Judge Caine stood as they entered and came around from behind his desk, offering Pete a hand, which he shook. While spacious, the office furnishings were unpretentious, with bookshelves that looked like they'd been purchased at IKEA. But the desk and chairs, while plain, appeared sturdy, which was also Pete's first impression of the judge.

"Ms. Mills tells me you're looking into Virginia's death," Caine said, shaking Zoe's hand after releasing Pete's.

"I am," Pete replied. "Her body was found in my township."

Caine gestured at a sofa and a pair of matching chairs, one of which he lowered into. "I still can't believe she's gone. What on earth was she doing way out there?"

A slight catch in the judge's voice made Pete wonder how close he'd been with his secretary. Pete glanced at Zoe and decided to put off answering the question. For now. He opened his notebook. "How long had Virginia Lowe worked for you?"

"Quite a while. Let me think. She was here for eight years, if I'm not mistaken. Then she left for a couple of years before coming back. That was about four years ago."

"Why did she leave?" Pete knew the answer but wanted to know if Caine did.

"She got married," Caine said, his voice clipped.

"What do you know about her husband?"

The judge's face took on the same sour-milk expression Pete had come to associate with those acquainted with Virginia's ex. "He worked for our coroner's office as a forensic pathologist. Charles Davis."

"How well do you know him?"

"Not well. Not personally, at least. Professionally, he seeks the limelight too much for my taste."

"How about his and Virginia's marriage?"

Caine removed his glasses and held them in his lap. "She didn't work here then."

"She didn't say anything to you about it, about why it ended, when she came back to work for you?"

The judge's eyes narrowed. "Why are you asking about her marriage to Charles Davis? Do you think he might have something to do with her murder?"

Pete didn't answer but felt Zoe watching him. He was grateful she kept silent.

Caine brought his eyeglasses up to his face, but instead of putting them on, he tapped one stem against his chin. "The bastard made Virginia's life a living hell. I remember he treated her like gold when they were dating. Would bring flowers here to the office for her."

Davis? Pete wanted to ask but controlled his reaction.

"He insisted she quit her job once they married. At that point, I mostly lost touch with her. I ran into her in town a couple of times, though. She looked miserable. I think the only reason she stayed with him as long as she did was because of the money. She'd been a single mom with a young son, so money was always tight before Davis. He gave her a nice home, but he was an ignoramus. Pushy. Controlling."

Pete couldn't help but think this was a lot of information for simply running into Virginia in town a couple of times.

"Her son was the reason she finally walked out on him. Davis treated the kid like dirt. I don't think he ever struck the boy, but he never had a kind word for him, either. Virginia was a good mother. She wouldn't put up with having her son abused, even emotionally or verbally. Davis, of course, made sure she got nothing in the divorce settlement. When she came to me asking for her old job back, I was more than happy to have her. She is...was...an excellent secretary." Caine fell silent, lowering his glasses to his lap once more and studying them intently.

"Do you know if she had any contact with her ex-husband recently?"

Caine kept his face lowered and shook his head. "She wanted nothing to do with him. I know she was overjoyed when he left his position here."

Pete decided to change direction. Temporarily. "Judge, to your knowledge, had anything changed in Virginia's life in the last few weeks or months?"

Caine appeared to consider the question. "Nothing to speak of."

Pete sensed he was omitting something. "What about her relationship with her son?"

"Alex? They got along well." Caine hesitated. "At least as well as any teenage boy and his mother get along."

When the judge didn't elaborate, Pete pressed. "What does that mean?"

Caine folded the stems of his glasses and shifted in his chair. "Alex is a good kid, don't get me wrong. But he's had...issues with the law in the past. I know he's trying to get his act together, as he would say, but..." The judge tapped his forehead with the glasses. "Boys that age, their prefrontal cortex has yet to mature. They tend to make bad decisions. Act. React. Think

88

about consequences later."

Pete thought about the time between Alex leaving for coffee and returning to the motel and hoped like hell they could track down the girl he claimed kept him distracted. "When I asked you about recent changes in Virginia's life, you said, 'nothing to speak of.' It sounds like there was something."

The judge looked pained and shifted in his seat again.

"You know as well as I do the smallest thing can have a big impact on a case." Pete softened his tone. "Tell me."

Caine unfolded and refolded his glasses. "It's nothing really."

Pete fixed him with a hard stare and let his silence apply the pressure.

It worked. Caine exhaled loudly. "I was supposed to have dinner with Virginia Saturday night. She called me late in the afternoon to cancel. She said she had to deal with something but wouldn't tell me what. The next day, I received the news." His voice grew raspy. "She was dead. In a motel room in Monongahela County. If only I'd insisted we still go out to dinner. If only I'd demanded to know where she was going. I might've been able to stop her."

Dinner with his secretary. Pete had suspected there was a relationship between the two. Now he knew for certain. He waited a beat before asking, "Why do you think she came to Monongahela County?"

"I don't know."

Pete didn't believe everything the judge had told him, but he believed this.

Caine inhaled and sat up straighter. He looked from Pete to Zoe. "You're the county coroner there?"

"I am," she replied with a glance at Pete, "and Charles Davis is my chief deputy."

The judge's eyes shifted as he processed this news. "Davis is in Monongahela County now?"

"Yes," Pete said.

Softly, as if thinking out loud, the judge said, "And that's where Virginia was killed." He locked eyes with Pete. "She did not go there to see him."

"No, she didn't." Pete tipped his head toward Zoe. "She came to see my wife." He went on to give a brief rundown of what Alex had told him about his mother's plans. "Do you have any idea what Virginia might've wanted to say to her?"

Caine replaced his eyeglasses on his face. "I wish I did." He looked at Zoe. "I'd have done my best to talk her out of going anywhere near the man, no matter what she thought you needed to know." He came back to Pete. "You say Alex thinks Davis is responsible for Virginia's death?" He cocked an eyebrow. "So do I."

* * *

They walked back to the car in silence, Zoe mulling over what Caine had said. And what he hadn't said.

Once they reached the Forester, Pete chirped the car open. Zoe stood at the passenger door as Pete rounded to the driver's side. She made no move to get in.

He looked at her over the roof. "What?"

She struggled to reply but did. "Do you think Davis...?"

When she didn't complete the question, Pete filled in the blank. "Do I think Davis killed his ex-wife? You work with the man. Do you?"

She pondered her response, squirming inside. "He's a pain in the ass. Self-righteous. Holier-than-thou. But a murderer? I saw the condition of Virginia's body. Whoever did that was in a red-hot rage."

"You don't believe he's capable of losing control?"

She thought of all the times Davis had launched into a tirade aimed at her or one of the staff. But she'd never been afraid of him. On the contrary, it had taken every ounce of control she could muster to quell her desire to choke the man. Then she thought of the autopsy suite's office door slamming open, following Knight and Wayne questioning Davis. That had been a different level of anger along with the contempt in his voice when he'd whispered, *"I'm not going anywhere. The only way you'll get rid of me is if you resign."* Maybe she should be afraid.

Especially if he was also responsible for Doc's "accident."

She met Pete's gaze, but instead of answering his question, she said, "I really wish I knew what Virginia wanted to tell me."

* * *

Pete entered the address he had for Virginia into his phone's GPS, clamped his cell into the phone holder, and followed Google's directions out of town.

Virginia Lowe's dilapidated single-story bungalow was barely visible through overgrown shrubs and grass in dire need of mowing. What he could see of the structure needed a new coat of paint. Pete pulled into a gravel driveway that ended at a paved slab next to the house. No garage. No silver Honda Civic.

"What a sad-looking place," Zoe said from the passenger seat.

He shifted into park, but left the motor running and climbed out. "Wait here."

"What are you doing?"

"Paying a condolence call on the son, if he's home." Pete knew he wasn't fooling her. The fact was he didn't know what he was doing. Just that he had to do it. He strode along an uneven walkway to the front entrance. The pitted aluminum door creaked when he opened it, and he noticed the latch was broken. He knocked and waited. There was no sound from inside. No television. No music. No footsteps.

He tried the knob. It didn't give. He bumped his shoulder against the wooden door. It didn't give either. Letting the storm door swing shut, he retraced his steps, but stopped outside the picture window. He shielded his eyes from the glare to peer into a tiny, dark living room. The furniture was far from fancy or modern, but he had a sense of tidiness and order within those walls. He imagined Virginia in there mere days ago. The heart of the home. A hard-working single mom, trying to raise her teenage son while making ends meet. Now, the heart had left the house, rendering it a hollow, lonely place.

Zoe had lowered her window and rested one arm on its edge, watching him as he returned. "Well?"

"No one's home."

"You already knew that."

Did he? Alex hadn't wanted to move in with either of his aunts. Pete thought maybe, underage or not, the kid might have come back here. But after seeing the house and its location, Pete suspected this wasn't the place a teen would want to hang out, especially on his own.

Back in the Subaru, Pete removed his phone from the holder and tapped out a text to his colleague with the Pennsylvania State Police. "I'm letting Duncan know we're done here."

Pete's cell pinged as he reversed out of the driveway. He touched the message icon and read the reply. "He says he'll meet us for lunch at the Lucky Dog in Confluence."

Chapter Twelve

Pete had worked with Pennsylvania State Police Trooper Jim Duncan last November when Pete trailed a missing Vance Township couple to a cabin near Confluence on the Fayette County side of the river. They were gone by the time Pete arrived, and he had to turn over the evidence he found to Duncan. Pete and Duncan had exchanged a few emails and texts since then. Duncan invited him to go fishing. He responded that would be great. Both men knew they'd probably never find the time.

As Pete and Zoe stepped out of the Forester at the Lucky Dog Café on the banks of the Yough—pronounced "Yock"—he wished he'd thought to bring his fishing pole.

Duncan rose from the shady bench in front of the Lucky Dog and approached. "Chief Adams, good to see you again."

"Likewise." Pete shook his hand and introduced Zoe.

"As I recall, the last time we met, you were looking for the man who was supposed to bake your wedding cake."

"Yeah," Pete said. "We had to come up with plan B as far as the cake was concerned. But the wedding took place nonetheless."

"Congratulations."

Zoe smiled. "Thanks."

"Congratulations to you, too," Pete said. "I hear you're a detective now."

Duncan shrugged. "The powers that be got tired of me sticking my nose into the investigations anyway, so they let me join the team and made it official."

Pete eyed Zoe, who'd lowered her head to hide a guilty grin. Aiming a thumb at her, he told Duncan, "Someone else around here knows a little too much about sticking her nose into police business."

Duncan pointed to the restaurant. "I hope you're hungry."

"Starved," Zoe said.

They followed him inside, past the *Please Seat Yourself* sign, to a table in the corner. Pete claimed one of the chairs with his back to a wall. Duncan took the other, leaving Zoe as the only one without a view of the entrance. Pete noticed Duncan didn't need to look at the menu.

After the young waiter took their orders and disappeared into the kitchen, Duncan folded his hands on the table. "What brings you back to my neck of the woods?"

"We're both working cases." Pete looked at Zoe. "You go first."

"Okay." She rested both elbows on the table. "Do you remember a suicide case from about five years ago? A man by the name of Tanner Ferrari jumped from a bridge over the Youghiogheny."

Duncan leaned back in his chair. "I remember it well." He tipped his head toward the restaurant's front window. "The bridge is right there. If you hadn't pulled into the parking lot, you'd have gone over it."

"Oh." Zoe stood and moved to look outside.

"You can't see much from here," Duncan said.

She returned to the table. "I want to take a closer look once we're done eating."

"I'm not sure what you hope to see."

"Me either." She went on to tell Duncan about Rachel Ferrari approaching Doc Abercrombie about looking into her husband's death, Doc's not-so-accidental accident, and how the widow ended up in Zoe's office. "It's not my jurisdiction, obviously. I'm just doing the legwork for Doc."

"Did you happen to work on the case?" Pete asked Duncan.

"No, but I live here in town, so I was aware of it." He grinned. "And I may have done some unofficial snooping at the time."

"Unofficial snooping," Zoe echoed. "That's exactly what I'm doing."

The waiter returned with their drinks. They fell silent until he left.

Zoe stripped the paper from her straw and stuck it in the soda glass. "Is there anything you can tell me? Unofficially, of course."

Duncan's eyes narrowed in thought. "I recall having a lot of doubts about Ferrari's death, mostly because of the disappearance of the RP. A woman called 911 anonymously, reporting she saw a man jump from the bridge, but didn't leave her name or any other contact information."

"I understand she used a burner phone."

"That's right." Duncan took a long sip from his soda. "It never sat well with me. Not being able to interview her. But when the body was found downriver, and the coroner determined it was a suicide, no one dug any deeper."

"Officially," Zoe added.

"Officially."

"What about your unofficial snooping?"

"Like I said, I live here in town." Duncan again gestured toward the window. "As you can see, we're not in the middle of a city. Neither are we in a desolate area. Route 281 is well-traveled. There are almost always fishermen along the river. Granted, this happened early on a weekday, so there were fewer than usual, but you would think someone else would've seen a man on the bridge, climbing over the barrier, jumping...something. But no one I spoke with saw him."

Zoe drummed her fingers in a slow rhythm on the table. "Only the missing 911 caller."

"Yep."

When Zoe fell silent, Pete said, "You say he jumped early in the morning? How early?"

"Shortly after sunrise, as I recall."

"Do you know where the body was recovered?"

"Not quite halfway to Ohiopyle."

Pete pictured the map the Somerset coroner had shown them as well as the one he'd studied last night. "That's what...four, five miles?"

"Closer to four. If you want to take a walk or rent a pair of bicycles in town, I can take you to the spot." Duncan shrugged. "Or across the river from the spot, at least."

Zoe wrinkled her nose. "Any chance of renting a horse instead of a bike?"

"Afraid not."

"Then I think I'll pass. For now."

Duncan chuckled. "Suit yourself."

"Do you know anything about the victim?" Pete asked. "We learned he owned a restaurant near Seven Springs."

"That's true. I never ate there, but I understand it was amazing."

"Was?" Zoe asked.

"It closed soon after Ferrari's death. Something about financial problems, as I recall."

"Why Confluence?" Pete mused. "If he did die from suicide, why here? And if not, what was he doing here?"

The waiter's return with their food interrupted the conversation. Once he placed their meals in front of them and confirmed they didn't need anything else, he hurried away.

They fell into silence while they each dove into their burgers. Initial hunger sated, Duncan continued. "I didn't know Ferrari personally, but I learned he was a regular around here and Ohiopyle. Apparently, he was quite the outdoorsman. When he wasn't in the kitchen, he was out here fishing or hiking."

Zoe set her burger down. "If his restaurant was having financial issues, he could have been depressed."

From her sour expression, Pete knew she didn't like that option.

"He could have come here to his favorite place to escape and decided it was where he wanted to end his life," she said, her voice soft as she put her thoughts out there.

"Or," Duncan said, "he could've been enjoying the fresh air like he always did."

Zoe nodded slowly.

Pete dragged a fry through a puddle of ketchup. "As you were asking around, did you hear of anyone who didn't like him?"

"No, I did not. But I didn't have a chance to really dig into his personal life. The sportsmen around here, the merchants he frequented, all had nothing but nice things to say. If it'd been my case, I'd have talked to his family and his employees and might've gotten different answers."

They fell silent as food and thought engrossed them for several long minutes. Pete ruminated on his burger and on the information Duncan revealed. Zoe, Pete knew, had already talked to the man's wife. As for his employees, with the restaurant closed, its staff had likely dispersed like dandelion seeds in the wind.

* * *

After lunch, Zoe followed Pete and the trooper outside. Duncan led them across the gravel lot and narrow River Road to Route 281 and the bridge. On this side, a concrete Jersey barrier separated the roadway from the bike lane. Higher metal railing edged the bridge, keeping bikers from running off and into the river.

Checking for traffic, they crossed to the downstream side, where only the Jersey barrier edged the roadway.

Zoe looked over the low concrete wall to the river below. "Which side did he jump from?"

"Don't know," Duncan replied. "Remember, the only information we have is what the 911 caller reported. She didn't give us much."

The water beneath them moved fast. Not whitewater fast. Not even as fast as the flood waters she'd been all too close to almost a week ago. Zoe turned to face Duncan. "I heard the water was deep that day. Deeper than this?"

He frowned. "A little. It was spring. We'd had a lot of snowmelt and some rain, but it was still fishable."

Something else bothered her. "This bridge isn't very high."

"High enough."

"True, but—" She again looked down. Imagined climbing onto the barrier and jumping. "I'm trying to get into the mindset of someone wanting to end it all. If it was me, I'd want to make sure I succeeded and didn't merely end up in a wheelchair." She pointed. "This looks potentially survivable."

Duncan leaned over the barricade to follow her gaze. "Not if you dived in headfirst. There definitely wasn't enough water to cushion that kind of fall."

Zoe turned her back on the river, frustrated. Duncan was right on all counts. So far, she'd found nothing to add credence to Rachel Ferrari's claims.

Pete looked at her, eyebrow raised.

She shook her head. "I think I'm done. Your turn."

Duncan looked at him. "You mentioned you were working on a case, too. Another old one?"

"No, but I don't think you'd have any knowledge of the persons involved."

Duncan crossed his arms. "Try me."

"A woman by the name of Virginia Lowe came to Vance Township with her son, Alex, claiming to want to talk to Zoe about Virginia's ex-husband." Pete glanced at Zoe. "The ex-husband happens to be Zoe's current deputy coroner, Dr. Charles Davis."

"Now him, I've heard of." Duncan looked at Zoe. "Nothing good, I'm afraid."

She snorted. "Most of the glowing reports about Davis come from Davis."

"He used to work for the Somerset County Coroner's Office, so he was in the news from time to time. He liked the spotlight more than Ken Nicholson does."

"Sounds about right."

"Davis has been making a lot of unfounded claims against her," Pete said to Duncan while tipping his head toward Zoe. "Virginia apparently got wind of it and intended to talk to her. But her body was found bludgeoned to death Sunday morning in a Vance Township motel."

"You have no idea what she wanted to tell you?" Duncan asked Zoe.

"None."

"All we know is what her son had to say," Pete said. "It's pretty clear there's no love lost between the kid and Davis. Alex went so far as to accuse Davis of being his mother's killer."

Duncan scowled. "Alex. Alexander Lowe?"

"Yep."

"That's another name I'm acquainted with. He'd be...what...seventeen or so now?"

"That's right."

"I haven't had dealings with him for the last year or so, but he's no stranger to law enforcement around here. Underaged drinking. Driving without a license. Petty theft. Simple assault. That sort of thing. I had a long talk with him one night when I pulled over a car with six teenagers crammed inside. All under the influence."

"Alex was driving?"

"No. But he was the mouthy one of the group. I had another trooper for backup. After we called all the parents, Alex told me he better never catch me alone and out of uniform. I took him aside and pointed out where his life was headed if he kept on the way he was." Duncan gazed downstream. "Come to think of it, I do remember his mother showing up at the scene. I got the feeling she was at her wit's end with the boy. Being a single parent of a headstrong teenager isn't for the faint of heart."

Zoe thought of her friend Lauren and her foster son, Marcus. "No, it is not."

Duncan shook his head. "I'm sorry to hear about his mother. I hope he doesn't end up in the system."

"He's got two aunts," Pete said. "One of them lives here in Confluence. Name's Fiona something." He reached into his pocket and came up with his notebook.

Duncan beat him to it. "Fiona Roth?"

"That's her."

"Fiona...she dances to music no one else can hear."

"How so?"

"She takes no crap from anyone. She's about a hundred pounds soaking wet, but I swear if she took on a grizzly, I'd feel bad for the bear."

"I've met her," Pete said. "Law enforcement doesn't seem to intimidate her."

"Nothing intimidates her. Don't let her size fool you. She works as a river guide, and I'm pretty sure she could maneuver one of those big rafts through class four rapids without any help." Duncan leaned back against the Jersey barrier and crossed his ankles. "She lives in an old farmhouse off Ramcat Road. Bought the place after it'd sat vacant for almost a decade. Did the bulk of the repairs herself. It's not fancy by any means, but at least it's not ready to fall over anymore. Fiona does the whole self-sustaining way of life. Grows her own vegetables. She'll sic her dog on anyone who wanders onto her property uninvited, but she's just as quick to give the shirt off her back if someone in town needs it." His brow creased in thought. "You say Alex Lowe is her nephew?"

"He is."

"I don't recall ever seeing him near her house. Or seeing them together."

Pete looked at Zoe. "What do you think about taking a ride out Ramcat Road? If Alex is at his Aunt Fiona's place, I'd like to check in on him."

Zoe thought about Duncan's dog comment. "Aunt Fiona might not want company." She turned to the trooper. "What kind of dog does she have?"

"German Shepard. I can go with you. Fiona knows me. Doesn't mean she likes me though."

Pete snorted. "She knows me too, and I'm very sure she doesn't like me."

Zoe pictured all three of them running with a barking, snarling beast nipping at their heels. "Why don't you call first?"

"I'd rather not let her know we're coming."

The mental image remained in the forefront of Zoe's mind. "Okay. How about we call once we get there? From the driveway. Before we get out."

"Deal."

Chapter Thirteen

Back at the Lucky Dog, Zoe volunteered to sit in the back seat, allowing the state trooper to ride shotgun. She watched the scenery from the passenger-side window as Ramcat Road paralleled the bike trail, winding its way along the Yough. It wasn't hard to visualize someone caught up in the wide river's current, swept downstream, fighting to stay afloat in those deep waters. The Somerset County Coroner said there was no water in Ferrari's lungs. Had he struck his head in the fall? If that was the case, there would be no fighting the current. Or had he battled for his life only to be thrown into one of the rocks farther downstream?

Or, as his widow believed, had he never jumped at all?

Instead of coming up with answers to advance Doc's investigation, all Zoe was finding were more questions.

"There." Duncan pointed to a narrow lane shooting off to the left. A sign tacked to a post on one side of the driveway proclaimed *No Trespassing*. On the other side, another posted sign read *Beware of Dog*.

Disregarding both, Pete swung the Forester into the two-track. Duncan said the house Fiona bought had been long abandoned. Judging by the driveway, it still was.

Two more signs flanked the lane. Both read *Do Not Enter*.

Zoe leaned toward the center console. "I don't think she wants company."

"We're on police business," Pete replied.

In Zoe's Forester, which did not scream law enforcement vehicle.

The trees on either side gave way to an overgrown yard punctuated with raised beds surrounded by deer fencing. While the lawn needed to be mowed, the gardens appeared immaculate. But her attention was snapped away from what types of vegetables were growing to the mass of fur and fangs charging toward them, barking ferociously.

Pete braked to a stop and powered up the windows. *"Now,* we call her."

Duncan nodded. "Agreed."

The dog slammed against the side of the Subaru and leaped at the windows, claws scraping at the doors.

Zoe reached up and backhanded Pete's shoulder. "You're gonna owe me a new paint job."

"Now you know why I didn't volunteer to drive," Duncan deadpanned.

With Cujo making laps around the small SUV, barking and flashing his teeth, Pete punched a number into his phone and waited. "Voice mail," he muttered. "Ms. Roth, this is Vance Township Police Chief Pete Adams. I'm at your house right now. I was hoping to check on Alex and see if there's anything he needs." Pete left his number and a request that Fiona return his call ASAP.

The dog leapt against the passenger door. Duncan flinched and muttered something Zoe couldn't make out. Then, louder, he said, "I wouldn't hold my breath about that returned call. Nice day like this, she's probably out on the river with a group of rafters."

Pete glanced at him. "You could've told us that sooner."

"I figured you'd want to see where Fiona lives in case you wanted to track her down later."

The fanged beast had circled to Pete's side, adding more scratches to the driver's door while threatening to come through the window if given half a chance.

"You definitely owe me a new paint job," Zoe said.

"I'll have the guys at Kramer's buff it out." He looked at his phone. "I'm going to try Alex's number."

"How about you do that somewhere without an attack dog trying to rip my car apart."

He shrugged. "Fair enough." He tossed his phone into the cubby beneath the car's radio and shifted into reverse.

102

Cujo trotted after them until they entered the overgrowth between the yard and the road. From there, the dog stood silently and watched with what Zoe interpreted as a smug smile. She wondered if the dog's name happened to be Charles.

* * *

Alex Lowe's voice carried a healthy dose of trepidation when he answered Pete's call. "Do you have any news about my mom's killer?"

"Not yet, I'm afraid," Pete admitted. He'd moved Zoe's car to a gravel lot next to a launch area where a swarm of people were buckling into life jackets while a river guide barked safety orders at them. Pete studied the guide and a buff young woman whose commanding presence and fluorescent green t-shirt identified her as another employee of the Raging River Raft Tours. She was not Alex's aunt, although Pete could easily see Fiona in the role. Bringing his attention back to the phone call, Pete said, "I wanted to check in with you. See if you needed anything."

"I need my mom back." Alex's tone was at once angry and heartbroken.

"Where are you staying?"

"With my Aunt Darlene."

"In Uniontown?"

Alex grunted an affirmation.

Pete shot a glance at Zoe in the back seat. She nodded.

"Is your aunt at home today?"

There was a pause before Alex answered with a cautious "Yes."

"My wife and I happen to be in the area. Would you mind if we stopped in?"

Another pause. Another cautious response. "Why?"

"Like I said. I wanted to see how you're holding up."

"I'm fine. I don't need you checking up on me."

Pete noticed Duncan's expression and slight head shake. "I also was hoping to talk to your aunt. About your mother," Pete added quickly before Alex protested. "I hope she might be able to shed some light on the case."

"Oh. Hang on a minute." The line grew raspy, Alex's voice muffled. He'd covered the phone's mic. When the line cleared, he said, "Sure. Aunt Darlene said that would be fine."

After Pete ended the call, he looked at the state trooper in the passenger seat.

"It doesn't sound like the Lowe kid has changed much." Duncan pointed at Pete's phone. "Still defiant. Still cocky."

Pete thought of the devastated young man standing at the door to what had been his and his mom's motel room, taking in the bloody scene and falling apart. He also thought of the judge's comments about the kid acting and reacting, saving the thinking for later.

And he thought about Alex's as yet unsubstantiated alibi. "I hope you're wrong about that."

"So do I."

Pete returned Duncan to the Lucky Dog, thanked him for his help, and promised to keep him updated on both cases.

After walking around the Subaru, inspecting the new scratches, Zoe reclaimed her seat next to Pete, her face an illustration of deep thought. "Do you want to tell me what's on your mind?" he asked.

"Besides getting my car buffed out?" she said. "Coincidences."

He'd been pondering the same thing. "Tanner Ferrari allegedly jumped to his death less than three miles upstream from where Fiona Roth lives."

"Exactly."

"In this case, the coincidence may be convenient."

"Oh?"

"If I can ever convince Fiona to cooperate, she might be able to shed some light on your case."

Chapter Fourteen

Their mental health day at Ohiopyle State Park turned out to involve merely driving through the small town while dodging tourists doing exactly what Pete had hoped to be doing. Instead, he promised Zoe they'd come back when he wasn't working a homicide and spend an entire day. Maybe even a weekend.

Her short laugh was laden with skepticism.

At least they did take Route 40, the scenic Old National Pike, toward home, but with a stop in Uniontown first.

Pete had no problem locating Darlene Roth's residence, although the tangle of one-way streets had him driving in circles to get there. Located a couple of blocks off Main Street, Darlene's two-story home appeared well-maintained. A sign in front stated Darlene Roth was a CPA and that clients should use the side door. The wide, paved driveway easily provided room for three cars and ended at a detached, two-car garage with the doors closed. Virginia's—now Alex's—silver Honda was parked on the street in front of the house despite the abundant space available in the driveway. Pete parked behind the Civic.

Since they weren't clients, he let them in through a gate in the chain-link fence surrounding the yard and led the way to the porch and the door facing the street.

Before Pete could knock, Alex opened the door. He looked gaunt and pale. And uneasy, if Pete was any judge. The teen stood back, allowing them entry.

Pete introduced Zoe, who expressed her condolences. Alex thanked her but kept his hands stuffed in his jeans pockets, making no move to shake either of their hands.

Pete took in the living room. Low, acoustic tiled ceilings and a worn dark green carpet gave the space a cave-like feel. The wood paneling had been painted white at one point but now looked beige, either from age or from cigarette smoke permeating the stagnant air. None of the furniture matched, and Pete wondered if it was all hand-me-downs or if Darlene was simply frugal, shopping at yard sales and thrift shops.

Pete brought his focus to Alex. "Is your aunt here?"

"She's in her office." He tipped his head toward the rear of the house, indicating they should follow him.

Pete caught Zoe's arm and leaned close to her ear, whispering, "I want to talk to Darlene alone. Why don't you take Alex aside and ask about what Virginia wanted to tell you. He might remember something or know more than he realizes."

She nodded.

They passed through a kitchen with the same style as the living room. Paneling minus the paint, a white fridge and a black stove, scratched but clean cabinets, brown faux brick backsplash. Nothing fancy or modern, but everything was clean. Alex rapped lightly on a door between the appliances and pushed through it without waiting for an invitation. Pete followed.

Unlike the other rooms, Darlene's office was decorated with furnishings from the current decade, with the exception of the paneling. On the far wall, a second door led to the exterior of the house—the client's entrance indicated on the sign. A woman Pete assumed to be Alex's aunt sat wide-eyed behind a desk that looked like one of those build-it-yourself models sold at IKEA.

"Aunt Darlene," Alex said, his voice flat. "This is the cop I told you about."

"Chief Pete Adams, ma'am." He reached out a hand.

She eyed it as if it held a gun, but, after a moment, reached across the desk without rising. Her grip was tentative and quick and, he noticed, clammy. She withdrew her hand, placing both on her lap, out of view. "How can I help you, officer?" she asked softly.

Darlene Roth matched her living room perfectly. Mousey brown hair, sallow complexion, light brown blouse, dark brown suit jacket. Pete had a feeling she wanted to fade into the brown-paneled walls.

Rather than correct her about his rank, Pete offered her a soothing smile. "I wanted to ask you some questions about Virginia."

"Oh." She sounded surprised. "Okay."

Pete shot a glance at Zoe, who turned to Alex and said, "Let's go sit on the front porch while these two talk business."

He seemed surprised, too. He looked at his aunt. "Will you be all right?"

"I'll be fine." The anxiety in Darlene's wide eyes contradicted her words. "But don't go far."

"We'll be on the porch. I'll leave the door open. If you need me, call out."

"Thank you." After Zoe and Alex left the room, Darlene looked at Pete. "He's a good boy."

The fact she felt the need to say it made Pete question the comment's validity, but he chose to file it away for future reference. He took a seat, although she didn't invite him to, and opened his notebook. "You have my condolences on the loss of your sister."

Darlene appeared uncertain how to respond and finally settled once again on "Thank you."

"When was the last time you saw or spoke to Virginia?"

Darlene brought her hands up to the desk's surface. Pete noticed they were trembling. She reached for a cup filled with matching pens and rearranged them. "I can't remember. We weren't really close."

"Was it a month? Two? Six?"

"Six." She ran her tongue over her lips. "Maybe six. Like I said, we weren't close."

Which meant she wasn't going to be able to give Pete any insights on Virginia's final days on this earth. He tried a different angle. "Did you know her ex-husband well?"

"Which one?"

Pete remembered Abby saying Virginia's first marriage to Alex's father hadn't lasted long. "Her most recent."

"Charles," Darlene said flatly and reached for a bottle of water on her desk.

"Yes." Pete could tell this interview wasn't going to be easy. "Charles Davis. How well did you know him?"

She uncapped the water, took a long drink, and replaced the lid. As soon as she set the bottle back in its spot, she again shuffled the pens in their cup. "Not very."

Pete expected her to stop there, but she continued.

"He wasn't a nice man. Virginia made a mistake marrying him. But she had a son and not much money."

The judge had told him the same thing. "You say he wasn't friendly. To her? Or to you?"

"To anyone. He said mean things to me and my other sister. He didn't want Virginia to have anything to do with us either." Darlene lowered her eyes. "Me and her weren't really close before then. She's older than me and Fiona. But after she married Charles, I hardly ever spoke to her. Fiona and me, we believe he's the one who killed her." Her words carried no vitriol. No anguish. Simply a statement of fact. Or what she believed to be a fact.

Pete studied the woman. She was no longer trembling, but she still appeared as tight as an overwound spring. He lowered his voice. "To your knowledge, did Charles ever physically abuse Virginia?"

Darlene's head came up just enough for her to make eye contact through her bangs. "You mean, did he beat her?"

Pete remained still, not answering.

She lifted her face, but her eyes shifted to the keyboard, to the water bottle, to the pens, to the door. "I never saw it, but I'm sure he did. Virginia would never have told me. She was too..."

"Embarrassed?" Pete offered.

Now, Darlene looked at him. "Proud. She would never lower herself to asking for help. Then again, she never offered to help me neither."

* * *

Zoe sat in an old but sturdy rocker on Darlene's front porch and watched a sullen and tense Alex on the porch swing. The teen reminded her of Logan Bassi, her best friend's kid. She'd been a pseudo aunt to him, but she hadn't seen him in ages since he, his mom, and his sister moved to New Mexico. Logan, however, had outgrown this gangly phase and was now a confident young man.

"I understand your mom wanted to talk to me," she said.

"Yeah." He shot a glance at her before looking away. "It was my fault."

"How so?"

He took a few moments to contemplate her question. Then he swallowed hard. "I have a Google Alert set for Charles."

Not the answer she expected. "Why? I thought he and your mom divorced several years ago."

"They did."

"Was he still in contact with her?"

"No. But I didn't trust him. When she left him…it wasn't pretty. He made a lot of threats."

Zoe thought of the threats he'd made to her, but those didn't make her fear for her life. They simply made her life miserable. "What kind?"

Alex rolled his eyes and gave her a look that said, "Duh." "You know. Like you'll never survive without me."

Not really a threat to do harm.

"And if I can't have you, nobody can."

Okay, *that* sounded menacing. "So you signed up for a Google Alert?"

"I wanted to keep tabs on him. If he was ever coming back to work in Somerset, I wanted to know."

Smart kid. "But instead, you saw the reports about him and me."

"Yeah. If I'd have kept my big mouth shut, Mom would still be alive." A rush of tears seemed to take him by surprise. He choked and turned his face away, trying to hide his vulnerability from Zoe.

She avoided looking at him, giving him a chance to regroup. His breath sounded ragged for a couple of minutes. From the corner of her eye, she saw him use his t-shirt to wipe his face. Only when he seemed composed did she risk meeting his gaze. Gently, she said, "You told your mom about the news reports. Did she tell you what she wanted me to know?"

He shook his head.

Zoe recalled what Pete had told her. "Your mom called Charles and had an argument with him."

Alex's eyes glazed over again. "She told him if he didn't back off what he was saying about you, she'd go to Monongahela County and make sure everyone knew *he* was the incompetent one."

Zoe wished she'd had a chance to meet Virginia. "Do you know why she felt he was incompetent?"

Alex shrugged and gave her the duh look again. "Because he was."

She lowered her face to hide her smile. God, Alex reminded her of Logan. When she'd forced the grin from her lips, she looked at the teen. "Is there any specific incident you can recall? Something she might have mentioned in passing?" Like screwing up Tanner Ferrari's autopsy, she thought.

"No. Sorry. I wish I could help."

She did, too.

They fell into an awkward silence. Zoe listened to the soft squeak of the rocking chair, the distant rumble of traffic a few streets over, a peel of laughter from a house down the street. She strained to hear a snippet of conversation from inside, the sound of Pete's voice, but they must've been speaking too softly.

She searched for something to say to break the uneasy quiet. "Are you doing okay? Living here with your aunt?"

"I'd rather be home with my mom."

Zoe closed her eyes, inwardly chastising herself for the stupid question. "I'm sorry. I know you would."

He sighed loudly. "It's okay. I don't blame you for what happened."

She opened her eyes again, studying his young face. Despite what he said, she had a feeling he did hold her somewhat accountable. Virginia had been coming to her defense, after all.

"Living here isn't awful," he said. "It isn't great either. Aunt Darlene...well, my mom always said she was a little slow. She's crazy smart with numbers. When I used to have problems with my math homework, I'd always come here for help. But Mom also used to say Aunt Darlene was 'emotionally unsteady' and 'socially unstable.'"

"What do *you* think?"

He took a few moments, considering her question. "I dunno for sure, but...do you know what an autistic savant is?"

"Someone who's exceptionally good at one thing—music or math, for example—but doesn't have good social skills."

"Exactly. I read about it in school and immediately thought, that's Aunt Darlene."

"You might be right." Zoe realized Alex was more perceptive than she'd expected and decided to dig a little deeper. "What about your Aunt Fiona?"

He acted surprised. "You know my Aunt Fiona?"

"No." She tipped her head toward the door. "But Pete wanted to talk to her about your mom. We stopped at her house earlier, but she wasn't home."

"She's probably at work. She takes people down the river on those guided rafting tours." A hint of a grin crept across Alex's face. "I bet you met Bruno."

"The dog?"

"Yeah."

Zoe looked at her car parked in front of the house. "I have a fresh batch of scratches in my paint job, thanks to him."

"You should've obeyed the signs she has posted. When she says stay out, she means it."

"I guess so." Zoe brought her focus back to him. "Do you think she's an autistic savant too?"

From his expression, she gathered he'd never considered the possibility before. He shrugged. "Maybe. But she's not good at math or music, so I doubt it. Mom always called her crazy."

"Do *you* think she's crazy?"

"Not really." He contemplated his hands folded in his lap for several long moments. "Aunt Fiona is the youngest of the three sisters, but she's the one who's super protective. Of me and of Aunt Darlene."

"Was she protective of your mother?"

"She used to be. Until Mom married Charles. He hated my aunts. Both of them. Aunt Fiona kinda took it personal when Mom didn't stand up to him where she and Aunt Darlene were concerned. It hurt her feelings. So even after Mom left him, Aunt Fiona couldn't let it go."

Zoe could sympathize. Charles had a knack for driving wedges.

"Aunt Fiona wanted me to stay with her," Alex said, his voice low as if afraid his words might carry into the house. "When Mom was—" His voice broke. He swallowed hard. "Aunt Fiona insisted I come stay with her."

"Why didn't you?"

He huffed. "I told you. She's protective. Too protective."

Zoe gave him a grin. "I thought maybe it was because of Bruno."

"Nah. He's all right. If he knows you, he's cool. Anyway, I'll be eighteen soon and can do whatever I want then."

"Will you move back to your house in Somerset?"

"No. I don't know. Maybe."

From inside the house came the sound of voices, Pete thanking Darlene for her time.

Alex leaned forward, elbows on his knees, and fixed Zoe with an intent stare. "Look, you seem like a nice lady. I don't know exactly what my mom wanted to tell you, but I do know it got her killed. And I know it was Charles who killed her. You need to watch your back where he's concerned. I wish like hell I'd been able to keep my mom far, far away from him. You need to do the same."

Chapter Fifteen

"Y ou're being awfully quiet," Pete said as he drove them home along Route 40.

Zoe was watching the rustic landscape pass outside her passenger-side window while replaying Alex's words in her mind.

Staying far away from Charles was exactly what she wanted to do. But it wasn't possible. And their foray into the Tanner Ferrari case hadn't provided anything solid to help the situation.

"Zoe?"

She turned away from the scenery to see Pete shoot a worried glance her way.

"What did Alex say to you?" he asked.

"Not much, unfortunately. He has no idea what his mother intended to tell me. Did you know he'd set up a Google Alert on Davis?"

"No. But I'd wondered how he found out about the news stories."

"The more I think about it, the more I realize something else. Alex is genuinely terrified of Davis. Why else would he want to keep tabs on a man who was otherwise out of their lives?" Pete kept his focus on the road, but Zoe could tell he was thinking. She lowered her voice and added, "Alex is convinced Davis killed his mom." Zoe expected Pete to dismiss the possibility.

He didn't.

"You didn't tell me what you learned from Darlene."

"Nothing solid. But there's no love lost between her and her ex-brother-in-law."

"Alex mentioned she might be a mathematical autistic savant."

Pete's eyebrows rose. "That could explain her nervousness. I thought she was going to crawl out of her skin at first. But she eventually calmed down enough to tell me a little about her family dynamics."

Zoe listened as he shared about the estrangement between Virginia and the two younger sisters, courtesy of Davis. How Darlene felt Virginia was too proud to ask for help if he'd been abusing her. Darlene's obvious hurt because Virginia wouldn't help her either.

"I asked Darlene what she wanted Virginia to help her with," Pete said, "but she refused to say."

Zoe pondered his words. "Alex mentioned Davis hated Virginia's sisters, and she wouldn't stand up to him where they were concerned."

Pete huffed. "It's a good thing I'm not investigating Davis's murder. We'd have suspects by the dozens."

Zoe didn't reply. She didn't want to point out she would be high on the list.

"Before I finished speaking with Darlene, I asked where she was early Sunday morning."

Zoe caught the scowl on his face. "And?"

"She started fidgeting again. Said she was home alone but her neighbors could vouch she didn't leave the house."

"Basically," Zoe said, "this was a wasted trip. We should've just spent the day at Ohiopyle."

"It wasn't a waste. You have a better sense of what happened to Tanner Ferrari."

Did she?

Pete must've sensed her doubt. "You have Nicholson's files on the case."

"True. I hope Doc is feeling well enough to go over them with me. He's more likely to spot any irregularities."

Pete lifted a hand from the wheel. "There you go."

"But *you* didn't learn much more than you already knew about Virginia Lowe's homicide."

"Not true. I've seen where she lived and worked." He chuckled. "I learned

Davis has a weird romantic streak and courted her by bringing flowers to her office."

Zoe had forgotten about the judge telling them that. She thought about the flower arrangement on Juliann Holland's desk and wondered if they'd come from Davis.

"I learned she was having a relationship with her boss," Pete said and fell silent. Zoe suspected he was pondering the last revelation. "I know more about her family," he continued. "Alex's Google Alert intrigues me."

"Me too." However, what most stuck with Zoe about her conversation with Virginia's son was the last thing he'd said to her. She needed to stay far away from Dr. Charles Davis, but she wasn't about to share that tidbit with Pete. Having him go deeper into protective cop mode wouldn't help. She already avoided Davis as much as possible.

"We may not have wrapped up either case, but you never know. Down the road, something we picked up today may be the key to solving both."

Zoe leaned back into the passenger seat's headrest. He was right. The thought comforted her, and she closed her eyes.

Her phone rang, bringing her eyes open. A check of the screen revealed a number she'd become familiar with. A sense of dread tightened her chest. "It's Doc's wife," she told Pete, swiped the green icon, and tapped speaker so he could hear too. "Grace, is everything all right?"

"Yes, yes," came the chirpy reply. "I'm sorry if I scared you. Where are you right now?"

"On our way home from Ohiopyle." It was simpler than listing where all they'd been. "What do you need?"

"Lyle's memory has started to come back. He wanted me to call you and ask if you could stop by his hospital room."

Zoe looked at Pete. He nodded and said, "We'll be there in forty-five minutes."

* * *

Doc was sitting up in a recliner when they arrived, looking much better than the last time Zoe saw him. Grace sat in one of the visitors' chairs, beaming.

"How did things go in Somerset?" Doc asked Zoe as he shook Pete's hand.

She placed the envelope containing Ken Nicholson's reports on the bedside tray. "I'm not sure. I hope these'll shed some light on the Ferrari case."

Doc tipped his head toward the envelope. "I gather that's Nicolson's report."

"He was gracious enough to give me copies."

A rap came on the door frame behind her. She and Pete turned to see Wayne. "Did I miss anything?" he asked.

Doc waved him in. "Not yet. I was waiting until everyone was here, so I don't have to repeat this more times than I absolutely have to."

Wayne entered and stood next to Zoe. "You remembered the collision?" he asked, pulling out his notebook and pen.

"Not the collision," Doc said. "But I remember leaving the house. I saw that damned Toyota 4Runner parked across the street again." He shot an apologetic glance at Grace, who apparently had yet to forgive him for keeping her in the dark about his stalker.

"Did you see who was driving it?" Wayne asked.

Zoe expected Doc to say it was Davis.

"Yes," he said, then winced. "No. Not exactly."

"What does 'not exactly' mean?" Zoe asked.

"It was a young man, late teens, early twenties, but I didn't recognize him."

A young man, Zoe thought, disappointed. Not Davis.

"Can you describe him?" Wayne asked.

"No. That's what I mean by 'not exactly.' He had his head down, playing on his phone, and he had a baseball cap on, so I didn't get a clear look at him. I remember pulling alongside the 4Runner. My door was right next to his. I wanted him to look over at me. I could hear the bass beat of his music vibrating the whole vehicle. He had to know I was there. But he wouldn't lift his damn face." Doc's cheeks had reddened. "I should've gotten out of my car and pounded on his window."

"No, you should not," Grace said firmly. "He might've had a gun. He might've shot you then and there."

"If he had a gun, why not use it? He tried to kill me by running me off the road."

"Because," Pete said, his voice low, "if he shot you, he couldn't make it look like an accident."

No one replied. There was no arguing Pete's logic.

Wayne flipped a page in his notebook. "What else do you remember? Did you see him behind you? Do you remember the impact?"

Doc shook his head. "I remember seeing him in his car, willing him to look at me. I gave up and drove off. I don't remember anything after that."

Pete crossed his arms. "Can you think of anyone fitting this guy's description who might've wanted to do you harm?"

"No. Not at all."

Zoe noticed both Pete and Wayne turn to her.

"You work with him." Wayne gestured to Doc. "What about you? Have you had any cases where family members weren't happy with your findings?"

"No one who comes to us is ever happy." She thought about it. "If a grudge against our autopsy results is the motivation for the attack, why Doc? You'd think they'd come after me. I am the coroner." She glanced over at Pete, feeling the burn of his stare. He didn't say anything, but she had a feeling he was very glad the young man in the 4Runner hadn't targeted her.

Yet, she thought and tamped down the sudden chill wrapping around her brain.

Wayne shifted his focus to Grace. "How about you, Mrs. Abercrombie? Can you think of anyone who might be angry with your husband?"

She flung up both arms. "Hell, how would I know? He knew he was being followed for weeks now and never saw fit to tell me. I'm apparently the last to learn anything."

Zoe stepped over to her and rested a hand on her shoulder. "Maybe this has nothing to do with work. Have there been any neighbors who've been angry with him?"

"Angry enough to try to kill him?" Grace's voice sounded strangled. "No."

Doc shook his head. "She's right. Besides, I would've recognized the vehicle if it belonged to one of our neighbors." He pointed at Wayne. "You said it was stolen."

"It was."

"What about the prints on the mirror?" Pete asked.

Wayne shook his head. "No matches yet."

"So," Zoe said, "you're looking for a young male car thief in his late teens or twenties whose prints aren't in the database."

"That about sums it up." Wayne tucked his notebook back into his jacket pocket and turned to Pete. "How did your dive into Virginia Lowe's past go?"

Pete aimed a thumb at the door. "Let's step outside to discuss it. I think Zoe and Doc have some other business to take care of."

Once Wayne and Pete had left the room, Zoe rested a hand on the envelope. "You up for going over this right now?"

Grace cut him off. "No," she said firmly. "You need your rest."

"Hell, woman, I'm not going out for a run." To Zoe, he said, "Let's have a look."

Grace exhaled an exasperated growl.

Zoe shot an apologetic smile at her before picking up the envelope. She thumbed open the flap, removed the reports, and handed them to Doc.

He held out his free hand to his wife, wiggling his fingers. "I know you brought my spare glasses."

She huffed and retrieved her handbag from the windowsill behind her.

"My good pair didn't survive the crash," he told Zoe.

Grace dug into her purse and came up with the spares. "I'm glad you didn't suffer the same fate."

"As am I." Doc positioned the glasses on his face and started scanning each page.

Zoe pulled a chair away from the wall and sat facing him and Grace, angled so she could still see his expression.

His brow was furrowed as he read. He lingered over one page, and the creases between his eyes deepened. Zoe wanted to ask what he was thinking but kept still, letting him digest what he was reading. He flipped back to a previous page and re-read it. His eyes shifted, and she could tell he was pondering the words in the report. Without speaking, he continued.

After studying the final page, he gathered the papers and tapped them on the recliner's arm to align them. "I'm afraid there's nothing conclusive here."

Grace appeared deflated. "Rachel will be disappointed."

Zoe already was. She shouldn't hope her chief deputy had done a crappy job, but she did.

Doc shook his head. "Not necessarily."

"What do you mean?" Zoe asked.

He handed the reports back to her. "The injuries recorded here are consistent with the body being battered against rocks in the Youghiogheny. No water in the lungs indicates he was dead before he had a chance to drown."

"Which is exactly what Davis and Nicholson found."

"Right. There's no evidence here of foul play."

Zoe couldn't understand why he didn't believe the widow would be disappointed.

Her confusion must've shown on her face. Doc gave her one of the kindly smiles he used to offer her when she was in training. "There's also no evidence of suicide. Or that his death wasn't purely accidental."

She looked down at the papers in her hands.

"Nicholson shouldn't have ruled Ferrari's death a suicide based solely on those findings."

She thought back to her conversation with the Somerset County coroner earlier. "He told me he questioned Davis's findings, but Davis insisted the case was cut-and-dried."

"Because he based those findings on the 911 call."

"Exactly."

"Made by a witness, the police could never find to interview further."

Zoe realized where he was going. "Right."

"I'm disappointed in Nicholson." Doc shook his head. "The death should've been ruled as undetermined."

Zoe pondered Doc's words. "Don't be too hard on Nicholson. I got the impression Davis pressured him. He told me how Davis liked to remind him he was the one with the medical degree. Don't forget, I've been on the receiving end of Chuckie's bluster."

"I know you have. But when it comes down to the bottom line, you go the extra mile to make sure the victim receives justice." He gave her a tired smile. "I know your husband gives you grief about crossing the investigative lines. To be honest, I'm proud of you for it."

Heat seared her eyes.

"Franklin would be, too," he added.

Mention of her late predecessor pushed her over the edge and released her tears. "Thank you," she managed. But the current status of her job and her office quickly stemmed the flow. She cleared her throat to steady her voice. "What will you do now?"

"Me? Don't you mean we?"

"No, I mean you." She looked at Grace, whose face was the picture of innocence. Coming back to Doc, Zoe said, "Rachel Ferrari wanted to hire you as a freelance pathologist. I'm just a lowly county coroner from Monongahela County. I've already overstepped by meeting with another county's coroner on a case I have no jurisdiction over."

"On my behalf," Doc reminded her. "Which I appreciate. As far as I'm concerned, you're part of this investigation. My assistant."

"But I'm not. I have no legal—"

He interrupted her with a shake of his head. "I don't care." He lowered the recliner's leg rest and leaned forward. "I understand what you're saying, so okay. Your part of the investigation is unofficial. But we're both motivated to uncover the truth, and I need your help."

Motivated. Zoe rolled the word over in her mind. Finding irrefutable grounds to fire Dr. Charles Davis—grounds even Juliann Holland couldn't argue—was pretty good motivation. "All right then. What do we do next?"

A slow smile spread across Doc's face, and this time, the weariness was gone. He looked at his wife. "Call Rachel for me. Set up a meeting. If we're not going to find answers in the official autopsy results, maybe we'll get them from her."

Chapter Sixteen

Pete arrived at the station well before his shift. Taking a day off didn't mean the township's miscreants had done the same. Nancy wasn't in yet. He couldn't remember the last time he'd gotten to work ahead of her. Even so, she'd left a stack of pink call-back notes on his desk.

He did, however, have to make his own coffee. While it brewed, he thumbed through the messages, which Nancy had prioritized with the most urgent on top, working down to a request for a citizen ride along and a "business opportunity too good to pass up."

He crumpled the last one and fired it into the trash.

Any true emergencies had been handled yesterday by Abby or Nate, leaving Pete with those residents who insisted on speaking directly to the chief. The fourth pink call-back form indicated Isabella Elson had put in another appearance at the station. Nancy resorted to block printing at the bottom. **Contact ASAP**. Underlined.

A door slammed at the rear of the station. Only his officers and Nancy had the access code. Pete assumed graveyard Officer Seth Metzger was returning from his patrol. His assumption proved correct when Seth appeared at Pete's office door, sniffing. "I thought I smelled coffee." He pointed at the pot. "Do you mind?"

"Pour me a cup while you're at it."

"Roger that." Seth filled and placed Pete's favorite mug on the desk but didn't bother to take a seat across from him. "Make any progress on the Virginia Lowe case yesterday?"

Pete clued him in on the conversations with Virginia's boss and sister and about the other sister's guard beast. As he finished, the rear door slammed again. This time, two female voices carried down the hall.

Seth's face lit at the sound of Abby's lilting laugh. Pete expected the pair to announce their engagement any day now.

· "How's the house?" Pete asked. They had bought his old place a few blocks from the station. Sadly, a week earlier, Tropical Storm Iona had flooded it.

Seth's joy at his beloved's arrival faded to despondency. "Still waiting to get a check from the insurance company. We get the old 'the check is in the mail' line every time we call. The new hot water tank is supposed to be delivered tomorrow. A new washer and dryer are on backorder, so I'm making a trip to the laundromat later this afternoon. We can only hope the HVAC guys get to us before the snow flies."

Abby and Nancy appeared in the doorway. "You trying to talk the chief into buying back his house?" Abby asked, a grin on her face.

"No refunds," Pete said. "Seriously though, if you need a hand with anything, let us know."

"Get that in writing," Nancy said as the station phone rang. "I see you got your own coffee. I guess I don't need to come in early every day after all."

"Hey. Don't get ideas," Pete called after her as she headed to her office to answer the phone.

"I better get busy writing up my reports." Seth turned to Abby. "Be safe out there." He looked like he wanted to kiss her but not in front of their boss.

She apparently wanted the same thing. "I'll be right back," she said to Pete before ducking into the hall, Seth right behind.

"Take your time," Pete said.

His intercom buzzed, followed by Nancy's voice. "Detective Knight on line one."

Pete hit the button and picked up. "How can I help you, Detective?"

"I understand you did a little field recon on the Lowe homicide yesterday."

"I did."

"We have some new information on it as well. Care to come to HQ so we can compare notes?"

Pete checked his watch and did some quick math on how many phone calls he needed to return. "Does ten o'clock work?"

"See you then."

As the call ended, Pete wondered what new information the county PD had uncovered.

Abby reappeared in the doorway. From her flushed cheeks, it must've been some kiss. "How was your trip?" she asked.

"Too soon to tell." He leaned forward, resting his forearms on his desk. "Have you had any luck tracking down Alex Lowe's 'super cute girl'?"

"Yes and no. I've stopped at Burger Boy a few times and talked to some of the staff. I found out Heather's last name is Smith. She graduated from Phillipsburg High this spring and is taking a semester off before starting college at West Liberty. According to someone who knows her well, she and her family have been away for a couple of days but are coming home later today."

"Did you get a phone number or address for her?"

"I did."

"Good. Give her a call and set up a time to chat once she gets home."

"On it. Anything else?"

"Yeah. See if the manager at Burger Boy would be willing to turn over the security footage from Sunday morning. If he isn't, let's get a warrant for it. Just in case."

"Roger that." Abby disappeared from the doorway.

Pete sat back, picturing Alex and Heather hanging out at Burger Boy. He seemed like a good kid, but Pete couldn't shake Judge Caine's words. *"Boys that age, their prefrontal cortex has yet to mature. They tend to make bad decisions. Act. React. Think about consequences later."* Pete wanted Heather to confirm she'd written the note. That she and Alex had been together during the time in question. Pete wanted to clear Alex, so they could focus on other suspects.

Like Charles Davis?

Did he really believe Davis capable of murder?

Yes. Pete knew anyone was capable of murder under the right circumstances. But was a threat to Davis's job enough motivation? Pete felt his jaw tighten. If it was, Zoe was currently the biggest threat to the good doctor's career advancement, which placed her dead center of the crosshairs.

Pete decided to pay a visit to his wife while he was in Brunswick.

But for now, he brought his attention back to the message about Isabella. What the hell was going on with her?

He contemplated calling her but decided no. He'd swing through Elm Grove on his way to the city and try to catch her at home. If she wasn't there, he'd call and at least be able to assure her he was following through on his promise to keep an eye open for her stalker.

* * *

With an envelope tucked under her arm, Zoe arrived at the morgue earlier than usual, hoping Davis wasn't there yet. She pressed through the front entrance doors to find the lights out and the autopsy suite as silent as the dead who waited in the cooler. Relieved, she unlocked and entered the office and flipped on the lights to the small enclosure.

According to the reports on the desk, there had been three autopsies while she and Pete had been away. Two were traffic fatalities. One was a drug overdose. While there hadn't been any homicides overnight, there had been a shooting in downtown Brunswick yesterday afternoon, meaning only one postmortem to deal with this morning. A note in Davis's nearly illegible writing stated he'd scheduled it for nine a.m.

She had an hour before he got there.

She took a seat, placed the envelope in front of her, turned on the desk lamp, and studied the return address. Allegheny County Medical Examiner's Office. Zoe had made a quick stop at her temporary office and found Virginia Lowe's preliminary autopsy results had been delivered by messenger late yesterday.

Zoe unsealed the flap, slid the papers out, and read.

Virginia had received a brutal beating with a blunt object, resulting in a broken left ulna—one of the bones in her forearm. Probably a defensive injury. There were four fractures to the skull, including two to the temporal bone, one to the parietal bone, and the one determined to be the fatal blow to the occipital bone. The first three had been to her left side. The final and lethal fracture had caved in the back of her head, perhaps after she'd fallen. Cause of death was massive brain trauma. Manner of death—homicide.

There was a notation stating the instrument used was consistent with the brass lamp Pete had collected from the motel.

No surprises.

Heavy footsteps jarred Zoe's attention away from the report. She looked up to see lights flicker on in the autopsy suite as Davis stormed in from the rear entrance. He spotted her through the glass windows and stopped. Glaring, he headed her way.

She gathered the papers she'd been studying and crammed them back into the envelope.

He burst through the door. "What is that you're trying to hide from me?"

"I'm not *trying* to hide anything. I *am* hiding it. It's your ex-wife's autopsy report from Allegheny County." She expected him to puff up like one of those wild turkey toms in mating season and insist on seeing it.

Instead, he said, "Oh." He waved a hand dismissively. "That's none of my concern. Where are those interns? I want to get started."

"Thanks to you, the best one quit, remember?" Zoe eyed him. "You're early. You have the autopsy on the schedule for nine."

"Nevertheless, I'm ready. Get someone in here to assist." He wheeled and trudged out of the office.

Zoe watched him cross the autopsy suite to the counter, holding the tools of the trade, and begin to organize them according to his preference. She looked down at the envelope. Was he really uninterested in the medical examiner's findings? Or was it an act?

Or did he not need to see the report because he already knew?

Davis was an ambitious ass, but could Zoe really be working with a man who would kill to keep his job and reputation? Worse yet, should she be worried she was the one person keeping him from moving up the ladder to the position he relished?

Zoe picked up the phone and placed a call to the assistant who hadn't followed Nikki out the door.

"I'll be there as soon as I can," he said.

She ended the call, stood, and scooped up the envelope. Davis may have acted blasé about its contents, but Zoe didn't trust him to keep his hands off the case. Especially if he turned out to be guilty.

He had his back to her, still preparing the surgical tools for the job ahead.

"I'll be back in a minute," she called over her shoulder as she headed out to lock the envelope in her car.

*　*　*

Isabella's red Corolla was parked under the carport when Pete approached her house. He was surprised, although he wasn't sure why. He'd come to disbelieve everything she said, from what kind of car her stalker drove to whether she had a stalker at all. He realized he even doubted the address she'd given him.

He slowed and looked around, making sure there were no white SUVs of any make or model lurking nearby.

There weren't.

When his gaze came back to the house, he spotted Isabella striding intently toward the road, waving. He braked to a stop and powered down the passenger window. "Good morning," he said.

Unlike the previous times he'd seen her, this morning, her long, dark hair hung loose, she was wearing yoga pants and an oversized shirt, and she wore no makeup, giving her a more youthful appearance. She stepped up to the Explorer and rested her arms on the window ledge. "I'm glad to see you," she said with a smile.

"I told you we've been patrolling more often. I had a message at the station to contact you. What's going on?"

The smile faded as a flush crept into her cheeks. "I—" she stuttered, "I just wanted an update."

"Have you seen the white SUV recently?"

Pete sensed the question took her by surprise, but she recovered quickly. "No. At least not this morning. Not yet."

"Good. If you see it around again, call us immediately. And it would be a big help if you can get the plate number or a photograph of the vehicle without putting yourself in danger."

"I'll do that." She tipped her head in the direction of her house. "Why don't you come in for a cup of coffee? I made a fresh pot."

He studied her. She didn't sound or act flirtatious in spite of the invitation. "Thanks, but I'm on my way to a meeting in Brunswick."

She looked disappointed. "Oh. How about lunch sometime? Or dinner?"

He still didn't get the feeling she was propositioning him. Her tone sounded perfectly innocent. Then again, he hadn't been able to get a good read on her since day one. "You do know I'm married, right?"

Isabella's cheeks flushed. "No, I didn't mean—" She stepped back, clearly flustered. "I wasn't asking you out on a date. I just wanted to—" She shook her head. "Never mind. Thanks for stopping by."

Pete watched her wheel and hurry away. What the hell was going on with her? And why did he suddenly have the feeling he'd seen her before?

No. Not Isabella. She reminded him of someone. But who?

He dropped the shifter into drive and pulled away. He'd try to figure out Isabella Elson later. For now, he needed to focus on getting to county HQ and solving Virginia Lowe's homicide.

Chapter Seventeen

The desk sergeant at Monongahela County PD directed Pete to the incident room and told him he'd let Detective Knight know he'd arrived.

Pete strode up the center aisle, which divided rows of tables with chairs facing a podium and a pair of whiteboards. He selected a seat in the front row but paused to study the boards before sitting.

Virginia's case was drawn out before him in black marker. One board listed the timeline with her time of death at midpoint. Details about when she checked into the Vance Motel, what time Alex left and returned. The second board held a list of names, including Alex, both of Virginia's sisters, and Charles Davis.

Voices from behind him drew Pete's attention. Max Knight, Wayne Baronick, and four uniformed officers entered and moved to the front of the room.

Knight carried a binder, which he set on the podium before positioning himself between the two whiteboards. "Good to see you, Adams."

Pete lowered into the chair. "I appreciate you inviting me to sit in."

Baronick claimed the seat next to Pete while the four officers sat across the aisle from them.

"We have some new information to address," Knight began and turned to Pete. "But first, Chief Adams made a trip to Somerset yesterday, correct?"

With a nod, he told them about meeting Virginia's boss, who Pete suspected was also her boyfriend.

Knight added Judge Caine to the list of names on the second whiteboard.

Pete continued, telling of his failed attempt to make contact with Virginia's youngest sister and of his conversation with Darlene.

"I'll get in touch with the Uniontown Police and have them do a knock and talk with her neighbors to confirm her alibi." Knight opened the binder on the podium. "Next, I want to update everyone on Ms. Lowe's autopsy report."

As Pete listened to the ME's findings, he wondered if Zoe had received a copy.

When Knight finished, Baronick turned to look at Pete. "Any luck locating the missing lamp from the motel?"

"If there was, you'd have heard about it."

"I assumed as much." Knight flipped to another page in the binder. "Next, we've discovered Virginia Lowe has a quarter-million-dollar life insurance policy."

Pete whistled. Someone was about to profit quite nicely from Virginia's death. "Who's the beneficiary?"

Knight and Baronick exchanged a look before Knight responded. "Her son. Alexander Lowe."

* * *

Zoe sat in one of the visitors' chairs and watched as Doc, in his recliner, studied the Allegheny ME's report on Virginia's death. After several minutes of reading and re-reading, Doc returned the papers to the envelope.

"What do you think?" Zoe asked.

"I think it's not our case."

"Neither is Tanner Ferrari's, but that hasn't stopped you."

He shot a dirty look her way. "Don't be a smart aleck."

She watched him, waiting.

"I *think*," Doc said, emphasizing the word, "Ms. Lowe made someone very angry. The beating she took required a lot of rage."

"Pete believes the weapon used was a brass lamp from the room's nightstand."

"Weapon of opportunity," Doc mused, echoing Zoe's thoughts. His expression turned puzzled. "I didn't think hotels still used freestanding lamps anymore."

"Most don't. But this is the Vance Motel. The owner hasn't modernized the place in decades."

"The killer likely wasn't counting on finding a murder weapon handy when he arrived, which rules out premeditation." Doc must've noticed the grin on Zoe's face. "What's so funny?"

"Everyone accuses me of exceeding my investigative boundaries. You're sounding more like a cop than a pathologist."

"We've already established this is Allegheny County ME's case. I'm just making an observation." Doc narrowed his eyes knowingly. "One I'm sure you've already toyed with. Tell me what you're thinking."

Zoe debated putting her suspicions, her fears, and possibly her paranoia into words. "There was no sign of forced entry. Virginia knew her killer and let him in."

Doc remained silent, his eyes unwavering.

Zoe drew a breath for courage. "The only reason Virginia was at the Vance Motel was because she wanted to meet with me. To talk to *me*." She waited a beat. "About Davis."

Doc remained silent.

"I asked her son about it. He's convinced Davis killed her to keep her from speaking with me."

"What do you think she was planning to tell you?"

There it was—the big question. The one Zoe had been asking herself and feared she might now know the answer to. "Possibly, she knew about Davis screwing up the Tanner Ferrari case."

Doc brought a hand up to rub his chin.

"According to Alex, Virginia called Davis a charlatan. She was married to him at the time of Ferrari's death. She might've been aware Davis was derelict in his duties, labeling it a suicide based on unsubstantiated claims made by an anonymous caller. Maybe..." Zoe rose from the chair and began pacing the room, her mind spiraling now that she was sorting her jumbled thoughts. "Davis goes to the motel to talk her out of seeing me. She's not about to be dissuaded. He goes ballistic, grabs the lamp, and starts swinging."

"You believe he's capable of killing his ex-wife to shut her up?"

"To save his ass?" Zoe didn't have to think very hard. "Yeah. I do."

Doc continued to rub his chin, his gaze shifting to the window. "I've been thinking about the Ferrari case. Beyond what was and wasn't in the coroner's report." He brought his eyes to hers. "You were there yesterday, where it happened. What's your assessment of the situation, having seen the bridge and the river?"

She pondered the question for the umpteenth time. "The barrier at the edge of the bridge was low enough for someone to climb over and jump. The bridge itself wasn't all that high, but high enough that if he landed headfirst, his skull would've been caved in as stated in the report. The river was higher than normal, because of melting snow. It makes sense he was swept downstream, and his body snagged where they found him."

Doc thought about it. When he spoke, his voice was soft. "If Tanner Ferrari really did jump from the bridge as reported, the injuries could be exactly what were found during the postmortem. The lack of water in his lungs is totally unimportant. He would've died on impact."

"The injuries *could* be?"

"I keep picturing the fall in my mind. You've seen the location, so you might be better suited to determine if my concerns are reasonable. If he jumped headfirst, for example, yes, there would be skull fractures, but I would think there might also be a broken neck. Had he jumped feet first, there might've been fractures to his heels and ankles."

"Are you saying you don't believe he jumped?"

"I'm not saying that at all. I simply have questions an investigation at the time would have answered." He looked at Zoe. "Since the only witness, the 911 caller, has never been found, never been questioned, you have to be my witness. Tell me what else you saw yesterday."

She wasn't sure where he was going with this but played along. She closed her eyes and pictured the bridge. The river. "There were fishermen out in the middle of the water. But according to the state trooper who was helping us, it happened early in the morning on a weekday. There probably weren't a lot of others around."

"Think. What were they wearing?"

She realized what he was getting at and opened her eyes to see a faint smile curling Doc's mouth. "According to the report," she said, "Ferrari was wearing a fishing vest and waders."

Doc shifted in the recliner and winced in pain. Once resettled, he said, "Which brings up another question that isn't addressed in Nicholson's report. Ferrari was found wearing chest waders and a fishing vest with his fishing license pinned to it. His wallet with cash and driver's license were zipped into a waterproof pocket in the vest, and he had assorted fly fishing accoutrement in other pockets."

"Right."

"Make that two questions." Doc held up one finger. "If he was planning to commit suicide, why gear up for fishing?"

Zoe thought about it. "I don't know. Maybe he wanted one last day of fishing before ending it all?" she suggested doubtfully.

"I might buy your theory, except—" Doc held up a second finger. "What happened to the rest of his gear? At the very least, he would have a rod and reel. Maybe a tackle box. Were they found left behind on the bridge or in his car?"

"I don't know. It might be in the police report."

"Which we don't have."

"But it should be recorded somewhere." She pondered his words. "Davis declared the death a suicide," she said slowly, as much to herself as to Doc, "so there was no police involvement *after* his ruling. But the police would've been at the scene while it was still a search and rescue—or search and recovery mission."

"Correct."

Zoe's phone rang. Pete's face and name lit the screen. "Hold that thought," she told Doc and swept the green button. "Hey."

"Hey, yourself." Pete sounded tired. "Where are you?"

"I'm in Doc's hospital room."

"I'll be there in about ten minutes." The call ended without a goodbye.

She stared at the phone. Normally, she'd be thrilled by the idea of seeing her husband, but she sensed there was more to his impending visit.

"What's wrong?" Doc asked.

"Nothing. Pete's on his way here." She brought her thoughts back to the topic of Ferrari's death and the non-existent investigation, thanks to her current chief deputy coroner. The case wasn't within her jurisdiction, something Juliann Holland would surely remind her of once she got wind of Zoe helping Doc's probe. If she and Doc could prove Davis had taken short cuts, possibly even been negligent, it might be worth it. As for the investigation into Ferrari jumping from the bridge, Zoe knew of someone who might get his hands on those early police reports. Maybe even do a little unofficial snooping.

A few minutes later—fewer than the ten he'd promised—Pete's voice carried into the room as he greeted the officer standing guard in the hallway.

He entered and crossed first to Doc to shake hands. "You're looking good."

"Thanks. There's talk of releasing me later today or early tomorrow, depending on my latest test results."

"Glad to hear it." Pete turned to Zoe and bent to kiss the top of her head.

"What were you doing at HQ?" she asked.

"They wanted to know what we found out yesterday."

"Which was basically nothing."

His face was drawn into a troubled scowl.

"Pete?"

"Did you get a copy of Virginia's autopsy report?"

"Yes." Zoe noticed Doc's eyebrows lift in interest. "There wasn't anything beyond what we expected," she said.

"I know."

She eyed Pete suspiciously. "What's going on?"

With a sigh, he told her about Virginia's life insurance policy.

"Makes sense though," Zoe said. "Alex is her son. Who else would be her beneficiary?"

"It's not the 'who' that concerns me. It's the amount."

"It is a lot of money."

"Especially for a kid who's used to living as austere a life as he and his mom have." Pete folded his arms. "You saw their house in Somerset."

"You can't honestly believe Alex could do that to his own mom. Even for two hundred and fifty grand." From Pete's expression, Zoe gathered he could.

"I've seen people—family members—murdered for a lot less," he said.

Zoe pictured the boy she'd talked to on his aunt's front porch. She thought of the body in the motel room. While she knew Pete was right, she hoped like hell this wasn't one of those situations. "What are you gonna do?"

"Same as we've been doing. Try to confirm his alibi. Keep looking at other suspects."

"Like Charles Davis." Zoe hated to think she'd been working with a killer.

Pete shrugged. "He's still on my list."

"He's on our list too." Doc winced as he shifted in his recliner.

"The Ferrari suicide?"

"*Alleged* suicide," Doc corrected. "Davis may not be guilty of murder, but I believe he's potentially guilty of letting a killer go free. He's definitely guilty of misconduct."

Zoe's phone chimed with a text. She opened it to find a message from the EOC with an address. She sighed. "It seems my services are needed over in Mt. Prospect Township. Traffic fatality." She reached over and touched Pete's arm. "Before I go, I have a question I wanted to ask you. Do you think Jim Duncan might be willing to look into some old police files and ask a few questions around Confluence? Unofficially?"

Chapter Eighteen

Pete entered his station through the rear door, bypassed the evidence room, and strode into the bullpen.

Abby looked up from her computer. "Learn anything?"

"Alex Lowe is the beneficiary of his mother's life insurance policy."

"Not surprising."

"Her two-hundred-fifty-thousand-dollar policy."

That got Abby's attention. "Whoa."

"Yeah."

She narrowed her eyes at the computer in front of her, but Pete had a feeling she wasn't seeing the image on the screen. "A quarter mil. That's a fortune to a kid."

"It's a fortune to a lot of people."

"True. It's also a hell of a motive." She winced. "But is it enough to kill your mother?"

"That's the big question, isn't it?" At least until they were able to confirm Alex's alibi. "What about you? Have you found anything?"

"The manager at Burger Boy gave me copies of the security videos from Sunday morning, from six a.m. until eight thirty." She pointed at her screen. "That's what I've been doing."

Pete circled to stand behind her. "And?"

"I haven't watched all of it yet." She tapped her keyboard, switching away from the image she'd been viewing to another. "Here." She pointed. "This shows Alex arriving at Burger Boy. Time stamp is 6:08."

The footage on the monitor was from the parking lot. A light-colored

Honda Civic pulled into a spot. A young man stepped out. Alex left the car and walked inside.

Abby clicked a few keys to switch to an inside view. As Alex had told them, the lines were long, especially for a Sunday morning. Abby tapped fast forward and the people in line jauntily progressed to the counter, including Alex. By now, the time stamp read 6:16. Alex placed and picked up his order, then headed for the door.

"Unfortunately," Abby said, "I haven't been able to find him for a while after that."

"What do you mean? He couldn't have just vanished."

"No, and I still haven't viewed all the footage." Abby pulled up a new angle from outside the front entrance. "See this?" She pointed at an umbrella covering a table. "I suspect he's sitting there, possibly with Heather Smith, but the umbrella blocks the view." Abby clicked to another camera mounted on the front of the restaurant, this one facing the parking lot and the street. "His car is still there at six twenty-seven," she said, aiming a finger at the image. "I have a lot of footage to watch yet."

"Keep at it and let me know." Pete started to straighten, but a passing vehicle on the monitor caught his attention. "Wait. Go back."

Abby paused the video. "Why? What'd you see that I didn't?" She rewound.

"Stop. There." He reached around Abby to advance the video frame by frame until he reached the one he wanted.

She leaned in, squinting. "What?" she asked, still puzzled.

It had to be one of those coincidences he so hated. He touched the screen and the frozen image of a dark Toyota 4Runner.

When he hit play, the SUV appeared to be traveling well above Phillipsburg's twenty-five mile-per-hour limit, and it was headed south. Away from the Vance Motel. Toward Brunswick.

"That," he said, "is the same kind of vehicle that ran Doc Abercrombie off the road."

"A 4Runner?" Abby looked up at him. "Do you know how many of those are on the road around here?"

Pete straightened again. "A lot."

"Not to mention the fact this one is in Phillipsburg. Doc Abercrombie's collision was fifteen miles away."

"Fifteen miles," Pete mused. *Only* fifteen miles. The 4Runner he was looking at on the computer was in Phillipsburg at six-twenty-eight. Doc had been run off the road shortly after seven. Was it likely to be the same vehicle? No.

Was it possible? Hell, yes.

Nancy appeared at the door. "There you are." She looked and sounded annoyed. "Detective Baronick is on line one. Says it's important."

"I'll take it in my office." Pete tapped Abby's desk.

"I know," she said. "I'll keep at it."

Back at his own desk, Pete picked up the phone. "Adams here. What's—"

Baronick cut him off before he got the question out. "Any chance you can come to Brunswick ASAP?"

The detective's tone tensed every muscle in Pete's body. "What's going on?"

"We're at Charles Davis's house. Juliann Holland discovered him unconscious on his living room floor."

Pete sat in shocked stillness. "What the hell?"

"He left a suicide note confessing to killing his ex-wife and attempting to kill Doc."

Baronick's words thundered inside Pete's brain, bouncing off the facts they'd uncovered. "You said Holland found him unconscious. Is he—?"

"He's alive and at the ER, but he hasn't regained consciousness. He's got a nasty head wound."

"Head wound?"

"Can you meet me at his house? I could use your take on the crime scene."

"I'm on my way."

* * *

Charles Davis lived in Brunswick on a quiet, tree-lined street a block from the university campus. Pete pulled his Explorer over to the curb behind a marked Monongahela County Police vehicle. Baronick's unmarked sedan sat directly in front of the stately two-story brick home.

A uniformed officer stood at the front door, which he opened for Pete. Bracing a shoulder against the doorjamb, he slipped protective booties over his shoes before crossing the threshold.

The updated, modern interior didn't mesh with the house's historical exterior. Pete stepped inside a wide-open space with the front half furnished as a living room with a massive kitchen at the rear. Baronick and a second uniform entered through another doorway.

"Glad you could make it." The detective's voice didn't carry even a hint of sarcasm. "CSU is on its way, so we haven't touched anything." He pointed to the floor next to a glass-topped coffee table. "Davis was found lying there. Other than transporting him outta here, everything is how we found it."

Pete approached slowly, taking in the scene. What appeared to be spilled wine, along with glass shards from a broken wine bottle, were scattered around the spot where Baronick indicated Davis had fallen. Blood smeared the corner of the coffee table.

"Check this out." Baronick approached the kitchen island and gestured to its countertop.

Pete joined him. A used wine glass perched next to a package of over-the-counter sleeping pills that had been ripped open. What was left of the drug was scattered around a sheet of printer paper. He pulled out his reading glasses, settled them on his nose, and leaned over to read.

I've been a cruel, deceitful man and can't stand to go on this way. I killed Virginia to keep her from telling my secrets. I tried to kill Dr. Abercrombie. I need to stop before I hurt someone else. Taking my own life is the only way I can do that.

There was no handwritten signature, only *Charles Davis* typed at the bottom.

"What do you think?" Baronick asked.

Pete took another look around. "It appears he came to see the error of his ways, took a bunch of sleeping pills, and chased them with a bottle of wine. He tried to make it to his couch but fell on his way and cracked his head on the corner of the coffee table."

"It does appear that way, doesn't it?"

Pete knew the detective was thinking the same thing he was. "I'm not buying any of it."

"Neither am I."

Pete reread the note. "I don't know who wrote this, but it wasn't Davis."

"Cruel and deceitful?" Baronick said. "He's never thought of himself in those terms."

"Not to mention, Doc Abercrombie saw the guy driving the 4Runner and said it wasn't Davis."

"Yeah…" Baronick dragged out the word. "About that." He beckoned for Pete to turn away from the island and look at the counter opposite it, on which was a Toyota key fob.

Pete stared, his jaw tensing at the implications. "Davis drives a Lexus."

"I know. So what's he doing with a Toyota key? Especially when we have a black Toyota 4Runner in our evidence garage and no key for it."

"It's a good question."

"One I wish like hell I could ask him. Until then, I can't wait to find out if this key starts our SUV."

Pete took another long look at the key, the letter, and the pills before removing his glasses and surveying the living room, the coffee table, and the debris around the spot where Davis had fallen. The wording of the note bothered him. "Have you contacted Zoe about this?"

"Not yet. I thought you might want to handle that."

Pete hated where his cop's mind went next. "Do you know what time this happened?"

* * *

The Mt. Prospect traffic collision was one of those that broke Zoe's heart. Two vehicles. One, a newer model pickup, made the twenty-some-year-old Chevy she used to have look like a compact by comparison. The driver reeked of alcohol even at this early hour. Had he been wearing a seatbelt,

Zoe suspected he would've survived. But he hadn't been and suffered fatal head and chest injuries. The second vehicle was a minivan driven by a mom with two youngsters strapped into car seats in the rear. The children had cuts and scrapes, but would be fine. The mom? The firemen were still trying to cut her lifeless body from the mangled wreckage.

Gene had already loaded the pickup's driver into the coroner's van. He stood silently at the rear of the vehicle, arms crossed, waiting. Zoe wandered toward her Subaru in search of some quiet to call her chief deputy.

Davis didn't answer.

Zoe blew out a frustrated breath and waited for the beep. "I need you in autopsy for two victims of a traffic collision. Let me know when you'll be available to do the autopsies." She hesitated before reluctantly adding, "Please." As much as it pained her, she needed him. At least for now.

She'd no sooner pocketed the phone when it vibrated. Expecting Davis was calling her back, she paused when Pete's face and name lit the screen. "Hey."

He didn't respond with his usual comeback. "Where are you?" He'd asked the same question when he'd called earlier. This time, there was an edge to his voice.

"At the traffic fatality in Mt. Prospect. What's up?"

Pete didn't reply. From the muffled voices and scrapes in the background, Zoe guessed he'd covered the phone's mic. The line cleared. "Where were you this morning before you visited Doc?"

Zoe knew from his tone this wasn't idle conversation. "I was at the morgue."

"With Davis?"

"Yes. What's going on?"

Pete still didn't answer her question. "What time did you leave?"

"A little after noon."

"Was Davis still there?"

"No. He left as soon as we finished the autopsy, about eleven thirty."

"Was anyone at the morgue with you after he left?"

The annoying questions were fast becoming frightening. "My intern. We left together. Pete—"

Before she could ask why he was interrogating her, he had one more question. "Did you see Davis after that?"

"No. And no more questions until you tell me—"

"Davis has been transported to the hospital."

Pete's words stole Zoe's breath. She stuttered out three attempts before she could force out, "Why?"

There was another pause as the background noise grew softer. She pictured him moving to a quieter spot. His tone was gentler as he told her about Holland finding him unconscious in his living room, the broken wine bottle, the pills, and the letter.

Zoe's mind raced, trying to process Pete's news. Charles Davis? Suicide? He'd been his usual overbearing self during the postmortem. Or had he been? She'd told him about Virginia's autopsy results. He appeared uninterested, but had it been an act? As Zoe thought about the morning's work, she realized he'd been brusque but hadn't insulted her or the intern. While far from pleasant, Davis had come as close to tolerable as he ever did.

But that didn't make him suicidal.

"Are you still there?" Pete asked.

She blinked. "I'm here. Just trying to wrap my head around Davis attempting to take his life."

"Did he seem different to you?"

"That's what I was thinking about. He seemed less antagonistic, but he didn't appear distraught." All of Pete's earlier questions clicked in her mind. "Wait. You were asking where I was and who I was with as if checking my alibi. You don't believe it was an attempted suicide. You think it was staged?"

His silence was all the answer she needed. Pete was investigating a potential assault, an attempted homicide, of her employee. An employee with whom she had a publicly contentious relationship.

Good thing she had a solid alibi.

Still, Pete was in cop mode, and she could be considered a suspect. There was no way he could talk to her about the case.

"I get it," she told him. "I'm on the other side of this one. I can give you my intern's name if you want to verify my whereabouts."

"Stop it." Pete sounded irritated. "I know you didn't try to kill Davis. I just wanted answers in case one of the other investigators around here did."

"Understood."

"Besides. You'd have done a better job of it."

She could hear the smile in his voice. "You're a smart ass, you know?"

"So I've been told. If you hear of anything, call me."

"Of course." She wanted to tell him to do the same but knew better.

After they ended the call, she pondered the news. Davis was in the hospital, unconscious. Someone wanted him dead. Wanted him to take the fall for Doc's so-called accident and for Virginia's murder. While Zoe had questioned whether her chief deputy could be a viable suspect in either case, this development definitely took him off the suspect list.

Unless he truly had written the letter left at the scene.

Zoe looked over at the minivan with its roof folded back. The firefighters were close to extricating the collision's second victim. She had two victims for autopsy and no forensic pathologist.

Chapter Nineteen

Pete shared the timeline Zoe had given him with Baronick, who added the information to his notes.

"He left the morgue around eleven thirty," the detective said. "I wonder if he came straight home. Alone."

"This case is all yours." A fact for which Pete was grateful. Considering Zoe's history with Davis, Pete wanted as little to do with this investigation as possible. "I have total faith you'll fill in the blanks between when Zoe last saw Davis and when Holland found him."

Baronick snorted. "Thanks." He waved his pen toward Davis's living room, where the CSU techs gathered fibers and assorted evidence samples. "If the note is legit, it wraps up two of our cases."

Except Pete would bet a month's salary, the entire scene was staged, especially the note.

Later that afternoon, back in Vance Township, he looked up from his desk to find Abby in his office doorway, looking like she'd scratched a winning lottery ticket.

"Heather Smith finally got back to me. She said she'd meet us at the Burger Boy in fifteen minutes."

"Good." Maybe they'd be able to cross Alex Lowe off the suspect list.

Pete and Abby arrived early and claimed the same outside table under the umbrella where they believed Alex had sat with Heather.

"Here she comes." Abby pointed at a young woman who fit with Alex's description of a "really cute girl" strutting across the parking lot. Long honey-colored hair, a crop top, and shorts revealing lots of tanned skin, and a very curvy figure.

"How do you know for sure?" As soon as he asked the question, he knew the answer.

"Social media," Abby replied.

He grunted.

Sure enough, the young woman stopped in front of them. "I'm Heather Smith. I understand you wanted to talk to me?" Her tone was tentative, strained. From the lightly veiled fear in her dark blue eyes, Pete judged she either wasn't accustomed to dealing with law enforcement or was overly accustomed to it.

Since he hadn't encountered her before, he suspected the former. He stood, offered a hand, which she hesitantly shook, introduced himself and Abby, and gestured to an empty seat.

Heather slid into the plastic chair and tucked her hands beneath her thighs as if keeping them from trembling. Instead, one knee bounced.

"Did you have a nice vacation?" Abby asked.

"Yeah. It was okay." She rolled her eyes. "As okay as spending time with your parents and no cell service can be."

"I know, right? How did anyone survive before the internet and cell service?"

Pete resisted the urge to laugh, knowing she was trying to put the young woman at ease. He pulled out his notebook and pen. "I'm glad you had a good time. I promise we won't keep you long. We have a few questions for you about Sunday morning."

Heather swallowed. "Okay."

"Why don't you start by running through the morning hours for us?"

She looked puzzled. "I had plans, so I got up early. Like five o'clock? I took a quick shower—"

Pete held up a palm to stop her. "Let me be more specific. I understand you were here a little after six?"

"Oh. Yeah."

"Tell us what happened."

Her eyes darted toward Burger Boy's entrance and back. "I don't know what you mean. Nothing happened."

Abby must've sensed Pete's growing frustration and jumped in. "You said you had plans. Did you meet up with friends?"

She wrinkled her nose. "I was supposed to, but once I got here, they texted me they were running late."

Abby gave her a sympathetic nod. "Did you talk to any strangers?"

Heather's eyes widened with understanding. "Oh. You mean that boy?"

"What boy?"

Pete noticed Heather's knee stopped bouncing. She clearly preferred speaking to Abby over him.

Heather sighed. "Some boy came over and started talking to me. What was his name? Alan? Anthony? No, it was Alex. He had picked up some takeout food for breakfast and started hitting on me."

"Hitting on?" Pete asked.

"Yeah. You know. Flirting. Acting cool."

Abby rested her forearms on the table. "Where were you sitting when he started hitting on you?"

"Right here."

"Did he join you?"

"Yeah. He sat there." She tipped her head toward Pete.

"What time was this?" Abby asked.

"I dunno exactly. About six twenty or so?"

Pete jotted the time in his notebook. "How long did he stay?"

Her knee started bouncing again. "Not long."

"What do you consider 'not long?' Five minutes? An hour?"

"Oh, no. Not that long." She squirmed. "Five minutes at most. I wasn't interested, you know?"

Not the answer Pete had hoped for.

"Did you write something down for him?" Abby mimed scribbling with an invisible pen.

"He wanted my number, so I wrote down a fake one. Just to get rid of him, you know?"

At least that much of Alex's story was true.

"Then what?"

"He left."

"Did you see where he went?"

Heather shook her head.

"Did you see what direction he went?" Pete asked.

"I dunno." She removed one hand from under her thighs and flapped it in the general vicinity of the laundromat next door. "That way, I think."

Pete looked at the building she'd indicated and wondered if it had security cameras. "Did you see him after that?"

She shook her head. "I was here until my friends picked me up around eight-thirty."

"You're sure you didn't see Alex again?" Abby asked.

"Positive. He was too flirty. I already have a boyfriend. I didn't want to give this Alex guy the wrong idea."

Abby thanked her for her time and gave her a business card in case she thought of anything else.

Heather stood, reading the card. Then she looked at Abby. "Is he in some kind of trouble? Alex, I mean?"

"Probably not," Abby said. "We're trying to pin down some loose ends on a case is all."

Heather lowered her face and headed toward the restaurant's front door.

"Pinning down loose ends is exactly what we didn't do," Pete grumbled and climbed to his feet.

Abby stood, too. "You can't really think Alex might've done that to his own mother, especially since Dr. Davis confessed to it in his suicide note."

"Alleged suicide note. As for Alex, I don't *want* to believe the kid's capable of killing his mother." Especially in such a brutal fashion. "But I've been in this line of work long enough that nothing surprises me."

* * *

At the morgue, Zoe performed the intake work on the two bodies, recording weights, taking photos, washing away the blood and debris, before parking both in the morgue's cooler. It was all she could do without a pathologist.

She exited into the hospital basement hallway, locked up, and headed for the elevators. When the doors swished open, Juliann Holland stepped out, nearly body slamming Zoe.

"Excuse—" Zoe started to say but stopped when she saw the county commissioner's pale and tear-streaked face turn livid at the sight of her.

"You," Holland said, her voice raspy and accusing. "I was coming to see you. This is all your fault."

Stunned, Zoe opened her mouth, searching for words.

Before she could find them, Holland raised a clenched fist. "You drove Charles to this. To try to kill himself. You did this."

"I didn't—"

Holland took a step closer, forcing Zoe to back up. "You don't belong here," the commissioner said in a growl. "The only reason you have the title county coroner is through nepotism, pure and simple. You're a cop's wife, nothing more."

Every muscle in Zoe's body coiled. She'd shifted from feeling sorry to shocked to defensive. If ever she was going to throw a punch, this might be the moment. But she forced her jaw to relax and ran her tongue over her dry lips before speaking in the calmest voice she could muster. "I realize you're under a lot of stress right now, plus you're new here." She caught the spark of anger in Holland's eyes and pressed on. "But I've been with the coroner's office for three years. I started as a deputy. Then Franklin Marshall promoted me to chief deputy before he passed away. He intended for me to take over his position all along. And for your information, all of that happened well before I married my husband. So, Madam Commissioner, I absolutely belong here."

Holland now looked ready to throw a punch. Zoe wished she would. For one thing, on her farm, Zoe handled thousand-pound horses that tried and failed to push her around. She was certain she could take Juliann Holland.

Holland's lips moved, but words didn't reach them.

Having said her piece, Zoe decided to take the higher road. "I'm very sorry to hear what happened to Dr. Davis. I truly hope he makes a full and speedy recovery."

Holland was trembling, her eyes gleaming, but Zoe wasn't sure whether it was from rage or sorrow. The commissioner's voice dropped to a strained whisper. "If he dies, I'll see that you pay dearly. Either way—" Holland moved closer, leaned in, and whispered, "I won't rest until I see you out of the county coroner's office."

Zoe held her gaze, unblinking. "Good luck with that."

Holland pivoted, apparently intending to step back into the elevator, but the doors had closed. Without missing a beat, she spun and strutted down the hallway toward the parking entrance.

Zoe watched her go before pressing the up button. From Holland's haggard appearance, Zoe wondered just how serious Davis's condition was.

She took the elevator up two floors to the ER and located her favorite emergency department physician, Dr. Fuller, scowling at a computer on a rolling cart. "How's Charles Davis?" she asked.

"You know I can't tell you anything," Fuller said gruffly.

She did. "Can you at least tell me if he's being admitted?"

"Since you could get that much from the front desk, yes." Fuller looked up. "He's been moved to ICU." He studied her before adding in a soft voice, "It doesn't look good."

Zoe may not like Davis, but she hated that he required intensive care. She wanted to fire him. She did not want him dead.

Hopefully the DA and the detectives on his case knew that.

She thanked Dr. Fuller and returned to the elevator.

Several floors up, Zoe found Doc Abercrombie alone in his room, seated in the recliner and staring out the window.

"Getting bored?" she asked with a forced smile.

"Damned straight. I was hoping they'd let me out today, but now they're saying tomorrow. Which is the same thing they said yesterday."

"I was hoping they'd let you out today, too. I guess we're too high for me to tie you a rope out of bed linens."

"Sixth floor? Yeah. I wasn't good at rope climbing—or lowering—even when I was in high school phys ed class." He chuckled.

Zoe didn't echo the laugh. She'd been borderline serious.

He grew serious as well. "I heard about Charles on the news. Attempted suicide? It's hard to believe."

"Very."

"What are you getting at?"

She flopped into a chair and pressed her hands to her face, massaging her forehead. "I don't know." Lowering her hands, she looked at Doc. "Did he ever seem suicidal to you?"

"No, he did not."

"Did you hear about the note?"

"A suicide note?" Doc looked surprised. "No."

Zoe winced. "If the news isn't reporting about it, the police are probably withholding that tidbit."

"I won't say anything."

Except to Grace, Zoe thought. But it was too late to take it back. "Davis confessed to trying to run you off the road."

Doc's expression darkened. "He did not. I saw the driver, remember? Not his face. But enough to know it wasn't Charles behind the wheel."

"Exactly. He also confessed to killing Virginia. I admit, I've thought it might be possible. Davis going into a rage, grabbing the lamp." Zoe shook her head. "But now?"

"What do the police think?"

"Pete couldn't tell me officially, but he thinks it was staged."

Doc lifted a hand to rub his jaw. "That's not the only thing going on, is it?"

She wasn't sure what he meant.

He pointed at the TV, which was on but muted. "The other thing I saw on the news. A traffic collision?"

She thought of the scene she'd left not long ago. The main reason she'd come to see Doc. "Pickup versus minivan."

"How many fatalities?"

"Two. I have two bodies in the morgue, and Davis can't do the autopsies." Doc studied her. "I hate to tell you this, but even if I get kicked free in the morning, I'm not going to be physically capable of performing two postmortems. I doubt if I could do one."

"I know." Zoe bent forward, bracing her elbows on her knees and planting her face in her hands. No Doc. No Davis. And a long list of pathologists who'd been alienated by Holland. "I'm going to have to send them off to Allegheny County like I did with Virginia."

"Nonsense."

She lifted her face to look at him.

"Dr. Maneet Patel," he said.

Zoe huffed a humorless laugh. "She'll never set foot in our morgue again. Not after Davis convinced her I was an unprofessional idiot."

Doc shook his head. "I know Maneet. I'll call her for you. Tell her the truth about Davis's antics and about what happened today." He reached for his phone with a grunt of pain.

Zoe hoped Maneet Patel had enough respect for Doc to overpower the discomfort of the last time she'd agreed to fill in. Zoe listened to Doc's side of the conversation, which started with easy laughter and a brief catch-up on his health and on Grace. He launched into a professional apology for Davis's behavior, an explanation of what had been going on, playing down the conflict within the coroner's office. He confirmed what Maneet must've already heard on the news and told her he would consider it a personal favor if she'd agree to step in until he got back on his feet. The conversation dissolved into Doc saying "uh-huh" several times. "I completely understand...yes, that would be fine...I appreciate it...yes...dinner and drinks on me." He thanked her and ended the call.

"Well?" Zoe asked.

"Maneet will be at the morgue at ten tomorrow morning."

Zoe exhaled a relieved sigh. "Thank you."

"One other thing." Doc placed his phone on his bedside table. "Grace called Rachel Ferrari. She's agreed to come back for another meeting tomorrow evening. And before you can try to worm out of it again, let me remind you I think of you as my assistant in this case. I want you there when I talk to her."

With Davis currently fighting for his life in ICU, Zoe no longer felt the urgency to dig up more dirt on him, but she'd already come this far. Not to mention the curiosity driving her to find out what really happened to Tanner Ferrari. "Tell me when and where."

"Six o'clock. Hopefully, at my house, provided the doctors don't decide I need more tests to prove I'm alive."

Chapter Twenty

Had someone told Pete ten years ago that he'd be mucking stalls on a horse farm after putting in a full day at the station, he'd have asked them what illicit drugs they were taking. But here he was, doing exactly that, when he heard Zoe's Subaru rolling into the driveway. A minute later, she appeared at the open barn door, taking in the scene.

Before she could ask the inevitable question, he said, "Lauren had to leave. Marcus called. Apparently, his attempt at some skateboarding trick didn't go well."

"Is he okay?"

"She's taking him to the urgent care place." Pete dumped a manure fork full of damp bedding into the wheelbarrow. "Marcus claims his ankle's not broken but says he can't put any weight on it."

"Ouch." Zoe turned to go. "I'll change into my barn clothes and be right back to help."

"Don't bother. I'm almost done." He scooped up the last pile of horse manure, dumped it on top of the rest, set the fork down, and hoisted the handles.

When he returned from depositing the load out back, he found Zoe perched on a bale of hay, her gorgeous baby blues fixed on him. "What weren't you telling me on the phone?"

He'd have put money on that being the first question out of her mouth. Technically, he was wrong. She asked about Marcus first.

Pete parked the wheelbarrow in its usual spot next to the feed room, leaned a shoulder against one of the support posts, and folded his arms.

"Abby and I viewed the security footage from Burger Boy this morning."

"To clear Alex."

"That was the idea."

"You didn't clear him?"

"He sat outside at a table with an umbrella, where the camera didn't pick him up. That was at six seventeen. He didn't reappear on the footage until he walked back to his car at eight twenty-one."

Zoe rested the fingers of one hand lightly on her upper lip, thinking. "What about the girl he said he was with?"

"Heather Smith?" Pete shook his head. "According to her, he was only there about five minutes before he walked in the direction of the laundromat."

"Did the video back her up?"

"No, but there are a lot of blind spots in their security cam coverage, including most of the sidewalk right in front of the building. The cameras are aimed at the front doors and the parking lot. I assume since the building there is all brick with no windows to break, they don't consider it a security threat."

"What about cameras at the laundromat?"

"I asked. They haven't worked since last winter, and the owner never replaced or repaired them."

"So you have nothing to verify Alex's story?"

"Just the opposite. He claimed he was talking to Heather the entire time he was at Burger Boy. Claims she's why he lost track of time."

"Could Heather be lying?"

"Good question. I'm not sure what she'd gain by lying, but I can't rule it out." Pete watched his wife, pondering the information. "While we didn't see Alex in the security footage, we did see something else that may or may not be related."

The baby blues came back to him.

He told her about the black 4Runner.

She stared at him as if waiting for him to continue. When he didn't, her expression turned skeptical. "You know it can't possibly be the same one that ran Doc off the road."

"I admit it's not likely, but it is possible." He dug out his notebook and started going down the timeline he and Abby had worked out. "We caught the 4Runner on video, heading south through Phillipsburg at six twenty-eight. What time did Doc leave his residence?"

Zoe shifted to one hip to tug her phone from her pocket. Scowling at the screen, she replied, "It was seven oh five when I asked him to come to the morgue. My second call, which he didn't answer, was ten minutes later."

Pete added the times to his notebook. "Let's say he left as soon as you called. That's thirty-two minutes to get from Phillipsburg to his house on this side of Brunswick."

"Okay. Not impossible. But still, there are dozens of black 4Runners in this area."

He couldn't argue the fact. "There's something else I didn't tell you on the phone."

She looked at him, an eyebrow raised expectantly.

"We found a Toyota key on Davis's kitchen counter. Baronick called me a little while ago. They tried it on the 4Runner in evidence. It started."

"Oh." Zoe's eyes narrowed.

"What are you thinking?"

She didn't reply immediately. Pete knew from her expression she was trying to put the pieces together. She plucked a piece of hay from the bale on which she sat and studied it. "We know for a fact the 4Runner the police have in evidence is the one that struck Doc's car. Paint transfer proves it."

"Right."

"Now you're saying the keys for that 4Runner were found at Davis's residence."

"Right," Pete said again.

"Doc, however, insists it was a young man behind the wheel. Not Davis." A light sparkled in her eyes. "Davis was afraid of whatever Virginia was planning to tell me. What if he drove the 4Runner out to the Vance Motel, killed his ex, and then headed back to Brunswick, stopping to pick up Alex along the way. What if it was Alex behind the wheel outside of Doc's house."

"What motive does Alex have to try to kill Doc? He benefited financially from his mother's death, but I see no ties between Doc and the kid."

"Unless they were working together." Zoe's lips slanted into a frown. "No. You're right. It's a stupid idea."

"Not really. To be honest, I toyed—*briefly*—with the scenario of the two of them working together and dismissed it."

"Why dismiss it?"

"Too many moving parts. Davis and Alex working together? The kid despises Davis."

Zoe leaned forward. "Or so he says. He wouldn't admit otherwise." She fingered the piece of hay. "It would be ingenious, really, if Davis killed Virginia and then Alex killed, or tried to kill, Doc."

"Ingenious," Pete echoed back to her. "You realize you're talking about Charles Davis, right?"

She sat back with a sigh. "I see what you're saying. Davis thinks he's brilliant, but he's not. Devious? Yes. But I can't honestly picture him putting together that kind of plan."

Exactly the conclusion Pete had reached. He recalled the note left in Davis's kitchen.

"What are you thinking?" Zoe asked. "I can see on your face that there's something else."

"Words," he replied. "Ingenious. Brilliant. Those are words Davis would use to describe himself."

She chuckled. "He would, yes. But no one else." After a thoughtful pause, she added, "With the possible exception of Juliann Holland."

"In the first line of Davis's alleged suicide note, he wrote he's been cruel and deceitful. That's what convinced me he hadn't written it. I can't imagine he'd admit to being either of those things. Not even to himself."

Zoe brought the piece of hay to her lips. "Cruel and deceitful? No way. He's not that self-aware."

"Exactly." Which meant the only viable suspect they had was Alex Lowe, and Pete was having a hard time picturing the kid as being that cold blooded. "If not Davis, who wrote the note and planted the 4Runner key in his kitchen?"

Zoe pressed up from the hay bale, dusted off her backside, and flicked away the piece of dried grass. "Didn't you tell me the note confesses to both Doc's accident *and* Virginia's murder? Sounds like Davis's attacker thinks the 4Runner you saw in Phillipsburg is the same one that ran Doc off the road." The sparkle in her eyes told Pete she was thinking well beyond those two cases.

As was he. "Sounds like Davis's attacker *knows* they're the same vehicle, because he was the one behind the wheel. Anything else is too much of a coincidence."

"I know how you hate coincidences." She crossed the barn aisle to him. "Maybe you can catch the Phillipsburg 4Runner on another camera and get a look at the plate number or even the driver."

He smiled at his beautiful wife. "I've already put Abby on it." He put his hands on Zoe's waist and drew her close. "You're thinking more and more like a cop."

She lifted her face to his. "I'm a death investigator now, too, you know. Plus, I think your inherent cynicism and distrust of the general public is rubbing off on me."

He groaned. "God, I hope not. I keep hoping your ability to see the best in people will rub off on *me*."

Her mouth curled into a sensuous grin. "Since you're done out here, what do you say we go take a shower together and work on the whole *rubbing off on each other* thing."

"Exactly what I was thinking." That was a coincidence he could get behind.

* * *

Well rested and cheerful thanks to the previous night's shower-for-two and subsequent intimate time with his wife, Pete made his morning rounds of his township before returning to the station. He hadn't yet made it to the door when a dark sedan pulled in next to the Explorer. He waited as Baronick climbed out. The detective leaned back into the car and came up with two large cups from Starbucks.

Baronick bearing gifts. Pete wondered what he wanted. Not that he ever refused coffee.

Inside, Nancy was on the phone and handed him a couple of call-back notes without making eye contact. He continued down the hallway to his office and his battered chair. Baronick set one of the cups on the desk in front of Pete before taking a seat across from him.

"What brings you here?" Pete picked up the cup and took a sip. Not exactly piping hot. Wayne's gifts from the coffee chain never were. The nearest one was a half hour away in Brunswick.

Baronick gestured at the cup. "You're welcome, by the way."

Pete grunted around a second sip.

"I assumed you'd want to know what we found at Charles Davis's house."

Pete set the cup down and waited without replying.

"Not a whole helluva lot. No fingerprints on the keys or the packaging for the sleeping pills."

"None?"

"None."

"Not even Davis's." Pete didn't pose it as a question. He'd hoped for prints but didn't expect they'd belong to the pathologist.

"Not even Davis's," Baronick echoed. "Someone wiped the place down."

"What about the note?"

"We confiscated Davis's computer and printer. Our tech guys determined they were used to create and print the document. No prints, though."

Pete ran a finger over his freshly shaven upper lip. "I wonder if the sleeping pills belonged to Davis."

"My guess is no." Baronick withdrew his notebook from his pocket and thumbed through the pages. "I questioned Juliann Holland, who apparently is well acquainted with Dr. Davis."

Pete choked. Those two were a match made in hell, but he wasn't going to share those feelings with the detective.

"According to Ms. Holland, Davis had no problems with insomnia." Baronick flipped a page. "Getting back to fingerprints, we did lift a few from the wine glass. Those matched the victim, and we got some smudges and partials from the broken bottle. Nothing we've been able to match to anyone yet." The detective looked at Pete. "But the one partial definitely was not a match to Davis."

Pete held Baronick's gaze. "What about Holland?"

"I thought the same thing, but no. We did find her prints elsewhere, but they didn't match those on the bottle."

"Elsewhere?"

"Kitchen. Living room. Bathroom." Baronick looked smug. "Bedroom."

They were venturing into territory Pete did not want to think about.

"She provided us with some interesting information, though."

Pete waited.

"The wine," Baronick said. He clearly wanted Pete to press for details. Which he wasn't about to do.

The detective gave in, as Pete knew he would. "The bottle at the scene was an inexpensive—or, as Ms. Holland put it, cheap—bottle of red. Cabernet Sauvignon to be exact."

"Two Buck Chuck," Pete mused.

"Pretty much. Ms. Holland insists..." Baronick raised one finger. "...Charles Davis would never lower himself to drink anything but the best, and..." He raised a second finger. "...Davis is a Chardonnay man." Baronick lowered his hand. "A check of his wine collection in his basement confirmed it. Only white wines with the exception of two bottles of Pinot Noir. For guests, according to Holland."

Davis had guests? Pete shook his head before he could verbalize his sarcasm. "Any sign of forced entry?"

"No. But there were two open windows in the rear of the house. Holland admitted he tended to leave them open for fresh air. She claimed she'd told him he shouldn't do that, but he dismissed her concerns for his safety."

Pete huffed a short laugh. "Maybe that'll teach him to listen to good advice."

"If he lives."

The gravity of Baronick's tone stunned Pete. "You've checked on his condition?"

"Before I left the city. He's still unconscious. They may have to do surgery to relieve pressure on his brain."

Pete leaned back in his chair, ashamed of how he'd assumed Davis's notoriously hard head would save him. Pete didn't like the man, but he didn't wish this kind of injury—or death—on him either.

"All this brings us to the big questions," Baronick said. "Did the same person who tried to kill Davis also try to kill Doc? And successfully kill Virginia Lowe? And if so, who?"

Pete thought of the conversation he and Zoe had last night in the barn.

Baronick scowled at him. "I know that look. You suspect someone. Spill it."

"Zoe and I discussed one theory. I would call it implausible at best, but…"

Baronick crossed an ankle over one knee and leaned back. "But?"

Pete sighed. Implausible or not, he shared the idea of Davis and Alex Lowe working together to bump off both Virginia and Doc.

The detective listened in silence and remained quiet after Pete finished. He'd expected Baronick to burst into laughter. The fact that he didn't unsettled Pete.

When he finally spoke, Baronick said, "There's one big problem with that." Only one?

Before he could voice his concern, they were interrupted by Abby's appearance in the doorway. "Oh, sorry," she said. "I didn't realize you had company." She shot a quick, dirty look at her brother before regaining her professional demeanor.

"Did you find any more security cameras in the vicinity of the motel?" Pete asked. That had been one of her assignments while she was out on patrol.

"I spotted one on a residence. It looked like it could potentially have picked up the traffic coming and going. I stopped and rang the bell, but no one answered. I'll try again later. Nothing else, though. The houses out there are spaced pretty far apart and sit back from the road."

"I knew it was a long shot."

"One other thing. I made a sweep through Elm Grove. No sign of a white SUV. No sign of Isabella Elson either. The house was dark. No car in the driveway."

Baronick set his coffee on the edge of Pete's desk. "Is this your stalker you're talking about?"

"She's not my stalker," Pete said. Was she? He forced his focus back to the interrupted conversation. "You were saying something bothered you about Zoe's theory."

"What theory?" Abby asked.

"Charles Davis and Alex Lowe plotting Virginia's and Doc's murders together," Baronick said to his sister before facing Pete. "First and foremost, Davis's attempted suicide."

Abby stepped into the office to stand at her brother's shoulder. "What's going on with that case?"

Baronick gave his sister an update while Pete sipped his coffee and pondered the three incidents.

"What do you think?" Baronick's voice cut through Pete's musings.

He realized he'd zoned out and missed something. "About what?"

"Suspects. We've all but eliminated the theory of Davis and the Lowe kid working together. Davis doesn't play well with others. Plus, this attempt on his life rules him out."

"Does it?" Abby asked.

Pete looked at her. "What are you thinking?"

Abby crossed her arms. "Alex. His alibi washed out for his mother's homicide. He matches the description Doc Abercrombie gave us of the 4Runner's driver. Maybe they *were* working together, but whatever agreement they had fell apart."

Baronick shifted sideways in his chair to look up at his sister. "You're suggesting the Lowe kid murdered his mother—or plotted her murder with his ex-stepdad, whom he hates—ran Doc off the road and tried to kill Davis?"

"You have a better idea?" Abby glanced at Pete before coming back to her brother. "You say Alex hates his stepdad. Are we sure about that? All we have to go on is Alex's statement."

Pete recalled Zoe's comment about the same thing. "Alex is the one who told us about Davis's connection to Virginia in the first place. He believed Davis killed her. If they were in some sort of plot together, why would he do that?" As soon as Pete voiced the question, he knew the answer.

Abby beat him to saying it out loud. "To throw Davis under the bus."

"Especially if having Davis kill himself and confess to the crimes was the plan all along," Baronick added.

They sat in silence. Pete knew the two Baronicks were also puzzling over the new hypothesis. Finally, he said, "We don't know where Alex was from the time he left Heather at the Burger Boy until he showed up on camera getting into his car a little before eight-thirty. We don't definitively know the key was planted in Davis's kitchen or if he actually had possession of it. Nor do we know who was driving the 4Runner that ran Doc off the road."

"Or," Abby added, "if it was the same 4Runner we spotted in Phillipsburg."

There was more they *didn't* know than what they *did* know.

The one thing Pete knew with any certainty was he needed to have another talk with Alex Lowe.

Chapter Twenty-One

By the time Maneet finished the last of the day's autopsies, it was well into the afternoon. Zoe thanked her, gathered her notes, and locked up the morgue. In the hallway, she paused. Rather than head toward the parking lot, she strode to the elevators. A few minutes later, she stood at the closed steel doors at ICU.

What the hell am I doing here?

A sign on the doors stated in no uncertain terms No Unauthorized Admittance. Another sign next to a phone between the doors and the waiting room explained family members could use the phone to check on their loved one's condition or request a visit.

Zoe was not a family member, and Charles was not a loved one.

So why did she feel the need to see him for herself and make sure he was still alive?

Suddenly, the doors swung open, and a nurse barreled through. Zoe stepped back before they collided.

The nurse stopped and blinked. "Zoe?"

"Tracy?" Zoe recognized her from her days on the Monongahela EMS. Tracy had worked on her crew briefly.

"How are you?" she asked with a wide smile that quickly faded. "Oh, I'm sorry." She gestured toward the doors as they closed behind her. "Who are you here to see?"

"I'm not—" Zoe stuttered. "I'm not family, but—I was wondering..."

Tracy gave an understanding nod. "You're checking on Dr. Davis."

"How is he?"

"We have him in a medically induced coma due to the subdural hematoma and the increased pressure inside his skull."

In other words, not good. Zoe hated to ask her next question. "Is he going to make it?"

Tracy stuffed her hands in the pockets of her scrubs. "You know I don't have a crystal ball. We can only do so much. The rest is up to him."

A lump rose in Zoe's throat. Why did she care? Davis had never been anything but antagonistic toward her. If their positions were switched, he would be cheerfully clearing out her office and having his name engraved on the door. But despite it all, she wanted him to pull through, to be whole and well.

Tracy glanced around furtively before leaning closer. In a whispered voice, she asked, "Do you want to see him?"

"Yes." The word escaped Zoe's lips before she gave it full consideration.

Tracy punched a code into the keypad, and the doors whooshed open. She gestured to Zoe. "Follow me."

Zoe had been in the ICU once before, years ago. It was a sterile place with glass-enclosed cubbies, patients attached to wires and tubes, monitors beeping, and medical staff, some in biohazard gear, keeping watch. This was the one unit where hospital personnel outnumbered patients.

She trailed Tracy to one of the small rooms. They stopped outside. "If you want to go in," Tracy said, "you'll need to gear up. The risk of infection is too high—"

"That's fine. I'll stay out here."

Tracy laid a hand on Zoe's arm. "We're doing our best for him."

"I know." It struck Zoe that Tracy thought she and Davis were close. Friends more than colleagues.

If she knew the truth, she'd have run Zoe off rather than invite her in. Or maybe Tracy knew Zoe well enough from their ambulance days to feel comfortable with her decision.

"Don't stay longer than five minutes," Tracy told her before turning and walking away, her footsteps soft whispers on the industrial tile floor.

Davis didn't look like Davis. Even through the glass, Zoe could tell his face was unnaturally pale. Bandages swathed his head. She'd never seen him flat on his back before. It was just wrong. He was supposed to be upright and belligerent. Despite the tears he'd caused, the grief he'd dished out, she did not want him to die.

"Fancy seeing you here."

She spun to find Wayne standing behind her. His expression was all cop with none of his usual jocularity. She almost blabbed about a friend letting her in but didn't want to risk getting Tracy in trouble. Instead, she chose silence and again faced the patient behind the glass.

"How's he doing?"

She repeated what she'd been told.

"You do know you shouldn't be here. It really doesn't look good."

She looked up at him, stunned and speechless.

His expression softened. "Look, I know you didn't have anything to do with what happened to Davis, but considering your very public feud with the man, *this*..." He pointed to the floor on which she stood. "...is a bad idea."

She knew he meant her being here, outside Davis's room.

"If Juliann Holland happened to show up—"

Zoe held up a hand, stopping him. "I hear you. You're right."

A hint of a grin crossed his lips. "Of course I am." The grin faded. "But I'm glad I ran into you."

"Oh?"

He looked around. "I need to get an update from the nurses. You get outta here. I'll catch up to you in a few minutes in the waiting room."

Zoe took one more look through the glass at her chief deputy and turned to go.

Which was the moment bells and alarms started screeching. She froze as nurses, orderlies, and a woman in a lab coat—Zoe assumed a doctor—raced toward Davis's room. In the midst of the din, she picked up on two shouted words.

"He's crashing!"

* * *

Pete sat behind the wheel of his Explorer in Isabella's driveway. He'd already knocked on her door. No answer. He'd called the number she'd given him. It went to voice mail. He'd walked around the house. Nothing. Her car wasn't there. The place felt empty. Abandoned. Curtains still hung in the windows, but—he realized—the red, white, and blue wreath was missing from the door. He tried to shake off his unease. Perhaps the wreath had been placed there to celebrate the Fourth of July. Now that it was past Labor Day, Isabella had taken it down, intending to replace it with something more reflective of autumn. Regardless, a missing decorative item and an empty carport were not indicative of something amiss.

Except she'd come to him about a stalker.

He'd put off digging deeper for long enough and shifted to face his onboard computer. Running her plates hadn't given him a thing. This time, he opened a web browser and pulled up Facebook, territory he usually left to Abby.

For good reason. Isabella Elson's profile page contained nothing personal. A few pictures. Dozens of memes of cute puppies and kittens. No mention of her relationship status. No list of friends. At least nothing available to the public. He picked up his phone.

When Abby answered, he said, "I need your help."

"What can I do for you?"

"I'm looking at Isabella's Facebook page and it seems to be lacking in information."

"You want me to see what I can find out."

"Yes."

"No problem."

For her.

"I'll check other social media platforms too. Some people don't like Facebook but will pour out their entire life on Instagram or TikTok."

"Call me if you find anything interesting."

"Roger that."

He ended the call and took one more long look at Isabella's house. He hoped Abby could unearth this woman's background online so he could determine what was going on with her. His gut told him she didn't have a stalker. Nor did he buy Baronick's ridiculous theory about her stalking Pete. But there was something going on with her.

He just didn't know what.

* * *

Zoe sat with Baronick in the waiting room outside the ICU.

She felt odd. Out of place. Others huddled in family groups around the large room, waiting for news about loved ones. For a chance to go to their bedside. Praying that chance would come.

Zoe waited for news about a man who, until yesterday, she'd desperately wanted out of her life. If she'd never seen or heard from Davis again, she'd have counted it as a win.

But not this way.

She looked at the detective next to her. He'd slipped out of his suit jacket and slung it over the back of the chair next to him and sat, leaning forward, elbows resting on his knees. He gazed downward toward his interlaced fingers or the floor.

Waiting.

She broke the silence. "You said you were glad you ran into me. Why?"

He sat up, frowning as if he'd forgotten. "Oh. Yeah." He shifted slightly toward her. "It's probably nothing, but a thought occurred to me."

Under different circumstances, she'd have quipped about the rarity of such a thing. Pete probably would've made a crack about it regardless. But she knew, as did Pete, that Wayne Baronick was one of the best at his job.

He counted on his fingers as he spoke. "Virginia Lowe. Doc Abercrombie. Dr. Charles Davis. I really don't want to believe we have three killers running around the county." He let his hand drop to his lap. "Going on the belief the same person is behind all of the attacks, we've been trying to figure out who has ties to all of them."

"I've been doing the same thing. Problem is, when it was just Virginia and Doc, Davis was the name I kept coming up with."

Baronick held her gaze. "Now I have another common denominator."

She waited for him to name his prime suspect. Instead, he raised an eyebrow at her. She inhaled a gasp. "Me?"

"You have to admit, you are connected to all three."

"I never met Virginia before I was called to the motel. She was dead by then."

He shook his head. "You misunderstand. I'm not saying I think you had anything to do with her homicide or the other two attempted homicides. I'm saying you need to watch your back."

Zoe pondered his words. "You think..."

"Virginia was coming to see you. Doc and Davis work for you. I know it's a long stretch, but it's not out of the realm of possibility you could be a target, too."

She snorted. "It's a very long stretch. What motive could one person have to want all of us dead? If they have a beef against the coroner's office, why take out Virginia Lowe?"

Wayne looked away. "If we could answer the *why*, we'd know the *who*." He came back to her. "But do me a favor and be careful, okay?"

"I'm always careful."

Tracy appeared in the doorway. Zoe watched her scan the room and settle on them.

She nudged Wayne. "I think there's news."

They stood as Tracy approached, her face giving nothing away. "Dr. Davis is still alive. But he suffered a stroke. We're rushing him into surgery to try to relieve the pressure inside his skull."

"What are his odds?" Wayne asked.

Tracy glanced at Zoe before replying. "Worse than they were an hour ago."

Chapter Twenty-Two

"Y ou two should go home," Zoe told Paulette and Elizabeth after giving them the update on Davis's condition. "It's almost five, and I don't have the budget to pay overtime." What she did have was a pile of paperwork from the day's autopsies to finish.

Paulette and her probationary replacement filled one more packing box with the most recent files. She looked at Elizabeth. "You're free to leave. I want to finish up here. The movers are coming Monday morning, and I'll be damned if I'm going to come in over the weekend. I have plans."

Elizabeth picked up another file and slid it in the box. "I don't mind sticking around a while longer. I'm meeting my daughter for dinner here in town at six-thirty."

Zoe's phone rang. "I appreciate both of you. I may not be able to pay you, but I'll take you out to eat one day next week."

"Not necessary," Elizabeth said.

Paulette snickered. "Speak for yourself. I never turn down a free meal."

Caller ID showed Doc's name and number. "Please tell me you're being discharged," she said, not bothering with hello.

"I'll do you one better. I'm already home." He sounded perkier than he had in a week. "How did it go with Dr. Patel?"

"Good. She was tense around me at first, but after the first postmortem, we were getting along fine. She agreed to be available until you're back on your feet. Or…" Zoe let the other option hang.

Doc filled in the blank. "Or until Davis gets out of the hospital."

"Something like that." She debated telling him about the stroke and decided against discussing it over the phone.

"If it's a race to recovery, I'm betting on myself," he said. "Anyway, Grace contacted Rachel. She's coming to our house this evening. Can you be here?"

Zoe looked at the reports waiting for her on her desk. "What time?"

"Seven."

In the background, she heard Grace saying something.

Doc chuckled. "Grace says she's fixing the pork tenderloin you like, so come early."

Bribery. Zoe weighed her options. "Tell her thanks, but I'm not hungry. Late lunch. And I have a ton of paperwork that has to be done, but I'll be there by seven."

As soon as she ended the call, she keyed in Pete's number.

"Hey," he answered.

"Hey, yourself."

"You sound exhausted."

"Sounds aren't deceiving."

"How did it go with the new pathologist?"

She repeated what she'd already told Doc, but included what she knew about Davis's condition...although she left out the part about sneaking into the ICU.

"A stroke?" Pete's voice dropped to almost a whisper. "As much of a pain in the ass as he's been, I hate to hear that."

"Same here. I want to fire him, not..." She stopped before saying *bury him*. "Never mind. The reason I called is I'm going to be late getting home."

"Another fatality to investigate?"

"No. At least, not yet. Doc called me. He's been released from the hospital, and Grace set up another meeting with Rachel Ferrari for this evening. Doc wants me to be there."

"I'm on my way to Brunswick anyway. How about I bring you supper?"

Everyone was trying to feed her this evening. "I've already turned down Grace's pork tenderloin."

"Tenderloin? Hell, I was just going to bring Chinese takeout. Mind if I stop by to visit my beautiful wife?"

"I don't mind at all."

"See you in about twenty minutes."

* * *

Pete stepped off the claustrophobic elevator in the historic office building where Zoe's temporary office was housed and started down the hallway. The door ahead was open, and feminine voices lilted out. He recognized Zoe's, and as he drew closer, he identified Paulette's. He checked his watch. Zoe must be paying her employees overtime.

He stopped in the doorway, and took in the room. There had been stacks of boxes the last time he was here. There were more now, even on the desktops. Except Zoe's. Her desk was stacked with papers on which she was working.

She spotted him and smiled. "There's my handsome husband."

Paulette and another woman, whose back was to him, were working together, loading yet another box at the desk reserved for Zoe's deputies. Zoe had told him about her new hire. Paulette's replacement. Elizabeth something.

"Chief Adams," Paulette called out. "Good to see you."

"Likewise," he replied.

The third woman didn't turn, but he could see her back muscles tense. Even without seeing her face, he sensed a familiarity about her. The same feeling he had when he'd encountered Isabella.

Zoe pushed up from her chair and had started toward him when the third woman turned to face him.

"Hi, Pete," she said.

Thirty-some years vanished in a flash, landing him back in high school. In the back seat of his beloved '87 Monte Carlo. Making out beneath the bleachers at the basketball games. His throat closed. "Liz?"

In his peripheral vision, Zoe froze.

"It's good to see you," Liz said in a slightly deeper, even sexier version of the sultry voice he remembered.

He blinked and crashed back into the present. Zoe stood halfway between him and her desk, her wide blue eyes darting from him to Liz and back. Zoe always joked he could read her mind. At that moment, he feared she could read his. Dear God, the last thing he wanted was for her to have seen those stupid teenage hormone-riddled memories that had flashed through his brain just now. But from the shock and confusion on her face, she may have.

"You know each other?" she said, her voice strangled.

"We do," Liz replied without taking her dark brown eyes from him. "We go way back."

If Zoe hadn't read his mind, Liz's low purr on the word "way" left little to the imagination.

Pete was rarely at a loss for words. His police training taught him to be ready for any situation. He'd stared down gun barrels and still been able to maintain a conversation with the person gripping the weapon. But facing this woman from his past stole every intelligible word from his vocabulary.

Liz prowled toward him. For a fleeting moment, he feared she was going to slide into his arms and kiss him in front of his wife. He shifted his weight away one step, instinctively moving into a position known as blading, his sidearm angled away from the advancing threat.

He doubted she recognized the meaning of the move—even though he had no plans to shoot her and didn't expect her to try to disarm him—but she stopped a few feet away. "You look good, Pete. The uniform definitely works for you."

She looked good too, but he wasn't stupid enough to say it.

Liz pivoted to face Zoe. "I lost my virginity to Pete."

This snapped him out of his bout of aphasia. "Dammit, Liz."

She looked at him, a perfect eyebrow raised. "It's the truth."

But Zoe didn't need to hear it.

"I'm pretty sure you didn't lose yours to me, though," Liz added.

"Enough." He closed the distance between them and gripped her arm. "What are you doing here?"

"I work here. Your wife hired me to be her new secretary."

He glanced at Zoe, whose face had blossomed into a bright shade of red. "Probationary secretary," she said. "You're fired."

Paulette issued a ragged and loud exhalation but said nothing.

"That's fine," Liz said with a shrug. "I expected my time here was limited."

"Why?" Zoe asked the question before Pete had the chance.

"I knew you were married to Pete. I wanted to find out how good a marriage it was before I decided whether I should simply stop in at the police station to say hi and catch up." She brought her attention back to Pete. "Or if I had a chance at rekindling old fires. Considering Zoe's long hours at work, I'm still not sure."

He looked at his wife and her clenched fists. "Zoe," he said, hoping she picked up on his unspoken caution. *Don't do it.*

"I know I should've done this long ago," Liz continued. "But my husband passed away last March. He was a good man. A good father. But once he was gone, I felt my daughter deserved to meet her biological father." Her lips curled into a knowing smile. "That would be you, Pete. My daughter is also *your* daughter."

He should've known the first moment she walked into his station. She'd looked vaguely familiar. He realized the familiarity was a combination of seeing Liz in her face, but also seeing something of himself there. "Isabella."

Liz didn't reply. She didn't need to.

Mouth dry, he looked at Zoe. Usually, he could read her, but not now. Her face was as still as granite, her eyes frozen in a wide-eyed stare, her lips pressed tightly closed. He wasn't sure if she was ready to burst into tears or rip Liz to shreds. He willed her to look at him. He wanted to know she was all right. That *they* were all right.

Instead, she turned away and walked stiffly back to her desk. She braced a hand on it as she circled to collapse into her chair, her eyes lowered. When she lifted her face, she looked at Paulette. "Get her out of here."

Paulette crossed to Liz. "I'm so—" Paulette sounded like she was about to apologize but thought better of it. "You need to leave. Now."

"Understood." With the fluid movements of a panther, Liz strode to

Paulette's desk and retrieved her handbag from the bottom drawer. On her way to the door, she stopped next to Pete. "Your wife has a meeting this evening. I'm having dinner with Isabella. I know she'd be thrilled if you joined us."

He looked at Zoe and had no problem reading her now. If looks could kill, Liz would be on her way to the morgue. To Liz, he said, "Not happening."

She shrugged. "We'll be at Andre's if you change your mind. Our reservation is for six thirty." And she sashayed out the door.

The room fell into silence as the click of Liz's heels faded down the hall.

He kept his gaze on Zoe, who still refused to look at him. He took one step toward her.

She bolted out of her chair and stood there, gripping the desk with one hand as if afraid she might fall. She lifted the other, aiming her palm at him. "Don't."

He stopped. "Zoe. Look at me."

She gave her head one quick shake. "I can't." Her voice was barely audible. "I...need time to think."

He glanced at Paulette, wishing she'd followed Liz out the door so he could have some privacy. Some time to assure Zoe she had nothing to worry about. Surely, she knew that.

She gathered her purse from the back of her chair and turned to Paulette. "If you don't mind, lock up when you're done."

"Of course."

Good, he thought. He and Zoe would go somewhere quiet and talk. Except she gave him a wide berth on her way to the door. He reached out to her, but she juked away, both hands raised, clearly saying *don't touch me*. He wanted to grab her. Shake some sense into her.

But he let her go.

She paused in the doorway. "I'll be at Doc and Grace's," she said over her shoulder before vanishing in the same direction Liz had gone.

Did she mean for this evening? For overnight? Pete looked at Paulette as if she might know.

"I'm so sorry, Pete." The secretary had tears in her eyes. "If I'd had any inkling of who Elizabeth Preston was—"

"You had no way of knowing." If anyone should have, it was him.

Elizabeth Preston. Isabella Elson. Neither of those last names was the one Liz carried in high school. Isabella definitely bore a strong resemblance to her mother. He thought he saw himself mirrored in her face as well. But a year and a half ago, Zoe had been convinced she saw her father's memory reflected in a man she desperately wanted to be her brother. Her conviction turned out to be tragically wrong. Pete wasn't about to make the same kind of mistake.

For a fraction of a second, he considered Liz's invitation. Only as a way to get answers. But he recognized a horrendous idea when he had one. No. Zoe needed time to think. So did he.

Tonight, he would go home to the farm and wait. And hope that Zoe showed up sooner rather than later.

Chapter Twenty-Three

Zoe desperately needed to regain her composure, but after nearly running a red light to the blare of horns, she realized the foolishness of being behind the wheel. She'd seen the results of distracted drivers, both as a paramedic and as coroner. Ending up in an ambulance or the morgue wasn't a viable solution to any of her problems.

Grace had invited her to come early, but Zoe didn't want to dump this mess on Doc or his wife. Zoe reached their neighborhood without any more close calls but parked shy of their house. It struck her Doc's stalker may have done the same thing. Maybe he sat in this very spot. But no. She couldn't quite see their house from here. The driver of the 4Runner would want to be closer.

She turned off the Subaru's engine and leaned back in her seat, eyes closed. Pete had a daughter.

Elizabeth Preston...Liz, or whatever the hell her name was...had accepted the secretarial job to get close to Zoe and to determine whether Pete was happily married or susceptible to an old love. Her rational side knew the former was true. When she thought back to her own high school days, she cringed at the memories of the boys she'd gotten too up close and personal with. She and her best friend from back then were wild. Some would say "easy." Neither of them was proud of their pasts. Rose had gotten pregnant twice and been fortunate enough to find a good man to marry and raise those kids as his own. Zoe had avoided the whole unwed pregnancy thing. At the time, she'd thought she was lucky. Years later, she learned she would never be able to carry a baby to term.

She'd lived with it—pushed the idea of kids aside, especially when Pete assured her he still wanted to get married, children or no children. Now he had a daughter. Not a baby, but a grown child. With a woman he must have once loved.

Had he? Or had it been like Zoe's high school flings? Hormone-driven with no thoughts of a future together.

No. She'd seen his face when Elizabeth turned around. Pete had been in love with her back then. As "in love" as two teenagers could be.

So, what had happened? Pete hadn't known about the pregnancy. Zoe knew him well enough to be certain he'd have done right by his girlfriend. Why hadn't Elizabeth...Liz...told him?

Questions Zoe perhaps should have asked before kicking the woman's ass out of her office.

A sharp rap on her passenger window jolted her eyes open. An older man, concern etched deep in his lined face, peered in at her.

"Are you okay, miss?" he shouted through the closed glass.

Zoe fumbled with the key and turned it to on without starting the car so she could power down the window a few inches. "I'm fine." She thought how she must look to a stranger and plastered on a smile. "I'm having dinner with the Abercrombies and got here too early, and I'm really tired, so I thought I'd close my eyes for a few minutes." She realized she was babbling and winced.

He didn't appear convinced. "As long as you aren't sick or anything."

Heartsick didn't count. She thanked him and started the engine. He backed away and waved as she pulled out to drive the short distance to Doc and Grace's house.

In the driveway, she stepped out of the Subaru and braced herself, pushing Pete, Elizabeth, and their now-grown love child out of her mind.

Doc opened the front door. Other than the bandages on his face and a stiffer-than-normal posture due to his wrapped ribs, he didn't look like a man who'd been in a wreck and unconscious for a day and a half. He ushered her in and guided her toward the kitchen from which the most mouthwatering aromas wafted.

"Zoe, so glad you could make it." Grace stood at the stove, stirring a pot. "I should've told you to invite Pete."

Zoe hoped she kept the stabbing pain from showing. "He's busy."

From the questioning scowl on Grace's face, Zoe knew she'd failed.

Thankfully, Grace let it drop, and from all appearances, Doc never noticed.

Dinner conversation surrounded the doctors' orders from the hospital. Doc mostly dismissed them, claiming he'd never felt better, except when he laughed.

Instead of laughing, though, he grew serious. "Has there been any word on Davis's condition?"

Zoe set down her fork. "He had a stroke late this afternoon."

"Mercy." Grace brought her napkin to her lips.

Doc shook his head. "The man may have been a contentious blowhard, but no one deserves what he's going through."

Zoe's thoughts exactly.

The topic was dropped when chimes echoed through the house.

Grace rose, depositing the napkin onto her plate. "That's probably Rachel. I'll let her in."

Zoe scooped up the last of her mashed potatoes and gravy, trying to ignore Doc's intent stare. "Is everything all right? With Pete, I mean," he asked, his voice low. Apparently, he had noticed.

Not in the least, she thought. As she chewed, she covered her mouth and mumbled, "Yeah."

"Uh-huh." His expression told her he didn't buy it.

A few minutes later, Doc, Zoe, and Rachel sat in the living room. Grace promised to join them momentarily, as soon as she cleared the table. Zoe offered to help, but she turned her down.

"Thank you again for looking into this," Rachel said before they started. "Even if nothing comes of it, I'm grateful you're taking the time to at least try."

"We're not done yet." Doc leaned forward and, from the coffee table, picked up the files Kenneth Nicholson had given them. "I've had an opportunity to study your late husband's autopsy report."

Rachel leaned forward. "And?"

"I'm afraid they're inconclusive. The injuries listed are consistent with him being swept downstream. Whether he jumped or not? We can't tell from this."

Her face lowered. "Oh." She looked up again. "What about exhuming his body? I'm willing to sign whatever papers I need to—"

Doc shook his head slowly. "I appreciate that, but I doubt it would help. I'm not calling the forensic findings into question but rather the conclusions that were reached. Yes, it could have been suicide. It could also have been an accident or homicide. I believe the manner of death should've been ruled undetermined. As you pointed out when we spoke earlier, the moment the Somerset Coroner's Office ruled it a suicide, no further investigation was done."

"Which is why I called you." Tears glimmered in Rachel's eyes, and her voice rose in pitch. "It was not a suicide. I know that. And I don't believe it was an accident either."

"The only other option," Zoe said, "is murder."

Rachel met her gaze. "Exactly."

"Who would've wanted your husband dead?" Zoe asked.

A sob escaped Rachel's throat. "I don't know."

Zoe glanced at Doc. She didn't want to overstep. This was his case, after all. She shouldn't even be a part of it. But he gave her the go-ahead with a nod. "Tell me about his work," she asked Rachel.

"You mean the restaurant."

"Yes."

Rachel sat back with a sigh. "There's always conflict in the restaurant business. It's hard work in a hot kitchen. Fast-paced. Chefs have huge egos, as the best of them should. They take pride in their food."

"Does that include Tanner?"

A memory danced across Rachel's face in the form of a smile. "Absolutely. He was very proud of his food and his restaurant. But it was difficult. There's competition with other restaurants. Unhappy employees. Unhappy diners, although Tanner worked very hard to avoid those. He had a lot of regulars."

People would travel from all over to eat his food."

Zoe recalled Nicholson saying the same thing. "I heard the restaurant was featured on a Food Network show."

"It was." Rachel beamed at the memory. "Tanner was extremely proud of that."

"What about the staff?"

Rachel's smile faded into a thoughtful scowl. "I would say there was a love-hate relationship in many cases. Tanner could lavish praise on an employee who'd done a good job. But he could dress down poor performance like no one I've seen."

"Was there anyone in particular who performed badly?"

"None that I can recall. If there were any slackers on staff, they didn't stay long, and Tanner never dwelled on it."

"Did you help out at the restaurant?" Doc asked.

"On occasion. If it was especially busy, I'd go in and help the hostess seat people and take reservations. That's about all."

Zoe thought about something State Trooper Jim Duncan had said. "I heard the restaurant closed shortly after Tanner's death."

"Yes. I tried to keep it running. I hired a chef Tanner spoke highly of, but we couldn't make it go."

"I understand there were some money problems?"

"Well, yes. Business dropped off, no fault of the new chef. Diners loved Tanner. It was never the same once he was gone." Rachel brought her fingertips to her lips, thinking. "Wait a minute. I wasn't involved in the business end of things prior to Tanner's death, but now that you mention it, I do remember him being upset about something with the finances. I also remember he said he'd handled it."

Nothing Rachel said screamed motive for murder. Zoe wondered if Davis had been right. Maybe it was suicide.

The widow must've seen the doubt in Zoe's face. "I know my husband wouldn't have jumped from that bridge. He wouldn't have left me and our kids alone like that. I can't even get his life insurance payout because of his death being deemed suicide." Rachel leaned forward, imploring. "Please.

Nothing will bring Tanner back. I've come to terms with that. But a killer has gone free for too long. Granted, I can certainly use the insurance money, but more importantly, I want justice for my husband."

Zoe looked at Doc. This was his case. He had the final say. Doc, in turn, looked at Grace, who'd slipped silently into the room and perched on an armchair, listening.

"How are you feeling, dear?" she asked him.

His bewilderment over his wife's question was evident.

"What I mean is," Grace went on, "it's going to be another week at least before the doctors clear you to go back to work. But if you're feeling up to going for a ride, I don't see what harm would come from visiting Seven Springs and Confluence."

"I feel fine as long as I don't laugh, cough, or sneeze. Even my headache is gone thanks to extra-strength acetaminophen. You'll have to drive. The doctor hasn't cleared me to operate a motor vehicle either."

Grace shook her head. "Not me. You need to have Zoe with you. I'm no investigator. She is."

All eyes turned her way.

Zoe opened her mouth to protest. She'd already been to Confluence. She hadn't found anything useful. But an avalanche of thoughts rolled over her. Yes, she'd been to Confluence, but she hadn't spoken to Virginia's sister, Fiona, who lived along the banks of the Yough and who worked in its waters. She might've heard something back then that could shed light on what happened.

And while she and Pete had toyed with the idea of going to Tanner Ferrari's now-closed restaurant, they hadn't gotten that far.

Pete.

Zoe's mind crashed back to the thought of him and Liz sharing a daughter. That child—although grown—would bind them forever. Would bind Zoe to Elizabeth and Isabella as well.

If Zoe went home, faced Pete now, she might say things she'd regret. Things she couldn't take back. She didn't want to do that.

She needed time to digest having two more women in Pete's life.

Grace mistook Zoe's silence. "Why don't you invite Pete along? Two investigators would be even better."

"No," Zoe said quickly. Too quickly. Both Doc and Grace gave her a perplexed frown. "He's working on the Virginia Lowe case and can't get away."

Grace seemed to buy the excuse. Zoe didn't think Doc did, though.

The mention of work brought another obstacle to mind. Davis was out of commission. Maneet may have been willing to help in his and Doc's absence, but leaving her in charge was pushing the limits. "I don't think I can do it. The Coroner's Office is already shorthanded."

"I'll call Dr. Patel—" Doc said.

"She's only filling in. I can't dump the entire operation of the morgue on her."

"She'll be fine. Paulette has the new secretary to help with paperwork. Gene may be your deputy in charge of transportation, but he's had the full training. For a day or two? He could be acting coroner."

Zoe's brain hiccuped at the mention of Elizabeth. "I had to let the new secretary go. She wasn't working out."

"Oh. I bet Paulette's disappointed."

Zoe was sure of it. "As for Gene, he's never expressed an interest in being more than a driver."

Doc tipped his head toward her. "Not to you, maybe. But he has to me."

"Really?" Zoe mulled it over. Gene, with his basset hound jowls and perennially sluggish pace, working an autopsy?

"Yes, really." Doc reached for his phone. "Here's what we'll do. I'll call Dr. Patel. You call Gene. Provided they're both in agreement, we'll leave tomorrow morning."

Chapter Twenty-Four

P ete prowled the farmhouse, waiting for Zoe to get home. He'd called her twice. Both times, the calls went to voice mail. He knew she had a meeting with Tanner Ferrari's widow at Doc's house and contemplated ringing the Abercrombie residence. His better sense won out. As big a shock as learning he had a daughter was to him, it was perhaps bigger for Zoe.

He had no interest in rekindling any kind of relationship with Liz. Zoe would realize that too, once the initial shock wore off.

He needed to give her time and space when he really wanted to pull her into his arms and reassure her.

From outside came the crunch of gravel and the soft rumble of Zoe's Forester. His chest ached with a mixture of relief—she'd come home—and dread of what came next. He checked the clock. Almost nine. He strode to the kitchen door. Nudging the curtain aside, he watched her climb out of the car and, lit by the dusk-to-dawn light, head to the barn. She always checked the horses when she got home late.

So why did he sense she was avoiding the house and him?

Ten minutes passed. He took a seat at the table. Finally, he heard light steps on the porch. The door eased open, and she slipped inside, giving him a cautious glance.

Without thinking, he asked, "Are you okay?"

Her short laugh sounded strangled. "No."

"Sorry. Stupid question."

She hung her purse on the back of one of the other chairs and tossed her keys onto the table—a small deviation from her routine. Normally, the purse was hung on the hall tree behind the door, and the keys on the hook next to it.

"Do you want to talk?" he asked.

She crossed to the kitchen sink and stood, her back to him. "Have you spoken to Elizabeth—Liz—and Isabella?"

"No." He would at some point, but not yet.

She turned to face him. From her expression, his answer had been the right one. Leaning back against the counter, she said, "Doc and I are going to the Laurel Highlands tomorrow to dig deeper into the Ferrari case."

Pete noticed she didn't ask him to join them. "Okay."

Zoe lowered her gaze. "I'm gonna pack an overnight bag and head back to Brunswick. I'll sleep in my office. That way I don't have to drive all the way into town in the morning plus drive all the way to Seven Springs."

Her plan made sense. After Doc's head injury, he wouldn't be allowed to share the driving chores. But her plan also meant she wouldn't share Pete's bed tonight. He feared that carried more weight in her decision. "Okay."

She brought her face up. Her eyes held no tears, but the puffiness around them and the redness indicated it hadn't been long since she'd sobbed her heart out. "I'm not angry."

"Okay." He winced. His vocabulary had shrunk to one word. It was the only safe one he knew at the moment.

"But I'm afraid I might *get* angry if we talked right now. I don't want that."

Rather than utter his single safe word, he stayed silent.

"I need time to get my head on straight. Working this case might help."

"Okay."

His limited vocabulary must've struck her as at least minimally funny. She smiled. For a second. Then it was gone. "Could you do me a favor?"

"Anything."

"Call your friend, the state trooper who helped us on Wednesday."

"Jim Duncan."

"Yeah. See if he's able to meet with me and Doc tomorrow."

"I can do that. I'll send his number to your phone."

The fleeting but tight smile returned. "Thank you." She pushed away from the counter and crossed toward the doorway leading to the living room.

He knew she was heading to the second floor and chose the longer route rather than using the other doorway leading directly to the staircase. The shorter route would take her past him. He would've stopped her to pull her into his embrace, which she knew. It was a small thing, like not putting her purse and keys away, but it spoke volumes. The few feet between the two passageways from the kitchen to the rest of the house represented the million-mile gulf between the two of them. He braced an elbow on the table and buried his face in his hand.

A feather-soft footstep made him look up.

Zoe stood in the doorway to the living room. "While I'm gone," she said, her voice raspy, "I think you should meet with your daughter."

Even his safe word wasn't a safe response this time.

"I have a lot to think about," Zoe said. "But so do you."

Then she turned and was gone.

* * *

Zoe had a feeling she wouldn't sleep well in her office. She needn't have worried. No sooner had she spread her sleeping bag in a corner behind a wall of packed boxes than her phone rang. A late-night Brunswick drug deal gone bad had escalated into two men firing guns at each other. One was reported on his way to surgery. The other was a case for Zoe.

City, County, and State Police had the scene well in hand when she arrived. Detective Knight stood nearby, as she prepped the victim for transport. Once she and Gene had loaded the decedent into the van, she asked her deputy if he had any questions for her, since he'd be overseeing the autopsy.

"Don't think so," he said. "It's been a while, but I've kept up my training." He gave her as close to a smile as she'd ever seen on his usually sullen face. "Besides, I've heard good things about Dr. Patel. We got this, boss."

Zoe watched the van pull out, relieved her office was in good hands while she skipped out for a day and, at the same time, felt superfluous.

Her phone rang again as she parked behind her office building. A traffic collision with fatalities a half hour away.

The entire night went like that. By morning, she had more bodies in the cooler than she'd had hours of sleep.

Dawn delivered flat gray skies promising rain. Zoe bought a large mocha with an extra shot of espresso before leaving the city to pick up Doc, thinking of every coffee shop—and restroom—on the way to Confluence.

Her phone chirped with Pete's text as she pulled into Doc's driveway.

Duncan agreed to do some checking on case details. Call him when you get there.

Pete included a phone number.

She texted back.

Thx. Just got to Doc's. Be in touch.

She clicked send, hesitated, and added, **Love you.**

Before she reached Doc's front door, her phone chirped again.

Love you more.

She smiled. They would be fine. Their vows had been anything but traditional. Instead of through good times and bad, she'd promised *"I will walk at your side in the sunshine and in the rain"* and quickly realized how sappy it sounded. Either way, this thing with Elizabeth and Isabella was one of those rainy times. They'd get through it and be stronger for the challenge.

The first kiss of drizzle settled on her face and the front door swung open as she stood at the bottom of the porch steps. Grace looked concerned. "Are you all right?"

Zoe made her way onto the small concrete slab, holding up her phone. "Just texting my husband."

"Oh, good." Grace stepped aside, letting her in. "I had a feeling last night you two might've had a disagreement."

"Not exactly." Zoe didn't want to invite questions. She was feeling a little better about the situation this morning, but still carried an ache in her heart.

Grace caught her arm and leaned close to her ear. "I'm sure you're already aware, but make-up sex is amazing."

Zoe faced the older woman, who fluttered her eyebrows suggestively and choked a laugh.

Doc approached them, carrying a satchel in one hand and a Thermos in the other. "What's going on out here?"

"Nothing," Zoe and Grace said in unison. Zoe tacked on, "You ready to go?"

He held up the canvas case. "I think so. I've got the coroner reports you picked up from Somerset County. I've got my own notes on my laptop. And I've got coffee."

"Sounds like we're all set. Let's hit the road."

* * *

The text from Zoe left Pete feeling slightly better. He'd lain awake all night, acutely aware of the void beside him. The tabby cats seemed to miss her too, curling up on the half of the bed where she should have been.

He made it to the barn to feed and water the horses before the clouds opened. With his third cup of coffee in hand, he settled into one of the Adirondack chairs on the porch to listen to the thrum of rain on the roof.

And to contemplate Zoe's request.

Saturday was a day off, provided nothing major happened within his township. As chief of a small, rural municipality, days off were never a given. Should he spend it trying to connect with Isabella?

His daughter.

Or was she?

Liz hadn't given him her number. Thank God. He could picture Zoe's face if she had. She'd been devastated enough by the news and by Liz's invitation to dinner.

He didn't have Isabella's number either. He could easily get it. She'd phoned the station, so there would be a record. He knew where she lived, although yesterday the house had looked deserted. He could take a drive past it. Check to see if her car was there.

But what if Liz's car was there too?

His desire to meet—really meet—his daughter was growing, but he did

186

not want to encounter Liz. At some point, he'd have to. But not today. Not until he and Zoe had a chance to discuss the situation at length.

Besides, Zoe had urged him to meet with his daughter while she was away. She hadn't said anything about his high school sweetheart.

He picked up his cup for another sip of coffee only to find it empty. At the same time, his phone rang. He hoped to see Zoe's name and face on the screen. Instead, it was Detective Max Knight.

He thumbed the green icon. "Knight. What can I do for you?"

"Thought you'd like to know. I believe we've found your murder weapon in the Virginia Lowe case."

Pete came to the edge of his chair. "The lamp from the hotel?"

"Yep."

"Where?"

"In the weeds along the road. A bicyclist out for an early-morning ride spotted something wrapped in a pillowcase about ninety minutes ago. When he opened it, the lamp was inside." Knight's gruff chuckle rattled through the phone. "Funny thing. It was found outside Rogers Mine, about a quarter mile from where we found the black Toyota 4Runner."

Thoughts of a Saturday off dashed, Pete stood and entered his kitchen. "We spotted a dark-colored 4Runner on security cam footage in Phillipsburg the morning of the homicide."

"Baronick mentioned that. Did you happen to catch a plate number?"

"No. We couldn't make out a driver either. It was just a coincidental blur on the footage while we were trying to confirm the son's alibi."

Knight grunted. "Did you? Confirm the kid's alibi, I mean."

"No."

"I'd like our tech guys to take a look at the video."

Pete knew they wouldn't find anything. Abby was as good or better than any tech geek at County. "I'll bring it with me when I come to check out the lamp."

"It's at the lab."

"Perfect. Then, I'll check out the lab results. Be there in an hour." Pete ended the call before Knight could argue and charged upstairs to change out of his faded jeans and sweatshirt and into a clean uniform.

Virginia Lowe's murder and Doc's attempted murder were linked by a 4Runner with a young man behind the wheel.

The keys had been found in Dr. Charles Davis's possession, but Doc insisted Davis hadn't been driving.

And no alibi for Alex. Could the kid and his ex-stepdad be co-conspirators after all?

Chapter Twenty-Five

Zoe was ready for more caffeine by the time they arrived at the Lucky Dog Café in Confluence. Doc said he still had some in his Thermos. He popped open his umbrella and wandered across the road to the bridge while she went inside and ordered another large with an extra shot. She texted the number Pete had given her for Trooper Duncan as she waited, letting him know they had arrived.

He texted back. **Be there in 5**.

Coffee in hand, she stepped out onto the café's deck and flipped her hood over her head. Through the drizzle, she spotted Duncan in his rain jacket, jogging toward Doc. She had to wait for a string of cars to pass before crossing Route 281. By the time she joined Doc and Duncan, the men had introduced themselves and were discussing the likelihood of Tanner Ferrari choosing this spot to jump to his death.

Duncan nodded at Zoe. "Good to see you again."

"Likewise. We appreciate your help."

"You and Pete made me curious after your visit. I managed to get my hands on the police report, such as it was."

Doc watched another car speed past. "And?"

"Ferrari's car was parked down at the Ramcat boat launch." Duncan looked at Zoe. "That's where we turned around after being accosted by the attack dog."

Doc scowled at her. "You didn't tell me anything about being attacked by a dog."

"We weren't. Not really. You may have noticed the scratches on my car..."

189

"Now that you mention it, I did."

"That's what happens when Pete ignores the *Do Not Enter* and *Beware of Dog* signs. No blood was drawn." To Duncan, she said, "His car was parked all the way down there? No one thought that was strange?"

Duncan shrugged. "It's three miles from here. An easy walk for anyone who's in good shape."

"Which Ferrari was," Doc said. "But it does seem odd. If you're planning to take your own life, why park three miles from the bridge when there's lots of parking right here?" He gestured at the Lucky Dog's rapidly filling lot and the public parking along the river.

"I agree," Duncan said.

"What about his fishing gear?" Doc asked. "He was wearing waders and a fishing vest when his body was recovered. What happened to his pole and any tackle boxes or such?"

"There was no report of anything left behind here on the bridge, but to be honest, other than his rod and reel, he probably didn't carry anything else. Fly fishermen keep all their necessities attached to them."

"Okay," Zoe said. "The rod and reel, then. If not on the bridge, what about in his car?"

"Nothing was found there either."

Doc was shaking his head, still gazing downward. "If I was despondent enough to kill myself, I'd want to be sure to accomplish the job. Not merely break a few bones. If I was determined jumping was my suicidal method of choice, I'd damned well find a higher bridge."

Zoe studied the rocky river bottom, visible through the current. "That's what I thought too."

He turned his back to the barrier and watched more cars stream past. "Is this road always this heavily traveled?"

"It's one of the main routes into town from Route 40, so yes." Duncan watched two pickups hauling campers rolling toward town. "Confluence might not be the hotbed of tourist activity that Ohiopyle is, but we have the Yough Dam and lake access, a couple of campgrounds, several rafting outfitters, and the Great Allegheny Passage Trail."

"Yet no one saw Ferrari jump," Doc said.

"I've asked around town this week." Duncan shook his head. "Locals remember the story and the search for the body, but no one admits seeing anything."

Doc's face had turned stony. "I want to see where his car was found."

Duncan eyed him. "You want to walk?"

"No," Zoe answered for him. "He got out of the hospital yesterday after having his car run off the road."

Duncan pointed at the bandage on Doc's forehead. "He was telling me about that. If Zoe's willing to risk her car again, we should drive."

"Absolutely," she said.

Doc raised both hands. "I'm not arguing. Three miles might not be much for you young folks, but if I'm going to put in that kind of distance, it's going to be on the golf course. Even then, I rent a cart."

Back in Zoe's Forester—she behind the wheel, Doc in the passenger seat, and Duncan in the rear—she drove the same narrow road as Pete had three days ago. As they passed the almost invisible entrance to Fiona Roth's driveway with its *Keep Out* signs, Zoe remembered she wanted to speak with the young woman. She did not, however, want to go anywhere near Cujo. Instead, she continued along the road to the same gravel lot from which Pete had called Alex.

Duncan leaned forward toward the center console. "This is where Ferrari's car was found. According to the report, it was locked."

Doc opened the file he'd brought with him and skimmed through it. "His keys were found on his body in a zipped pocket of his fishing vest."

Zoe studied the parked vehicles. "He plans to kill himself. Locks his car, zips his keys into his vest, and walks three miles to jump off a bridge."

"Seems like a lot of effort," Doc said.

"Unless he wanted to walk the trail one last time," Duncan said with a shrug. "It is a pretty trail."

It was all perfectly plausible. Yet none of it felt right.

Duncan's attention shifted to another group of rafters at the launch area, preparing to set out. The guides wore the same fluorescent green t-shirt emblazoned with the Raging River Raft Tours logo as the ones on Wednesday. "Drive over there," he said, pointing to a spot closer to the rafters.

She eased the Subaru to the edge of the gravel and into an empty space, giving them an unobstructed view.

Duncan grunted. "There's your girl."

"Who?" Zoe asked. "Fiona?"

"Yep."

Zoe hadn't seen her before and only had Pete's description to go on. Wiry. Tough. Short dark hair. From where they sat, Zoe could tell only one of the guides was a woman, and she matched the picture Pete had painted in Zoe's mind.

Zoe looked over her shoulder at Duncan. "Should we approach her here?"

He gave a short laugh. "Not we. *You*. You're the one who wants to talk to her. If she sees me, she's likely to tell you to go to hell. Or worse."

Zoe looked at Doc. "You coming, or are you leaving me to face her alone?"

He unclipped his seatbelt. "I'm not sure what you expect to find out."

"Probably nothing. But Ferrari allegedly jumped three miles upstream. His body was found a few miles downstream from here. Fiona works on the river and lives not far from it. If the cops didn't interview her..." Zoe shot a questioning glance at Duncan.

"Not as far as I've been able to determine."

"Then I think it's time we find out what she has to say."

Zoe offered a hand to Doc as they picked their way down a dirt path to the ramp.

He waved her off. "I'm good."

She wasn't buying it. Less than a week ago, he'd suffered a concussion and broken ribs. If he slipped and fell, Grace would have Zoe's head on a platter. "Well, I'm not." She took his arm, acting as though she needed the support when, in fact, she could tell if he wobbled and could steady him.

If he was wise to her ploy, he didn't let on.

The buff young man in the raft tours t-shirt spotted their approach and held up a hand, stopping them. "I'm sorry, folks. These rafts are full. You'll need to sign up for a later tour at the office."

"We're not here to raft." Zoe motioned toward Fiona. "We need to speak with your co-worker for a minute."

Fiona noticed them and looked as inviting as her dog.

"Fee," the young man yelled. "Come here." To Zoe, he said, "Only a minute. We have a schedule to keep." He strode away as Fiona walked toward them.

"I'm working," she said. "What do you want?"

Zoe extended a hand and introduced herself. "I'm the Monongahela County Coroner."

Fiona stuffed both her hands in her pockets without shaking Zoe's. "Monongahela County? You arrest my sister's ex for her murder yet?"

Zoe let her hand drop. "The police haven't made any arrests, I'm afraid." She tipped her head toward Doc. "This is Dr. Lyle Abercrombie, my forensic pathologist."

Doc gave Fiona a somber nod. "We're very sorry for your loss."

She eyed him warily. "If you don't have any news about Virginia, what do you want from me?"

"We're looking into another case," Zoe said. "One from about five years ago. You were living here at the time, right?"

"Yeah. So?"

Doc stepped in. "Do you remember a man by the name of Tanner Ferrari? He was reported to have jumped from the bridge over Route 281. His body was recovered a few miles downriver from here."

"I heard the news reports. Everyone was talking about it."

"Exactly. We thought you might've picked up some of the local gossip."

"What kind of gossip?"

"Like who the anonymous caller was."

Fiona held Zoe's gaze. "Why don't you talk to the police? They must know."

"No, they don't."

"I'm afraid I don't know anything about the caller." Fiona took a long look at Doc before coming back to Zoe, her expression relaxing. "The locals said the dude was despondent. He came here for one last day of fishing at his favorite holes. Then he jumped. You ask me, it ain't a bad way to go."

Zoe looked out at the green mountains kissed with a hint of early autumn gold and orange. Listened to the relaxing whoosh of the river. The way Fiona described Tanner's last day made sense.

"What about his gear?" Doc asked.

"What gear?"

"You said he came here for one last day of fishing. What happened to his pole?"

"I dunno. Probably got washed down the river, too."

Doc considered it, scowling, then shook his head. "I'm trying to picture him climbing up on the concrete barricade on the bridge. He was wearing his waders, so it couldn't have been easy. Would he carry his pole up there with him? I don't think so."

Fiona removed her hands from her pockets and crossed her arms. "Then he must've left it somewhere."

"The police didn't find it on the bridge or in his car," Zoe said.

Fiona shook her head. "Sorry. I can't help you."

"Were you working the raft tours that day?" Doc asked.

"Hell, I don't remember. Probably. Look, I gotta go. I *am* working today, and we have a schedule to keep to."

"Before you go, can you do me a favor?" Zoe dug her business card from her pocket and held it out. "Can you ask around? Any of your co-workers who were in the area at the time. If you hear any rumors or gossip about who made the 911 call, could you please contact me?"

Fiona eyed the card before cautiously taking it. "Sure. But don't hold your breath. Most of these kids I work with were still in grade school back then."

"Still, maybe they remember something their parents said. When things like this happen, people talk. There have to be theories about the identity of the mysterious caller."

"Maybe." Fiona pocketed the card. "But, like I said. Don't hold your breath." She turned to leave. Then turned back. "For the record, I wish you were working to put Charles Davis behind bars for smashing in my sister's head instead of digging into some poor schmuck's suicide from years ago." Fiona clearly hadn't heard about Davis's attempted suicide or subsequent stroke.

As she strode away, Zoe could see her point. But Virginia's murder investigation was out of her hands. Zoe faced Doc. "That was a total waste of effort."

He stared out at the river, much as she had a few minutes ago. "Not really."

"How so?"

He turned to face her. "Something Ms. Roth said." He shook his head. "No, not what she said. What *I* said because of what she said."

Confused, Zoe waited.

"He kept his waders on while he climbed up on the concrete barrier?" Doc shook his head.

"Maybe he wanted to be certain he didn't float?" Zoe suggested. "Those things fill up with water, they drag you down."

Doc narrowed his eyes. "I highly doubt that was a concern. No. I now feel a hundred percent certain. Tanner Ferrari did not jump from that bridge."

Chapter Twenty-Six

Pete found Knight and Baronick waiting for him as he entered the County Police HQ.

"Did you bring the security footage?" Baronick asked.

Pete withdrew a flash drive from his pocket.

Baronick accepted it. "I'll run this down to IT." To Knight, he said, "Meet you both in the incident room."

As Knight led the way down the hall, Pete updated him. "I have my officers canvassing the homes and businesses between the motel and Phillipsburg. It's a long shot, but maybe someone else captured an image of our vehicle."

"Good. We could sure use a break."

"What are the odds of it being the same 4Runner?" Pete mused, as much to himself as to the detective.

"Doesn't seem likely, does it?" Knight opened a door and ushered him into the same room where they'd met two days ago.

Instead of two, there were now four whiteboards. The third contained information on Doc's "accident," especially the 4Runner. Someone had drawn an arrow from the vehicle's description to Virginia's boards along with a trio of question marks.

The fourth had the words *Dr. Charles Davis's Attempted Suicide* written across the top with notes about the pills, wine, fingerprints, and the keys listed below. A similar arrow connected the keys to the other boards.

"By the way," Knight said as Pete studied the newest notes, "Uniontown PD spoke with Darlene Roth's neighbors."

"And?"

"As far as they've been able to determine, she was home."

Pete looked at him. "As far as they've been able to determine?"

"The residents on Ms. Roth's street aren't big believers in neighborhood watch. According to the patrol officers, they made a point of minding their own business. The consensus is Ms. Roth isn't very friendly toward them, so they see no need to be friendly in return."

Pete thought of his meeting with Darlene. "Alex Lowe claims she's on the spectrum. Having spoken with her, I have to agree."

"A few of the neighbors corroborated that much. But they all confirmed her car never left the driveway."

Baronick bustled into the room. "While I was downstairs, I stopped at the lab." He held up a folder. "We got a match on the fingerprints from the lamp."

"Anyone we know?" Knight asked.

"No one we know *yet.*" Baronick slapped the folder down on the front table. "They didn't match anything in AFIS."

Knight glowered at him. "But you said—"

"We got a match. Yes." Baronick opened the folder. "To the prints found on the 4Runner's rearview mirror."

Pete swore. So much for the Toyota on Burger Boy's security footage being a coincidence.

"The Lowe and Abercrombie cases really are linked," Knight muttered.

"It would appear so."

Pete looked from Knight to Baronick. "Neither set of prints matched Alex Lowe?"

"We don't have his on record," Baronick said.

Icy claws wrapped around the base of Pete's neck. "I told him to stop here on his way home from the motel and get fingerprinted for elimination purposes."

The detectives exchanged looks. "He didn't," Knight said.

Baronick's expression darkened. "Maybe he was afraid we'd find them somewhere we shouldn't."

"Which we may have," Knight said.

Pete moved to stand in front of the whiteboards, studying the timeline. "Alex could not have been in both places at the same time."

"Unless he had help," Knight said.

The discussion Pete and Zoe'd had in the barn Thursday evening whispered in the back of his brain. "Davis?"

Knight picked up the dry-erase marker and used it as a pointer. "Alex Lowe leaves the Vance Motel in his mom's car at six o'clock Sunday morning. Dr. Davis arrives in the 4Runner shortly afterwards, let's say six-oh-five. Kills his ex-wife." The detective turned to Pete. "What time did you say you spotted the Toyota on the security footage?"

"Six twenty-eight. Heading south, away from the motel."

Baronick stared at the timeline, rubbing his chin. "How long does it take to get from the motel to Phillipsburg?"

"I clocked it as six or seven minutes," Knight said.

Pete thought for a moment. "That's about right."

Knight returned to the board. "Let's say Davis and Alex meet somewhere in Phillipsburg to swap drivers. Davis turns the Toyota over to the kid, who drives it to Dr. Abercrombie's residence and eventually follows him and runs him off the road."

Baronick moved to Knight's side. "Doc and his wife confirm he left their house a few minutes after seven o'clock. It takes maybe twenty-five minutes to get to his house from Phillipsburg."

"Tight." Baronick shrugged. "But do-able."

"I admit, on the surface, it doesn't make sense," Knight said. "But that might be the point. Davis came up with a plan to muddy the investigative waters."

Pete rubbed the space between his brows where a headache was threatening. Knight's theory was on target with Zoe's. Pete had dismissed it then and didn't like it any better now.

The detective raised one hand at Pete. "Hear me out. Davis knows his job is in peril. Hell, his whole career. How would it look if Zoe fired him? It would be a huge black mark on his resume. He decides to get rid of Dr. Abercrombie, thereby solidifying his position in the coroner's office." Pete started to cut him off, but Knight repeated, "Hear me out."

"Go ahead."

"Davis knew the kid was used to just scraping by. Virginia's insurance payout could change his life. Dr. Abercrombie would recognize Davis, so he has Alex follow Abercrombie until the opportunity arises to take him out. But Davis wouldn't expect him to kill his own mother, so that part of the plan is up to him."

Pete shook his head. "I've seen Hitchcock's *Strangers on a Train*. You're forgetting something. Doc has been aware of the 4Runner tailing him for weeks. Virginia only decided Saturday night to come here and talk to Zoe."

Knight smirked. "According to Alex."

Pete started to argue but stopped. Abby had made the same point. Everything he knew about Virginia learning of Zoe and Davis's dispute had come from Alex.

"The conflict within the coroner's office isn't new," Baronick said, keeping his voice low. "Everyone knows about the grief Davis has been giving Zoe for months."

Knight nodded. "Davis figured it was only a matter of time before Zoe had enough of him."

Pete faced Knight. "You're saying Davis enlisted his stepson, who claims to despise him—"

Baronick raised a finger. "*Claims.*"

Pete gave him that one and started over. "You're saying Davis enlisted Alex weeks ago to follow Doc Abercrombie with the intention of eventually killing him?"

"In exchange for Virginia's life insurance payout." Knight must've seen the doubt still embedded on Pete's face and returned to the timeline on the whiteboard. "Just bear with me. Once Alex ran Dr. Abercrombie off the road, he drove back to Phillipsburg to return the 4Runner to Davis. What time did you say he showed up on video again to get in his car?"

Pete frowned. "Eight twenty-one."

Knight raised both hands. "More than enough time." He capped the dry-erase marker and dropped it in the board's tray. "I rest my case."

"You've missed something," Pete said. "The fingerprints on the lamp match those in the 4Runner." As soon as the words were out of his mouth, he knew the answer to his own question. He sighed. "Alex spent the night in the room and could've turned the lamp on or off at any time."

"Exactly," Baronick said. "I expected both prints to match Davis, but his are on record. No match. He probably wore gloves."

With a growl, Pete faced the timeline. Knight was right. It all fit.

Except it didn't. Not in Pete's gut. In order for both crimes to have happened this way, to have been planned weeks in advance, Davis would have to be a mastermind genius.

Manipulative? Narcissistic? Condescending? He was all of those. But a genius?

Hell, no.

* * *

Zoe watched the raft tour shove off. It looked like fun, paddling out into the wide, smooth Youghiogheny, even in the drizzle. Smooth here at Ramcat. Downstream? Not so much. If the rafters weren't wet already, they would be soon. She decided she'd rather view the world from the back of her horse than from an innertube on steroids. She turned to Doc. "Let's get back to the car."

She took his arm again, letting him believe he was helping her instead of being steadied by her.

"Learn anything?" Duncan asked once they'd climbed into the Subaru.

Doc shook off his umbrella, closed the door, and buckled his seatbelt. "Ferrari didn't jump from the bridge."

Zoe caught the trooper's surprise in her rearview. "Fiona told you that?" he asked.

"No." Doc shared his thought process on the matter.

Duncan watched a family in rain gear, unloading various-sized bikes from a rack on the back of their SUV. "I doubt that would hold up in court."

"You're right, of course." Doc shook his head in disgust. "I wish like hell

Davis had done his job."

Zoe remained quiet, thinking of a few wishes of her own. She wished she knew what Virginia intended to tell her. She wished she knew why Kenneth Nicholson had signed a non-disclosure agreement.

She wished Pete hadn't fathered a child when he'd been in high school.

Zoe shook her head. *Focus.*

Her phone rang. As if Pete had known she was thinking of him, his name lit the screen.

She considered letting the call go to voice mail but noticed Doc watching her. She swiped the green icon. "Hey."

"I need you to do me a favor." Pete sounded on edge.

"What do you need?"

"I'm texting you a photo. Show it to Doc and ask him if he recognizes him. Then call me back."

"Okay." Before she could ask what this was all about, the call ended. She looked at Doc.

"I heard," he said.

Her phone chirped. She opened the text and clicked on the attached photo. Alex? Perplexed, she handed the device to Doc.

He squinted at the screen, pulled out a pair of reading glasses, shoved them on his face, and looked again. "Who is this?"

She almost told him but didn't. "Does he look familiar?"

Doc studied the photo again before shaking his head. "No. Should he?"

Zoe reclaimed her phone. "I guess we'll find out." She tapped the call icon. Pete answered immediately. "Well?"

She put the call on speaker. "He says he doesn't recognize him."

"Who is he?" Doc asked.

The reason for the call, the photo, and the question struck Zoe. "You think Alex was driving the 4Runner?"

"That's what I want Doc to tell me," Pete said over the speaker. "Is this the young man you saw behind the wheel of the Toyota parked in front of your house?"

Doc looked at Zoe. "Can you pull it up again?"

"Sure." She kept Pete on the line as she found and enlarged the image.

Doc took the phone from her and scrutinized the picture. Finally, he shook his head. "It may be him. Then again, it might not be. I can't tell for sure. He wore a ball cap pulled down and had his head lowered."

Pete's frustrated sigh filled the air. "Thanks anyway, Doc. Zoe, have you talked to Jim Duncan yet?"

The trooper leaned toward the center console. "I'm right here. What do you need?"

"I'd asked Alex Lowe to stop here at Monongahela County HQ to get fingerprinted since we knew he was in the motel room where his mother was murdered. He never did."

"You want me to remind him?"

"We *need* his prints."

"Alex couldn't have been driving the 4Runner," Zoe said. "He was in Phillipsburg at the time."

"I hope that's true. If it is, and if we eliminate his fingerprints, I'll feel a lot better."

"He still staying with the aunt in Uniontown?" Duncan asked.

"As far as we know."

"I'll head over there later this afternoon and talk to him."

"Thanks," Pete said. "While you're at it, ask him where he was between six sixteen and eight twenty-one the morning his mother was killed. The girl he gave us as his alibi denies being with him all that time."

"I'll handle it."

"Let me know what he says. And, Zoe?"

She sensed he was about to ask if she would be home tonight. Quickly, she said, "Talk to you later," and ended the call.

Zoe caught Doc studying her with the same intensity he'd used on the photo. She forced her mind from Pete and Alex back to the case at hand. "About Ferrari, assuming you're right and he didn't jump, how did he end up in the river? Did he slip and fall in?"

"Maybe. But I doubt it." Doc retrieved the folder from the map pocket in the passenger door and set it on his lap. "The skull fracture, the lack of water in his lungs, doesn't fit the scenario."

Zoe looked at him, knowing what he was getting at.

From the back seat, Duncan said, "But being struck over the head and killed, then dumped in the river does."

"Yes, it does."

She blew out a breath. "I've known all along this was a possibility. But how do we find a killer five years after the fact?"

"Same as we do with any cold case," Duncan said. "We go back to the beginning."

Doc shook his head. "Not we." He turned to look at the trooper. "You, maybe. As for me, I feel comfortable recommending the Somerset County Coroner's Office change their ruling." He shot a look at Zoe. "If Davis ever wakes up, he will be pissed."

Chapter Twenty-Seven

Pete, alone in the county police incident room, stared at his phone, the screen indicating Zoe had hung up on him. He'd wanted to ask how things were going with the Ferrari case, but if she had any news, she'd have told him.

Wouldn't she?

The device vibrated in his hand. For a second, he thought she was calling back. But no. The incoming call was from Keegan Ireland, his weekend officer.

"Chief, I may have something." Keegan sounded breathless. "I've been canvassing the residents and businesses between Phillipsburg and the Vance Motel, and I found out Bert's Garage has a pretty decent security system."

Pete knew the place. At one time, well before Pete had moved to Vance Township—possibly before he'd been born—Bert's Garage had been a thriving gas station servicing the same travelers who'd stayed at the motel in its heyday. That was before they put in the four-lane. Now, the gas pumps were long gone. Bert's was a one-man business offering state inspection services, oil changes, and repairs to a dwindling clientele.

"One of his cameras is aimed at the pull-off area in front of the building," Keegan was saying. "It picks up road traffic as well."

"Is Bert willing to hand over the footage?"

"Yep."

"Have you looked at it?"

Keegan's breathless excitement dissipated. "Only enough to make sure it really did pick up the road traffic."

"Good." Pete considered the timeframe. "Get a copy of last Sunday morning from 5:30 until 7:30. Take it back to the station and start going over it. I'll call Abby and see if she can come in on her day off to give you a hand." Or an extra set of eyes. "I should be back in about forty-five minutes."

"On it, Chief."

Pete ended the call and pulled up Abby's number. She answered with a too-cheery "What's up?"

"You busy?"

She huffed. "Just more post-flood cleaning."

Guilt jabbed at him. "Okay," he told her. "Never mind."

"No. Wait," she called out before he could hit the red button. "If you need me to do something, please ask. I'm sick to death of scrubbing this basement with bleach."

Pete chuckled. He told her about the video Keegan had snagged. "You're probably equally sick of watching hours of security film, and this is your day off—"

"I'll get changed and meet him at the station."

He thanked her and ended the call. Pocketing his phone, Pete debated his next move. The county IT nerds were handling the Burger Boy footage. The newly discovered video from Bert's was in good hands. Zoe and Doc were chasing leads in Confluence. Jim Duncan was going to make sure Alex Lowe got fingerprinted.

Pete checked his watch. Early afternoon on a Saturday. Would Isabella be home?

* * *

The rain had stopped by the time Zoe parked in front of the Lucky Dog, and Duncan climbed out. He leaned on the open passenger window ledge. "I'm heading to Uniontown to talk to Alex Lowe and get his fingerprints. What's next on your agenda?"

"I'm going to call Ken Nicholson," Doc said. "Maybe he can meet with us this afternoon. But beyond giving him my recommendation, I don't see there's much more for me to do."

"And Somerset County is out of my coverage area, so I guess I'm done with it too." Duncan looked at Zoe. "Keep me posted, though. Ferrari died practically in my backyard. I'd like to know how it all shakes out."

"Will do," she replied. "Thanks again."

Duncan straightened, slapped the window ledge, and strode away.

Doc made his call to Nicholson and placed his phone on speaker. The Somerset County coroner answered but was out at a death scene and doubted he'd be able to meet. Doc shared his findings and conclusions. Nicholson sounded uneasy and only promised to *consider* Doc's recommendation, not act on it. Once again, Zoe wondered about the non-disclosure agreement Nicholson had with Davis.

Doc's tone had grown terse by the time he ended the call and faced her. "You ready to head home?"

She wasn't, but didn't realize her expression gave away more than she intended.

"What's going on between you and Pete?"

Zoe swallowed. "Why would you ask that?" But she heard the guilty squeak in her voice when she'd meant to sound blasé.

He fixed her with a look. "I'm not stupid. Out with it."

She exhaled. "I told you I fired the new secretary."

"Yes."

Closing her eyes, Zoe spilled the story of Elizabeth and Pete. And their daughter.

When she finished, Doc stared straight ahead, clearly mulling it over. After several silent minutes, he turned to her. "Pete had no idea he had a child with this woman?"

"None."

"Excuse me if I'm being obtuse, but why are you upset with him then? This happened long ago. He's not been keeping anything from you."

Doc was right. "I'm not upset with him. I'm just...upset. In general." And furious about how Elizabeth had handled it. Zoe wasn't going to dump all of her rage on Doc, but she realized she really wanted to—*needed* to—dump it on Elizabeth.

But for all their sakes, not now.

"I told Pete to talk to Isabella. I need to give him space to do that."

"Which is why we're here," Doc said slowly. "You're giving him 'space.'"

"Yeah."

"Or are you giving yourself space?"

"Both."

"Gotcha." Doc wiped a hand across his mouth. "You know what? I'm hungry." He pointed at the Lucky Dog. "But I don't think I want to eat here."

He was getting at something, but Zoe wasn't sure what.

"You know what else? I've never been to Seven Springs. It's not all that far, is it?"

She smiled, now knowing where his mind was. "You realize Tanner Ferrari's restaurant has been closed for years."

Doc shrugged. "So? I'm sure there are other restaurants in the area. It's a resort town, after all." He waved a hand. "Let's go. Lunch or dinner or whatever it ends up being is on me."

* * *

Pete made the same detour on his way back to Vance Township as he'd made on his way to Brunswick yesterday. Except this time, Isabella's red Corolla was parked under the carport. He braked at the end of the driveway, his grip tightening on the steering wheel. He should pull in. Knock on the door. Sit down with his daughter.

His daughter. Sit down with her, and then what? How could he expect to catch up on a life he'd only learned about yesterday? She'd known about him. It's why she'd come into the station reporting a non-existent stalker. It's why she wanted his personal attention on the case. She'd wanted to believe he would protect her.

And he'd brushed her off as a lunatic.

He looked away from the house, down the road in front of him, and battled the desire to jam his foot on the gas pedal. He wasn't ready for this meeting.

He wasn't ready to face his own offspring. But when he glanced at the house, Isabella stood on the front stoop, arms crossed, as if she sensed his desire to run and was once again disappointed in him.

Pete exhaled a growl and pulled into the driveway. He turned off the ignition, braced himself, and stepped out. Isabella watched his approach without a word, her expression giving nothing away. He stopped at the bottom of the three concrete steps leading up to the small stoop on which his daughter stood looking down at him, arms still folded. For the second time in as many days, he was at a loss for words. He had no idea how to begin this conversation. She didn't appear to even consider helping him out. But what could she say? *Hi, Dad?*

What could *he* say? He started with "Isabella."

Her mouth slanted into the same disappointed sneer he remembered seeing on Liz's face. "Chief." That one word oozed sarcasm.

"How about you try calling me Pete."

Her expression shifted back to neutral. "Pete."

"I gather you've spoken with your mother."

"We speak all the time."

Dammit. She wasn't going to make this easy. "Do you want to talk? Or would you rather I stayed the hell out of your life?"

"I could ask you the same question," she said. "I'm here, aren't I?"

"So am I."

The stoic mask softened. "I have coffee on, if you want to come in."

"I'd like that."

A few minutes later, he was sitting at the island in his daughter's kitchen, watching as she filled two large mugs. A plate with breadcrumbs and an empty water bottle on the counter before him was evidence of Isabella's lunch.

She set both mugs down before picking up the plate and placing it in the sink. "Sorry about the mess." The bottle crinkled in her hand as she tossed it into a garbage can at the end of the counter. Staying on her side of the island, she said, "I have creamer if you want."

"Black is fine." He took a sip. "Good coffee."

"Thanks. I take mine black, too."

One thing they had in common, he thought. It was a start. "I apologize for the last time I was here." He remembered mistaking her invitation to share a meal as a sexual proposition, her storming away, frustrated and in tears. It made sense now.

She lowered her eyes to her mug. "I'm the one who should apologize. Looking back, I think of what I must've sounded like." She shook her head.

"Let's just call that one a draw."

She lifted her eyes, and he gave her a smile. "Deal," she said.

Pete drew a breath and decided it was time to dive in. "I hope you realize I never knew I had a daughter. Nothing against your mother, but she never told me."

"I know. She said she didn't want you to feel obligated to her."

Obligated?

Isabella must've seen the pain on his face. She waved a hand. "Mom admitted she didn't want to be tied to you either."

He winced. But thought about it. Liz may have been the more mature of them back then, thinking well ahead of teenage pregnancy repercussions. "How long have you known?"

"About you?" Isabella took a sip. "Mom told me Dad—the man who raised me—wasn't my biological dad when I turned thirteen. I guess she figured I was old enough to understand by then, but I'm not sure I was. She didn't tell me who you were until years later. Even then, she didn't tell me much. Just that she'd gotten pregnant late in her senior year of high school. She wanted me to know she hadn't been raped or anything like that. Two hormone-driven kids, she'd said."

"You never pressed? Never asked for more details?" Pete made sure to keep his voice soft, not accusatory.

"Not until after Dad died. Then Mom and I sat down for a long talk. Several long talks." Isabella met his gaze with a hesitant grin. "I probably shouldn't say this, but it was during those talks that I realized Mom still carries a torch for you."

He flashed back to yesterday in Zoe's office. Liz had brazenly said as much.

In front of his wife.

"I know," Isabella said. "You're married."

"Yes. I am."

"I understand. I'm not so sure Mom does. She can be...persistent."

Pete remembered that about her. It had been attractive when they were seventeen. Now? Not so much. He leaned toward Isabella, resting his forearm on the countertop. "I hope you do understand. I want to get to know you. To be a part of your life as much as you're willing. But that doesn't include your mother."

Isabella nodded. "How does your wife feel about all of this? I don't mean about my mom. I mean about me."

He sat back and considered his answer. "We haven't had a chance to really discuss what's happened."

Isabella hiked an eyebrow.

"This has been a shock. To both of us, but especially to her." Pete didn't mention the way Liz had dropped the bomb on them hadn't helped. "She's out of town for work today, but before she left, she told me to talk to you."

Isabella turned to look out the window, thinking. After several long moments of silence, she said, "I'd like to meet her. Your wife."

"Zoe," Pete said.

"Zoe," she echoed.

"She'd like to meet you too."

At least, Pete hoped so.

A phone rang, and Isabella reached back to retrieve her cell from her jeans pocket. "It's Mom," she said with a sheepish grin. "Excuse me while I take this."

Pete watched her retreat into the next room and wondered if his daughter would tell her mother about his visit.

His daughter.

A fragment of doubt whispered inside his head. Isabella was his daughter. He was certain. Almost one-hundred-percent certain.

Almost.

A new question occurred to him. Would Liz intentionally claim Isabella was his daughter in order to drive a wedge between him and Zoe? Even if Liz knew full well Isabella was not his flesh and blood?

He looked around to make sure Isabella hadn't returned before digging out one of the nitrile gloves he always carried in his pocket. Silently, he used the glove to pick the water bottle from the trash, then slipped the same glove inside-out over the bottle, protecting it and the DNA on its mouth from contamination. By the time Isabella returned, he'd stashed his evidence safely within his jacket pocket.

Chapter Twenty-Eight

As Zoe drove north from Confluence, the rain began falling again. This time, in earnest.

Zoe quickly realized she had no idea where she was going. They didn't have an address for the long-closed restaurant. They didn't even have a name for it.

Doc managed to reach Rachel on his phone. "Tanner's Bistro," he repeated to Zoe, along with the address. Before he ended the call, Zoe heard him say, "Yes, we know it's closed."

Twenty minutes later, they sat in an empty parking lot, looking up at the vacant structure set on a hillside surrounded by forest. All dark wood and windows, it blended perfectly with the surroundings and reminded Zoe of a mountain chalet. She could imagine diners looking out over the valley below. It was gorgeous.

"Too bad it's closed." Doc opened his door and popped open his umbrella. "Let's take a closer look."

Zoe shut off the motor, climbed out, and followed him. For sale signs filled the windows, leaving only a narrow gap in the glass. Doc peered in, squinting against the reflection. Zoe did the same, using her hands to frame her face against the glare.

The interior was in shadows, but Zoe made out the haunting shell of the business. A bar stretched along the right side, the shelves behind it barren. Rustic light fixtures hung from the ceiling. But what must've been a massive dining space was void of furnishings. No tables. No chairs. The space was too dark for Zoe to see the cobwebs she was certain had taken over.

Doc backed away. "I guess it really is closed."

"You didn't believe the owner's widow?" She looked around and spotted another business, less grand and rustic, about a hundred yards down the sidewalk. "How do you feel about going for a little walk?"

He followed her gaze. "Doesn't look like a restaurant."

"No, but I bet whoever works there can recommend a place."

"Good point. Let's go."

The sign painted on the side and front of the squat brick building identified it as Jewel's Gift Emporium. An electronic chime welcomed them as Zoe opened the door and stepped inside. Shelves and glass cases displayed a variety of knickknacks and postcards, all boasting a mountain or ski theme, along with some interesting items labeled as the work of local artisans.

Doc shook the water from his umbrella, careful to contain the droplets to the industrial-grade rug at the door. "Tourist trap," he said under his breath.

A young woman with short platinum hair and a pierced eyebrow stood behind a counter in the center of the shop, talking to an athletic-looking young man. She turned away from him and flashed a perky smile. "Hello. Is there anything I can help you find, or are you just browsing?"

"We're from out of town and looking for someplace to eat," Doc said. "Do you have any recommendations?"

The young man gave a bored sigh, a poor attempt to hide his annoyance at their interruption.

While the pierced blonde jotted down some restaurant names for Doc, Zoe wandered over to the display of locally made gift items—some pottery and a few leather goods—and leaned in for a closer look. One hand-thrown mug grabbed her attention as a potential Christmas gift for Pete.

"Aren't those lovely?"

Zoe spun to find the blonde behind her. Doc remained at the counter, the note in one hand, his phone in the other. The young man had wandered over to a nearby display.

"Yes, they are." Zoe pointed to the mug in question.

As the blonde removed a coiled plastic keychain from her wrist to open the case, she asked, "What brings you and your father to town? Staying at the resort?"

"He's not my father." Zoe extended a hand. "I'm Zoe Chambers-Adams, Monongahela County Coroner. He's my forensic pathologist, Dr. Lyle Abercrombie."

The young man glanced her way, vaguely interested.

The blonde feigned a shiver. "Coroner. Forensic pathologist. You guys deal with dead people?"

"Yes, we do." Zoe accepted the mug and studied it, but her mind was racing elsewhere. "How long have you worked here?"

She brightened. "Seven years now. Hard to believe. And I don't just work here. I own the place. I'm Jewel."

"Nice." Zoe noticed the young man dig out his phone and walk toward the back of the store.

"Don't mind him," Jewel said, her voice low. "He's my cousin. His girlfriend dumped him, so he's hanging out with me." She laughed softly.

Zoe acknowledged the comment with a nod before getting back on topic. "Were you open when Tanner's Bistro was still in business?"

"Oh, yes. I'm so sorry it closed. I used to get takeout from them for lunch all the time."

Doc must have heard their conversation and joined them.

"Do you know anything about what happened? I know the owner died, but I understand there were problems before that."

Jewel wrinkled her nose apologetically. "I really don't know any details. There were rumors of big-time money troubles, but that's just gossip."

"Do you know of anyone around here who worked there and might know about those financial problems?" Doc asked.

Jewel scowled, then brightened. "Now that you mention it, yeah." She pointed at the note Doc still clutched. "The one place I told you about? Mountaintop Tavern? Several of the waitresses from Tanner's got jobs there."

Doc grinned at Zoe and held up the paper. "I've decided where I want to eat."

* * *

Pete returned to the station after his visit with Isabella and checked in with Abby and Keegan, who were huddled over their computers in the bullpen, studying the security footage from Bert's. Leaving them to their work, he retreated to his office, placed the glove-encased water bottle on his desk, and pondered what to do with it.

DNA testing was notoriously slow and expensive. Very expensive. Did he doubt what Liz had told him? It was one hundred percent possible that he was Isabella's father. She definitely looked enough like him. But the way Liz had dropped the bomb on him and Zoe made his high school girlfriend less than trustworthy in his mind.

He reached into one of the desk drawers and withdrew an evidence bag. After a moment's hesitation, he wrote *Isabella* and *Personal* on it and stuffed the bottle inside. Then he unlocked the top file cabinet drawer and tucked the "evidence" all the way in the back before relocking it. For safekeeping, he told himself, just in case.

As he started a new pot of coffee, he thought about Zoe. Where was she? Had she and Doc learned anything in Confluence? While the Mr. Coffee gurgled, Pete sat down with his phone.

It rang before he could pull up Zoe's number. The incoming call wasn't from his wife.

"Knight," he said. "What've you got?"

"Maybe nothing," the detective replied. "You know how many black 4Runners are on the roads around here."

"But?"

"But my IT guys spotted one on your Burger Boy video, heading north through Phillipsburg at 5:44 a.m."

North. Toward the Vance Motel.

Pete flipped through his notes to find the timeline. "Before Alex left to get breakfast. Can you make out the driver?" If they could identify Davis behind the wheel, they'd know their crazy theory might be right.

"Unfortunately, no. Can't make out the plate either, so it's possible—no, probable—it isn't the same 4Runner as the one we have in the evidence garage."

Just as probable it wasn't even the same one he'd spotted later in the morning. "Why can't the bad guys drive unique cars?"

Knight chuckled. "It would definitely make our jobs a lot easier." His voice grew serious. "What about the footage your officer found?"

"Still looking through it."

"Keep me posted."

"Roger that." He ended the call, pulled up Zoe's number from his favorites list, and tapped the green icon. For a few painfully long moments, he thought she wasn't going to pick up.

"Hey." Her voice sounded light, not tight and reserved, as he feared.

"Hey, yourself. Where are you?"

"Near Seven Springs."

"What?" Not what he'd expected.

"Doc and I decided to come up here for something to eat. And before you say it, yes, I know Tanner Ferrari's place is closed."

"Is Jim Duncan with you?"

"No. We left him in Confluence. He was planning to go to Uniontown like you asked him to."

Pete wanted to ask when she'd be home, but before he had the chance, she launched into telling him about having located some of Ferrari's old employees, and that was where she and Doc were headed.

Then she fell silent for a beat before asking, "Have you had a chance to talk to Isabella?"

"I did." He decided to keep his plans to test the water bottle to himself until he got the results. "It was awkward at first. But I think we're in a good place for now."

"Good." Zoe sounded like she meant it.

"She'd like to meet you."

There was a moment's hesitation before Zoe replied. "I'd like that."

Relieved, he answered the question she didn't ask. "I have not seen Liz again. Nor do I intend to."

"Good," Zoe said again, although this time, her voice wavered.

Time to change the subject. "You didn't say before...did you try to track down Fiona?"

"Yeah." Zoe told him about encountering her at the Ramcat launch area. "But she didn't know anything."

"It was a long shot."

"I know. I asked her to check with other outfitters and rafters and gave her my card in case she hears anything."

Pete thought of the brusque young woman he'd met at the motel. "Don't hold your breath."

"I'm not."

Footsteps in the hall drew his attention, and Abby, face flushed, appeared in his doorway. "We've got—" She noticed he was on the phone and clamped her lips closed before whispering, "Sorry."

Pete held up one finger to her. To Zoe, he said, "Duty calls. Let me know what you find out."

"Will do."

"Love you," he said, but realized he was speaking to dead air. She'd already ended the call. He sighed and lowered the phone.

"I'm so sorry," Abby said.

Pete waved off the apology. "What have you got?"

"An image of the 4Runner." She beamed. "And the driver."

* * *

Mountaintop Tavern had the same rustic vibe as the vacant Tanner's Bistro but with a full parking lot. Doc accepted Zoe's offer to drop him at the door, saying he'd get them a seat or at least get their names on the list. She looped the lot twice before finally snagging the only available spot well away from the entrance.

She found Doc seated on a bench inside, along with almost a dozen other waiting patrons.

"They told me fifteen minutes," he said, sliding over so she could squeeze in next to him. He handed her a laminated menu.

She thanked him and scanned the restaurant's offerings. One side of the single page listed a few choices each of appetizers, soups, salads, sandwiches, and flatbreads. She flipped to the other side to find dozens of craft beer selections and about ten varieties of wine.

"Their priorities don't seem to be the food," Doc said softly and chuckled.

Zoe looked up and surveyed the room. "Mine isn't, either." She was more interested in the staff.

She returned the menu to Doc, rose, and approached the hostess at the reservations desk. After introducing herself—leaving off the coroner part—she said, "I'm friends with Tanner Ferrari's widow. The man who owned Tanner's Bistro?"

"Oh, sure," the hostess replied with a smile. "Everyone around here knew Chef Ferrari."

"I understand some of his employees work here now. Are you one of them?"

The hostess glanced beyond Zoe to a couple who'd come through the door. "No. I never worked there."

"Is there anyone on duty right now who did?"

She held up one finger to Zoe and addressed the new arrivals, informing them of the wait and taking their names. Once they'd turned away, the hostess came back to Zoe. "Let me see…" Her gaze swept the room. "Yes. Doug over there." She pointed to a dark-haired man in his mid-twenties. "And Stacy." She indicated a woman in her forties with brown hair pulled into a short ponytail.

Zoe's mind raced. Doug would've been barely out of school when the Bistro was still in operation. "Is there any chance you could make sure we get seated at one of Stacy's tables?"

The hostess studied her seating chart, her expression exhibiting doubt.

Zoe reached into her purse and pulled out a ten-dollar bill, which she placed on the desk, partly covered with her palm. "I'd appreciate it."

The woman eyed the money. "You might have a slightly longer wait."

Zoe's growling stomach complained. "No problem."

The hostess nodded. "I'll handle it."

Chapter Twenty-Nine

Pete and Keegan stood behind Abby, looking over her shoulder at the computer monitor. She'd paused the video on one frame, which showed the area in front of Bert's Auto where gas pumps had long ago resided. A 4Runner was parked there, the open passenger-side window toward the camera. Beyond, the security camera also caught the two-lane road. The timestamp in the corner read 5:59.

"Looks like the same SUV." Pete didn't mention it also looked like a hundred other dark Toyota 4Runners.

Abby wouldn't have come to him, flushed with excitement if there wasn't more. "Watch." She touched her keyboard. The video advanced. For a full minute, nothing happened. Then a car entered the frame. Abby hit pause and pointed. "That's Alex in his mother's silver Honda."

The timestamp read 6:00, exactly when he'd claimed to have left the motel to get breakfast.

She clicked play and the car zoomed past, never stopping, never slowing down. Freezing the video again, she swiveled to face Pete. "No indication of him acknowledging the 4Runner being there."

Which proved nothing. Pete glared at the monitor. "I thought you said you had an image of the driver."

"I do. Sort of."

"Sort of?"

She faced the computer and advanced the image, frame-by-frame.

Through the open passenger window, something—some*one*—moved into view. The driver was leaning over, apparently opening the glove box, digging inside. Abby paused the video.

Pete leaned closer. A Steeler's ball cap shielded the driver's face.

"What do you think?" Keegan asked. "Could that be Dr. Davis?"

Pete had never seen Davis wearing a ball cap. Or any hat, for that matter. He had seen Alex wearing one. Sandy Giden had said she'd seen him wearing a Steelers' cap when his mother checked in at the motel.

But they'd just seen Alex drive past, in the Honda.

Hadn't they?

Pete reached over Abby's shoulder to point at the monitor. "Is that the best image you can get of the driver?"

"Afraid so. I've been all over this footage. Right after this, he pulls out, headed toward the motel. I spotted what appears to be the same 4Runner heading south toward Phillipsburg at 6:21. We picked it up on the Burger Boy security cam at 6:28, so the timing aligns."

Approximately twenty minutes to commit Virginia's murder. It fit about as well as a jigsaw puzzle piece pounded into place with his fist.

Pete pulled his phone from his pocket and found Doc in his contact list.

"Pete?" Doc sounded surprised. "Do you want to talk to your wife?"

He did, but he had more pressing matters right now. "I need to talk to *you.*"

"Oh. Okay. What's up?"

"The driver of the 4Runner that was tailing you. You said you couldn't see his face because he had a ball cap pulled down over it."

"That's right."

"Did you happen to notice what kind of ball cap?"

Doc fell silent. Pete could almost hear him trying to dredge up the memory. "Now that you mention it," Doc said at last, "I think it was black and gold. Through the tinted windows, it was hard to tell for sure. Steelers? Pirates, maybe."

Which didn't really mean anything. There were more people in southwestern Pennsylvania wearing Steelers and Pirates attire than driving Toyota 4Runners. "Thanks, Doc." Pete ended the call and scrolled through his contacts for another number. Trooper Jim Duncan.

"Adams," he answered. "What can I do for you?"

"Have you had a chance to talk to Alex Lowe yet?"

"Funny you should ask. I'm looking right at him."

"Did he happen to tell you why he didn't give us his fingerprints as requested?"

"Says he forgot about it until he was almost to Uniontown. I'm about to walk him over to the police station and get it done."

"Is he resisting?"

"No. In fact, he's eager. When I pressed him about not being at the burger joint as long as he'd claimed, he freaked out. Insists he was there the whole time, and the girl, Heather, is lying if she says otherwise."

"Now, why would Heather lie?" Pete asked, as much to himself as to Duncan, and made up his mind to pay another visit to the young woman. "When you get his prints, make sure to send them to Detectives Wayne Baronick and Max Knight at Monongahela County Police."

"Will do."

Pete ended the call and noticed both of his officers watching him. Looking at Abby, he said, "I realize it's your day off—"

"I'm happy to keep working on this." She pointed at her computer.

"No." He turned to Keegan. "I want *you* to keep working on this." To Abby, he said, "I want you to come with me. I want to have another talk with Heather Smith, and I think she'd be more willing to cooperate if there's another woman in the room."

"Good cop, bad cop? I get to be the good cop?"

"Yes to good cop, bad cop. But I think this time, you get to be the bad cop."

* * *

The hostess called out, "Abercrombie. Table for two," the moment Doc lowered his phone from talking to Pete. Zoe waited until they were seated before asking about the call.

"All he wanted to know was what kind of ball cap the man driving the 4Runner was wearing. You heard my response."

"Yeah." Zoe sighed. "A man in a Pittsburgh sports ball cap driving a black 4Runner. Really narrows it down, doesn't it?"

"Not at all." Doc reached up to rub his head and flinched.

A rush of guilt hit her. "I shouldn't be dragging you all over the Laurel Highlands with you fresh out of the hospital. As soon as we finish eating, we'll head home."

"I'm fine. It's not like I'm doing anything strenuous." He picked up his menu—the same one they'd already looked at—and studied it as if the chef might've added to it in the last five minutes. "But we should head home. You and Pete need to sit down and have a long talk."

Doc was right, but she wasn't sure she was ready yet. All day, she'd intentionally pushed thoughts of Isabella and Elizabeth from her mind rather than make any effort to come to terms with the new members of Pete's family. Of *her* family.

The waitress, who the hostess pointed out to Zoe earlier, arrived at their table with two glasses of ice water, which she sat in front of them. "Hi. My name's Stacy, and I'll be your server this afternoon." She deftly wiped her hands on her apron and pulled an order form and pen from a pocket. "Can I get you started with something to drink? Appetizers?"

Zoe ordered coffee, and Doc asked for iced tea and an order of meatball parmesan skewers. He shot a look at Zoe. "Don't you dare tell Grace I'm eating red meat."

"Your secret's safe with me."

Stacy laughed. "I'll put that in and get your drinks."

She started to turn away, but Zoe reached out. "Excuse me, Stacy. I understand you used to work at Tanner's Bistro?"

"That's right."

"If you have a minute, we'd like to ask you a few questions about it."

Stacy appeared wary. "I'm pretty busy right now."

"We're working for Tanner Ferrari's widow, so any time you can spare would be appreciated."

The wariness vanished. "Rachel? She was such a sweetheart. Let me take care of my tables. Then I'll come back."

Zoe spent the next several minutes watching Stacy bustle around the dining room. She dropped off the coffee and iced tea with a flash of a smile before hurrying off again. A young man delivered the skewers. Zoe started to think Stacy was going to avoid them.

But then she arrived, slightly out of breath, at their table. "I can take your order whenever you're ready, and I should have a few minutes to answer your questions."

Zoe didn't want to announce their professions with other diners nearby, so she merely said, "We're looking into Tanner's death for Rachel."

Stacy huffed. "It's about time someone questioned what really happened. I never did buy into the suicide story."

Zoe glanced at Doc before asking the waitress, "What do you think really happened?"

"I don't know. But Tanner loved life, and he loved Rachel. He wouldn't have cut out on either."

"I understand there were some financial problems with the Bistro?"

"Financial problems? I guess that's one way of putting it."

"How would *you* put it?"

"Embezzlement. Plain and simple. Tanner didn't let on to the rest of us, but we knew. I don't think he realized what was happening until it was almost too late. The place was on the verge of bankruptcy."

"How could he not know?" Doc asked.

Stacy considered her words before replying. "I think—and I'm only guessing, mind you—he knew something was off, but not how far off. Tanner was the kind of man who always saw the best in people. He never wanted to believe an employee would do something like that."

"What happened when he did realize what was going on?" Zoe asked.

"He fired her."

"Her?"

"His bookkeeper." Stacy snorted. "While Tanner was cooking in the kitchen, she was cooking the books and lining her pockets in the process. So he got rid of her and brought in a firm specializing in situations like this. They were great. Things were getting back on track. At least until Tanner's death. The Bistro couldn't recover from his loss."

Which went along with Rachel's story. Zoe felt a tingle across her shoulders. She shifted in her seat to lean closer to the waitress. "Do you know the name of the bookkeeper?"

Stacy caught her lower lip between her teeth, thinking. She shook her head. "I can't remember. She wasn't exactly friendly. Came in, did her work, and left."

The tingle ignited into a flame. "Thanks for your help."

"Do you want to place your order now?" Stacy asked.

Zoe had lost her appetite.

Doc apparently had not. "I'll have the steak fajita flatbread." He looked at Zoe.

"Grilled chicken sandwich," she said. After Stacy had walked away, Zoe looked at Doc. "Call Rachel."

"Why?" he asked, but he reached for his phone.

"Maybe nothing." Zoe watched as Doc placed the call. Once Rachel answered, Zoe held out her hand.

"Zoe wants to talk to you," he said before handing over his phone.

"Hi, Rachel. Last time we spoke you mentioned Tanner had been upset about the finances but had handled it."

"That's right. I didn't get the impression it was a big deal."

Zoe repeated what Stacy had told them about the embezzlement.

From Rachel's tone, the news rattled her. "Oh, dear." She sighed loudly. "Although I'm not really surprised. Tanner didn't like to bring his work troubles home with him."

"Do you remember who this bookkeeper was?"

"No. I probably knew at the time, but it's been so long."

"Rachel, I need you to think really hard."

"It's that important?"

"It may be."

Rachel fell silent for several agonizing moments. "It was…I don't know… Dorothy? No. Deborah? Denise? Seems to me the name began with a D."

Zoe closed her eyes. "Darlene? Darlene Roth?"

"That's it." Rachel sounded excited. "I only met her once. She seemed very shy."

"Thanks, Rachel. We'll be in touch." Zoe ended the call and returned the phone to Doc.

"Who the hell is Darlene Roth?" he demanded.

"Besides being an embezzler? She's Virginia Lowe and Fiona Roth's sister."

Chapter Thirty

Pete and Abby's first stop was Heather's favorite haunt. Burger Boy. She wasn't there.

"What's her home address?" he asked Abby.

She thumbed through her notes. "Wilson Street. Four eighteen."

Only a few blocks away.

The Smith residence was a well-kept brick two-story surrounded by yellow, orange, and pink chrysanthemums. A newer blue Mustang was parked in front of the closed garage doors. Pete pulled in beside it and shut off the engine.

The front door swung open before he had a chance to knock, revealing a woman wearing a concerned expression. "Can I help you, officers?"

"Vance Township Chief Pete Adams." He introduced Abby, who appeared to have already shifted into bad cop mode. To the woman, he said, "You're Heather Smith's mother?"

Concern shifted to puzzled. "Yes."

"Is she here?"

"She's on the back patio with her boyfriend. Is there a problem?"

"We need to talk to her about a case we're working on."

Mrs. Smith stepped aside and allowed them to enter. "Follow me." She led them through a spotless house to a pair of slider doors that opened onto a patio with a view overlooking Phillipsburg. "Heather?" she said as they stepped outside. "The police want to talk to you."

Pete had heard the same edge in the woman's voice from many mothers standing between him and their child. It reeked of *what have you done now?*

He recognized the young man seated next to Heather on a glider. Pete had busted him three times in the last few years. Once for speeding. Once for underage drinking. Once for being involved in a throw-down with another kid on school grounds. "Jack," Pete said. "Keeping out of trouble?"

"Yes, sir."

Pete didn't believe him. From the look on Mrs. Smith's face, she had no idea her daughter's boyfriend was acquainted with local law enforcement. Pete slid a chair from one of the outdoor seating areas, placed it directly in front of the young couple, and sat. Abby took up a standing position behind him, arms crossed, looking stern.

Jack came to his feet. "I have to go." To Heather, he said, "Talk to you later, babe," and hurried around the corner of the house toward the driveway and, Pete assumed, the Mustang.

Mrs. Smith moved to her daughter's side. "I'd like to stay, if you don't mind."

Pete already knew Heather was eighteen. "Actually, we'd prefer to speak with her alone."

Mrs. Smith scowled. "I'm not comfortable with that."

"It's okay, Mom. I'll be fine," Heather said, saving Pete from having to insist.

Mrs. Smith eyed her daughter, then Pete, then Abby, before coming back to Heather. "I'll be inside if you need me."

Pete had a feeling Mrs. Smith would be hovering just inside the screened sliding door.

Once the mother was gone, Abby took the seat the boyfriend had vacated. "Heather, you lied to us."

The young woman recoiled, her eyes widening.

Paydirt, Pete thought.

"You told us Alex Lowe was only with you at Burger Boy for five minutes, but that wasn't true, was it?" Abby asked, an edge to her voice.

Last time, Heather had been more willing to talk to Abby. This time, with Abby applying pressure, she looked to Pete for help. "I couldn't tell you the truth."

Keeping his voice soft, he asked, "Why not?"

Heather's gaze darted toward the screen door. Obviously, she also suspected her mother was listening from inside. Meeting Pete's eyes, she whispered, "Jack."

Pete glanced at Abby before coming back to Heather. "What about Jack?" He kept his voice low enough to keep eavesdropping parents from hearing.

"He's possessive. Jealous. If he knew I'd spent that much time with another boy, he'd go ballistic on me."

Pete hoped like hell she was exaggerating. "How do you mean? Go ballistic?"

She shifted uncomfortably. Abby put a hand on her shoulder. "It's okay. You can tell us."

So much for bad cop.

"He has a temper. Can we leave it at that?"

"Okay," he said without adding *for now*. "You lied because you were afraid your boyfriend would find out."

Heather nodded.

"Tell us what really happened Sunday morning."

She looked down at her hands in her lap. "That boy—Alex—showed up right when I said he did."

"About six twenty?"

"Yes. He was cute. He asked if he could sit with me, and I said yes."

"How long did he stay?"

"A couple of hours. We hit it off, you know? I didn't realize how much time had passed until he checked his phone and swore. He said his mom was waiting for him to bring her breakfast and was upset because it was cold by now. He was gonna toss it and buy more but was outta money. I told him to ask at the motel's front office if he could use their microwave, since he said there wasn't one in their room."

"So, he was with you until eight twenty?"

"About that. Yeah."

Which was exactly what Alex had claimed. He hadn't killed his mother. Nor had he driven the 4Runner that ran Doc off the road. "Heather, is there anything else you haven't told us?"

She shook her head. "I'm sorry I lied to you the first time. I'm really sorry it got Alex into trouble. I just couldn't have Jack finding out." She appeared on the verge of tears. "Can you keep it quiet? I mean, you don't have to make it public I was Alex's alibi, do you?"

"We'll do our best." Pete thanked her for her help and climbed to his feet.

Abby did as well. They moved toward the screen slider only to have Mrs. Smith open it before they got there.

"I overheard," she said to them once they'd stepped inside. "I never liked that Jack."

"We'll have a chat with him," Pete said.

"You do that, but trust me, he won't be seeing my girl again anytime soon." From the tone of her voice, Pete had no doubt this was true.

Neither he nor Abby spoke until they were back in the Explorer. She clicked her seatbelt and turned to face him. "We know it wasn't Dr. Davis who ran Doc Abercrombie off the road, and we now know it wasn't Alex behind the wheel. If not either of them, who?"

"Good question," Pete replied. Before he had a chance to regroup, his phone rang. Jim Duncan's name appeared on his caller ID.

"Pete," Duncan said, his voice tense. "I thought you should know. We have a bit of a situation here in Uniontown."

"With Alex Lowe?"

"Not exactly. I drove the kid to the station and had him printed. No problem. But when I was ready to drive him home, his aunt, Darlene Roth, charged in and grabbed the kid."

Pete tried to make sense of what he was hearing. "She kidnapped him?"

"No. More like she was trying to protect him. She was babbling he didn't do anything."

"She's probably right. We just verified Alex's alibi for the morning of his mother's homicide."

"He'll be glad to hear that. But it didn't end there. Alex managed to free himself. Then Roth started screaming about the whole thing being all her fault. Said she should've killed herself long ago like she wanted to. I'm talking full-fledged mental breakdown. She dove at one of the uniforms and tried to grab his gun."

Pete closed his eyes. "Christ. Don't tell me they shot her."

"It didn't go that far, but they did have to take her down and restrain her. She was screaming at the top of her lungs, demanding to see her sister."

"Which one?"

"She didn't say. As crazed as she was, I thought Virginia. She kept repeating her sister would take care of her. Except Alex told me Darlene and Virginia weren't close."

"Darlene told me the same thing when I spoke to her. She must mean Fiona." Pete tried to imagine Alex witnessing his aunt's meltdown. The aunt he was living with after losing his mother. "Where's Darlene now?"

"Sitting in one of the holding cells waiting to be transferred to the hospital. She's completely shut down. They have an officer keeping an eye on her. When I checked on her a few minutes ago, she was catatonic, sitting in the corner, hugging her knees and rocking."

"Have you tried to reach Fiona?"

"That's another weird thing. I tried her cell. It went straight to voice mail, so I contacted the rafting outfitters she works for. We'd seen her this morning getting ready to take a group down the river. Zoe and Doc Abercrombie talked to her. From where I was sitting, she seemed fine."

"What do you mean? She *seemed* fine?"

"When I called the outfitters, I was told she'd gotten deathly sick shortly after they launched. They'd had to send someone to pick her up after the raft dropped her off along the shore. Said she refused to go to the hospital and drove herself home."

"You should check her house."

"I already sent someone to do a wellness check. She's not home, and her car's gone."

"Did the dog let them close enough to be sure?" Pete asked, not entirely in jest.

"That's what really struck me as odd." Duncan's voice grew even edgier. "The dog wasn't there either. Granted, lots of people take their dogs with

231

them. Hell, I take mine with me all the time. But I only saw Fiona taking Cujo for a walk in town once, and it was all she could do to control him. I thought for sure he was going to eat a couple of kids playing in the town square. Even worse, judging by the look on Fiona's face, I was afraid she was going to let him. He's not so much a pet as a weapon."

Chapter Thirty-One

By the time Zoe and Doc finished their meals, left Stacy a generous tip, and reached the restaurant's front doors, the earlier drizzle had given way to a downpour. Memories of the hurricane seized her neck and shoulders, but she pushed those thoughts aside. She looked toward her Forester at the far edge of the parking lot. "Wait here while I get the car."

"Don't be silly." Doc sniffed. "I have my umbrella."

She imagined him trying to hurry through the parking lot, not only getting soaked but slipping and falling, causing further injury to his ribs and head. "Wait here," she repeated, firmer this time. Holding out a hand, she added, "But you can loan me the umbrella."

He exhaled loudly but acquiesced.

The umbrella was no match for the windblown deluge, and Zoe was soaked by the time she reached her car. She pulled around to the restaurant's entrance, feeling vindicated as Doc shuffled the few yards to the Subaru.

"Don't you dare say I told you so," he grumbled as he buckled his seatbelt.

"I wouldn't think of it." Before leaving the curb, she programmed a route home into her phone's GPS. Instead of heading south to Confluence, the way they'd come, it directed them north along a winding road toward the Pennsylvania Turnpike.

"Do you know where you're going?" Doc asked as they pulled out of the parking lot.

"Home," she offered weakly and pointed at the phone. "As long as my app knows the way, we're good."

Doc grunted and made a point of glancing upwards at the charcoal-gray clouds. "I hope your app's right. This looks more like a paved goat path than a road."

Vivid lightning, followed by a ground-shaking rumble of thunder, lit the narrow two-lane. "I hope so too." She clicked the wipers on high and swore. "I had enough rain a week and a half ago with Hurricane Iona."

"At least this shouldn't last as long." Doc had his phone out, apparently checking the weather app.

During the remnants of Iona, Zoe had been driving in familiar territory. This evening, she was negotiating a winding two-lane mountain road with minimal visibility. She pictured being blinded by the downpour, missing a bend, and plummeting over the hillside, and wondered if Doc was having flashbacks to last Sunday.

Adding to Zoe's jangled nerves, headlights appeared behind her. The vehicle closed the distance but thankfully didn't ride her back bumper. At least one other driver was out on this "paved goat path."

The road leveled out at the bottom of a valley, and she blew out a relieved breath. As another sizzling lightning bolt split the darkness, the Subaru sputtered. "What the hell?" Her trusty Forester had never done anything like this before. She pressed the accelerator.

The car stuttered and died.

"Crap."

Doc used stronger language.

She drifted the car to the edge of the road, grateful they were low in the valley rather than teetering on a mountainside. She tried to restart the engine. The ignition ground but didn't catch. She looked at the instrument panel and noticed the fuel gauge. "What the hell? We're out of gas."

"You brought us out here in the middle of nowhere without filling the tank?"

"Of course not. I topped it off before I picked you up this morning. We still had over half a tank when we got to the restaurant." With the storm and the unfamiliar roads, she hadn't checked it since.

She shouldn't have needed to.

"I'm calling my motor club," Doc said, tapping his phone's screen. "Son of a bitch. I can't get the call to go through."

Zoe looked up through the rain-streaked windshield at the surrounding green mountains silhouetted against the roiling black clouds. Being broken down in a valley no longer seemed so beneficial. She glanced into the rearview mirror. A car was stopped directly behind them, headlights off. Zoe remembered the vehicle following them and realized it hadn't passed when she pulled over. It must be the same car. "Someone's parked behind us."

Doc turned to look. "Thank God. I don't suppose there's much traffic on this stretch of road. We could wait for an hour for someone to happen along."

But a knot was forming low in Zoe's belly—what Pete might call a gut feeling or her mother might call women's intuition. Back in her teens and early twenties, she'd unwisely ignored it too many times.

In the rain-streaked mirror, she saw the car's door open. She turned in her seat to look back, but the view through the rear window wasn't any better. She turned the key to on. The dash lights lit, and she turned the dial on the end of the wiper control to engage the rear wiper. It made two swipes as the driver approached through the downpour. He was thin and had his head down, the bill of his ball cap shielding his face from the rain.

The bill of his Steelers ball cap.

"Didn't you say the guy driving the 4Runner wore a Steelers hat?" she asked Doc.

"Yeah." He turned for another look. "Son of a bitch."

Zoe slammed the door lock as the man reached the back of the Forester. She twisted the key in the ignition, praying for there to be fumes enough to start the engine. But it ground and nothing more.

The man in the ball cap stood outside her door and rapped on the window with the butt of a flashlight.

Zoe looked at Doc and whispered, "Is that him?"

"Hell, I don't know. I never saw his face."

She still couldn't see it. Maybe she was being paranoid. Maybe this really was a good Samaritan who happened to be a sports fan. She hit the button to lower the window a few inches.

Which was when she realized it wasn't a flashlight he'd used to rap on her window.

It was a gun.

* * *

Pete wasn't sure what was going on with Fiona but was damned sure he didn't like it. After he got off the phone with Duncan, he pulled up Zoe's number. The call went straight to voice mail without ringing. He liked that even less. She and Doc had talked to Fiona that morning. Then Fiona got sick—or so she claimed—and left a raft trip. Now, she and Cujo were missing.

And Zoe's phone was turned off.

Or she was in a dead zone in the Laurel Highlands. Definitely the more likely possibility.

After dropping Abby off at the station, Pete headed for Uniontown, a drive that normally took a good hour. He hoped to make it in half that. Thanks to the cloudburst he encountered after crossing into Fayette County, it took forty-five minutes. He was becoming a pro at speeding through inclement weather. During the trip, his mind kept replaying the events of the last week. Virginia. Doc. Davis. All with ties to the one person he cared most about in this world. From the Uniontown PD parking lot, he tried Zoe's number again with the same results.

"Dammit. Where the hell are you?"

Pete found Duncan waiting inside the buff brick building.

The trooper shook Pete's hand. "I was surprised you said you were coming. Don't trust us to handle it?"

Instead of responding to the question, Pete said, "I can't reach Zoe. Her calls go straight to voice mail." He told Duncan about her plans to go to Seven Springs.

"Cell coverage is spotty in a lot of places up there. I wouldn't worry."

"There's more to it." Pete told him about Davis's alleged attempted suicide. "First, Virginia Lowe comes to town to speak with my wife and is murdered before she has the chance. Then Doc Abercrombie is run off the road and nearly killed. Now Davis is in the ICU with a head injury after ingesting sleeping pills and wine."

"Why do you think his attempted suicide was 'alleged?'"

"I know this guy. He's never seemed the suicidal type. The note he supposedly wrote?" Pete shook his head. "Doesn't sound like him at all."

Duncan folded his arms. "You think the same person's behind all three incidents."

"And all three victims are linked to my wife. You can understand why I'm concerned about not being able to reach her." Pete looked around the small seating area. "Where's Alex?"

"Back at his aunt's house. He was pretty shaken up by Darlene's meltdown. But I told him about you verifying his alibi. That settled his nerves." Duncan tipped his head toward a door leading from the reception area to the interior of the station. "I assume you want to talk to Darlene."

That was the main reason Pete had driven here, but the mention of Darlene's house triggered a memory. Something Max Knight had said that morning. "Darlene's driveway," Pete said under his breath.

"Excuse me?"

"According to Monongahela County Detective Max Knight, the Union-town Police questioned Darlene's neighbors. They said Darlene's car never left her driveway last weekend."

Duncan held his gaze, waiting for more.

"You've been to her house," Pete said. "Why would she keep her car in the driveway? She's got an oversized two-car garage."

The trooper shrugged. "There's a guy on my street who has a big garage with no room in it for his car. It's little more than a storage unit."

"I know lots of people like that. But answer me this—was Darlene home when you picked up Alex earlier?"

"He said she was in her office with a client."

"Was her car in the driveway?"

Duncan thought about it. "No."

"It wasn't there when Zoe and I stopped to talk to Alex on Wednesday either."

"What are you thinking?"

"I'm not sure, but I hope Darlene has snapped out of her stupor and can give us an explanation."

* * *

The Fayette County Booking Center occupied half of the same building as the Uniontown PD. Pete followed Duncan through the maze of hallways and heavy steel doors to an interview room where Darlene had been taken to meet with her attorney, a dark-haired young woman with large, gentle brown eyes. She rose when they entered and introduced herself as Val Mercer. After they shook hands, she reclaimed her seat next to her client.

"Darlene?" Pete asked softly. "Do you remember me? I visited you at your house earlier this week."

Her eyes remained fixed straight ahead. Pete feared she wasn't going to respond. But then, in a small, childlike voice, she said, "I remember."

He exchanged a glance with Duncan before bringing his attention back to her. "Do you mind if I ask you a few questions?"

She didn't agree. Nor did she say no.

He eased into the chair across the table from the women. "I'm here to help you. If you'll let me."

No response.

"I want you to know Alex isn't in any trouble. We know he had nothing to do with his mother's death."

Darlene shook her head emphatically. "Charles killed Virginia. Fiona said so."

"Fiona?"

"My sister. Fiona takes care of me. She's always taken care of me. Fiona says Charles killed Virginia."

"How does she take care of you, Darlene?"

238

Darlene swiped her nose with one hand and sniffed. "I should've killed myself back then. But Fiona fixed it."

"Back then? When?"

She shook her head again. "Not allowed to say."

Pete glanced up at Duncan, who'd remained standing. Pete hoped the trooper had some clue what she was talking about, but he shrugged.

"I need my sister," Darlene said, whimpering.

"Virginia?" Pete asked.

"Virginia's dead. Charles killed her."

At least she wasn't so far removed from reality that she wanted to see a ghost. "You want to see Fiona?"

Darlene rocked back and forth in her chair. "Fiona takes care of me. She won't let them hurt me."

"Who wants to hurt you, Darlene?"

"That path—" She stuttered and scowled. "Pathol—"

A chill gripped Pete's spine. "Pathologist? Forensic pathologist?"

She nodded vigorously. "He wants to hurt me."

"Dr. Abercrombie?"

Darlene kept nodding. "Fiona took care of it."

Pete's chest tightened. "What did Fiona take care of?"

"Everything. She keeps me safe. She won't let him hurt me."

Questions roared through Pete's mind. Why did Darlene think Doc Abercrombie wanted to hurt her? But extracting answers from her was likely to take time. Time Pete suspected they didn't have. "Darlene, listen to me. How did Fiona take care of Doc Abercrombie?"

"Not allowed to say."

He ran his hand through his hair and realized the hand was trembling. "Did Fiona try to kill Dr. Abercrombie?"

For the first time since Pete and Duncan had entered the room, Darlene met Pete's gaze, her eyes wild. "Not allowed to say," she said firmly.

He feared pressing her any harder about Doc might cause her to shut them out completely. Time to change direction. "When I was at your house last week, I noticed what a nice garage you have."

Darlene returned to staring blankly at the tabletop. "Thank you."

"You've been keeping your car outside in the driveway."

She nodded.

"Why keep your car outside when you have such a nice garage?"

"No room," she said.

Maybe Duncan had been right, and she was using the garage as a storage unit.

Darlene hiked her shoulders, eliciting a loud pop before saying, "Fiona was keeping her cars in there."

Not the answer he expected. "Fiona's car?"

She nodded again. "Both of them."

A glance at Duncan revealed this was news to him as well. "I didn't know she had two cars," Pete said to Darlene.

"She did. For a while. Her Nissan."

Pete knew about that one.

"And the Toyota 4Runner we stole."

Chapter Thirty-Two

"Get out."

The femininity of the voice behind the gun startled Zoe. She fleetingly considered ignoring the demand and closing the window. But then what? She couldn't very well speed away. She then considered ramming the door into the person with the gun, throwing her off balance, kicking the gun away, and wrestling her to the ground. But that only worked for television or movie heroes.

"I said *get out.*"

Zoe opened the door slowly. The woman holding the gun must have anticipated Zoe's plan and kept her free hand on the doorframe. Zoe couldn't have rammed her with it even if she'd decided to play television hero.

The rain pelted Zoe as she stepped out. Had she survived Hurricane Iona only to be gunned down in a mountain rainstorm a week later?

The gun-wielding woman gestured at Doc. "You too. Get out."

For the first time, Zoe caught a glimpse of the face beneath the ball cap's bill. "Fiona?"

Her head jerked up, her fierce eyes burning into Zoe's. But only for a moment. Fiona stepped back, shifting her aim from Zoe to Doc and gesturing with the gun for him to come around to the driver's side of the car.

He squinted at her. "You're the one who ran me off the road?"

"Too bad you didn't die then. Now I have to get rid of both of you."

Zoe's mind raced back in time. Doc had claimed all along the 4Runner's driver was a young man, although he admitted he'd never gotten a glimpse of his face beneath the ball cap. Now, Zoe took in the woman holding the gun. A boyish haircut. Slender, but with broad, well-muscled shoulders. Without an ounce of fat on her frame and small-chested, Fiona could easily have been mistaken for a teenage boy.

"But why?" Zoe asked. "We've never done anything to you."

"This has nothing to do with me." Fiona pointed the pistol at Doc. Zoe feared she was going to gun him down right there on the side of the road.

Dear God, Zoe pleaded in silence, let another car come along. Now. Preferably, one with a cop behind the wheel.

Instead of shooting, Fiona told him, "Give me your phone."

"I left it in the car," Doc said.

"Get it." She aimed the gun at Zoe's face. "If you try anything, she's dead."

Zoe knew she was going to be dead soon anyway.

"Is your phone in there too?" Fiona asked her.

"Yes."

She looked at Doc. "Bring both of them."

He trudged around the front of the car, leaned in, and came up with both devices.

"Come back over here and give them to me."

He did as he was told and held both devices out to Fiona.

She started to reach for them but stopped. "No. You." She looked at Zoe. "Take the batteries out."

Zoe exhaled. Fiona was no fool. Without the batteries, their phones couldn't be pinged. Couldn't be tracked. With rain dripping from her bangs onto her trembling hands, Zoe thumbed her phone from its protective OtterBox case, pried off the back, and popped out the battery.

Fiona used the gun to gesture toward the woods. "Toss it."

Zoe wished she could think of a way to fake it while secretly pocketing the device and battery. But Fiona was watching her intently. Zoe flung them over the roof into the weeds.

"Now, the other one."

She repeated the process with Doc's phone and whispered, "I'm sorry," to him.

"Don't apologize," he replied. "You're only here because you agreed to help me."

"Shut up," Fiona barked. "He's right, though. You weren't part of my plan."

Zoe held Doc's phone and battery in her palm and again pitched them over the roof.

This time, she didn't throw as hard, hoping they'd land close enough to the car that, given the chance, she could retrieve them.

"Good," Fiona said. She waved the gun between them and her car. "Let's go."

Zoe swiped her hand across her eyes in a futile attempt to wipe away the water. Go? In Fiona's car. Words of warning learned as a teen screamed in her brain. If accosted, never get in the attacker's car. Never let yourself be taken to a second location.

"Now," Fiona growled.

Zoe started toward the Nissan, moving slowly. There were two of them and only one of Fiona.

Plus, the gun. It counted as two.

Still, if one of them distracted Fiona, they could jump her. Overpower her. Fiona might be all muscle, but Zoe was no weakling. She handled thousand-pound horses. Had lifted stretchers holding obese patients onto the ambulance.

But Doc? He was fresh out of the hospital with broken ribs and a concussion and was older. Even on a good day, his idea of physical activity was a round of golf. But he had size on his side.

They needed to make a stand before being forced into the car.

As they neared the Nissan, something inside hit the driver's door. Fierce barking drowned out the roar of the rain.

Cujo.

Fiona had her dog with her.

Crap.

Fiona opened the driver's door, and the beast bounded out. It started toward Zoe, barking and baring its teeth.

She stepped back, stumbling into Doc.

"Bruno. Stay," Fiona ordered.

To Zoe's shock, the dog obeyed.

But if Fiona's gun counted as a second person in Zoe's escape plan, Bruno ranked as an entire platoon armed with razorblade teeth.

"You." Fiona pointed the gun at Zoe. "Get in the passenger seat. You." She pointed at Doc. "Drive."

There was no way Zoe could take down Fiona with her dog present. Resigned, Zoe rounded the front of the Nissan and climbed in. Doc slid in behind the wheel. Fiona and Bruno got in the back seat. Zoe could feel the dog's hot breath on her shoulder.

Doc cleared his throat. "My legs are longer than yours. I need to move the seat back."

Fiona pressed the muzzle of the gun into the back of his head. "Go ahead. Just don't try anything cute."

Like slamming the seat backward into her.

Maybe Doc was planning an escape as well.

He fumbled for the control and eased the seat into position.

"Everybody comfy?" Fiona's voice oozed sarcasm. "Good. Now drive, old man."

* * *

Ms. Mercer stopped the questioning and asked for a few minutes with her client.

In the hallway, Pete tried again to call Zoe. The robotic voice informing him the number he was calling wasn't available immediately kicked in. At the beep, he said, "Zoe, call me. *Now.*"

"Still not answering?" Duncan asked.

"No." Pete ran a hand through his hair. "Doc reported seeing a young man behind the wheel of the 4Runner." Pete remembered the first time he'd seen Fiona at the Vance Motel. Thin, but wiry. Short hair. Angry. "It wasn't a young man at all. It was Fiona."

"I can understand the mix-up," Duncan said.

"Then you can also understand my concern. For some reason, Fiona believes Doc is a threat to her sister and has already made one attempt on his life. Now my wife is with Doc, Fiona's in the wind, and I can't reach Zoe on her phone."

"Oh, I get it. Believe me."

Another thought floated to the surface of Pete's tumultuous mind. "Dammit."

"What?"

He looked at Duncan. "We have security footage of the 4Runner near the motel where Virginia Lowe was murdered. You know this woman. Would she be capable of killing her own sister?"

The trooper's eyes narrowed in thought. "My first reaction is no. You heard Darlene. Fiona believes Davis killed her."

"And Davis left a suicide note confessing to the homicide." Pete fixed Duncan with a hard stare. "In the same note, he confessed to attempting to kill Doc."

Duncan swore. "You think Fiona killed her sister, tried to kill Abercrombie—"

"And wrote the suicide note we found with Davis. Meaning, she's the one who tried to kill him too."

The door to the interview room opened, and Mercer stepped out. "Gentlemen," she said softly, "I've tried to explain the situation to Ms. Roth. I'm not convinced she completely understands what she's facing by confessing to car theft."

Pete held up a hand. "I'm not interested in seeing her charged with stealing the 4Runner." He shot a glance at Duncan, who nodded in agreement. "We're only interested in finding out what she knows about her sister, especially where Fiona is at this very moment. It could be a matter of life and death."

Mercer appeared to consider his words. "Fine. But if she confesses to anything else—"

"I have a feeling any criminal activity Darlene has been involved in was precipitated by Fiona."

Mercer reached for the door. "You may be right."

As Pete followed the attorney back into the room, he wondered what Darlene had told her while he and Duncan stood in the hallway.

Once they returned to the same chairs in which they'd sat earlier, Pete used every bit of self-control he could muster to not lean over the table toward Darlene. Instead, he leaned back, crossing an ankle over a knee. "Tell us about Fiona and Doc Abercrombie."

Darlene shook her head. "Not allowed to say."

Pete clenched his fists.

But Mercer placed a hand on Darlene's arm. "These men are trying to help."

"No." Darlene's face contorted, and Pete wasn't sure if she was going to burst into tears or into a rage. "I want Fiona. I need Fiona. She takes care of me."

Pete relaxed his hands and forced his voice to stay calm. "Darlene, do you know where Fiona is right now?"

She shook her head.

"Would you be willing to call her for us?"

Another headshake.

"If we knew where she is, we could bring her to you." Not entirely a lie, considering their current location.

He could tell Darlene was considering it. "I don't think she'd like that."

"You said she protects you. I know you're scared. Wouldn't she want to be here to protect you now?"

Darlene wrapped her arms across her chest and began rocking. "I should've killed myself back then. I should've killed myself back then." She repeated the line twice more.

Pete cut in. "Back when, Darlene? Why do you think you should've killed yourself?"

She kept rocking. "I was in trouble. I got fired. I didn't think I was doing anything wrong. I'm good with numbers. Fiona always told me that. I'm good with numbers. She showed me what to do. I didn't think I was doing anything wrong. I got fired."

"Fired from where?" Pete asked.

"From my job."

"What job?"

"At the restaurant in Seven Springs."

It all clicked. Pete looked at Duncan, and at the same time, they both said, "Tanner Ferrari."

* * *

As dusk approached, the rain had once again eased to a steady drizzle, but the roiling clouds overhead promised Mother Nature was not done with them.

Zoe glanced at Doc next to her, his knuckles white as he clenched the wheel. It occurred to her he hadn't been cleared to drive. Yet, here he was, piloting a small, unfamiliar vehicle along a narrow and winding mountain road. In the rain. With an armed crazy woman and her attack dog in the back seat.

Zoe wasn't sure which part of the equation scared her more. Bruno's head protruded between the front seats, his breath hot on her neck, reeking of a wet dog in need of a bath. If the stench didn't choke her, his jaws clamped on her throat would definitely be the end of her.

She didn't dare turn her head, but in her peripheral vision, saw Fiona, who appeared remarkably calm, directly behind Doc, gun in hand, loosely aimed at him.

Fiona had a plan for them, although Zoe hadn't a clue what it was. Silent except to direct Doc to turn one way or the other at the crossroads they encountered, Fiona either knew where they were going or wanted Doc to keep driving until she made up her mind.

Either way, Zoe needed to come up with a plan of her own. It wasn't easy. She couldn't do something as simple as grappling with Fiona. Bruno would tear her apart. Nor could she attempt to bolt into the wilderness when given a chance. First, she couldn't outrun the dog. Second, she couldn't leave Doc behind to fend for himself.

That was her biggest obstacle. She wasn't simply trying to save herself.

And she couldn't discuss strategy with him.

Pete. Did he even know where she was? He certainly didn't know she was in trouble. No one did. What was Fiona going to do with them? Shoot them and leave them in the forest? Hunting season was almost here. Woodsmen, out to bag a buck or doe, would stumble across their decomposing bodies. Or not. It could be years before someone happened upon them. Pete and Grace would be left wondering what had come of them. Would they even suspect Fiona was behind it? Zoe hadn't.

"Fiona, why are you doing this?" she blurted without thinking.

"You don't know?" Fiona asked with a grunt.

Zoe risked Bruno's wrath and turned to look at the woman in the back seat. "No. I don't."

Fiona pointed the gun at the back of Doc's head. "Because he's too damned smart. I couldn't have him investigating Ferrari's suicide."

A piece of the puzzle clicked. "Because it wasn't a suicide. You killed him."

"She's the one who called 911 on a burner phone, too, I bet," Doc said.

"See? I told you. He's too smart. I knew he would figure it out. That idiot brother-in-law of mine didn't. At least not right away. He was in too much of a rush to sign off on the case. When he did figure it out, he was never going to admit to getting it wrong."

Zoe faced forward again, thinking. Davis had taken the word of the anonymous 911 caller. "He knew you were the one who called it in."

"He put two and two together eventually, but never said anything. If you're thinking Charles kept quiet to protect me, you'd be wrong. No. He was afraid of tarnishing his precious reputation. He hated me. Same as he hated Darlene. He thought we were both stupid." Fiona snorted a laugh. "Boy was he wrong. Darlene's brilliant with numbers, but for all that brilliance, it took me to show her how to cook the books at the restaurant."

Zoe had already pieced together that much. "She was the embezzler."

"Yep. We were making a pretty penny with her mad math skills, but that damned Ferrari busted her. He could've just fired her, but no. He planned to go to the police. Darlene was a wreck, threatening to kill herself. I figured I'd been the one who got her into the mess. I had to get her out."

"By killing him."

"I knew he liked to fish around Ramcat. I'd see him there all the time. So, I watched for him. That morning, he was along the bank, bright and early. No one else around. I walked over to him. I don't think he knew I was Darlene's sister. We started chatting about the river, and when he was focused on bringing in a trout, I picked up a rock and bashed him in the head. Then I tossed the rock in the water and slid him in, too. The current did the rest."

"Why report a jumper?" Doc asked. "Why not merely walk away?"

"Because I didn't want the police involved. He'd recently fired Darlene. If they looked at her, sooner or later, they'd come around to me. By calling 911 and saying I saw someone jump, there was no investigation. I knew Charles wouldn't put any effort into it, and I was right." Fiona nudged Doc's shoulder with the gun. "Turn left here."

The left turn put them on an even narrower road, more gravel than pavement, that climbed steadily upward.

Another piece of the puzzle clicked into place. "This is what Virginia wanted to tell me," Zoe said.

Fiona blew out a noisy breath. "Stupid move. Somewhere along the line, she'd figured it out. Part of it, at least. She was determined to tell you how inept Charles was, to give you the ammunition to fire his ass. I followed her to the motel to talk her out of it. But she was one stubborn bitch. Insisted on putting an end to his incompetence and bullying. I couldn't let her do that."

"Because it might bring up the Ferrari case," Doc said.

"Which you were already about to dig into."

"You stalked me," he said.

"I needed to learn your routines to figure out how best to deal with you."

Zoe's whirling thoughts circled back to her chief deputy. "Davis's attempted suicide and the keys they found there," she said. "That was you."

"Yes." Fiona made the word sound like a hiss. "I always knew he was self-absorbed, but if he got scared his laziness might be made public, he'd try spinning the story to his own benefit. And that would include throwing me to the wolves. I had to shut him up permanently." She swore. "I can't believe I botched that up. I thought the pills in the wine I gave him would be enough, but he tasted it and realized what I'd done."

"Why would he drink wine you gave him if he hated you so much?"

"I knew his tendency to leave a window open for fresh air. Sure enough, I found one in the back of his house. My plan was to doctor the wine, plant the keys, and leave. He'd think his girlfriend had left the bottle for him, not me. But he came home while I was there. I told him we should drink a toast to poor dead Virginia. Like you said, though, he didn't want to. So I told him if we shared one toast in Virginia's memory, I'd leave. That's when he tasted the pills in the wine. When he turned his back, I picked up the bottle and whacked him good. He hit his head on the coffee table on the way down." Fiona snickered. "Even better. Made the staging more realistic."

Zoe felt a jab in her left hip. Doc had nudged her with his thumb—quickly so Fiona didn't notice. Zoe turned her head ever-so-slightly toward him. Without meeting her eyes, he reached down and touched his seatbelt. She already had hers buckled. She always did, having witnessed too many traffic fatalities that didn't have to be. So, what was he trying to tell her?

Then she knew. She might not have come up with an escape plan, but he had, and he wanted her to be ready. She shot a glance out her window. There was no guardrail, no barricade. Only a flimsy-looking fence, trees, and rocks protruding from a steep drop. Overhead, a flash of lightning warned of another storm.

"Virginia," Fiona said, sounding as if the name tasted sour on her tongue. "My sweet sister Virginia. I didn't go there to kill her, but she just *had* to talk to you. She said stopping Charles was the 'right thing to do.'" Still clutching the gun, Fiona made air quotes. Sputtering, she added, "Right thing for *her*. For *you*. Not for me." Fiona flopped back into the seat like an insolent child.

Doc chose that moment, when Fiona was distracted by her own temper, to act. Zoe saw him yank the wheel hard to the right. The car veered, throwing Zoe toward Doc. The seatbelt bit into her hip. And she had a fleeting sensation of being airborne.

Chapter Thirty-Three

Pete listened as yet another call to Zoe went to voice mail. Darlene's attorney hadn't allowed her to elaborate about what had gotten her fired from Ferrari's restaurant. She didn't need to. Pete had figured out enough of it. What he didn't know was where his wife was.

Or Fiona.

He had a terrible ache in his gut. If he found one, he'd find the other. Zoe was with Doc. Doc had been Fiona's target. Zoe and Doc had spoken with Fiona at Ramcat earlier. Fiona had left the rafting expedition shortly afterward and disappeared.

Duncan strode down the hall toward Pete, two cups of coffee in hand. Pete waved it off. Duncan shoved one at him. "It's going to be a long night. You'll need this."

Pete accepted it, although staying awake wasn't an issue. The level of adrenaline coursing through his veins would be a thousand times more effective than even the most potent caffeine.

"I gather Zoe still isn't picking up?"

"No. We need to make Darlene call her sister."

Duncan shook his head. "After you stepped out, I tried again. She refuses. But here's the thing. Darlene doesn't have her phone on her. It's at her house."

Pete locked onto his gaze. "Alex is at her house, too."

"That's what I was thinking. Once Alex learns it was his Aunt Fiona who killed his mom, I bet he'll be more than willing to help. Let's get over there

251

and talk to him."

Pete shoved the untouched coffee back at Duncan. "Not us. Me. I need you to rally your fellow state troopers. When I last talked to Zoe, she and Doc were headed to Seven Springs to check out Ferrari's restaurant."

"That was hours ago."

"It's a start." Pete dug his notebook and pen from his pocket and jotted the Forester's plate number on a blank page. Then he flipped back to find Fiona's car's information, scribbled it onto the new sheet as well, ripped it out, and handed it to Duncan. "Get BOLOs out on both of those vehicles."

"On it." Duncan turned away and called over his shoulder. "Stay in touch."

"You do the same."

* * *

Alex looked horrible when he opened the door at Darlene's house, his red eyes in stark contrast to his ghostly pale skin.

"Where's my aunt?" he demanded.

Pete stepped inside, not waiting for an invitation. "She's still at the station."

"She was just trying to protect me. She doesn't know how to behave around people. I've told you that."

Pete took him by the shoulders. "Listen to me. There's more going on with your aunts than we realized. Darlene has admitted to some things, but she has a good attorney, and considering her mental state, I don't see her being in any major legal trouble." He knew he was making a huge assumption there, but he needed Alex to focus. "Fiona is the one I'm concerned with. Alex, we're pretty sure she's the one who killed your mother."

Pete expected the teen to launch into a rant, claiming Pete was crazy, denying his aunt would or could do such a thing. Instead, Alex's face contorted. A soft whimper escaped his trembling lips, and his knees buckled. Pete tightened his grip to keep him upright.

"Oh, God. I—I had a feeling," Alex stuttered through the tears. "Something seemed hinky when she showed up at the motel right after Mom—died. I didn't believe it. Didn't want to believe it. But—you know when you asked me who else knew Mom was at the Vance Motel? I should've said something then. Aunt Fiona knew. She'd called me, and—and I told her." He lowered his face and sobbed. "I'm so sorry. I didn't know. It's all my fault."

Pete guided him to the worn sofa and eased him down. The kid had every reason to curl into a fetal position and weep uncontrollably. But Pete didn't have the time to let him.

Zoe didn't have the time.

Pete dragged an ottoman over and sat, facing him. "Alex," he said, trying to control his voice. "I need your help."

But Alex remained doubled over, his shoulders shaking with each sob.

"*Alex*," Pete said, firmer this time. "We think Fiona may be going after my wife and Doc Abercrombie."

Alex lifted his tear-streaked face.

"I need you to pay attention. We need to find out where Fiona is right now. Can you call her?"

After a moment of struggling to regain control, he nodded.

"Here's the thing. We need to know where she is, but I don't want her to know why. Do you think you can get the information from her without tipping her off?"

Alex took a deep, raspy breath. He dug his phone from his cargo pants pocket, thumbed the screen, and waited. A moment later, he made a face and tapped the device, putting it on speaker so Pete could hear the request to leave a message. At the beep, Alex said, "Aunt Fiona, please call me ASAP. Aunt Darlene and I are in big trouble." He ended the call and looked at Pete. "Okay?"

"That was fine, son," Pete said, but wished Fiona had picked up.

Alex's eyes brightened. "Wait a minute." He pushed up to his feet. "I can do better than that. Let me get my computer."

* * *

The sensation of weightlessness lasted only a second before Zoe watched the ground rush up at her. The impact flung her forward. The shoulder belt

253

cut into her collarbone. The car exploded.

No. Not the car. The airbags, filling the air with an acrid stench and smoke. From the corner of her eye, she spotted a large, furry missile hurtle through the gap between the front seats. The world erupted in a deafening screech of metal. Shards of glass rained in on her.

But they continued downward. She closed her eyes. Waited for the end. Something heavy and warm slammed into her. Bounced away. She didn't want to see.

Even without looking, she knew they were upside-down, right-side-up, upside-down, spinning like an amusement park ride. Moments of floating punctuated with jolts and pain. And screams. Tossed violently forward. Restrained. Thrown back into the seat. Toward the driver's side. Jerked back. Slammed into the door. Hot flames of pain shot through that shoulder. Her knees. Her neck.

The sensation of flying ended. Now, they were rolling. Sideways. Down.

She kept her eyes squeezed shut. Waiting for it all to stop.

Waiting to die.

One more horrendous impact. A booming, deafening thud.

And all went black.

Chapter Thirty-Four

Zoe's first waking sensation was of excruciating pain, as if her entire body had been run through a meat grinder. The second moment of awareness, beyond the realization she wasn't dead, was the unearthly howl coming from...somewhere. She opened her eyes. Or thought she did. But all she saw was darkness. Maybe she really was dead.

No. Dead wouldn't hurt this much.

Nor would dead reek of gasoline and...was that gunpowder?

Maybe she was blind. The glass had cut her eyes and left her sightless.

Her right arm was useless. But she could move her left. She raised her hand to her face, gingerly touching her eyelids. The hand came away warm and sticky. Her eyes, however, didn't hurt.

That was the one part of her body that didn't.

She opened her eyes again and waited. No, she wasn't blind. It was dark outside. Even darker inside.

How long had she been unconscious? Long enough for dusk to have drifted into night.

Gradually, her sight acclimated, and shadowy images came into hazy focus. Her mind cleared as well.

The car—what was left of it—was on its side. Her side. Slowly, cautiously, she turned her head to look upward. To look at Doc. Motionless, he was draped above her, suspended from his seatbelt harness. His head and one arm hung down like a rag doll.

She reached toward him, touching the side of his face. His skin was cool.

Her paramedic training kicked in. Don't move him. His neck could be broken. She gently felt for his throat. His carotid artery. Her practiced fingers found the groove. She rested them there, waiting, holding her breath.

There. A faint pulse. Weak, but definitely there.

She moved her hand to his shoulder and gently squeezed. "Doc."

No response.

She tightened her grip and raised her voice. "*Doc.*"

A groan.

She closed her eyes and exhaled. Opened her eyes again and focused through the darkness. "Doc," she repeated, firmer. Louder. "Can you hear me?"

Another groan. The rasp of a deep inhalation. "Yeah." His voice was labored. "Zoe? You all right?"

Under other circumstances, she'd have quipped, "Define *all right.*" Instead, she said. "I think so. You?"

She made out movement. He brought his dangling arm in against his chest. His head swiveled slightly. He looked down at her. "Been better."

She huffed. "Same here."

The unearthly howl rose into the air once more.

"What the hell is that?" Doc asked.

Zoe searched her memories. Wolf? Doubtful. Coyote? Maybe. Then she remembered. "Bruno. The dog." She tried to look into the back seat, but the seatbelt and the pain limited her movement. She recalled the large furry projectile hurtling around inside the car as it crashed and rolled down the hill. "Fiona?" she called out.

Only the howling responded.

Zoe thought of the gun. Where was Fiona? She wasn't hanging from her seatbelt behind Doc. That much, Zoe could see. Had she even been wearing her seatbelt? Was she crumpled in the back seat? Had she climbed out? Or been thrown?

As crazed as Fiona had been, Zoe didn't want to think she was dead.

Nor did she want to think of Fiona out there with her gun.

"We need to get out," Doc said. "Can you move?"

"I don't know." The engine compartment had been rammed into the passenger space by the first impact and was pressed against Zoe's shins. She moved one leg. Then the other. Pain raced up each and sizzled up her spine. But she wasn't paralyzed. Wasn't pinned. "Yeah. I think I can. What about you?"

"Well…" He grunted. "Maybe. I can't really tell. If I release my seatbelt, I'm going to fall onto you."

Doc wasn't a small man, and Zoe already hurt enough. Besides, he had broken ribs and a concussion, no doubt exacerbated in the crash. One last drop might be the final straw. "Okay. Don't do that. Let me see if I can get out." She used her left hand to fumble for the seatbelt release. Found it. Pressed it. The harness recoiled.

At least part way. Her immobile right arm was caught in it and something else. She fingered what felt like a sheet of fabric half enveloping her.

The now-deflated airbag. *That's* what smelled like gunpowder.

She batted it away, then tried to free her arm, but the knife-sharp pain choked her.

"What's wrong?" Doc asked.

She took a few deep, slow breaths—the kind she used to instruct laboring mothers in her ambulance to do. Once the pain became manageable, she said, "My shoulder is either broken or dislocated."

"That's not good."

"Better than my neck or spine."

"True."

She unzipped her jacket, not quite all the way. Carefully, she used her good hand to pick up the dead weight of her right arm and disentangle it from the seatbelt. Then she tucked her useless forearm into the front of the jacket, gritting her teeth as the pain launched fireworks inside her shoulder and into her eyes. "Here goes nothing," she said.

She squirmed her knees in toward her chest, extracting her legs from the carnage. Wiggling and doing her best to keep her right arm tight against her, she managed to twist and writhe until she sat on the door, her back against the crumpled roof.

If only she had a flashlight. She kept one in the glove box of her Forester.

Did Fiona keep one there as well?

Zoe swatted away the airbag and gingerly ran her fingers along the broken plastic dash where she remembered seeing the latch. Found it. She pulled. It wasn't locked, but it was jammed and unwilling to give. Gritting her teeth, ignoring her shoulder, she yanked again. It budged, but not enough. She tugged and heaved until it finally released. After all that, she damned well hoped to find what she was searching for. Her fingers closed around a metallic barrel. Yes!

She wrenched it free from the other contents and flicked the switch. It worked. Shining the light at the rest of the glove box's contents, she spotted a coiled length of woven strapping. She snatched it, stuffing it into her jacket pocket. Nothing else appeared helpful. Sunglasses. Instruction manual. Crumpled papers.

She turned the beam toward Doc, whose face was streaked with blood. He closed his eyes against the brightness. "Sorry." She swung the light to survey their predicament.

Now able to see into the back seat, she confirmed it was empty. The back window was missing. Fiona was gone.

As if sensing someone was thinking of his mistress, Bruno let out that ungodly howl again.

"He must be hurt," Zoe said.

"Sounds like it."

She imagined the poor beast lying broken and bloody out there.

Doc must've read her mind. "I know you have a soft heart, but that dog was vicious under normal circumstances. Injured? You don't want to mess with him."

He was right. She sighed. "I know."

Doc met her eyes. "How do you plan to get out?"

She looked around, assessing her options as best she could by the narrow beam. She couldn't very well climb out over Doc. The roof was too caved-in for her to climb into the back seat. That left one choice. "I have to kick out the windshield." Which was somehow still intact. The light sparkled over the ripples, and spiderweb cracks spread across it. "I need to cover you with

258

something, or the glass might fall in on you."

"I have a feeling I already look like a glass-shard porcupine. Besides, it's laminated glass. Hopefully, you can kick out your side and get the rest of it out in one piece."

She'd watched the fire department do that at accident scenes. But they had the tools needed for the job. She had two feet and one arm. "Okay." She took another look at Doc and noticed his deflated airbag hanging from the steering wheel. Touching it, she said, "Hold this over your face to be safe."

"Good idea." He pulled it close and draped it over his head, looking eerily like a ghost.

Zoe wriggled onto her back again. This time, she drew her knees in, took a breath, and struck out with both feet. The first impact did little, but she felt the shattered glass give ever so slightly. She kicked again. And again. And a fourth time, roaring like a trapped bear.

The entire side of the windshield broke free from its frame.

"Got it." Biting her lip against the sensation of having her arm torn from its socket, she scrambled onto her knees, braced her good arm against the loose glass, and pushed.

She managed to create a big enough space to slither through, like a chick exiting its egg.

Outside, she staggered unsteadily to her feet. Her head ached. Hell, everything hurt, but with the exception of her right shoulder, nothing appeared to be broken. She took a deep breath and swept the flashlight beam through the night. She had no idea how far the car had traveled once it left the road. Doc must have waited until they'd cleared the trees before veering, because they'd come to rest on a steep, grassy hillside. The light didn't reach far enough for her to see the road, but the flattened grass indicated the path they'd taken.

No passing motorist was likely to spot them down here. At least not until daybreak. Maybe not even then.

She took another quick look around. No Fiona. Had she been ejected near the top of the hill? Zoe didn't see Bruno either. She thought about calling to him, but what if he was still mobile? Would he charge in her direction, hurt and angry?

First things first, she decided. Doc had to be her top priority. But how to get to him?

She bent down, set the flashlight on the ground, grabbed the edge of the windshield, and tugged. It didn't budge. She readjusted her grip and tried again. Same result. If she could use both hands, she'd have a better chance, but with only one, there was no way. She gave up, retrieved the flashlight, and looked for other avenues.

The roof was a crumpled sheet of steel. Could she climb it with only one arm? Not likely. She clambered around the demolished car to the undercarriage side. At least the engine wasn't smoking. Thank goodness for small blessings. She tentatively touched the rough, rusted metal. They'd been here long enough for the engine and its workings to have cooled. Its array of brackets, pipes, and tubing offered a better option for hand- and footholds.

A better option for someone with four functioning limbs. Zoe imagined trying to climb the steel jungle gym. Getting cut on the rusty metal. Losing her footing, not being able to hold on, falling.

"What are you doing?" Doc called from inside.

"I'm trying to figure out how to climb up to you."

"For crying out loud, be careful," he replied.

"Yeah," she said under her breath.

Before starting her ascent, she set down the flashlight, retrieved the strap from her pocket, and created a makeshift sling to better immobilize her injured arm. Pulled tight and knotted, the strap stabilized her shoulder, bringing the pain down to a tolerable level. Then she tucked the flashlight into the sling, hoping she could keep it angled upward to let her see what she was grabbing.

She reached up and wrapped her fingers around a pipe. Tested its strength. Whatever it was, it held. Then, she placed one foot on a piece of protruding steel. It also held. She heaved herself up and found a lip for the toes of her second foot. So far, so good.

Except, now what? She needed to reach up but couldn't let go, couldn't use her right hand. She pressed her body against the undercarriage, trying to keep her balance forward. Trying not to tumble back. She located the next pipe she wanted to get to. Inhaling, she released her grip and made a grab as gravity did its best to drag her back and down.

Her fingers closed around the pipe. She closed her eyes, exhaling in relief. She repeated the process twice more. Almost there.

But whatever her right foot was braced on broke with a metallic crunch. She dropped. Her one good arm supported her full weight as she scrambled to find a new foothold.

The pipe she was clinging to groaned. She felt it give. Just a little.

Then it buckled, and she tumbled backward, slamming to the earth.

* * *

Zoe couldn't see. The flashlight had flown from her sling and gone dark. She couldn't breathe either. This was it. The end. She was going to die on this godforsaken hillside in the pitch black of night. She gasped, but nothing entered her lungs. She tried again. And again.

After what felt like a decade, her lungs filled, and she sucked in the night air.

She wasn't dying. Not yet, at least. She'd merely had the wind knocked out of her. She remembered the sensation from when she'd taken a bad spill off a horse long ago. Back when she was young and able to pop back up, remount, and keep riding.

Tonight, there was no popping up. Her head hurt like hell. Her shoulder, on the pain scale of one to ten, was a forty-five.

"Zoe!" Doc's frantic shouts made their way into her consciousness.

"I'm okay," she shouted back. A baldfaced lie.

"Good," he said, and then added in a voice so soft, she wasn't sure she heard him right, "I'm not."

"What?" She struggled to her feet, picked her way around to the front of the car, and felt for the small opening she'd made in the windshield. Dropping to her knees, she stuck her head through the gap. "Doc? What's wrong?"

She couldn't see him but heard his humorless laugh. "You mean besides hanging from the seatbelt in a wrecked car?"

"Yeah. Besides that."

He exhaled a breath that sounded like gravel. "There's no use trying to free me."

Not what she wanted to hear. "Why?"

"Because I tried to get myself loose. I can't move my legs. Can't feel them either."

Heat rose behind Zoe's eyes. Did Doc have a spinal cord injury? Was he paralyzed? Were his legs broken? Or merely pinned in the wreckage?

She wished she had the first aid kit she carried in her Subaru. Wished she had her phone.

She wished she was at home in her bed with Pete at her side instead of stuck on this hillside in the dark.

Adding to her sense of despair, Bruno, also out there in the dark, let out another mournful howl.

"I know how you feel, boy," Zoe said.

Where the hell was Fiona?

"I'm going to try to find the flashlight," Zoe told Doc. "Then I'll crawl back in there and try to figure out what's going on with your legs."

"No."

"No?"

"No," he said firmly, although Zoe heard the fear in his voice. "Find the flashlight and then climb up to the road and try to flag down someone. Have them call for help."

"I don't want to leave you here alone."

"We don't have a choice. It's hours until daylight, and I really don't want to be stuck that long."

She tried to think of a better option.

"Look. You can't get me out. If I release the seatbelt, I'm going to be hanging by my legs. As uncomfortable as I am, that sounds even worse."

Zoe couldn't argue the point.

"I need rescue equipment. I need *you* to go get help."

He was right, and she knew it. "Okay. I'm going." She looked up at his shadowy form and imagined she was looking into his eyes. "But don't you die before I get back."

"You have my word."

She wasn't convinced.

After she'd backed away from the shattered windshield and the crumpled car, she returned to the undercarriage side and lowered to a tripod version of all fours. Crawling and feeling for the flashlight, she prayed she didn't grab a snake or some nighttime marauder with teeth. She was about to give up when her hand fell upon the familiar-shaped metal barrel. She sat back on her heels and clicked the switch. Nothing happened. She shook it and clicked again. Still nothing.

"Crap."

"Did you find it?" Doc called.

Forcing cheeriness she did not feel, she replied, "Yes. I'm heading up toward the road."

"Good luck."

"Be back soon."

She was about to toss the broken flashlight but reconsidered. If nothing else, she might be able to use it as a weapon if she encountered Fiona.

Or Bruno.

Zoe tucked the flashlight back into her makeshift sling. Drawing a breath for courage, she began to climb.

Chapter Thirty-Five

The ascent would've been difficult on a good day. The hillside was steep, the grass chest-high and slick from the rainstorm. Zoe followed the path made by the car as it had careened downward. But the path was also gouged in places, non-existent in others, the result of being intermittently airborne.

Clouds obscured the moon and left her wishing for the nighttime vision of her cats. She fumbled to keep her balance with only one functioning arm.

How far had she come? How far did she still have to go? She couldn't tell.

A random rock poking through the turf tripped her. She went down hard, skinning her already bruised knees. Her head pounded. Her injured shoulder felt as though it had been partially severed from her body. Her good hand was scraped and raw and burned as if someone had poured acid on it. Cursing under her breath, she regained her footing and pushed onward.

Every so often, Bruno's woeful wail joined the chorus of nighttime insects, reaching a crescendo that raised the hair on Zoe's neck. She had no clue which direction the howl came from. It echoed against the hillside and through the valley below.

Where was Fiona?

She stopped to catch her breath. Once Bruno fell silent, Zoe realized she hadn't heard a single car pass by. Was she still that far down the hill? Or was there absolutely no traffic? Neither was good.

The chilly night air seeped through her jacket and made her sweat-soaked shirt feel like ice. Keep moving. At least the strenuous climb warmed her.

Another twenty feet, another skinned knee from stumbling over a rock, and Zoe heard it. She froze, listening. In the distance, but growing louder, the whispered hum of an approaching vehicle. She scrabbled upward, ignoring the overwhelming pain, blindly plunging ahead.

The hiss of tires on pavement, the thump of hitting potholes, grew into a rumble of what sounded like a pickup truck.

Her heart raced. How much farther? Winded and exhausted, she pushed on. Above her, the vehicle's headlights lit the sky. She wasn't close enough. Couldn't reach the road in time.

As the pickup rumbled by, still a good twenty feet away, Zoe drew a deep breath and bellowed as loud as she could. *"Help!"*

The truck continued down the road, the red gleam of its taillights fading.

She stood motionless, watching her best hope disappear into the night. Turning, she sat with a choking sob and buried her face in her abrased hand. She pictured Doc, still hanging from his seatbelt, his legs pinned. Pictured Pete, wondering what had become of her. Was Grace at home, worried, trying and failing to reach her husband by phone?

From somewhere not far off, the dog's mournful cry rose, carried on the air currents. Zoe knew exactly how he felt.

The distinctive pop of a firearm exploded in the night. Simultaneously, the dog gave a sharp yip.

Then nothing.

Zoe stifled a cry. Fiona was out there, and while the valley echoes made determining her location impossible, the gunshot had sounded terrifyingly close. Even worse, Fiona had shot her own dog.

But why was Zoe surprised? Fiona had killed her own sister. Maybe she'd discovered the dog mortally wounded and had put him out of his misery.

The thought did nothing to comfort Zoe.

Fiona was out there. Armed. And perfectly willing to kill without an ounce of regret.

Zoe needed to move. To get to the road. To find help. But the sound of rustling froze her in place. Fiona? Zoe wanted to believe, no, it was a deer. Hell, she'd almost prefer a bear over the crazy woman with the gun. Would she rather die from a gunshot or from being eaten?

A shadow moved in the darkness not far downhill. Zoe remained motionless, trying to make out what it was. Not a deer, for sure.

Too thin for a bear.

The moment Zoe knew for sure not what, but *who* it was, another shot rang out.

"The next one isn't going to miss." Fiona's voice sounded strained.

Or maybe it was the ringing in Zoe's ears.

Fiona stood below her. It was difficult to judge in the darkness, but Zoe guessed her to be about thirty feet downhill from her. How good of a shot was Fiona? Zoe had fired handguns at the range and knew most people weren't accurate at that distance, even if they could see their target. Zoe could only make out Fiona's shadow, so the reverse had to be true.

Zoe's mind raced. She should run. Except she couldn't. Not on this steep terrain. She could continue her climb and pray Fiona wasn't that good with a firearm. After all, she'd bludgeoned her sister to death with a hotel lamp, killed Tanner Ferrari by bashing him over the head with a rock, and used a vehicle in her attempt to kill Doc.

A line from one of Pete's favorite movies echoed through Zoe's consciousness.

"I said I never had much use for one. Never said I didn't know how to use it."

But sitting there, doing nothing, wasn't a good alternative either.

Zoe drew her feet in closer, getting ready to stand. If she kept climbing the hillside, but at an angle, the chances of Fiona's bullets hitting their target lessened.

"Don't move," Fiona ordered.

Had she seen Zoe preparing to rise? Or had she heard the scrape of Zoe's boots on the ground? Zoe hoped the latter. She was counting on darkness to even the playing field.

"I told you, don't move." The shadow took an unsteady step toward her.

Was Fiona hurt, too?

Of course. She had to be. She'd been inside the same car as Zoe. Had either been thrown out or climbed out. If she'd climbed out, why hadn't she confronted Zoe sooner? No. Zoe believed Fiona and her dog had been tossed from the vehicle as it crashed and rolled. Zoe's experience as a paramedic told her, if that was the case, Fiona was injured even worse than Zoe was.

Zoe closed her fingers around the barrel of the flashlight, still tucked into her sling. She needed to be close to use it. Leaving it where it was, she launched to the left and up, refusing to look back.

The explosive pop of the handgun was immediately followed by the tick of the bullet striking stone. Fiona had missed, however Zoe realized there was a secondary threat of a ricochet.

"*Stop.*" Fiona's voice sounded strangled, desperate.

Zoe wasn't about to comply. Stumbling, slipping, Zoe groped her way up the hill. Toward the road.

Away from Fiona.

Fiona, however, was also on the move, grunting and cursing as she climbed.

Another shot. Another miss, although this one kicked up earth close enough to spatter dirt into Zoe's face. Fiona might be a better shot than Zoe had anticipated. Or she was getting lucky. But Zoe was lucky, too. She hadn't been hit.

Yet.

Uneven footstep by uneven footstep, she ascended the hill, grabbing handfuls of weeds to leverage herself upward. She sensed the road getting closer. Once she reached pavement, she would take off, running as fast as she could. But which direction? The way they'd come was miles from civilization. She couldn't remember seeing a house. The opposite direction was likely even more desolate, since she doubted Fiona had been directing them into a town to kill them and dump their bodies.

And if anyone—please, God—happened to be coming to look for them— fat chance—they'd be coming from the same direction Zoe and Doc had.

Wouldn't they?

In her limited nighttime vision, Zoe spotted the fence. The same spindly broken fence Doc had driven through. She'd made it.

267

Her foot hit a rock. A smooth one. Her boot slipped, and she went down. Instinctively, she protected her injured shoulder, instead landing on her other elbow. Her second foot lost traction, and suddenly, Zoe was tumbling, sliding down rain-slicked ground. The flashlight went flying. Her right arm was ripped from its makeshift sling. Pain drove all other thoughts from her mind.

Until she bowled into something. Someone.

The collision took Fiona's legs out from under her. She slammed down on top of Zoe. For the second time that night, Zoe had the wind knocked out of her.

Fiona flailed, grabbing Zoe's injured arm. In a jumble of thrashing arms and legs, both women rolled downward. Zoe's head—and the world—spun at a dizzying rate, but she couldn't think beyond catching her breath and battling the sensation of having her arm severed.

Fiona let out a primal wail…one that ended with another gunshot.

* * *

Pete fought the urge to press the gas pedal to the Explorer's floorboards. Instead, he held the vehicle to a reasonable speed, searching the narrow road ahead of him for some sign of Zoe or Doc or even Fiona in the beams of his headlights.

Alex sat in the passenger seat, the window wide open in spite of the drizzle. He clutched his cell phone, staring at its screen. "We're close. Real close."

Back at Darlene's house, the teen had brought out his laptop. He told Pete he acted as tech support whenever his aunts needed help with their computers. In doing so, he'd acquired their Google passwords. As Pete watched, Alex logged into Fiona's account, brought up her Google Maps app, and tapped on her timeline for the day. Zooming in, Alex showed Pete the path Fiona had taken from her home to the Ramcat boat launch, down the river for a short distance, and then back to her home, where she stayed for a couple of hours. Then she hit the road again and traveled to Somerset, where she stopped at the Mountaintop Tavern. When she left there, the line took her along the same road Pete was now driving with Alex, who'd pulled up Fiona's map timeline on his phone when Pete asked him to come along.

"Close?" Pete saw nothing but mostly bare trees lining the road's edge.

"Slow down," Alex said. "She's right here."

Here?

The trees gave way to black nothingness on the right side of the road.

"*Here,*" Alex repeated emphatically.

The crack of a gunshot ripped through the night, and Pete steered the Explorer as close to the edge as he could, jamming the brakes and spewing gravel.

Alex reached for the door, but Pete caught his arm. "Stay in the car. Call 911." He pointed at the map on Alex's phone. "Give them our location. Tell them 'Officer needs assistance. Shots fired.' Can you do that?"

"Yes, sir."

Pete exited the Explorer, pausing to grab his portable searchlight and wishing like hell he had one of those FLIR nighttime vision gadgets he'd once borrowed from Baronick. At the edge of the road, he flipped the switch. The steep drop-off lit up. He swept the beam across the ground and spotted movement about a hundred yards below him. Two figures were engaged in a wrestling match. He caught a glimpse of blond hair. Heard an agonized scream. Zoe's. Pete's worst nightmare. Fiona had shot his wife.

"Police!" he bellowed.

He launched downward through the high, wet grasses, sliding, battling to maintain his feet while keeping the light on the two women grappling. If they were aware of his approach, neither indicated.

"*Police!*" he shouted again.

His feet shot out from under him on the rain-slicked ground. He landed hard on his hip. Bounced up and kept going. Gravity helped and hindered him. He didn't dare draw his weapon. Not yet. If he fell and accidentally discharged it...

He couldn't risk hitting Zoe. Fiona had already shot her, but Zoe was still alive. Still fighting. Her cries and curses grew louder as he grew closer.

He slid, stumbled, staggered. Fifty yards. Thirty. Twenty.

Within the beam of his light, Fiona straddled Zoe, who was on the ground. Fiona's hands were around Zoe's throat.

Fiona looked up, her expression shocked, as if she'd been unaware of Pete's presence until he was almost upon them. She squinted into the light.

"Police! Let her go and show me your hands!"

There was movement, so fast he almost couldn't register what happened. With one hand, Zoe reached up between Fiona's arms. Snatched a handful of her short hair and yanked, jerking Fiona's head around. Throwing her off-balance. Breaking her hold.

Pete lunged at them. He grabbed Fiona, slipped, and spun her, face down onto the ground. In one quick motion, he placed the searchlight on the ground aimed at Fiona and wrested both her arms behind her back. He expected more of a battle. Instead, she went limp with a childlike whimper. He snatched his cuffs from their holder at the small of his back. As he secured Fiona, he looked toward his motionless wife.

"Zoe?" he shouted.

"I'm okay."

She didn't sound okay. "Were you shot?" he asked.

"No."

With Fiona restrained, he picked up his light and swung it toward Zoe. She struggled to sit, cradling her right arm close to her body, her face etched in agony. "What happened?" he asked.

She was looking downhill into the night. "Doc. He's pinned in the car. Down there. I was trying to get to the road to flag down help."

Pete hoisted Fiona to her feet. "How bad is he?"

"It's his second crash in a week. It's not good."

Pete glanced up the steep hillside. "Can you make it to my car? I'll secure her in the back." He shot a dark glare at Fiona. To Zoe, he said, "You can sit up front with Alex and wait for the ambulance."

Zoe shook her head vehemently. "I'll wait here so I can show the EMS crew where the car is. Besides, I don't trust myself in the same car with her." The look in Zoe's eyes was as deadly as Pete had ever seen in his wife. "She shot her dog."

Fiona spat. "He was gonna die anyway. Stupid shit mutt. I shoulda let him tear you and that doctor apart."

Zoe closed the distance between them in one long stride and struck out. The slap echoed across the valley. Fiona yelped.

Had it been anyone else, Pete would've made a case for assault since his prisoner was already in custody. Zoe clearly was thinking the same thing. She held out the arm she'd used to belt Fiona. "If you want to handcuff me, you'll need to do it with my hands in front. I think my shoulder's broken."

"Handcuff you? For what?" He shrugged. "I didn't see a thing."

Chapter Thirty-Six

Zoe perched on the edge of the ambulance's jump seat, wrapped in a wool blanket, her right arm immobilized, bound tight against her torso with a sling and swathe. She'd applied this same type of bandage more than once during her time working for Monongahela EMS but had never been on the receiving end before. The paramedics had left the back doors open when they'd gone to attend to Fiona's injuries. Zoe overheard talk about Fiona having sustained suspected fractures of her facial bones, and she'd lost a lot of blood from several deep lacerations. The hospital would have to determine the full extent of her injuries.

Outside, the steady rain continued, backlit by the headlights of the fire/rescue truck parked behind the ambulance. Voices filtered through to Zoe. They'd located the car with Doc still inside and were in the process of freeing him. No word yet on his condition. She studied the storage bins above the stretcher, taking inventory of the familiar first aid supplies. She remembered her time in a similar rig. The adrenaline rush of roaring to a scene, lights, and sirens. Charging to rescue the sick or injured. Comforting patients. Stabilizing them. Getting them to the hospital.

Saving lives.

From the corner of her eye, she spotted movement in the doorway. Pete stood there, holding two bottles of water.

"Mind if I join you?" he asked.

With her good hand, she patted the spot on the bench next to her.

He climbed in, unscrewed the lid of one of the bottles, and handed it to her.

She thanked him and took a sip.

"How's the shoulder?"

"Better now. But it hurts like hell when I move my arm."

"You're going to the hospital." His tone made it clear he expected an argument.

Zoe wasn't about to give him one. "Yes, I am." She tipped her head toward the door. "Have you heard anything about Doc?"

"They're still working to extricate him. I hiked down to the car. I'm amazed you both survived."

She flashed back on the awareness of being airborne. The jolt and metallic crunch of the impact. The stomach-curdling sensation of rolling, being flung around inside, pinned by the seatbelts and airbags.

"I can't believe you made it all the way back up here in your condition, either," Pete said, his voice soft.

"I had to get help for Doc." She noted the worry in Pete's pale blue eyes. "How did you find us?"

He leaned toward her and pressed a kiss to her forehead. "I'll tell you all about it later. I'm just glad I did."

"So am I."

He sat back and looked at her, a strange expression on his handsome face. "About Liz. I had no idea she was pregnant. No idea I had a child out there."

In the terror of the last few hours, the fissure that had opened in their relationship had receded to the far recesses of Zoe's mind. She placed the water bottle on the floor and reached up to touch her fingers to his lips, silencing him. "There'll be time to talk about that later, too."

Pete wrapped his hand around hers, moving it down to her lap. "But there almost wasn't time."

He had a point.

"I don't want to let things go unsaid between us. Not the important stuff like this. I do want to get to know my daughter. But I have no intention of…" He made a pained face, searching for the word. "…*reacquainting* myself with Liz."

"You may not have a choice. You share a daughter." A surge of tears rushed into Zoe's throat and eyes. "That ties the two of you together for the rest of your lives." Her voice cracked, and she looked away.

Still holding her hand, Pete squeezed gently. "No, it doesn't. Yeah, if Isabella was still a youngster, there would be parental decisions to be made. But she's an adult. There's no reason to have to deal with Liz."

Zoe couldn't meet his eyes. He was being short-sighted. Isabella had major life events ahead of her. Perhaps a wedding. Children—Pete's and Elizabeth's grandchildren—and God only knew what other occasions might draw them all to the same place at the same time.

"I mean it." Pete reached up to touch Zoe's chin and turned her head toward him. "Look at me."

Reluctantly, she gave in.

"I love you. *You.* I hoped you knew that by now."

"I do. I love you, too. More than life." She blinked away the tears blurring his face. "I'm sorry I took off. I never doubted you. I just had a lot to get my head around."

He gave her his cockeyed grin. "Same here. I have a grown daughter. I'm not old enough to have a grown daughter."

She choked a laugh. "I have news for you, bub. Yeah, you are."

A shout went up outside. Pete gave Zoe a quick kiss on her lips and released her hand. "Let me see what that's about." He stepped down from the patient compartment and looked toward the gorge. "What's going on?" he yelled.

Zoe heard a voice reply, but the thrum of rain on the roof muffled the words.

Pete brought his attention back to her. "They've freed Doc and are bringing him up. Looks like he has two broken legs but no apparent spinal injuries."

Zoe blew out a relieved breath. But her relief was tempered by thoughts of Fiona's other victim. "Have you heard any news about Davis?"

"No. Do you want me to call and find out?"

"I'm not sure I want to know." She thought about sitting beside Doc, listening to Fiona in the back seat, recounting her role in all that had transpired. "Fiona's responsible for Davis's situation, too." Zoe gave Pete an abbreviated version of Fiona's confession and reasoning.

Midway through, Pete climbed back inside the patient compartment to get out of the rain. Once Zoe finished, she watched as he mulled it over. He shook his head. "I'm not giving her any slack, mind you. Fiona's a stone-cold killer through and through. But I have to wonder if you can really say she's the one responsible for Davis's situation."

Zoe gave him a quizzical look.

"Back when Tanner Ferrari's body showed up in autopsy, Davis didn't bother to look beyond the obvious. Had he simply declared the manner of death as undetermined, the police would've uncovered Darlene's embezzlement and eventually come around to Fiona."

"Which is why Fiona placed the 911 call claiming to see Tanner jump. She knew she'd be found out eventually if his body simply showed up."

"If Davis had done his job, Fiona would've gone to prison, and none of this would've happened."

"Another thing I wonder about," Zoe said. "Was Kenneth Nicholson aware of it? Or at least have suspicions?"

"I'd love to know what's behind the non-disclosure agreement between Nicholson and Davis."

"So would I. But I doubt we ever will. Those secrets could bring down Nicholson and the whole Somerset County Coroner's Office." She gingerly touched her injured shoulder. "They might still bring down Monongahela's Coroner's Office."

"What do you mean?" Pete looked confused. "You and Doc uncovered the whole mess."

"At what cost? I'm out of commission for the foreseeable future. So is Doc. Not permanently, I hope. Then there's Davis. Fiona has managed to put most of my staff on the disabled list." Zoe left off the part about Paulette, who essentially was no longer employed as her secretary, and Zoe had fired her replacement.

Another yelp filled the night air.

"Now what?" Zoe asked.

Pete bolted from the ambulance and vanished around the corner. He was gone for what felt like an hour, giving Zoe time to conjure several horrible scenarios. Doc going into cardiac arrest while being hauled up the steep and slick hillside. One of the rescuers getting hurt in the attempt to save him. Fiona breaking free and disappearing into the night.

The clomp of footsteps brought Zoe's attention back to the open doors as Pete returned, a look she couldn't define on his face.

"What?" she asked.

"They found another victim."

Zoe ran the statement through her mind and started counting. Doc. Her. Fiona. "The dog," Zoe said, remembering his mournful howling, the gunshot, the yip. The silence. "Fiona shot him."

"Yes, but her aim sucked. He's alive."

Chapter Thirty-Seven

Three days had passed since the nightmare on the hillside in the Laurel Highlands. Despite having her right arm in a brace, Zoe stood in the wide hallway of the recently opened county building, gazing at the full-glass windows and double doors etched with Office of the Coroner and her name in smaller print below.

"Looks like we're going to be neighbors."

Zoe turned to find Juliann Holland, leather briefcase in hand, glaring at her. "Ms. Holland." Zoe was in no mood to deal with the commissioner today. Or any day. "Not exactly neighbors. Your office is two floors down. What brings you up here?"

"I heard about your ordeal. I wanted to make sure you were well enough to do your job." Her voice carried no hint of concern.

"I have a good team in place to handle what I can't." Zoe fought the urge to say more and instead asked, "How's Dr. Davis?"

The question took Holland aback, and Zoe caught a fleeting glimpse of tears in her eyes before she blinked and lifted her chin. "He's making good progress. I'm sure he'll be back to work soon. Until then, I wish you well in your new offices." Holland pivoted and hurried away, before Zoe could press the validity of her statement.

She sighed, faced her office door, and fumbled with the key in her left hand. Her attempt to insert it in the lock resulted in her dropping the darned thing.

"Crap." She wished she could put full blame on her injury, but knew she'd be kidding herself. Nerves played the bigger role and not because of Juliann

Holland's visit.

"Let me get that," came Paulette's voice from behind her. She stooped and snatched the key from the floor. "I didn't expect to see you here." Paulette returned Zoe's key to her and used her own to unlock the door.

"I could say the same to you. I thought you'd retired." Zoe followed her inside, where a cherrywood counter divided a small reception area from the rest of the office space.

"I did." Paulette unlatched a swinging half-door at one end of the counter and sauntered through. She turned, holding the half-door for Zoe. "But my replacement didn't work out." Paulette winced. "Sorry. I didn't mean to bring her up."

Easing past Paulette, Zoe moved to the middle of the large space. "No need to apologize." She had to get used to the mention of Elizabeth Preston.

Paulette dropped her handbag into a drawer at the receptionist's desk. "Anyway, I've placed another help-wanted ad. I'll do a more thorough background check on the next one."

"So, you're not leaving me high and dry?"

"Franklin would haunt me if I did." Paulette looked around. "Speaking of Franklin, he'd be impressed with this place."

Zoe wasn't so sure. He'd loved his little office in the basement of his funeral home. If he was still alive, he'd probably have passed on the offer of the new space.

"You didn't say what *you're* doing here," Paulette said, crossing her arms. "You have a concussion."

Zoe fingered the side of her head. "The doctor refused to clear me to play football, but as a rule, I don't get tackled much around here."

"Smart aleck. What about your shoulder?"

"It was just dislocated. They were able to do a closed reduction. No surgery. I'm not allowed to drive until I get out of this brace, but they cleared me for work as long as someone else does all the lifting."

"If you're not allowed to drive, how'd you get here?"

"Pete. He has a meeting at County Police Headquarters this morning. He dropped me off and went to get coffee. He'll be back." Hopefully, before the guest he'd invited to join them.

Zoe did a slow three-sixty, taking in the new office. She'd been here several times over the last month, watching the progress as it took shape. But she'd missed yesterday's move-in day thanks to a very long appointment with the orthopedist. Today, the new desks, new file cabinets, and new carpeting were all in place. It even smelled new. At the rear of the office was a pair of solid doors stained to match the cherry of the counter. A plaque on one read County Coroner. On the other, Chief Deputy Coroner.

Despite Holland's claims, that one would never be occupied by Dr. Charles Davis. Zoe had spoken with Tracy at the hospital earlier this morning regarding his condition. While he had regained consciousness, the stroke had dealt him a cognitive blow, one which would require months of therapy. She had no intention of adding to his misery by pressing the whole Somerset County dereliction of duty thing.

At least not until he recovered and decided to force the issue.

"Nice digs," Pete said from the doorway where he stood with two cups of coffee.

"Beats the 1950s office we were using." Paulette opened the half door and waved him in.

He entered and held out one of the coffees to Zoe. To Paulette, he said, "Sorry. I didn't know you would be here, or I'd have brought you one." He held out his cup. "I haven't taken a drink yet if you want this."

She waved a dismissive hand at him. "I had plenty before I left home."

Another set of approaching footsteps drew their attention. Zoe's heart lurched, expecting someone else, but Grace breezed in, carrying a floral arrangement in a vase. "I'm glad to see you all here," Doc's wife said, a lilt in her voice.

Pete pointed at the flowers. "For me?"

Grace snorted. "Silly man." She set the vase on the counter and smiled at Zoe. "Lyle and I wanted to give you an office-warming gift."

"They're beautiful. Thank you. And thank him for me, too."

"How's he doing?" Paulette asked. "I hear he has two fractured legs to add to his broken bone collection."

"He's at the rehab facility by the old mall." Grace gestured in the general direction. "And he's complaining like mad. Insists he's fine to go home."

Zoe sipped her coffee. "One broken leg? Sure. You could handle that. But both? It's gonna take time and a lot of PT."

"True. But he wanted me to assure you he'll be back in the morgue as soon as he's able. Until then, I understand Dr. Patel has agreed to fill in."

"She has. I spoke to her while I was still in the ER waiting for my x-rays."

"It's too bad about Davis, but I still have a hard time mustering up a lot of sympathy for him." Grace wrinkled her nose. "He brought most of his woes on himself."

Zoe couldn't argue.

Grace fluttered a hand. "I almost forgot. Lyle and I spoke to Rachel Ferrari last night. She wanted to thank you for all you did to put things right with Tanner's death."

"I didn't do much." Except to unknowingly present Doc to the murderer and end up nearly getting them both killed.

"Yes." Grace fixed her with a solemn stare. "You did. Now, Rachel will be able to get the payout from Tanner's life insurance policy and pay off her debts. *And* you saved Lyle's life."

"Not really." Zoe had tried, but it was Pete, guided by Alex, who'd ultimately saved Doc. And her.

Grace stopped her with a raised palm. "Don't argue with me."

Zoe would never win and knew it.

Grace shifted her focus to Pete. "What about that woman? The one behind everything?"

"She's still in the hospital. But she has two officers at her door round-the-clock, and as soon as she's released, she'll be transferred to the jail."

"What about Darlene?" Paulette asked.

"She'll face charges, but I don't expect her to do any time." Pete took a sip of his coffee. "She has a good attorney and a good case for diminished capacity."

"And Alex has agreed to stay with her," Zoe added. "Even after he turns eighteen."

Pete gave her a subtle eye roll. She understood his unspoken comment about the teen. Neither Paulette nor Grace were aware of the dog situation, so there was no need to tell them, but Alex had also agreed to take in Bruno, aka Cujo. The poor creature had some serious injuries, including a non-life-threatening gunshot wound. Pete had talked it over with Alex and pledged to cover the dog's vet bills. He'd also pledged to have the scratches in Zoe's paint buffed out. Her Subaru was safely in the shop getting that done as well as the gas lines replaced after Fiona had cut them.

"That poor boy." Grace shook her head sadly. "He's been through hell."

"He has," Pete said, "but he's going to be fine. He did a helluva job helping us with the case against Fiona. Once he accessed her GPS timeline to help me find Zoe, we were able to track her movements over the last couple of weeks. It placed her at all the locations where Doc remembered seeing the 4Runner, as well as at the Vance Motel and at Davis's house the day she broke in and tried to kill him. I'm not sure how much of it will be admissible in court, but there's plenty of other evidence."

"Not to mention everything she confessed to me and Doc," Zoe said.

"To be honest," Pete said, meeting her eyes, "I don't give a damn about the GPS timeline being admitted or not. I'm just glad Alex had access to it that night."

Zoe didn't reply. Didn't need to. She and Pete had already had a long talk, sharing their fears about what might have been had he not arrived on the scene when he did.

Grace turned to her with a puzzled scowl. "One thing I don't understand. How did that woman know where to find you and Lyle?"

"I can answer that," Pete said. "During interrogation, Fiona admitted receiving a call from a friend in Seven Springs who spotted them in a gift shop."

Zoe recalled the young man at Jewel's Gift Emporium, who had wandered off to use his phone.

"Apparently, since Fiona knew Doc was investigating Ferrari's death, she'd called in favors with a number of friends and acquaintances around town. She had her own personal early warning system."

Zoe shivered. "It worked and almost got us killed."

"But it didn't." Pete must've sensed her need to change the subject. He leaned on the counter. "Who are you going to promote to chief deputy?"

It was an easy question to answer. "Gene. He did a great job over the weekend."

Paulette clapped enthusiastically. "Excellent choice. He's so quiet, it's easy to overlook what a good worker he is."

A knock at the door drew their attention. A tall woman with long dark hair stood there, looking hesitant. Paulette started to ask, "How may I help—"

But Pete strode toward the woman, waving *never mind* at Paulette. "I'm glad you could make it," he said to the newcomer.

Even if Zoe hadn't known Pete had invited his daughter here this morning, the moment Zoe took a good look at her, she'd have known who she was. The dark eyes and hair no doubt came from her mother, but the slightly off-kilter smile, the shape of her nose...

Zoe had seen those before, every time she looked at Pete.

He guided the young woman inside, his gaze sweeping across Grace and Paulette to settle on Zoe. "Ladies, I'd like you to meet my daughter. Isabella." He introduced her to the two older women.

Zoe braced herself, strode forward, and extended her left hand. "Isabella. I'm Zoe."

Isabella took Zoe's offered hand. "I've heard a lot about you."

Zoe wondered how much of it was from her mother but wasn't going there. Not today.

As if reading her mind, Isabella grinned. "I'm only giving credence to the parts I've heard from Pete."

Pete leaned toward them. "Which were all glowing."

Zoe gave him a faux haute look. "I would hope so."

"I have to be going," Grace said and pointed at the flowers. "Thank you again. Stop in and see Lyle when you get a chance."

"Will do," Zoe said as Grace headed for the door.

The phone rang. Paulette raised her hand. "I guess the new office is officially open for business." She picked up the receiver and punched the blinking red button.

Pete checked his watch. "I need to get to my meeting." He looked from Zoe to Isabella and back. "Are you two going to be okay?"

"We're going to be fine," Zoe assured him before turning to his daughter. "Let's go into my office and get to know each other."

Isabella fell into step beside her. "I understand you have horses. I worked in a boarding stable when I was a kid, so I could get to ride every once in a while."

"Really?" Zoe looked back at Pete, who gave her a knowing wink.

"I hope I can come over to your farm and get a fix of horse smell. I've always thought it was a better scent than perfume."

"I totally agree."

Yep. They were going to be just fine.

Acknowledgements

This book and the two previous Zoe Chambers Mysteries would never have happened had I not signed with Dawn Dowdle of Blue Ridge Literary Agency. She encouraged me to continue with the series and found a new home for it with Level Best Books. Losing Dawn left a hole in my heart and in those of all her clients. I'm grateful for the too-few years we had together and to the team at Level Best for helping me keep Zoe alive.

As always, I'm beyond grateful to my critique buddies, Jeff Boarts, Liz Milliron, and Peter W.J. Hayes, for taking my rough early drafts and helping me polish them into coherent stories. And I want to give an extra shoutout to Liz for allowing me to borrow Jim Duncan from her Laurel Highlands mystery series to help Pete and Zoe catch a killer. If you haven't read Liz's books, you should remedy that right now.

I want to thank my friend, Anne Tiller, who once again beta read this book and caught a ton of my mistakes.

Since I'm not a cop or a coroner, I have to thank my technical advisors, retired coroner Chris Herndon and (recently) retired police detective Adam Richardson for answering my procedural questions. Any errors in this book are my fault and mine alone. Also, if you're an aspiring mystery author with police procedure questions, check out Adam's Writer's Detective Bureau podcast and his Writer's Detective School online courses.

I owe a huge debt of gratitude to Dru Ann Love for her never-ending support of not just me, but of the entire mystery community. Thank you, my friend.

Several books back, Sandy Giden won a contest to appear in Fair Game. I brought her namesake character back in this one, so I must thank Sandy again for allowing me the use of your name.

Two organizations have proved vital to my career. Thanks so much to the members of Pennwriters and Sisters in Crime. I wouldn't be here without you!

And a big thank you to my readers, fellow authors, friends, and family who keep my Facebook group, "Annette Dashofy's Detectives & Friends" lively and active and who make me laugh daily with the antics of "The Clubhouse Squirrel." Don't ask. Just find us and join.

Finally, I couldn't do any of this without the love and support of my husband, Ray. Thanks for putting up with me.

About the Author

Annette Dashofy is the *USA Today* bestselling author of the Zoe Chambers mystery series and the Detective Honeywell series. She won the 2021 Dr. Tony Ryan Book Award for excellence in Thoroughbred racing literature for her standalone, *Death By Equine*, and has garnered multiple Agatha Award nominations. Her short fiction has also earned a Derringer nomination. Annette and her husband live on ten acres of what was her grandfather's dairy farm in southwestern Pennsylvania with their very spoiled cat, Kensi.

SOCIAL MEDIA LINKS:
  https://www.facebook.com/annette.dashofy
  https://www.instagram.com/annettedashofy

AUTHOR WEBSITE:
  https://www.annettedashofy.com

Also by Annette Dashofy

Zoe Chambers Mysteries:
Circle of Influence
Lost Legacy
Bridges Burned
With a Vengeance
No Way Home
Uneasy Prey
Cry Wolf
Fair Game
Under the Radar
Til Death
Fatal Reunion
Helpless

Death By Equine: A Dr. Jessie Cameron Mystery

Detective Matthias Honeywell Mysteries:
Where the Guilty Hide
Keep Your Family Close

Printed in the USA
CPSIA information can be obtained
at www.ICGtesting.com
LVHW091314150524
780222LV00002B/186